CHOICES OF THE HEART

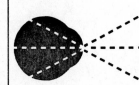

This Large Print Book carries the
Seal of Approval of N.A.V.H.

THE MIDWIVES, BOOK 3

CHOICES OF THE HEART

LAURIE ALICE EAKES

THORNDIKE PRESS
A part of Gale, Cengage Learning

GALE
CENGAGE Learning·

Detroit • New York • San Francisco • New Haven, Conn • Waterville, Maine • London

GALE
CENGAGE Learning®

Thorndike Press® Large Print Christian Historical Fiction.
The text of this Large Print edition is unabridged.
Other aspects of the book may vary from the original edition.
Set in 16 pt. Plantin.

LIBRARY OF CONGRESS CATALOGING-IN-PUBLICATION DATA

Eakes, Laurie Alice.
  Choices of the heart / by Laurie Alice Eakes.
    pages ; cm. — (Thorndike Press large print Christian historical fiction)
  (The midwives ; book 3)
  ISBN-13: 978-1-4104-5662-5 (hardcover)
  ISBN-10: 1-4104-5662-5 (hardcover)
    1. Midwives—Fiction. 2. Large type books. I. Title.
  PS3605.A377C47 2013b
  813'.6—dc23   2013000516

Published in 2013 by arrangement with Revell Books, a division of Baker Publishing Group.

Printed in Mexico
1 2 3 4 5 6 7 17 16 15 14 13

For my mother. To say why would take at least a chapter's worth of words.

AUTHOR'S NOTE

Although most of the feuds of the Appalachian Mountains started after — and because of — the Civil War, not before (when my story is set), the practice of fighting between families came over from the Old Country, where warring clans were still the norm when many of these people immigrated to America.

This location is fictitious, but the beauty and wildness of the mountains in western Virginia are not. The reason for the beginning of this family feud happened in Kentucky. As I mention in these pages, local sheriffs and federal agents discovered that finding and arresting the perpetrators was nearly impossible. Getting lost in "hollers" or over a ridge was just too easy, and people didn't tattle on their kinfolk. Some feuds lasted for thirty years or more. For all we know, some are still going on.

When I was a graduate student at Virginia

Polytechnic and State University in the late 1990s, a friend from the area I've written about told me that some roads you come across you just don't go down without an invitation. Of course, he might have been pulling my leg.

I lived in Appalachia for many years and still have family there, and I can imitate the dialect. For ease of reading, I have kept idiomatic expressions and spellings to a minimum. The one I employ here the most, I still use myself upon occasion — the insertion of "right" as an adjective, adverb, or whatever one needs it to be. I figure if it charmed me as a younger, single female, it would charm my heroine.

There is therefore now no condemnation to them which are in Christ Jesus, who walk not after the flesh, but after the Spirit. For the law of the Spirit of life in Christ Jesus hath made me free from the law of sin and death.

Romans 8:1–2

1

Seabourne, Virginia
April 1842

Esther Cherrett removed the sketchbook from her satchel and lifted it to the highest shelf in the armoire. She didn't need pictures of men whose form existed simply in her imagination's portrayals, in colored chalks — not where she was going. And drawings of her family would only make her sad. Make her feel guilty.

She didn't need the satchel either. Its packets of herbs, rolls of bandages, and canvas apron for protecting her dresses during a lying-in would be of as little use in her new position as were the drawings. She started to hoist it up to the shelf too, but her arms shook as though the black leather bag weighed a hundred pounds instead of ten, and she let it drop.

It landed on the blue floral rug with a thud. The latch sprang open and poked up like an accusing finger. *You shouldn't be doing this,* it seemed to say in the voice of Letty O'Tool, the eldest congregant in the church. *You aren't answering to your calling.*

Esther snapped the latch back into place, then popped it open again, retrieved the sketchbook from its shelf, and shoved it amongst the instruments of the profession she had determined to leave behind in Seabourne. Leave behind with the scorn and ridicule she'd faced over the past four months.

"I'm ready now." She glanced around the room growing dim in the April twilight to see if she had forgotten anything essential for a 350-mile trek across the mountains and her new life beyond the Blue Ridge. Nothing on the dressing table, inside the armoire, beneath the bed. She had squeezed all she could manage into two carpetbags and an oilskin pouch. Everything else must remain behind.

"Except —" She dove beneath the bed and reached up between headboard and wall. Her fingers encountered stiff paper, and she yanked at it.

A bundle of foolscap and fine stationery tied together with a black ribbon dropped into her hand. She should either take the letters or burn them before she departed, whatever necessary so her parents didn't find the condemnatory, derisive, even threatening words from people they thought they knew well — her father's parishioners, her mother's patients. People her parents thought liked them and respected them, but who condemned them as well in the missives.

"Once I'm gone, they'll see it's not your fault," Esther said to the mental pictures of her parents.

She shoved the written messages into the oilskin pouch amongst her books, then turned to the door. The time had come to tell her parents about her plans to spare them all from more heartache.

Head high, knees wobbly, she descended the steps to the first floor — the ground floor, Papa called it in his confusing English way. At that moment, on that late April evening with the celebration of her youngest brother's wedding behind them and the guests about to depart, it was the crowded floor. Laughter and the clink of china cups on saucers rang out from the parlor. In the music room, someone played the pianoforte, accompanied by the chime of silverware in the dining room, where the maids cleared away the supper dishes. The scent of lilacs and squeals of delight drifted through the open windows as children chased moths through Momma's garden.

Momma herself stood in the front hall, a shawl flung around her shoulders and her satchel in hand. She glanced at Esther, and her heart-shaped face lit with the warmth of her smile. "Are you coming with me after all?"

"Coming with you?" Esther blinked. "There's a lying-in?"

"Yes, Mrs. Parker's time has come." Momma's eyes glowed as they always did at the prospect of bringing a new life into the world. "I thought you would have heard their boy come to fetch me. But no matter. I can wait a few minutes if you wish to come."

Momma's half smile, her downcast eyes, conveyed her longing for Esther to say yes, she would go. The cord that had held her to her mother's profession for nearly six years tugged at Esther's heart, urging her to go, to experience the moments she had found so precious. She took a half step forward.

Then she saw the words from more than one missive emblazoned on her mind's eye. *Jezebel* was the kindest of them. If she went, she could further harm the career of midwifery at which her mother had worked for over forty years.

Esther retreated to the first step, her back against the balustrade. "Thank you, but I . . . can't." Esther's eyes burned, and she looked away to avoid seeing Momma's tightened lips.

Six years ago — no, six months ago — she would have been the one waiting for Momma before dashing out the door. For most of her life, she had eagerly awaited the day she would become Tabitha Eckles Cherrett's new apprentice midwife, carrying on a family tradition that had been passed from mother to daughter for generations, beginning in England and continuing in America.

And now Esther must break the chain so Momma could continue her work of delivering babies and healing.

"I came down to — to speak to you and Papa for a few minutes," Esther added. "But if you must leave . . ."

She would have to tell Papa and let him break the news to Momma. Surely that would be easier than seeing Momma's heart break.

"It can wait a bit," Esther continued.

"Not if you're troubled." Momma set down her satchel. "I'll send the boy ahead to tell them I'm on my way. They're only across the square, so if there's a need for me to be there sooner, I can run over." She turned toward the kitchen, where the Parkers' servant would be waiting to accompany the midwife across the darkening town square. "Your father is in his office looking for a book."

"Her father is now in the hall to see why his two best ladies are talking about his whereabouts." Papa emerged from behind the staircase with the languid stride not in the least diminished by his fifty-seven years. "Going out, Tabby?"

Momma turned to him like a compass to the North Star, her mouth relaxing into a smile again, her eyes more shining blue than gray. "Yes, Mrs. Parker's time has come."

"That's wonderful news." Papa laid his hand on her cheek and kissed her on her widow's peak.

Esther clutched the newel post and fought a surge of pain in her middle strong enough to give her nausea. Since she'd turned sixteen, she had sought for a man who would make her look at him as Momma did Papa, and the other way around. She had conjured his image in her mind and set her dreams in colored chalks in her sketchbook. She observed her brothers courting, marrying, and the eldest two producing children. At the same time she watched the men on the eastern shore of Virginia shy away from her, call her Queen Esther behind her back, and end up marrying other females who didn't have an English marquess for an uncle, a mother who knew all the town's secrets, and a profession of her own.

Now the eligible young men simply ran from her as though fearing for their virtue.

"Are you going with her, Esther?" Papa turned to her, eyes wide.

"No, I —" Esther made the mistake of looking into his face, the eyes she dared not call beautiful since the same dark brown orbs with their gold flecks and ridiculously long lashes peered back at her from every mirrored surface, as did her own delicate version of his aristocratic features.

She flicked her gaze right and down, concentrated on a drift of lilac petals fallen from a vase and onto the polished floorboards. "I still can't. I —" She took a long, shuddering breath and gripped the newel post with both hands, curling her fingers into the carved leaf design like marlinespikes holding a sail line in place — holding herself in place before she raised her eyes to her parents' faces. "I'm leaving Seabourne."

Momma caught her breath and pressed her hand to her lips.

Papa's eyes widened further, and his chin hardened. "By whose leave, young lady?"

"Mine. That is —" A lifetime of obedience crowded down upon her shoulders. "I have to go. I have . . . no future here now."

"Of course you do." Momma spoke hastily. Perhaps too hastily. "Your sweet spirit will overcome the talk."

"When some new scandal comes along?" Esther cast her parents a smile that barely moved her lips up at the corners. "Perhaps in another thirty years or so?"

"Sarcasm is not attractive in a young lady," Papa said. Then he sighed. "But I wish it didn't hold at least a drop of truth." He closed the distance between them and rested his hand over hers on the newel post. "You aren't going to brazen this out, my dear? Have I raised a craven for a daughter?"

"I think so." Esther blinked back tears and would not meet his gaze. "I'm running away, I am well aware. And I see no other choice."

"You could have discussed it with us." Momma joined them at the foot of the steps. "If you want to go, we can send you back west with the Dochertys."

"I thought about that." Esther glanced toward the parlor and the remaining guests who had come for the wedding. "But they know."

"They'll never tell anyone," Momma said.

Esther nodded. "I agree. But they know, and perhaps they have their doubts about me. About whether or not I'm telling the truth." She removed her hand from beneath Papa's and backed up a step. "I just wanted to tell you of my plans so you wouldn't worry."

"As if we won't." Papa reached out his hand to her.

Esther's fingers twitched to take it and go down to him and Momma, let them hold her as they had when she was small, as they had four months earlier, as they had every time she hurt and needed comfort. The idea of living without their loving arms around her whenever she needed reassurance, which seemed like every day now, felt like a hole ripping open inside her.

She backed up another step, out of arm's reach. "I need to go where no one knows anything more about me than they need to."

"But you can't, child," Momma protested. "How will you live? You might not be safe on your own."

Esther bit down on her tongue to stop herself from reminding them that she hadn't been safe living at home.

"I won't be on my own," she said instead. "The families I'll be working for are coming to fetch me."

"Indeed." Papa's supercilious eyebrows arched toward a hairline now more silver than the deep brown shot with copper and bronze that Esther had inherited. "And when is this, and who are these families?"

Esther crossed her arms over her chest. "S-soon, and no one you ever heard of. They live on the other side of the commonwealth. I didn't want to leave without letting you know first."

"I suppose we are honored," Papa murmured.

Momma laid her hand on his arm. "Sarcasm, love."

"Ah, yes, my dear conscience." He smiled at Momma.

Esther's heart crushed down on her stomach, it hurt so much to see how deeply they loved one another even after thirty-three years of marriage. She had dreamed of having that kind of future with her husband. Now she would never have a husband.

"Please," she whispered, clasping her upper arms with her hands, "just let me go."

Papa gazed up at her, the corners of his mouth tight. "Esther, we would be neglecting our God-ordained duty if we let you go without knowing to whom and to where."

"And if they are godly men and women," Momma added before drawing her lower lip between her teeth. She failed to stop a tear from slipping from one corner of her eye.

Esther's own eyes burned. "I can't. I mean, I'd rather no one here know so the letters can't —" She clapped her hand over her mouth.

Papa's eyes narrowed. "What letters?"

"Nothing." She started to turn away.

"Do not!" Papa surged past her up the steps and blocked her way. "Esther Phoebe Cherrett, what letters?"

She looked up at him without meeting his eyes. "Some notes people have sent me, is all."

"And why were we not told about them?" Papa demanded.

Esther shrugged, realized how disrespectful that was, and shook her head. "Please don't make me tell you. They were mean."

"Did they suggest you leave town?" Momma asked.

Esther nodded.

Papa ground his teeth. "And you think you'll give in?"

"To protect all of you, yes."

"Protect us?" Momma began.

"Regardless of why," Papa said at the same time, "you will go nowhere without telling us where and with whom."

21

"Nor without us meeting —" Pounding on the front door interrupted Momma.

"Mrs. Cherrett," a shrill voice called through the panels. "Mrs. Cherrett, quick."

Momma dropped her head for a moment, then straightened her shoulders. "Dominick, I am so sorry to have to leave you, but duty calls."

"I know, Tabby. It is quite all right." Again he gave her that devastating smile that must have melted Momma's heart the first time she met him.

Esther closed her eyes and considered making a dash for the rear staircase while he was distracted with Momma's departure. She took a step down.

The parlor door opened, and her four brothers, their wives, and two guest couples spilled out, chattering and laughing and talking about joining the children on the lawn. People Esther loved so much she couldn't breathe. Her heart raced at what she was about to do, but she had no choice. She flung herself into their midst and followed them into the yard and the growing darkness. Behind her, Papa said something about her coming back. She ignored him. If she turned back and read the pain on his face, she wouldn't be able to leave for anyone's sake.

The cool, damp air of mid-spring wrapped its arms around her, a contrast to the cold fog that had clutched her as she ran home in January. Ran away from the disaster she had surely brought upon herself.

Run. Run. Run now and don't look back.

Not yet. She couldn't leave her things behind. She wanted to see her family one more time.

She ran to the garden gate and opened the latch. The wrought iron swung out on well-oiled hinges.

And two shadows detached themselves from either side of the opening.

She gasped, choking on a cry, and flattened herself against the gate, hand groping for the latch.

"You're safe." The voice belonged to a female, gentle and low with the hint of a mountain twang. "I'm Hannah Gosnoll. My brother Zachary Brooks and I are here to carry you west."

"But I thought — I thought —" Esther's breathing and heart raced as though she'd been running. She took a deep breath to steady herself. "I thought the Tollivers were coming to fetch me."

"They were." The voice of the taller shadow — presumably Zachary Brooks — was deeper, smoother than his sister's. "But our cousin Griffin suffered an unfortunate accident on his way here."

"An accident?" Esther's mind raced over the letter she had received from Mrs. Tolliver, the plea to take the work for the sake of her younger children. She had warned that life in the mountains could be difficult but not dangerous. "What sort of an accident?"

"Nothing serious," Hannah said.

"As long," Zachary added, "as that knife in his belly didn't go through his innards."

2

Miss Esther Cherrett caught her breath, started to say something. At least she made a noise in her throat like intended speech, but nothing emerged.

Hannah kicked Zach with the narrow toe of her boot. If he hadn't worn thick leather over his ankles, the strike would have crippled him for hours. As it was, he grunted from the impact, glared at her even though she couldn't see it in the dark, and opened his mouth to apologize for mentioning the attack on his cousin. He just blurted it out because, of course, she was expecting Griff and Bethann Tolliver, not just Zach and Hannah.

Zach opened his mouth to speak, but a gaggle of children ran across the lawn, calling Miss Esther's name.

"Midnight beneath the oak," she whispered.

The gate closed. The children swarmed

around her.

Zach sighed. "I shouldn't have told her."

"Maybe she won't come now that you did." Hannah turned toward the graveyard behind which they had sheltered the horses. "Either way, I'm not waiting here." Her feet swished through the grass.

Zach all but leaned on the fence in his attempt to listen to and watch the activities on the other side. The children wanted Esther to play some sort of game with them.

"For a little while," she told them. "But then you all have to get tucked up in your beds. It's getting l-late." Her voice broke and she sniffed.

"Are you crying, Aunt Esther?" a little girl asked.

"Of course not, Leah. What do I have to cry about? Now, let's play. You can help me count while the others hide."

She began to count in unison with the little girl, while the others scattered around the house and grounds. A man with an accent Zach recognized as English, due to visitors to the mountains, called out to Miss Esther, and she stopped counting. Several people drew closer to the gate. Zach stepped back into the shadow of the garden wall, poised to run if someone opened the gate.

Miss Esther disappeared into the gloom

of falling night.

Midnight. Four hours away. That meant her family did not want her to go, but she was coming anyway, coming despite him telling her what had delayed Griff.

Four hours to cool his heels in an unfamiliar town. It was a small town, he supposed, not like some they'd seen on their way east, but large enough no one had looked at him and Hannah oddly when they rode through. They could return to the public house on the square, have dinner, learn what they could of Miss Esther Cherrett. Maybe they could find out why a young lady living in a fine house, with people who wanted her around, would choose to answer Aunt Lizbeth's advertisement in the Richmond newspaper and come teach mountain folk like them. Aunt Lizbeth said it was a calling of the Lord, most like. Hannah and cousin Bethann both said it was something else. Zach thought it could be good to have her in their midst.

Zach joined Hannah with the horses, and they walked into the square. The public house looked crowded, noisy, and smoky. No place he wanted to take a meal.

"I don't mind it," Hannah said. She and her husband had lived in a town for a while. "I'll go in and get us supper." She disappeared into the sea of people.

Zach waited in the dark.

"Maybe she won't come," Hannah said when she emerged.

But she did. At midnight by the striking of the church clock bell, Miss Esther Cherrett appeared at the gate carrying two bags. "Mrs. Gosnoll? Mr. Brooks?" she called. "There's more. I'll change my dress and bring them down."

Zach moved the bags into the alleyway but remained by the gate waiting, watching the back of the house. She would come now. She wouldn't leave her things at the gate with them and not come back . . . would she?

No, she wouldn't. Past midnight, according to the church clock, she appeared as a shadow against the back of the house, more bags in her hands and a bundle over her arm.

She reached the gate, breathing a little heavily, and let her parcels fall to the ground with too loud a thud. "I'm ready to leave now."

Not a hint of a quaver, no hesitation. Only determination.

Beauty, courage, determination. As usual, Aunt Lizbeth Tolliver was right when she said Miss Esther Cherrett possessed the right character for the position.

And for a wife for either her son or her nephew.

"Her nephew," Zach mouthed, then stepped forward to lift the first bag. The oilskin sack proved heavier than its relatively small size implied. He hefted it onto his shoulder but gave Miss Esther a quizzical glance she couldn't possibly see.

"And I thought we were the ones with the lead mine," he muttered.

"Books," she said.

"Right wise of you. We don't have much in the way of books on the ridge."

And he hadn't read any of the ones in his mother's collection, not more than the bits she had made him read and take to memory. Of course this lady would be bookish. It was why Aunt Lizbeth had picked her for the position. And she would want a man who could discuss those books with her.

So he'd be catching up on his learning. Might be good for him with the mines and all. Maybe she could start his book learning along the way, give him an advantage over Griff.

First he had to get her on her way with them.

When she turned to latch the gate behind her, Zach realized the bundle over her arm

29

was her own skirt, or the extra fabric of the skirt. She wore a riding habit. He'd seen them on his few visits to a town. They did well for a lady riding sidesaddle.

Their horses weren't broke to a sidesaddle.

Zach's heart sank. She might refuse to go once he informed her she would have to ride astride for over three hundred miles. Might as well get it over with at once.

"Our horses ain't broke to a sidesaddle, Miss Esther."

She flashed him a smile. "Then it's a good thing I have lots of fabric in my skirt." She shook out the excess folds.

"You could make two dresses out o' that material," Hannah said. "Kind of a waste, isn't it?"

"Not to preserve my modesty, it isn't." Miss Esther sounded just a bit uppity.

Zach laughed. Hannah needed that jab now that her husband ran the mine and made more money than his in-laws did as yet, for all the Brookses and Tollivers owned it. He liked Miss Esther's spirit.

He liked her too much.

"Let's get goin'." He spoke sharply and turned his back on the women, expecting them to follow.

They did — down the alleyway and around the graveyard to a copse of trees

30

where four horses stood. Three served for riding and the fourth for supplies. They weren't about to waste money on inns in this fine weather. For this night, they needed to ride fast and far in case Miss Esther's parents came after them.

She had chosen to come. She said she was old enough to make the decision on her own, and if she wanted to stay, Zach wasn't about to stop her. But he longed for her to come with them, to save them all from destroying one another.

They mounted and headed through the quiet village. None of them spoke. Apparently Miss Esther could ride astride without too much complaint. Zach would find out how that came to be, there on the coast where ladies rode sidesaddle or not at all. Her back was straight, her head high, her ridiculous skirt draped over every inch of her legs right to the tops of her feet. In contrast, Hannah's legs showed from mid-calf down. Boots covered her. The practice seemed normal to Zach. Compared to Esther Cherrett now, it seemed vulgar.

If Miss Esther was appalled by them, she showed no sign of it. She remained silent, riding at an easy canter. All the way to Norfolk and beyond, to where the fine plantations began to march along the James River.

31

At dawn, they stopped in woods around one of those plantations.

"We'll have some breakfast here and rest the horses," Zach said. "I'll get a fire going while you and Hannah fetch water."

Miss Esther didn't follow Hannah to the creek. She stood beside her horse with her hands on her hips. "Tell me about this cousin who was stabbed."

Zach paused in the act of loosening the saddle cinch on his horse. Hannah halted halfway to the creek.

"Griff." Zach looked away, though she likely couldn't read his expression in the poor light. "He was ambushed on our way here. We stopped like this and went for firewood and . . ." He shrugged. "I best be getting that firewood or we'll be taking too much time."

She started to ask another question, but he entered the trees with a crunch of last year's pine needle carpet and scattered cones, drowning her out. Maybe by the time he returned, he could talk about the attack on his cousin long enough to satisfy Miss Esther's questions. They surely wouldn't be too many. She had come with them, after all.

Zach paused in the act of gathering branches from a lightning-struck, dead tree.

Aunt Lizbeth had said she hadn't told Miss Esther about the fighting for fear she wouldn't come at all. "Can't have her finding out and turning back halfway here."

He shouldn't have mentioned Griff's attack, as the bruise on his ankle from Hannah's kick indicated. Esther Cherrett had come anyway, strutting out of her parents' house in her fancy city clothes like she ran off every night.

But maybe she did, and that was why she needed to start again where no one knew how to find her. A fine female to take into the Tolliver household and teach the young'uns the right way to go on in the world.

Zach smiled and ripped several branches from the downed tree. They snapped off. Good. Not rotten to the core and likely to burn too fast. A fairly recent lightning strike then. Easy wood for the small fire he wanted, just good enough to fry up some bacon and boil some coffee.

He took too long gathering more wood. Sunlight was beginning to stream through the foliage as he returned to the clearing where Hannah had already begun a small fire and set water to boil. Miss Esther perched on a log to one side, her head bowed over her hands as though she were

33

praying. She looked up at his approach. A beam of sunlight shot between two branches and concentrated on her face.

Zach dropped the pile of branches in his arms. It crashed to the ground with a clatter, snap, and crunch of breaking, colliding wood. Hannah cried out a protest. He ignored her and stared.

Miss Esther Cherrett's beauty took his breath away. Her hair wasn't just dark brown. It was like fine wood polished and set with bands of copper and gold. Her skin was as fine and smooth as one of Aunt Lizbeth's china bowls that she prized like her children, and wide, dark eyes gazed at him from beneath ridiculously long lashes.

"You're staring," Hannah muttered out of the side of her mouth.

"Sorry." Zach glanced away, then back.

For less than a heartbeat, his eyes met Miss Esther Cherrett's. Then her eyelashes swept down to shield those gold-flecked orbs, and her cheeks paled.

"Will you stop acting like a loon and feed the fire?" Hannah commanded.

"Yea, sure." Zach crouched to feed more wood to the fire. When he heard footfalls heading toward the creek, he made himself concentrate on the burning branches and not on watching Miss Esther walk away.

"She's right pretty," Hannah said. "And in a heap of trouble, I expect."

"Yea, she came with us for some reason, sounds like. Even with me telling her about Griff." Zach raised his head to watch Miss Esther kneel beside the creek.

She splashed water onto her face. She then took a comb from her pocket and raised her hands to her hair to twist and tuck and pat every strand into place.

Yes, she was indeed a lady, to care so much about being neat on the trail.

He glanced up at Hannah. "She's got courage."

"Either that," Hannah said as she set the spider over the fire, "or her trouble's bad enough she's willing to risk being in the middle of our troubles."

"Should we bring her along after all?" Zach watched Miss Esther rise in one fluid motion, then stand staring down at the water, her hands clasped behind her back as though she contemplated deep thoughts, prayed, or perhaps simply admired the ripple of light on the water.

Hannah glanced over her shoulder. "I'm thinking she's wondering if she should come along."

"She'll come."

Zach didn't take his eyes off of her as she

straightened her shoulders, turned, and marched back to the fire with a long-legged stride of self-confidence. Her rounded chin was set firm beneath a half smile, though she looked past rather than at him.

"What may I do to assist you?" she asked.

Hannah smirked. "Can you make coffee?"

"Of course." Miss Esther set about pouring water into the battered tin coffeepot, spooned in grounds from a bag, and set the pot on the edge of the fire without a second's hesitation.

Zach glanced at Hannah, who stared at Miss Esther wide-eyed.

She looked up from her preparations and smiled. "Why are you so surprised I can make coffee on a fire? I told Mrs. Tolliver of my skills, which she said were why she wants me for the position. She said something about primitive conditions in the mountains. I can assure you, some of the conditions at fishermen's huts . . . where my mother and I . . ." She faltered for the first time. "Why — why are you staring at me?"

Zach didn't have words to express the sense of a dozen butterflies beating their wings around the inside of his ribs.

But Hannah laughed. "You'll do, Miss Esther Cherrett. You'll do right well."

"For a position as a teacher, yes, I am well-educated thanks to my parents —"

"No." Hannah sliced her hand through the air between them. "As a wife for Zach or Griff."

3

She should not have brought her sketchbook along after all. If Zach Brooks or Hannah Gosnoll found it, Esther would simply have to run farther west, off to the barely civilized plains, and take her risks with the Indians. Or maybe down the Mississippi to New Orleans or on a ship to the West Indies or Europe, anywhere to hide her shame.

Too many of her sketches — images conjured from dreams she had abandoned long ago — could pass as portraits of Zachary Brooks, right down to the wheat-gold hair and sky-blue eyes. If he saw those drawings, the colors shaded with chalks, he might, just might, think she agreed with his aunt that she would make him a fine wife. He already looked at her like she was one of her mother's candied violets.

She shuddered, and the temptation to head back east to Seabourne left her shaken and hollow inside. The two desires of her life ripped her in two — go home to parents who loved her and would now be worrying about her, or go on and worry herself over pushing away suitors while trying to civilize the younger children of the families, now that they had discovered lead on their land and needed an education to ensure no one swindled them. Now that the families had ambitions, apparently.

"Not me," Esther said between clenched teeth. She realized her error and added, "Not I. I have no intentions of marrying."

"Pretty girls always do," Hannah said.

She was a more than passably pretty girl herself with the same pale gold hair and blue eyes her brother possessed. But her skin needed protecting from the sun, as it had darkened to a honey brown, and lines at the corners of her eyes made her look all of her thirty or so years.

Esther rubbed a finger along her as-yet unmarred complexion and looked first Hannah and then Zach in the face. "I mean what I say. I am not coming to the mountains or going anywhere else to find a husband. The idea of marriage —"

She stopped before she said it sickened her. They either wouldn't understand or would understand too much.

"Does not appeal to me," she concluded.

Hannah and Zach exchanged glances, then burst out laughing.

"Can you teach me to do that?" Hannah asked. "I can use it on cousin Bethann when she gets on her high horse."

Esther blinked. "Teach you what?"

"How to look so hoity-toity." Hannah laughed again, a full-throated bellow of mirth. "I declare you could freeze butter in July with that look."

"I had no idea." Esther's face heated.

"Leave off, Hannah." Zach toed a fallen branch back into the fire and didn't look at Esther. "You're going to frighten her off."

"As if you telling her about Griff being stabbed did." Hannah snorted and began to dish up fried bread and bacon onto plates.

Esther leaped forward to snatch up the coffeepot, using some of her excess riding habit hem to lift the scalding pot, and poured the coffee into waiting mugs. The rich, dark aroma smelled heavenly. She inhaled the bitter scent she found so much more satisfying than tea, and a lump rose in her throat.

Papa never drank coffee. Momma never drank tea unless it was chamomile. The teakettle and coffeepot resided side by side atop the stove, as different as Momma and Papa and unimaginable not together.

Her body leaned toward the east, toward her home of four and twenty years, the church her father shepherded, the patients she and her mother tended, the people who had watched her grow up.

Yet they had called her a liar when she needed them to believe the truth the most.

She leaned back toward the west. "If you want me to continue with you," she announced, "no one must mention that I am marriage fodder."

"It's just a crazy notion of my aunt's." Zach shrugged. "And we're wasting time eating instead of traveling. I want to get as far as fast as we can and see if Griff's all right."

"He's all right," Hannah grumbled. "He's too stubborn to let a little knife do him in." Her mouth twisted and her nostrils pinched as though she smelled something unpleasant.

So Hannah didn't like her cousin, but Zach did.

"Who stabbed him?" Esther pressed, watching Hannah.

Hannah took a huge bite of bread and bacon and chewed with evident pleasure, her eyes half closed.

"Ambushed," Zach said. "Probably someone thinking to rob him." He touched his side. "They weren't very good with knife throwing, though. Anybody knows one should aim for the middle."

"Of course." Esther nodded. "One hits the bowel and the large artery there. If they don't bleed out, they'll die slowly of —" She gulped.

Hannah and Zach stared at her.

"You seen a man stabbed in the gut or something?" Hannah asked.

"No, I, um, learned a lot of medical things from my mother." Esther bit into her own bread and bacon so she needn't say more.

She didn't want to tell them that her mother was a midwife, didn't want to admit that she herself was a fully qualified midwife. She'd left healing behind when she ceased to heal.

"It's all them books," Zach muttered and rose to his feet in one sinuous motion.

Esther watched him stride away into the woods, carrying his plate. Hannah gazed after him too, her brows knit, her mouth pinched. "Momma owns three books. She tried to get Zach to read them, but he never would much. She said he'd regret it one day when Griff could read and he couldn't."

"We all regret disobeying our parents sooner or later." Esther surged to her feet and began to gather up the coffeepot and spider for cleaning. "We should be on our way."

She looked toward the east again. She had regretted her disobedience sooner rather than later. But here she was, going against their wishes yet again and wondering how long would pass before she once more regretted her actions, or if just maybe this time she was right.

Hannah and Zach should be on their way back from the coast by now.

Griff Tolliver came to full consciousness. Vaguely, through a haze of burning pain, he had been aware of the passage of days — sunlight, moonlight, and the in-between shades of gray and blackness — slipping past his fevered brain. Too many days for him to lie vulnerable in an abandoned cabin along the Old Wagon Road. A log cabin with no glass in the window and no lock on the door and his elder sister Bethann's inexpert ability with a rifle were not enough protection from whoever had tried to kill him.

"Who?" He groaned as he struggled to sit up. Corn husks whispered from the pallet beneath him. His head no longer throbbed. The rough stitching in his right side pulled, a far cry from the earlier, constant, tearing certainty that death would find him a willing companion. "Who?" he repeated on a sigh.

"Who what?" Bethann dropped to her knees beside him and slipped one arm beneath his shoulders. "You sound like an owl."

Griff focused on her face, pasty white save for a constellation of ruddy freckles across her slightly crooked nose. "Who did it? Who tried to kill me?"

"Zach, of course. Drink." She held a cup to his lips and tilted it so he had to swallow the bitter but cold draft or choke.

He swallowed, fighting dizziness and weakness. "Not Zach. Zach wouldn't."

"He's a Brooks and related to the Gosnolls, isn't he?"

"Sure, but —" He leaned on his left hand to spare his right side.

Zach, his friend, his cousin, would never harm him, despite his family. Together they had knelt in the makeshift church and prayed for God to forgive them for their part in the family dispute. They had vowed before God that they would stop the fighting, the violence, before any more of the men of Brooks Ridge were maimed or killed, and then they persuaded their mothers to hire a schoolma'am for the younger children to be properly taught how to read

44

and write and love their neighbors as themselves. Neighbors or family. Either counted. Miss Esther Cherrett sounded perfect — the daughter of a parson, educated by him with some fancy English education.

"Not Zach. He took a vow," Griff murmured.

Bethann snorted. "Since when does a Gosnoll or Brooks stay by a vow?" She rose with one fluid motion and stalked to the open door of the cabin, plain in face and form but as graceful as a mountain lion.

And as bitter as one of her herbal concoctions.

Griff slid back against the rough wall to keep himself from succumbing to one of those herbal concoctions. His side murmured a token protest at the movement. "So why do you think it was Zach?"

"Rest. You need your rest."

"I'm right rested, Bethann. I need to talk." The effort not to yawn nearly dislocated his jaw.

Bethann laughed, the sound like a saw blade striking metal. "You need to rest so's you don't open up that wound."

"It's healed well enough." He groped beneath the remnants of his shirt for the bandage wrapped around his middle.

No fresh blood soaked through the linen.

45

His touch on the slice through the flesh right above his hip bone didn't send him reeling into unconsciousness. A twinge. A simple twinge. He would be back on his horse in another day or two.

And continuing east to meet up with the party from Seabourne.

"Tell me why you claim Zach threw that knife at me," Griff persisted.

In the doorway, Bethann shrugged her narrow shoulders. "Who else was around who can throw a knife but him and Hannah?"

"Hannah couldn't hit the side of a barn with a knife if she was a yard away, let alone in the dark from fifty feet away." Griff stifled another yawn. "But why would Zach ambush me and slice my guts open?"

"To be rid of you, Brother. You die and it's all his — the woods, the mine, the farms."

"Not with our fathers still alive, and we have younger brothers and cousins who expect a share."

"Our fathers." Bethann kicked her booted foot against the door frame.

Dust and splinters shimmered in the last rays of the sun. With a ripping sound, the frame cracked up the middle.

"They'll kill each other off sooner than

later," she insisted.

"No. No, it's over, I'm right certain of that."

Bethann snorted.

"I can't —" Griff shoved his hair out of his face, finding only a line where a lump and a gash had rendered him unconscious. "No, I won't go around accusing Zach of trying to murder me without more proof than your guessing."

"You ain't up to believing proof." Muttering something about fetching more water, she slipped out of the door and beyond his line of sight.

The water bucket remained in one corner of the cabin.

Griff remained in the far corner, drowsing, aching in body and heart.

Not Zach, not the cousin who was closer to him than his brothers, fourteen and sixteen years younger. He and Zach had been born a day apart. Until ten years ago, they had spent more time together than with the rest of their families.

And we took that vow together.

Yet unfortunately, Bethann was right. Zach's father and brother-in-law had broken every vow they had made.

Including their marriage vows.

Still, Griff didn't want to tar Zach with

the same brush and continue the feud. Too many had died already. They didn't need to add to the numbers on the word of a bitter and resentful spinster, regardless of her reasons for her anger.

"Lord, get me out of here." He fell asleep propped in the corner and praying for a speedy recovery from his wound.

He awoke to Bethann attempting to pour more of her draft down his throat. He pushed it away. "Food, not that swill. I need to get up."

"You still need rest." In the dim morning light, her face glowed as pale as moonlight, her seemingly lipless mouth a slash of red like a cut.

Gently Griff took her arm and tried to push it away so he could get to his feet. She resisted. His hand shook with the effort to move her. Weakness. Humiliating, dangerous weakness. He couldn't lift a gun, throw a knife, or ride a mile if he couldn't move aside his thin sister.

But he managed to spill the contents of the tankard over his pallet.

Bethann grumbled and sighed and backed away. "Don't come crying to me when your side rips open and you bleed your veins out." She stomped from the cabin, her heels thudding dully on the dirt floor.

Griff used notches in the walls as handholds to pull himself to his feet. He staggered and swayed and moved with as much confidence as a baby taking its first steps, but he moved. The sun had risen by the time he reached the door. He longed for the strength to leave the cabin and walk far enough to stand in the bright rays, feel the warmth. A stream gurgled at hand, and the notion of diving into the icy water spread through him like hunger.

He was hungry. He wanted meat. Bethann brought him porridge. Even though they would not find the wherewithal to stay in inns along the route, more from habit than necessity, they had packed provisions of oatmeal and flour, dried meat and bacon. Bethann preferred sleeping in the open and cooking over a fire to crowding herself amongst people. Griff wanted a real bed and fresh food.

Bethann located some wild berries growing in a meadow. Lush and red, they satisfied Griff more than had the thick porridge. One more day passed by, then two, then three. Each one brought more strength.

They also brought the schoolma'am closer, gave her more time in Zach's company without Griff so much as knowing what she looked like.

"We're leaving tomorrow," he announced to Bethann over a bowl of cornmeal mush flavored with jerky. "No arguments. Either you come with me or I go alone."

She didn't argue. She didn't speak at all until, with some difficulty, Griff was mounted on his roan gelding and Bethann on her gray mare. Instead of heading her mount east toward the road that would take them to the pass over the Blue Ridge, she headed back the way they had come, back toward the New River and home.

He drew up. "Where are you going?"

"To give you your proof of Zach's treachery."

Sickness clenched his gut. "I'm not interested."

"In what? The truth? Griff." Bethann drew her brows together over her long, slim nose. "Knowing will save your life next time."

Griff remained stiff in his saddle, though the rigidity pained his side. "There won't be a next time."

"Why not? A Brooks hurt Pa and killed our other kin."

And paid for it with his life.

"The fighting has stopped," Griff insisted. "I won't be a party to it starting up again."

"You won't be a party to nothing if you don't pay attention to the signs." Bethann

50

dismounted and lifted a sheaf of cut pine boughs. "I laid these here where I found you so you can see for yourself. Look."

Griff didn't want to look. He wanted to ride east and find Zach and Hannah and the lady.

But he dismounted and looked. Not enough rain had fallen in the past three weeks to have reached through the canopy of branches overhead or the pine boughs of Bethann's making to hide the signs of where Griff had fallen as he attempted to dismount from his horse with a knife blade sticking out of his side. Leaves and pine needles lay crushed into a hollow. A brief outcropping of rock bore a splash of darkness. Blood. Nothing else showed signs of the ambush.

He scowled at Bethann. "I don't see any signs. In fact —" His hand pressed to his side. "What happened to the knife?"

"Good question, that." Bethann's upper lip curled. "Took it with him so's we didn't recognize it. But he left this behind when he pulled the blade out, I expect."

She lifted aside the bough of a cedar tree. Beyond it, the brambles of a wild rose wrapped around the outcropping of rock and struggled to reach the light. And from those briars dangled several strands of pale yellow hair. The butter-yellow of Zach's hair. Hannah's too. Hundreds of people's hair.

But hundreds of people hadn't been up the trail in the past three weeks. A few dozen, perhaps. Several possessed that gleaming pale gold. But few would have reason to duck into the depression beneath the tree.

Griff's gut ached from his belly to the mostly healed stab wound. "Not enough proof."

"Stubborn mule." Bethann bent and plucked something from a lower thorn on the wild rose. "What about this too?"

She held up a strip of buckskin perhaps a finger long and half as wide as a pinkie. Fringe from a hunting shirt. Plain, brown, well-worn. Nothing distinguished it from the shirt Griff wore now, as the homespun one he'd donned for the journey had been ruined.

Then Bethann laid it across his palm, and he saw the difference. Stamped into the underside of the leather were two letters — ZB. Their mothers had started stamping their clothes when they were small to help know whose was whose when they left bits behind at the swimming hole or a field or any number of places.

"Tiresome problem, him losing the one

bit of fringe with his letters on it," Griff mused aloud. He flashed a gaze at his sister's grim face. "Or does his momma put them on every fringe?"

Of course she didn't. No woman had that kind of time.

Bethann shrugged. "Can't change what I found. But with the fringe and the yeller hair, looks kinda bad, don't you think?"

"Right bad." Griff tucked the bit of fringe into his trouser pocket and returned to his gelding.

He turned the roan east to meet up with Zach and Hannah and Miss Esther Cherrett, to place as much distance between the ambush place and himself as possible. Out of sight, out of mind. When he met up with Zach, saw his cousin and friend's smiling, bright face, he would know for certain Bethann was mistaken. The ambusher was a stranger thinking to rob him, or one of Zach's cousins thinking to get rid of one more Tolliver out on the trail and away from the rest of the families. Anyone else. Despite the hatred reigning in the rest of the family, Zach and Griff refused to let it poison their friendship. Nothing, they had vowed before the traveling preacher and one another, would come between their efforts to bring peace back to the ridge.

He met up with his cousins and the new schoolma'am the following day. Wood-smoke aromas slowed their pace. A quarter mile down the road, a familiar giggle and accompanying light laugh joined that of another voice, something clear and sharp, a little brittle like new ice.

Griff held up his hand for Bethann to halt and reined in his own mount. "Zach? Hannah?" he called to them without approaching.

The merriment stopped. Underbrush rustled, and Zach's mop of yellow hair emerged from the trees. "Griff, you're a'right."

"Looks like it this time." Griff dismounted and paced toward his cousin, his hand on his own knife. "You got the lady?"

"Yep. Come have some dinner. Hey, Bethann." Zach lifted aside branches to reveal a flickering fire and two females perched atop a log on its far side.

Bethann didn't move off of her horse. "I'm not hungry."

"Bethann." Griff shot her a warning glance. "We've got a friendly invite. Step down and say hey to your cousins and the schoolma'am."

Not waiting for Bethann, Griff tethered his horse, then stepped into the clearing.

Hannah lifted a hand to him, but the other female stood.

"Miss Esther Cherrett," Zach said with a soft look toward the young woman.

A shaft of late afternoon sunlight fingered its way through the branches to find her face and make it glow as though she were lit from within. Even her eyes and hair, for all their dark brown color, sparkled with golden lights. Her skin looked like some fine bowls Pa had brought Momma from a trip to the city after they'd excavated the lead — as smooth as the glass they were putting into the new house, but with shades of cream and roses. His gaze flicked down a dusty riding dress, then quickly back to meet her eyes to stifle thoughts of how fine even a grimy dress could look on the right female.

She looked away from him, and her face lost the rose color. "Pleased to meet you, Mr. Tolliver."

Not half as pleased as he was to meet her.

He cleared his throat. "It's right glad I am to meet up with you all. Bethann?"

He turned to introduce his sister, but Bethann was gone.

4

Esther watched Griff from beneath her lashes, her body tense. She'd seen the flare of interest in his blue eyes — eyes the same sky-blue as Zach's, but more striking against his curly, dark hair and sun-darkened skin with the shadow of dark whisker stubble. Bold blue eyes that took her in at a glance, as though he assessed a horse for possible purchase at a fair.

She glanced at her mount. "Do we need to go look for your sister, Mr. Tolliver?"

"Not Bethann." Griff shrugged. "She'll get here when she chooses and not before. But I'm right happy to see you've come this far unscathed."

"Did you think we'd dump her in a river for the load of books she's carrying?" Zach stood with his legs splayed and his hands on his hips, not quite in fists but halfway there.

Griff laughed and strode forward to slap

his cousin on the back. "I didn't know if she could ride all this way without one of those fancy eastern saddles." He stood with one of his soft leather boots a finger's breadth from Esther's long skirt.

"I've managed perfectly well." She swept her skirt behind her. "Thank you."

Griff smiled at her, a smile that reached his eyes, then glanced at his cousin. "Her voice is as pretty as her face. Is she of a good temperament too?"

"Not at the moment." Esther enunciated each word with the English diction her father had fruitlessly tried to teach his children to use all of the time. They had sounded too out of place in Seabourne. There in the mountains, she sounded out-right ridiculous and fumbled for something less clipped.

But the others were laughing as though she'd made a great joke. Zach's stance relaxed, and together the two men turned toward the fire.

"Does she always talk like that?" Griff asked.

"Naw." Zach glanced at her out of the corner of his eye. "She's been perfectly amiable."

She'd been too weary to be anything else. Talking proved a staggering effort. And she ached in every limb. But they would reach the ridge in two more days, Zach assured her. If only she could survive for another forty-eight hours without collapsing in an ignominious heap under the hooves of her horse.

"I think it's right pretty," Griff said. "Kind of sweet and sharp at the same time."

"Like those oranges we had a couple Christmases back?" Zach suggested.

Cheeks hot, Esther snatched up the water bucket and headed for the sound of running water. Behind her, Hannah and then the men made a perfunctory offer to go instead. Esther ignored them and pushed aside some fir tree branches to another clearing with a stream sparkling through it over a jumble of rocks — the endless rocks of the mountains catching one's heel, blocking the straightness of a path, rising like monuments in the middle of a patch of wild strawberries.

A woman knelt on one of those rocks, a flat one worn smooth by years of spring floods. She splashed water on her face but still looked pale.

"May I help you?" Esther made the offer by instinct.

The woman jumped and lost her balance. She caught herself in the shallow water, but the rippling stream soaked the front of her dress.

"I'm so sorry." Esther dropped the bucket and rushed forward to take the woman's arms to help her upright.

She jerked free and crossed her arms over her middle. "I don't need no help like you've given me already." Her voice was high, a little nasal, her features sharp. She'd be rather pretty with a little more flesh on her bones. Flesh and a smile. Her pursed-up lips tightened the skin over her cheekbones into the semblance of a skull mask.

Esther shuddered and retrieved the bucket. "Suit yourself. I'll be here for a few minutes if you need someone to help you up." She selected her own flat rock onto which she could kneel and set the bucket to fill with the swiftest part of the creek flow. "Are you Bethann Tolliver?"

"I am." The woman hadn't moved except to commence shivering.

"I'm Esther Cherrett."

"I know." Bethann stood and turned her back on Esther. "You're too pretty for anyone's good."

Esther sighed from the depths of her chest, where a constant ache reigned. "I know, especially mine."

Bethann cast her a narrow-eyed glance

59

over her shoulder. "You making fun of me?"

"No." Esther stood and lifted the bucket. "I'd rather look like —"

She stopped at the sound of footfalls crunching along the path.

"Me?" Bethann suggested.

"No, you're much too pretty."

Bethann snorted with a hint of genuine amusement. "Maybe you need glasses, child."

"Do you think they'd make me ugly?"

"Nothing," Griff Tolliver said from the trees, "could make you ugly, Miss Esther. Bethann, you all right?"

She faced her brother and shrugged, emphasizing the sharpness of her collarbone and shoulder points. Unlike her brother and cousins, the former of which had been laid low by a stab wound, she looked unwell, pasty-faced, and red-eyed.

Consumption? A cancerous growth? A blood disorder? The latter required lots of meat. Red meat. And red fruits like strawberries and grapes. People got well from some blood disorders that way, but not the other two. Esther could try to persuade Bethann of —

Of nothing. She was on this journey to teach younger children how to be — to use their mother's and aunt's words — civilized and book-learned. Esther had given up her role as healer. Bethann had summarized why in three words: *You're too pretty.* Mothers, wives, sisters, and sweethearts didn't want Esther around their menfolk.

Esther ground her teeth and took a step toward the path. "If you all will excuse me, I should get this back so we can get some food cooking."

"I'll take it for you." Griff closed the distance between them in a few long strides and removed the bucket from her hands. Then he glanced back at his sister. "You're going to join us, aren't you, Bethann?"

"I s'pose." Bethann's voice sounded choked.

Esther's training tugged her toward the stream. Griff's hand on her arm tugged her toward the path.

"Let her go," he murmured.

"But she's ill."

"Yea. Yes, I expect she is. But she'll be all right once we're home."

"If you're certain." Esther glanced back again.

Bethann had raised her hands to her face, and Esther caught her breath. She now knew why Bethann was so thin and unwell. Esther could help her. She must help her. If she continued to be ill and lose weight, she

61

would die.

Later. Esther would talk to her later.

"Have a care of the rocks, Miss Esther." Griff grasped her arm above the elbow.

Esther flinched away. "Please, don't."

"You were about to step onto that rock break."

"I'll . . . be more careful." Esther ducked her head under the pretext of watching for loose stones and more outcroppings of rock along the path, but it was more to mask her face, her muscles feeling tight enough to crack if she so much as brushed her cheek with a finger. Her head spun a little, and she felt queasy.

She would not be sick. The only thing worse than being touched was being sick in front of others. Neither must she show her weakness. Griff or Zach, once they returned to the clearing, would believe she needed assistance and would try to help her, take her arm again, hold her hand, lead her to a fallen log to sit.

Hungry. She was merely hungry. The sooner she helped Hannah prepare dinner, the sooner she could eat.

"I make the coffee," she announced to Griff.

"They make you work?" He shook his head as though disapproving.

"I volunteered."

"And a good job of it she does," Zach said.

He and Hannah already had bacon frying. Esther's nose wrinkled. She was hungry enough to eat it, but if she never saw another slab of pork after this journey, it wouldn't be too soon.

"I hope your coffee is better than Bethann's," Griff said. "She likes it so weak you may as well save money and have hot water."

"Is she all right?" Hannah asked.

"Are you all right?" Zach asked Griff.

Esther set about making the coffee while the three cousins talked. She'd thought earlier that Hannah didn't like Griff, but now she smiled with warmth when he assured her he was fully healed from his stab wound and the lump on his head.

"Who would've done that to you?" Zach asked. "We've been pondering that since we had to leave you."

Hannah paused in the middle of measuring cornmeal for the fried corn cakes they mostly ate, and Esther nudged her aside. "Go talk to him."

Hannah nodded and smiled her thanks, then joined her brother and cousin on the far side of the fire as Griff answered.

"I don't know. Someone thinking to rob me, I suppose."

"But they didn't." Zach stooped to add more wood to the fire. He met Esther's eyes across the flames and gave her his gentle smile.

It warmed her a bit, almost like when one of her brothers winked at her across the dinner table — but not quite. Just the message seemed the same. It was a gesture of "I'm not ignoring you."

She didn't care if the cousins talked while she worked. Zach had said something about needing them to get along, both families to get along, better than they had been. These three looked to be on the right path for that.

Then Griff said, "Bethann says it was you, Zach."

Zach dropped his armful of kindling with the crack and crunch of wood snapping.

Hannah gasped and pressed her hand to her throat. "That's nonsense. Zach wouldn't hurt a fly."

"I will if it gets in my dinner." He swiped at a handful of insects heading for the sweet cornmeal Esther was about to drop into the hot fat.

"You know what I mean." Hannah took a step backward and narrowed her gaze at Griff. "You don't believe it, do you?"

"No. But I've seen him kill a lot of fli—"

Hannah smacked his arm.

He grinned and caught her wrist. "You might be older, but you're smaller."

"Let her go." Zach's face was white, his mouth tight. "You know I wouldn't harm you. We took the vow together."

"I know." Griff patted Hannah's hand and released her. "Never fear, cousin Hannah, I'm not about to start thinking that Zach wants to start the feuding up again."

Esther's hand shook. Cornmeal batter slipped off of her wooden spoon and into the fire. It smoked and stank, and she jumped away. "I'm so sorry." She raised her hand to wipe her streaming eyes.

Griff caught hold of her hand. "You'll get that in your hair." He removed the batter-coated spoon from her hand but didn't move away. "Is something wrong?"

He held her gaze from six inches back. His breath brushed her lips.

She shut her mouth tight and turned her face from him without speaking.

"Of course something's wrong." Zach punched Griff's arm, breaking his hold on Esther's hand. "You just talked about the feud."

"Why shouldn't he?" Bethann stalked into the clearing, a beautifully woven shawl wrapped around her shoulders and hiding the wet front of her dress. "She's coming into it."

"There is no feud," Griff insisted. "No one's been hurt in over a year."

" 'Cept you," Zach murmured. His face twisted as though he were being stabbed.

"And he almost got dead," Bethann said. " 'Cause of you, Zachary Brooks."

"Bethann," Griff barked.

She ignored him and leaned over Zach, where he still squatted by the fire. "You stabbed my brother. I found the evidence. Your hair. Your —"

"Bethann." Griff reached out a hand as though intending to grasp hold of her and draw her away.

She slapped at him. "He may as well know we know the truth and you're just trying to protect him so's not to start the fighting again."

"No." Griff set his hands on his hips. "I don't believe it."

Zach and Hannah remained motionless, silent. Esther glanced from brother to sister. Their eyes were wide, their jaws tense in nearly identical expressions save for a muscle ticking at the corner of Hannah's jaw and her fingers twisting in front of her.

In the pan, the corn dodgers began to blacken and smoke. Esther dragged the spider off the flames and tipped it over into the dirt. The reek of scorching corn stung her nostrils. Her stomach heaved. She swallowed and returned her attention to the tableau on the far side of the now dying flames.

"What is this all about?" she managed to croak out past a parched tongue and lips.

The four cousins jumped and turned toward her as though they'd forgotten her presence.

"The feud," Bethann said. "Ever heard of one of those?"

"In Scottish history, yes, but not in Virginia."

"Told Momma it was a bad idea to bring her out here." Muttering something else, Bethann tramped to the far side of the clearing and the tethered horses. She began to rummage in a saddlebag.

"Well?" Esther challenged the other three with her eyes. "What's this all about?"

"I thought Momma told you." Griff scrubbed his hands over his face. His calloused palms rasped on his day or two growth of beard.

"She should have." Zach sighed and rose to join Esther. He reached out his hand to her, then let it fall to his side before he touched her. "We had no business bringing you out here without telling you the whole about the feud."

"It can't be a true feud." Pads of bandaging lint seemed to surround Esther. She brushed at her cheeks as though she were pushing them away. She took two deep, slow breaths. "You don't go to battle or anything, do you? Please tell me no."

"Do you want the truth or not?" Griff asked, his hands back on his lean hips.

"Truth." She could barely get out the word.

"Then yea, we do." Griff cleared his throat. "Yes'm, we did. Fifteen members of four families have died in the past ten years. That's why our mothers want you here — to learn — to teach the young'uns to grow up civilized."

"She knowingly brought me into a war?" Esther began to back toward Bethann and the horses.

She might manage to get back to Seabourne, or maybe Charlottesville. That wasn't far off. She could surely find work there as a serving maid in a tavern, if nothing else. Surely a town with a university would have lots of taverns needing maids to serve. Her parents wouldn't like it, but they'd like this situation less.

"Mrs. Tolliver wrote there was some

roughness up here, but not . . . fighting like that. I thought —" She took another step backward and trod on the overly long hem of her riding habit. It drew her up short. She stood on one foot in an attempt to free herself, tottered —

Zach's arm around her waist stopped her from falling. "Told you that dress was stupid."

She shuddered and glared at him, then Griff, then Hannah. "Why didn't one of you tell me before now?"

"You wouldn't have come," Hannah said. "Would you?"

"No. That is —"

If she admitted that she would possibly have done so even once she knew the whole tale, she would be admitting to them how much of a fix she was in at home. She had already let on too much.

"I expect I need to know more about this before drawing a conclusion." She sounded like her father again.

Griff laughed and grinned at her. "If you don't run away, I hope you'll teach me to talk like that. It'll give me something to confound those mineral factors."

"She sounds like some kind of uppity —" Hannah's mouth pinched. "We don't need to have her kind looking down her nose at us."

"Her kind is what Momma wants," Zach said. "And she's pulled her fair share on this journey, so she's not that uppity."

"Nor is she deaf," Esther interjected. "But she hasn't heard an explanation yet."

"Sit down," Griff directed. "Please."

Esther obeyed. She wobbled.

Griff poured her a cup of coffee and brought it to her. He squatted, his knees a hairbreadth from hers, and placed the tankard into her hands. Their fingers touched. He could have given her the mug without any contact. The contact was deliberate and lingered a second or two too long.

Esther's mouth parched like herbs in the oven. Drinking down the coffee in one gulp seemed like a good idea, except she'd scald herself in the process.

She swallowed and drew the cup close to her chest. "I'm listening."

"And so am I." Griff spoke in a low voice, a tone too low to carry farther than her ears. "Will you keep talking?"

Esther lifted the mug to her lips in response.

He sighed but did not move away. "This is rough country, you know. We're all loyal to our families. And sometimes a family member is so offended he just has to fight back. That's what happened. A man connected with the Brookses did something that offended my relatives and got wounded for it. Then his relatives went after mine for wounding him and killed my older brother . . . And that's how it starts. But Zach and I took a vow to stop the fighting once and for all. We took it before God and everyone at church."

"That's . . . barbaric." Esther sipped at the coffee to warm her cold insides. "No one right in his reason tries to kill someone. No one kills someone over an insult."

"They do if the insult's bad enough." Griff's gaze shifted right.

"Not a Christian soul," Esther persisted.

Hypocrite that she was for invoking the Lord when she had revoked her claims to a relationship with Him months ago.

"We seemed to forget all that." Zach spoke up for the first time. " 'Cept for Griff and me. We listened to the circuit preacher who comes through once a month or so, and we know it's wrong."

Both men wore identical expressions of intent sincerity — beautiful blue eyes wide, chins determined — handsome cousins so much alike in looks save for one fair and one dark. Not much older than Esther

71

herself but already bearing lines at the corners of their eyes. Mostly smile lines. Nice, kind young men who deserved the better way of life their mothers wanted for them. That God surely wanted for them.

She was most definitely not right for them. More suited to be that tavern maid, or so they'd think if they knew the truth.

"You won't come to harm up here with us," Griff assured her. He rose, brushed his forefinger across her cheek, and moved back before she could shy away.

She gripped the tankard so hard she expected the pewter to bow beneath her hands. She should ask what had started the fighting. If someone had stabbed Griff because of the feud, how safe could an outsider truly be if the fighting broke out again, despite these two scions of the families vowing they would stop it?

She couldn't form the words. She didn't want the answers. She must continue on with them. If matters grew dangerous, she would simply leave. She'd learned that lesson well.

Decision made, she rose. "I think we need to get some food prepared and be moving along then."

"Yea, we do." Hannah stooped to right the spider and let out a soft cry.

"Hannah?" Esther glanced down at the other woman. "Are you all right?"

Beside the fire, Hannah knelt in the dirt by the ruined dinner. She was cradling one hand with the other. On her palm, flaming red marks warned of blistering to come. "I grabbed the pan without a cloth." Her voice was a whimper.

"You should have said something." Esther tossed her cup aside and grasped Hannah's wrist. "Griff, hand me that bucket of water. Zach, fetch my satchel."

5

Without taking a moment to consider the consequences of her actions, Esther used the voice her mother had taught her to employ in the birthing chamber: "You need people to jump when you tell them to, not question why, so be authoritative."

Hannah crouched on the ground, sobbing through her teeth, though without tears, and her face was pale beneath the sun-tinted skin. Esther held her wrist in the water and spoke in the other kind of voice Momma had taught her to employ — the gentle, soothing one, almost like talking to a fractious child, without the exaggerated sweetness people tended to apply to little ones.

"I know it hurts. Burns always do. This will help. Thank you, Zach." She didn't raise her voice as he returned with her satchel. "Set that beside me. Griff, fetch some colder water. This is too warm to do much good."

"Won't do no good anyhow." Bethann returned to the gathering around the dying fire. "You need grease on that hand."

"No, cold water. Griff, please?"

With a nod, he trotted off with the coffeepot, the only large enough container besides the bucket.

"What are you?" Bethann called after him. "Her lapdog?"

Esther's mouth tightened, but she kept moving Hannah's hand around in the cool but not icy water.

Perhaps she should ask Bethann to stick her hand in the water to freeze it.

"He's helping my sister." Zach set the satchel on the ground beside Esther and flipped up the catch.

She rummaged in the bag with one hand, keeping eye contact with Hannah so she would know if the older woman might swoon at any moment. "I'm going to make a poultice with these herbs. Bethann, will you assist me?"

"Naw. All she needs is a little grease."

"My mother and I have never believed grease to be helpful for taking away the pain. Later it helps prevent the blisters from breaking, but at first, the colder the water —"

"You're going to kill her with that, I tell

75

you." Bethann began to scoop fat from the bacon tin. "I've been doctoring my family for years. I know what works and what don't. Never heard of water for a burn."

"I've used cold water, even ice if it's available, for years on pa—" Esther shut her mouth and turned her attention to Hannah, her tone a soothing murmur.

"I'll help you." Zach shot Bethann a glare, then turned his full attention on Esther, moving closer to her. Too close. His not entirely unpleasant odors of woods, horses, and perspiration filled her nostrils, her brain. Nausea touched her middle, spread as dizziness into her head.

"Please." Esther took a deep breath. "I need room to work."

"Sure." He moved back half a foot.

Not as much as she liked, but better.

"I mix the herbs in the grease," Bethann persisted.

"That might work." Esther set the envelope of elderflower leaves on her lap, then reached in to find her comfrey. "But we need that cold water first."

"Suit yourself. No one listens to me." Bethann slammed the lid on the bacon tin and stumbled away, looking ill. Beyond a curve in the path, her voice rang out. "You men are fools, and so is she."

"She knows what she's doing, that's clear," Zach responded.

Bethann grumbled something indistinct, then crashed away.

Another patient for Esther to tend. She should not be this ill.

Except Esther didn't want to be tending patients. She had left that behind. Yet she couldn't deny Hannah the care she needed, and Bethann appeared at the end of her strength.

Griff strode into the clearing with only a hitch in his gait to tell of his recent wound. He crouched beside Esther, and she flashed him a quick smile.

"Do, please, pour that water into the bucket. No, wait, let me pour some of this out. Hannah, I'm sorry." She drew Hannah's hand from the water.

Hannah hissed in her breath. "I declare the water is helping. It hurts more out of it."

"Of course it does. These herbs will help, though fresh would be better and aloe would be the best."

"What's aloe?" Griff asked.

Concentrating on studying the severity of Hannah's injury, Esther murmured, "A plant from northern Africa, though it grows all over the world now. It likes warm places, so we always grew a pot on our kitchen window sill." She plunged Hannah's hand into the water again. "Just a few more minutes."

"Why is aloe so good?" Griff pressed.

Esther glanced at him, eyebrows arched.

A dusky hue rose on his cheekbones, and he rubbed his cheeks. "I'm a farmer. Plants interest me."

Zach shuddered. "I'd rather be on the river."

"Perhaps you can take the river to someplace warm enough to grow aloe." Esther made the suggestion as a joke, but the cousins exchanged glances as though she were serious.

"That should do with the water for now." Esther removed Hannah's hand from the bucket and sprinkled herbs right onto the skin. "The elderflower smells nice, but the comfrey is like garbage. But nothing heals faster. Zach, hold your sister's hand while I wrap it."

He hesitated. "Why would you use something that smells bad to heal?"

"Because it works. Now take it, please."

"Sure thing." Zach slipped his hand between Hannah's and Esther's, his the size of both theirs together and even more calloused on the palm than Griff's.

Esther snatched her fingers free and dug in her satchel for a bit of gauze. The burns needed air to heal, but the herbs needed to remain pressed to the skin for several hours. "Griff, you should go look in on your sister. She's not well."

"Maybe you should." He was staring at her as Zach was too — with amazement. "You're the one with the doctoring skills."

More than he knew. More than she wanted.

"Men are doctors," she muttered.

"We don't got —" Hannah ducked her head. "I mean, we don't have no —"

"Any," Zach corrected.

Hannah sighed. "We don't have any doctors, men or otherwise, where we live. Just Bethann with some herbs and a midwife as old as Mr. Jefferson."

"Mr. Jefferson," Griff said, "is dead."

"Well, so should Granny Duval be." Hannah half smiled. "She's as old as he would be if he was still alive — about a hundred."

"You'll be welcome," Zach added.

Esther's skin broke out in gooseflesh as though the temperature had suddenly dropped from early summer day to late autumn night. "I am here to teach, not doctor. I just thought . . . burns need tending immediately."

And she couldn't abandon Bethann if she could help her.

Esther stood and brushed a few pine needles and herbs off of her lap. "I shall return in a few minutes." She turned and marched down the path. "Lord, don't let —" She stopped. No sense to pray for the men to remain behind. God didn't listen, let alone answer.

As though proving her point, boot heels crunched along the overgrown and leaf-strewn path. Zach or Griff? Long, easy strides eating up the ground. Griff. Zach walked faster with a shorter gait.

She stopped and turned. "Please, I'd like to talk to Bethann alone."

"Not sure you should." Griff smiled at her in that eye-crinkling way that made her insides feel like plucked strings on the church's old harpsichord. "She's taken a dislike to you."

And she wasn't going to like Esther any more in the next few minutes.

She hesitated. She need not go. Bethann wouldn't welcome her. Esther's aid hadn't been requested.

But she had watched her mother rush off at all hours of the day or night to help someone in need. And as Esther paused at the end of the path, Bethann moaned at the edge of the stream.

Esther spun on her heel and bounded to the other woman's side. Bethann stood bent over with her arms taut across her waist, her hands gripping her elbows as though she held her guts inside, which she just might feel she was doing.

"Bethann." Esther reached out to rest a hand on the older woman's shoulder but drew it back at the last moment. "I can help you. I have some gingerroot and peppermint oil in my —"

"Don't need any of your fancy know-it-all doctoring." Bethann turned her face away. "This'll pass."

"It should have passed already, and you're far too thin. You're not eat—"

Bethann turned on Esther with a sound like a snarl. She jumped back, glancing toward the end of the path to see if Griff remained in proximity. She might need his aid after all.

He stood there as still as the trees on either side of him, face tense, mouth grim.

"What would you know of this?" Bethann demanded. "Pretty little preacher's daughter who has to seek trouble because you don't know what it is?"

If only you knew.

Esther set her hands on her hips and

glared at Bethann. "You don't know any-thing about me, Miss Tolliver. I might be pretty, but that's not my fault, and I'm scarcely little. As for trouble . . ." She took a deep breath. "No, I haven't known the kind you're in, but I've seen my share —"

"Where?" Bethann snorted. "At tea par-ties and the like?"

"When I've examined women." Esther took a step forward to ensure only Bethann heard what she had to say. "I am a fully qualified midwife and have been for three years. I apprenticed with my mother for three before that."

For a moment, Bethann's eyes widened. Her jaw hung slack. Then she flung her head and shoulders back and her hands forward, palms slamming into Esther's chest. "You lie. You don't know anything. You can't. It's not true. Do you hear me? Not true."

"Four months." Esther managed the two words through chattering teeth and a haze of memories that wanted to intrude.

From the corner of her eye, she spotted Griff moving forward and waved him back.

"Maybe five," she added.

"No." Bethann shot her head forward like a chicken about to pick up a tasty bug. "I'll deny any such thing, and you'll be gone without an escort back to your momma."

"Of course I'll say nothing." Esther tried the gentle smile she'd practiced in the mirror to resemble Momma's. "It's part of my training to keep secrets."

"See that you do. This ain't nobody's business but mine."

And the father's. And God's. And perhaps Bethann's parents, despite her age, since she lived at home.

"You're right." Esther nodded. "It isn't any of my business unless you ask for my assistance." She held out her hand, palm up.

Bethann hesitated a moment, then touched her fingertips to Esther's in a feathery acknowledgment of their agreement. Then she stumbled away, past Esther, and along the creek.

The brush of Griff's heels on the ground cover joined Bethann's retreating footfalls in the brush as he approached Esther. "What was that about?"

"I gave her some advice." Esther smiled. "She didn't want it."

"Didn't look like it." Griff gazed past Esther. "Will she be all right? I mean, she ain't a-dyin' or anything, is she?"

Esther hesitated before responding. Women did die from the sickness that accompanied childbearing. They suffered so badly they couldn't eat and faded away. Sometimes they suffered a seizure and just collapsed, never to awaken again. Bethann attempted to appear vigorous though.

"I don't think so, if she eats more," Esther said.

Griff rubbed the back of his neck. "And she'll be better in a week or two?"

"Should be."

So he suspected what was amiss with this sister.

How it must distress him to have a sister, who must be eight or nine years his senior and unmarried, in a condition too many women in the East referred to as *delicate.* Despite her thinness, nothing about Bethann, from her forceful voice to her wiry arms, was delicate.

He dropped his hand and clasped the other one behind his back. "Miss Esther, my pa ain't — isn't well, and my older brother got himself killed with the feuding ten years ago. That leaves me the head of the family, and there are reasons why I gotta know the truth about Bethann."

"I promised her I'd keep her secret. You'll have to ask her."

Lightning flashed across his eyes. "Even if it means this could start the fighting again?"

"I keep my promises," Esther said. "And

my secrets."

"Even if it could get people killed?"

"How could it get people killed?"

"That's family business."

"And this is my business."

Even if she had vowed to leave it behind, it apparently wouldn't leave her behind.

Their eyes locked, held, neither so much as blinking for a full minute.

Then Griff ripped his gaze away and turned back toward the clearing. "I suggest you be praying no one's going to die over your honor, especially not you."

6

Not a polite thing to say to her. Griff knew it without his mother standing over his shoulder reminding him that just because he'd grown up in the mountains didn't mean he was raised without knowing how to treat a female right. Suggesting Esther Cherrett might be responsible for someone's death was certainly not treating her right.

Even if it was the truth.

He'd have to be ignorant of all around him to not suspect what was wrong with Bethann. And if she was breeding, the same man as before was all too likely responsible — Henry Gosnoll, Hannah Gosnoll's husband, Zach's brother-in-law.

The incident that had started a ten-year-long feud.

"Oh, Bethann, how could you be such a fool again?" He groaned the words aloud and paused on the path to lean against a tree and rub his face, his gritty eyes.

His side ached. His heart ached more. The instant Pa learned the truth, he would take his shotgun to Gosnoll and the fighting would begin again.

If it hadn't already.

Griff pressed his hand to his side and considered the possibility that someone in the Gosnoll family knew about Bethann and wanted vengeance against the Tolliver family for her interference.

Someone like Zach.

"Not Zach." It was a prayer, a plea, a cry for help. "God, this can't go on."

"God can do anything He wants." Miss Esther's voice purred through the afternoon stillness in the forest. "He has His reasons, and I'm not convinced they are all good for us."

Griff jerked around and stared at her. "Miss Esther, that's blasphemy."

"Perhaps." She shrugged. "Will you send me home for saying it, for not being the perfect lady of faith everyone expects the preacher's daughter to be?"

Her lips smiled. Her eyes did not. The canopy of leaves shadowed them, dimming the golden lights and turning them into bottomless pools. Cold pools like the one beneath the waterfall where he experienced peace and solace.

He wouldn't find peace and solace with this female, that was for sure. A quiet and biddable female she was not. She hadn't in the least backed down from Bethann's belligerence and, according to Zach and Hannah, hadn't complained or expected them to wait on her for the entire journey. Yet she was not — as Momma believed from mention of Miss Esther's father being a minister — a spiritual female. Unless he'd just been mistaken about the meaning behind her words.

"You don't believe God has our good in all He does?" he asked.

"I believe He has a purpose in all He does, but it may not be for our good." She bit her lip, then brushed her fingertips across her lower lids. "No, that's not right or fair. I'm worn to a thread, is all. I meant to say that I don't think it is always good for us . . . or something of the like. I can't think straight." Tears swam in her eyes, bringing back the gold lights.

Griff stared at her, quite certain she had made those tears appear and wasn't in the least sincere.

A chill ran up his arms, raising the hairs against his shirtsleeves like a cat's fur being rubbed the wrong way — enough to make him want to hiss out something sharp and probably unkind. Or send her packing back to her seaside village and preacher father to set the fear of God back into her soul.

Then she lowered her hands, and the shadows around her eyes were genuine, like bruises beneath her skin. She held her lips tightly together, but a muscle in her jaw twitched. Surely no one could make that happen to oneself.

He raised his hand to touch her cheek, re-assure her that soon enough they would reach the ridge and comfortable accommodations, at least in comparison with the road, and she could get her rest, write to her family, forget about unpleasant encounters with Bethann.

Well, maybe not that, with Bethann still at home.

And too soon, Bethann's condition would create chaos on the ridge, and her state wouldn't be the only condition around that was delicate.

Miss Esther flinched away from his hand the instant before it touched her cheek. "I apologize for saying anything untoward. Your sister's . . . situation has distressed me into saying foolish things." Casting him a half smile, she started up the path.

"I can guess what it is." Griff tucked his

hands behind his back. "It isn't the first time."

Miss Esther stumbled over a protruding root and grabbed an overhead limb for balance as she swung around and stared at him. "What are you saying?"

"Bethann has never been married. She has, however, been easily . . . persuaded to —" Heat suddenly crept up his neck. "I'm right sorry I said anything. This ain't — I mean isn't the way I was taught to talk to a lady."

"I'm used to such talk. You haven't offended me." She gave him a smile that drew the sunshine beneath the trees.

Griff's toes curled inside his boots, and he glanced away, focused on an empty bird's nest above her head. He must not be swayed by a pretty face. A more than pretty face. Look how it had gotten Bethann into trouble and about destroyed two families when she got herself persuaded by a well set-up man. Griff would not fall into the same danger, the same trap. He wanted his wife to love the Lord unconditionally, believe that all the Lord willed was good and right.

"We should get back," he said with an abruptness that verged on rudeness. "We haven't eaten and daylight's wasting."

"Of course." Her quick, light footfalls headed up the path.

After several moments, when she must have disappeared beyond the trunks and underbrush, Griff followed. By the time he reached the clearing at the pace of a tortoise, Miss Esther Cherrett was positioning the spider back over the fire and asking Hannah about her hand.

"It's much better, thank you. Scarcely a blister."

"Good. I'll put more herbs on it before we leave. Can you ride with only one hand?"

"Yes, ma'am, I can."

Hannah calling Miss Esther Cherrett ma'am? Hannah had at least five years on the newcomer. But Miss Esther possessed an authority, a sense of command. She directed. The rest of them obeyed. Good for the children, if she didn't preach her blasphemy.

Griff looked at the shadows beneath her eyes and shook his head. Maybe not blasphemy, but honest doubt. He understood honest doubt after too many years of watching friends and kinfolk die for no good reason. But what sort of misfortune could she have endured in her comfortable village?

Her hands steady, her face smooth, Miss

Esther appeared free of cares as she set about preparing dinner. Griff fed more sticks onto the fire and watched her efficient movements with knife and spoon, coffeepot and skillet. Her hands were small with long, slender fingers. They appeared delicate. With just one hand, she lifted the heavy iron spider and moved it as though it weighed less than the curl slipping from its pins to caress the nape of her neck.

"What's going on, Cousin?"

Intent upon watching Miss Esther, Griff jumped at Zach's question. "With what?" He made himself look at his cousin.

Zach arched one brow. "With Miss Esther and your sister."

"Oh, that." Griff shrugged. "Bethann being herself." Griff watched Miss Esther from the corner of his eye. Graceful and comfortable with what she was doing, as though she had cooked over a fire many times. "We should help her."

"We're keeping the fire going. That's more help than either of us trying to cook. Why is Bethann in a snit?"

"She didn't like someone else doing the doctoring, I expect."

The truth as far as that went.

"You know how she is — unhappy, so she works to make us all unhappy."

"Your pa should have married her off a long time ago." Zach's eyes drifted to the right. "Would have saved us all a lot of trouble."

"Yep, he should have. Or sent her away. She and Miss Esther aren't going to get on at all. I just hope the youngsters —" Griff stopped himself.

No need to tell Zach about his uneasiness regarding the schoolma'am, whether or not she was good for the children. Surely she would keep her religious views to herself and simply teach them what the Bible said. Maybe in doing so, she would come to the truth herself, realize God was always faithful no matter what.

"They'll like her right much," he finished.

"How couldn't they?" Zach stared at Miss Esther without even trying to disguise his expression — pure admiration, longing, need.

Griff's gut twisted ever so slightly. Too much for him to deny it was a twinge of envy, since Zach had a three-week advantage over him with the lady. Too little for him to convince himself he cared all that much, not enough to start trouble between him and his cousin over her.

"Are you thinking of courting her?" Griff asked.

Miss Esther glanced their way and frowned. Surely she hadn't heard them.

"May I have some more wood, please?" she asked.

Zach and Griff sprang to produce more dry sticks for her cook fire.

"I should do that," Hannah said from her log seat. "Better'n sitting here doing nothing."

"Let your hand rest." Miss Esther's face softened as she glanced at Hannah.

Griff removed himself to the far end of the meadow, where the horses grazed and dozed in the shadow of an oak. He untethered two of them and led them down to the creek. In the clearing behind him, Zach remained at the fire, alternating between feeding wood to the blaze and gazing up at Miss Esther Cherrett. He hadn't answered Griff's question, but the answer was obvious from the yearning expression on his face — yes, he wanted to court her.

"You may have your chance with her," Griff murmured beneath the burble of the stream and the drinking horses. "I won't cause more strife in this family than my sister has already."

If he could just stop himself from looking at her, from listening to her voice.

He returned to the meadow for the next

set of horses. The others were eating and waved him over to the fire, but he shook his head and proceeded to water all the mounts. By the time he finished with the two pack-horses, the others had finished their meal. Zach was burying the fire, and Miss Esther was tending to Hannah's hand like she truly did know what she was doing.

And she must. She carried herbs and the like with her. Though red with a few small white blisters along one side, Hannah's hand didn't look as bad as it might have.

Griff pulled up his sleeve to examine the scar just above his left wrist, where he had burned it half a dozen years earlier. Bethann had smeared it with lard, which hadn't done it a bit of good. The skin had blistered and wept, then settled into a ridged, red pucker. It didn't bother him now. It didn't hurt the use of his arm, but that kind of scarring could keep a body from using his hand well.

"What happened?" Miss Esther's voice glided across his ears, as soft and rich as that ribbon Pa had brought from the city for Momma and the girls before he got hurt.

He glanced up, caught a hint of a scent he didn't recognize, and looked away. "Burned it."

"That's apparent." Impatience rang in her tone. "How did you burn it?"

"Mule shed caught fire a few years back. I was in getting the stupid beasts out, and burning hay fell onto my sleeve."

"That must have hurt."

He shrugged as though it were nothing. In truth, he had been sick with the pain.

She hefted her satchel, passed it from hand to hand. "Did you save the mules?"

"Sure did." He grinned at her.

She blinked and darted a glance toward the horses. "When will we get home — to your home, that is?"

"We'll get there day after tomorrow if we ride late. The moon is bright."

"What about Bethann? She didn't take her mount."

"We'll leave it for her. She can make it on her own."

"Is that safe? I mean —" She shifted the bag a couple more times. "A female alone and all. Females alone aren't . . . safe."

As if she knew anything about danger.

He took her bag from her twitching fingers and started for the horses. "Bethann likes to keep to the shadows. She'll be right behind us."

"If you think so." Mouth tight, which made her lips look fuller instead of thinner like most people's, she trudged beside him. Her gaze flicked around the clearing's edges. Yes, somewhere out there Bethann likely lurked, waiting for them to head out. She would fetch her mount then and follow close enough that they could hear her scream if she encountered danger she couldn't manage herself.

Not that she was likely to encounter danger she couldn't handle herself. Even if the fighting had begun again, no Gosnoll or Brooks would harm a female or child.

At least not intentionally.

Griff strapped Miss Esther's satchel onto her horse, then waited for her to ask his assistance mounting. Ignoring him, she took the reins and led the mare over to the log by the fire, stepped onto it, and swung herself into the saddle. Not a bit of petticoat or ankle flashed from beneath the excessively long skirt of her gown.

So she mounted as well as she did everything else.

A lead weight seemed to settle around Griff's heart, dragging him down, for Zach too watched her, his eyes an intense blue like the sky on a sunny autumn day. Griff knew Momma and Aunt Tamar Brooks hoped the schoolma'am would be a good wife for either him or Zach. The mothers wanted at least one of the sons to marry someone more refined than the local girls now that the lead mine promised the families a bit of prosperity. For the sake of peace, Griff would let Zach try. He didn't know how much success his cousin would enjoy from a female who didn't like to be touched.

For a moment, Griff's blood raced with the potential challenge of simply taking Miss Esther Cherrett's hand without her flinching away from his nearness. At once he dismissed it as improper, unworthy of the kind of man Momma wanted him to be, unworthy of the vow he had taken to preserve or restore peace at any cost between the families on the ridge.

Annoying things were vows. When a body made them, he didn't know the cost they would demand.

7

If nighttime had not been so close, Esther pondered after two more days of riding and sleeping on the ground, she would have turned her horse east, north, south, anywhere but a continuing trek west. West and up. And up. She kept glancing back toward the east, where the land lay in darkness and the wind through the trees sounded like the sea.

She ached for the sea, the sharp tang of salt spray, the cleanness of the air. There in the mountain forests, she smelled nothing but leaf mold, damp earth, and the occasional whiff of pine. Not to mention her own reek of wood smoke, horses, and, horrifyingly, perspiration. She wanted a bath, a swim, a bar of her fragrant soap applied more lavishly than quick splashes while bent over a stream allowed. Clear, sweet-water streams, but cold and shallow streams nonetheless.

More than bathing, more than clean clothes, more than a day spent off a jouncing horse, she ached for her feather bed and lavender-scented sheets, a variety of food, and, most of all, peace.

"What have I done?" she asked the space between the mare's pointed ears. "What have I done?"

She had asked the question a few times after learning of a conflict between the families. But now that she had met Bethann and Griff, had been told that she could be responsible for someone's death if she said the wrong thing to the wrong person, all Esther wanted to do was run back to the shelter of Seabourne, home, Momma, and Papa. Except she wanted that home to be the one she'd enjoyed before she had gone to the Oglevies' house when Papa had said to wait for Momma.

She longed for the impossible.

So she remained facing west, perhaps a little south, and always climbing through lush, green forests and past racing streams. Then they reached a river that shimmered and sparkled in the last rays of the sun as though the stars had come out early and drowned themselves in the racing current.

Esther stared at the current, blinked, stared again. "It's flowing north. I thought rivers flowed south."

"This is the New River." Zach walked his horse back to Esther's. "It flows north to the Kanawha River."

"So does the Shenandoah," Hannah added. "Not to the Ohio, but it goes north."

"I didn't realize." Esther ran through all she had learned about geography. She could tell someone how to find Saint Petersburg in Russia but hadn't known about a river in the commonwealth of Virginia.

A fine teacher she would make for children growing up in these mountains.

"Do you live by this river?" was all she could think to ask.

"Another five miles away or so." Zach's face shone as bright as his hair. "My family operates a ferry. Has for fifty years."

"And the ridge is named for us." Hannah's voice rang with pride.

On his mount a dozen yards behind them, Griff said nothing and made no move to ride closer. A shadow on the path farther back suggested Bethann did indeed follow them and Griff remained in the rear to watch over her.

"Our father's people were here first," Zach explained.

He already had said so along the way. His mother and Griff's mother were sisters whose families had resided in the mountains since the Revolution. The Tollivers were relative newcomers, having only been in Virginia's mountains for the past forty years or so. "They've been in America forever, though," Hannah had admitted reluctantly. "Maybe lived around your people once."

"I don't know the name." Esther would have remembered any family related to Griff Tolliver if they at all resembled him.

For all Zach's golden good looks, Griff's dark attractiveness in contrast to his pale blue eyes left her restless and afraid of what she didn't know — him. It was quite enough to fear. Men who got themselves stabbed without knowing why made poor companions, surely. He made a poor one now, silent and too distant on his roan gelding. The horse blended into the surroundings as mist rose from the river and the sun sank behind the mountains on the other side of the water.

Esther pictured another man sneaking up behind her, resting his hands on her shoulders, grinning at her pallid reflection in the kitchen window.

She jumped and swung toward Zach fast enough to draw her horse into a sidle. "May we go? I want to get home. That is, to your house."

"You'll be stopping at the Tollivers'."
Zach's lips turned down a bit at his words.
"I wish you were coming to our house, but
they're further along with their building
than we are."

"They have the school building," Hannah
said. "And most of the mine, though my
husband manages it."

"He must be very intelligent," Esther
responded, as she had the other two times
Hannah told her this.

Hannah snorted. "Most of the time.
About mines anyway." She wheeled her
horse away from the riverbank and trotted
up the path.

"I'm sorry about that." Zach rode alongside Esther on this wide track along the
water. "He's not the best husband at times,
you may as well know. You'll hear soon
enough."

"I'm sorry." What else could she say?

She wanted to know nothing of these
people's lives beyond what she needed to
know. She should not have interfered with
Bethann, but a lifetime of observing her
mother and her own training over the past
six years had taken over her good sense, and
she had to give her advice when it wasn't
sought. She knew better than to do that.
But she'd felt so comfortable with Zach and

Hannah by then, she thought —

No, she hadn't thought.

"Lord, how can I ever —" She broke off the silent prayer before it was formed. Praying was before. God had failed to save her when she begged and pleaded. She wouldn't ask for His help anymore. Mistakes or not, she would manage her future on her own.

She plodded on beside and then behind the Brooks siblings. Darkness settled over them with stars seeming to hang upon the trees, guiding their way, until the moon rose in a brilliant shine to light the way to a fence created of upright saplings stripped of their bark so they gleamed white in the colorless light, and a gate also created out of whole tree trunks.

"A stockade?" Despite the warm summer night, Esther's skin rose in gooseflesh. "Surely it's not . . . dangerous here."

"Not now," Zach said with dauntless cheer. "But it used to be. The gate's never locked."

He dismounted and opened the massive portal. It swung outward without a sound, but suddenly chickens and children and the tallest woman Esther had ever seen swarmed into the yard beyond. Lanterns blazed, and Griff appeared in their midst with an embrace and a word for each person.

"Let me help you down." Zach reached Esther's side and held up his hand.

She took it and slid to the ground. The hard-packed earth tilted and swayed beneath her wobbling legs, but Zach's hand remained beneath hers, strong, hard from labor, not in the least something to flinch away from or fear touching.

She smiled up at him. "Thank you so much for coming to get me. I'm certain we will see one another again."

"Soon. Very soon. I'll bring my brothers to the school when it opens. Now come meet Aunt Lizbeth." He led Esther forward to the tall woman presiding over what seemed like a dozen children swirling around Griff.

The number of children proved to be only two girls and two boys between ten and fifteen years of age. The woman was almost as tall as her eldest son, with his pale blue eyes and remnants of dark hair, and a smile shining with warmth even in the flickering lantern light.

She held out a hand to Esther. "Welcome to Brooks Ridge, Miss Cherrett. So glad you decided to come and civilize these louts of mine."

"Thank you."

They were all too good-looking for Esther

to consider them louts, though their thick accents as they greeted her — a drawling speech with a hint of a twang — and their homespun clothes and bare feet might give others pause when meeting them on a street. Lead mines or not, they didn't look prosperous.

"Hannah, Zach," Mrs. Tolliver called out, "you all want to bide here overnight?"

"I'd like to get home," Hannah said. She drooped in her saddle like a flower left too long in a vase.

Zach frowned, then returned to his waiting horse. "Momma will want to see us. I'll call soon, find out about the school. Miss Cherrett, I'll be calling, if I may."

No, no, not call that way, Esther cried inside her head.

She inclined her head. "In a few days. I'll be occupied with the school right off."

"Hear that, girls?" Mrs. Tolliver turned toward her daughters. "Hear how pretty she talks? You can learn to talk that way too."

"Why'd I want to?" The younger girl, possibly thirteen or so, turned down the corners of her wide-lipped mouth. "Ain't nothing wrong with the way I talk."

"Except you sound like an ignorant mountain girl, Brenna," the older sister said. "Kind of like Beth—"

"That's enough, Liza." Griff laid his hand on his sister's shoulder. "Bethann's got her troubles." He looked at his mother. "Too many, it looks like."

"Where is she?" Mrs. Tolliver asked.

"She was right behind me. But there's — we'll talk after you get Miss Cherrett settled." He nodded at Esther. "Momma and the girls will show you your quarters."

"My . . . quarters?" Esther glanced around the part of the stockade she could see by the lantern light.

To one side stood a barn and a small board structure. The door to the latter stood open, and a rustling and muttered clucking inside suggested hens roosted there. A lot of hens. A half-built house of cedar shakes sprouted on the other side of the fenced area. Oiled paper instead of glass filled in most of the windows. With the children leading the way and Griff drawing up the rear with Esther's luggage, they swept across the yard, past a flourishing garden and the house under construction.

"You live behind the school," Mrs. Tolliver said. "You'll be more comfortable there than in the big house without any windows. We're hoping the glass comes before winter, but it's hard to get it up here."

Esther dropped the hem of her riding

habit and stumbled over the excess fabric. "I — I'm living alone?" She glanced around at the house, the barn and coop, the garden, the stockade fence. "I didn't realize . . . I never . . ."

"I'll trade with you," the younger of the two boys piped up.

"No one will trade with her." Mrs. Tolliver strode to the stoop of another log building. "You can take your meals with us, of course, and we're only a holler away, but you won't have no privacy in the house yet."

"She means you can't be in a room on the same floor as Griff," Brenna added. "Even if she does want him to marry you."

"She doesn't even know her." Liza's tone dripped with scorn. She sidled up beside Esther and whispered, "She don't — doesn't have any manners."

Esther smiled and whispered back, "They rarely do at that age."

Liza giggled. "Do you have a younger sister?"

"No, just know lots of girls that age back —" She stopped before she said *home.*

It wasn't home. Nothing was home. Especially not the log house the Tollivers showed her. Two rooms presented themselves to her, with one window in each. The windows had glass, true, but the building would be dark even on a sunny day. A fireplace took up most of the wall that joined the two rooms. A fireplace she would have to tend, no doubt, if she could lift logs big enough to fill it. On the bright side, it was a large enough hearth to heat a huge kettle of water, if she could acquire one.

Other than a few benches and a single table and chair, the front room lay empty. The far room, however, held a plain but highly polished wooden bedstead, a rocking chair, and a chest of drawers. A hand-braided rug covered the plank floor, and two quilts decorated the walls.

The quilts, pieced with care into intricate patterns of red, blue, and green, faded and appearing as soft as the finest muslin, made Esther's eyes burn, then tear. She blinked to get rid of the moisture. One tear fell down her cheek. She brushed it away with the back of her hand and tried to speak. But her throat had closed, and all she could manage was a smile she feared appeared far too wan to express how much those carefully hung quilts meant to her.

"They're lovely," she croaked out.

A wave of emptiness washed over her, staggering her. She missed her mother, her father, the grandparents she had never known, and the brothers who had teased her mercilessly.

Suddenly a hand gripped hers, as calloused and broad as a man's. "You all right, child?"

Esther flicked a glance up at Mrs. Tolliver, then down to the colorful rag rug on the floor. "Yes, thank you. It's all quite . . . nice. No, b-beautiful." She swallowed. "Th-thank you."

"It's us who thank you for coming out here. Not many was willing." Mrs. Tolliver patted her shoulder. "I'll have Griff bring you some hot water so you can have a bath, and someone will come down with your supper and give you any help you need."

"What kind of help?" Brenna demanded. "Bring her a towel she can mop up her — ouch, Griff, what'd you do that for?"

Esther snapped her head around in time to catch Griff just releasing the end of his youngest sister's pigtail. He was scowling at her. "Reminding you of your manners. Now git."

Face sullen, she turned and stalked from the room.

"I'll go see she does her chores," Liza said and followed at a trot.

Griff and his mother exchanged a glance, then he turned back to Esther. "Liza can sleep out in the other room if you're afraid of being alone out here."

"You needn't be," Mrs. Tolliver answered. "We close up the stockade at night to keep the animals safe, and there's a lock on this door."

Esther opened her mouth to say she would like that, then realized Liza would have to sleep on the floor in that barren chamber instead of her bed in a room possibly as lovingly set up as this one. More so.

"No, thank you. I'll manage quite well, thank you." She smiled at Mrs. Tolliver, then Griff.

The former nodded and tucked a stray tendril of hair into Esther's chignon as her own mother might have done — without thinking, a reflexive motion of tender care.

Griff said nothing. He didn't smile. He did catch her eye and hold her gaze for far longer than was necessary. Than was polite. Then he spun on his heel and strode from the room, from the building, with a speed suggesting he wanted to place as much distance between them as he could, but not because he disliked her as Bethann and now Brenna did. On the contrary. She had read the expression in his eyes and understood it, as she had experienced it herself.

His lingering gaze held the longing for something he knew he couldn't have — her.

8

Zach hated leaving Esther with the Tollivers. They would take good care of her and had more space for her to live comfortably, but Griff would see her morning, noon, and night, whereas Zach would need to find excuses to call on his cousins in order to see her.

"She's been in our company for more than three weeks," Zach mused aloud. "Kinda feel like we left her behind or something."

"She's not for the likes of you anyway." Hannah yawned. "I think it was a mistake to bring her."

Zach stared at her through the starlit path farther up the ridge to their holding — land better for grazing than farming, but even better for logging, and now just a wee corner for mining precious lead.

"She fixed up your hand right well. How can you say we shouldn't have brought her?"

"Because she fixed up my hand right well.

And she went to see why Bethann is so sickly." Hannah half turned in her saddle, leather creaking. "Zach, don't you find something odd about that, her knowing so much about herbs and having them with her?"

"No. Lots of womenfolk do."

"Up here where there aren't any doctors, yea, but not in the east."

Zach shrugged. "Be glad she does."

"Sure, but why wouldn't she say so when she wrote about the position? Why would she need to be teaching if her daddy is a preacher and all? I mean, her clothes are fine and that satchel of hers, all her baggage, is fine."

"So?"

"Don't you see?" Hannah's tone held impatience. "She's not poor. She don't need to earn her living."

"Maybe she just wants to." He grinned. "Or maybe she's looking for a husband."

Hannah snorted. "Up here? Females who look like her marry city men with diamond rings and such-like."

Queasiness gripped Zach's stomach. He feared his sister was right. Females who looked and talked like Esther Cherrett and came from the kind of family she did didn't go to the mountains for work or husbands.

Yet Miss Esther Cherrett, with her English father and American mother living in a quiet fishing village on the eastern shore, had answered an advertisement for a schoolma'am there in the Virginia mountains.

Not for the first time, he questioned her honesty. She might be telling them the truth about most things. She was certainly good enough for the work they wanted from her — to teach the youngsters good English and reading and writing so they could be more than men and women trying to eke a living out of the unforgiving rock of these hills. But Esther was too pretty, too comfortably off, too confident in herself, to truly belong amidst the mountain folk. She was more like those people who had come to ask questions and watch them, write in little books, then go away and print things they thought were true, like they were writing about some new breed of animal. And she was a bit old to not be wed, especially as pretty as she was.

Despite his doubts, Zach's heart twisted with the very image of her flashing through his mind. The sound of her voice made him quivery inside. He'd never felt that way before about any of the girls on the ridge, but he should leave Miss Esther to Griff.

Except Griff got everything — the talent, the charm, the ability to make even Zach's brother-in-law do what he wanted him to do.

Zach should seek a bride from the girls on the mountain. Some of them were just as pretty. Well, almost. They knew what they needed to about living without markets and dry goods stores close by — preserving meats and vegetables, weaving, stitchery. They could cook whatever they had and make do however necessary to keep a family alive in the lean times. Many were sweet, and some could sing like the angels must. They'd been tossing their caps for him since he was sixteen. He'd even courted a few from time to time. It had never come to anything when he thought about living with them the rest of his life, but he could change that.

Or he could try his luck at winning Miss Esther over Griff.

"You want to court her, don't you?" Hannah said as though she could read his thoughts.

She probably could.

Zach didn't answer.

"What if Griff wants to?" Hannah pressed.

" 'Course he does. Didn't you see how he was lookin' at her?"

"Thought so. And what if he decides you did stab him? Bethann says she has proof."

"It ain't —" He stopped. He needed to stop saying that. Esther never said *ain't.* "It isn't good enough for Griff to believe I'd harm him."

"He might with Bethann poisoning him against us." They rode into the light from a lantern hung on the family stockade gate in time to show Hannah's face twist with bitterness.

She despised Bethann, and with good reason. Hannah's husband had courted Bethann first, back when the older woman was younger and prettier, her face not twisted up with her own bitterness and maybe guilt. But the Brookses were more prosperous then with the ferry, so Gosnoll dishonored Bethann and started a feud.

"Henry married you, Hannah," Zach said gently.

"But I haven't given him children. If he could, he'd unmarry me for that." She slid from her horse with a thud and yanked open the gate. "We're home."

Momma, the two younger children, and Pa raced from the house with joyous cries of welcome.

Henry Gosnoll, Hannah's husband, didn't appear.

■ ■ ■ ■

"When did Brenna get so hateful?" Griff asked Momma as they tramped back to the main house, the kitchen, the tank of water always kept filled and hot behind the stove. "She's as miserable as —" He didn't supply the name. No need. They both knew to whom he referred.

Momma's shoulders slumped, and she suddenly looked all of her fifty-one years and more. "I don't know what's wrong with her. Ever since you left, she's gotten ornery, disrespectful. I tried to get your pa to speak to her, but he says she's a female and all females are ornery at that age."

"Liza wasn't." Griff opened the door for Momma.

"Liza is an angel. Never gave me a lick of trouble." Momma entered the kitchen and picked up two buckets. "Take these to Miss Cherrett. She'll be wanting a bath, no doubt."

"I'd rather not." Griff kept his gaze fixed on the far side of the room, where Pa had gotten shelves fixed to the wall in the past few weeks. "Those'll look right fine when they're finished. Is Pa feeling all right then to do that much work?"

"He's been well, but I make him go to bed early and get his rest." Momma thrust the buckets at Griff. "You take these, young man. That's an order."

"It's not a good idea, Momma." Griff took the buckets, then set them beside the stove before wandering to the shelves. "His back ain't hurting him none?"

"Isn't. Gotta stop saying *ain't.* And no, his back hasn't been too bad. Good enough for him to get after you if you don't do what I say, even if you are a man grown."

"I can't see her." Griff ran his hand along a smoothly planed shelf. Pa had been shot in the early days of the feuding. By whom, no one was sure. The wound hadn't been bad, but the impact had knocked him off a cliff and sent him tumbling thirty feet to land in some trees. Those branches broke his fall and saved his life, but his back hadn't been the same since. The eldest Tolliver son had died that same day.

If Griff hadn't been old enough to take over the farm then at sixteen, the family would have starved. They hadn't prospered until they realized the land to one end of the ridge, partly shared with the Brooks family, bore more lead than any of the families on the mountain could use for their own need — for the rifle bullets they'd been

118

making themselves for decades to keep meat on their tables when the land failed to produce enough crops for survival.

"Zach wants her," Griff added, bent over the wood to study the swirling grain of the pine board. From the corner of his eye, he caught a flicker in the window, the pale blur of a face. "She's his."

"He's already fallen for that pretty face?" Momma clattered the lid to the water tank. "I don't believe it. She's gotta be too smart for that. He don't know nothing about anything."

"He's kind, and maybe that pretty face is enough. Either way —" Griff turned. He had to tell Momma now, if that was Bethann outside the window. She'd come inside in a moment and say what had happened and make her accusations. If Momma believed her eldest daughter, if Pa believed Bethann, and if his own suspicions about his sister were right, the shots ringing over the mountain wouldn't be coming from hunting rifles.

And someone in either family would no doubt be dead.

"He got three weeks' acquaintance on me, you see," Griff blurted out.

Momma spun to face him. "How? You set out together."

"Yea, but I got stabbed along the way.

Ambushed."

The stove lid clattered to the floor. The back door burst open, and Bethann shot into the kitchen on a wave of warm air smelling of pungent farm animals and fragrant herbs.

"Did he tell you he's been stabbed?" Bethann demanded. "Well, did you tell her?" she asked Griff.

"He did." Momma frowned at Bethann. "I'm not much on that etiquette stuff, but I taught you better'n to interrupt a conversation like that. You can say howdy to all of us first."

"How do you do, Mother." Bethann spoke with exaggerated care in her words as though she were trying to imitate Miss Esther, then she started to curtsy like they'd seen some females do in a traveling player show, but her features twisted in pain and she staggered back a pace.

Griff caught her before she fell against the stove. "What's wrong?"

"Wasn't paying attention in the dark and got myself knocked off my horse by a tree branch." Bethann rubbed her lower back. "Just hurts a bit."

"Maybe you should go to your bed." Griff's gaze dropped to Bethann's middle, not showing any evidence of his suspicions yet, at least not beneath her layers of skirt and petticoats bunched up with a belt to accommodate for being too big for her. "You weren't well earlier."

Bethann shot him a murderous glare. "I'm right fine, thank you."

"I can rub some salve on your back," Momma offered.

"No." Bethann spun toward the door leading to the rest of the house. "Thank you," she added as an afterthought as she exited.

The door slammed behind her, hard enough to rattle some pieces of crockery and china on the shelves.

"What's amiss with her?" Momma asked. "You said she was sick."

"Not for me to say. Miss Esther talked to her about it. She seems to know a lot about healing herbs and the like."

"Does she?" Momma's dark eyebrows rose. "Imagine that. I'll have to ask her about it. But right now you need to get her that hot water and some food."

Griff opened his mouth to argue again, but then shut it. No use arguing with Momma. She and her sister Tamar were determined that either he or Zach marry the schoolma'am. Momma, of course, thought Esther would be right for her son.

Griff wished he didn't agree. He wished

his heart didn't feel stuck somewhere between his chest and his throat at the prospect of seeing her.

The attraction was only to her looks. He must remember that, tell himself that again and again. She didn't love the Lord. She wasn't particularly nice at times. She would grow weary of the mountains and go home within a month or two. All those things must convince him not to find her in the least attractive. They did convince him.

Until she answered the door to his knock and he saw her face, her form, the vulnerability in the shadows beneath her eyes, and a hint of redness suggesting she might have been crying.

"Do you have homesickness?" he asked, as though conversing with her was all right.

She blinked and gave her head a violent shake. "If I never again see Seabourne, Virginia, it will be too soon."

That wasn't a particularly bright thing for her to say. She knew it before she made the declaration, but the words slipped out anyway. Well, so much the better if they drove this unrefined yet too attractive mountain boy away.

"If that's even slightly hot water," she added as though she hadn't made the remark about home, "I will count you blessed forever."

"It's hot water." He smiled.

Esther winced. He shouldn't have such a nice smile crinkling up the corners of his eyes and making the blue appear like a sun-washed sky.

"Lovely. You may set it up wherever it's best."

There, treat him like a servant. Not that she had all that much experience with servants. She was just used to giving orders when necessary.

Ensuring that Griff Tolliver didn't like her was most definitely necessary.

"Do I get to eat?" she pressed on with her rudeness.

"I expect so." He set the buckets on the floor with a thud. "After I've had my supper. That's what I prefer hot — my vittles. The waterfall does well enough for me for bathing."

"Waterfall?" In spite of her resolve, Esther took an eager step toward him. "You have a waterfall?"

"About a mile from here. It's just a little one. I've heard tell of a big one in New York, but this is only twenty feet high or so. It has a pool as clear and deep as a crystal looks. It's cold too. But nothing feels better after a hard day's work than to dive in for a swim."

"Swimming . . ."

A vision of the Atlantic surged across her mind's eye. Bluegreen waves swelling up to white peaks foaming like the cream on syllabub. Her brothers showing her how to catch those waves and sail into the sandy beach with nothing holding her up but that power of water so cold and refreshing — after a day helping Momma preserve strawberries or her precious sugared violets, and later delivering a baby — with all the heat and effluvium of the birthing chamber washing away with the undertow.

Esther's stomach cramped, and she bent forward with the pain before she could stop herself. She grasped the bail of one bucket to cover up the impulse to ask Griff for the waterfall right then and there. On this warm May evening, ice-cold water would do well to wash away the grime of the trail.

Griff took the bail from her. "I'll get it for you."

"Thank you."

Either he hadn't noticed her moment of weakness — homesickness she wished she didn't feel — or he pretended not to have seen her pain. She liked him the better regardless of what he saw and his choice of reactions.

When he had gone and she scrubbed away dust and sweat and mud, she adored him for bringing the water. Adored him as she adored the farmer who had delivered cream just when she needed it most for something she was cooking, of course. She wouldn't like anyone here except for her students.

The younger Tollivers and Brookses were her reason for being in the mountains. Her new calling, if she must use that term Papa thought so appealing. He talked of the trouble he had caused when denying his calling, how Momma's calling had changed lives, how Esther had that calling too.

"No, I don't," she had cried out in January when refusing to go out on any more visits to expectant mothers. "I've failed in too many ways to enter another birth chamber."

Her bathwater, fragrant with her precious violet-scented soap, suddenly grew cold and greasy. She stood to rinse out her hair with a pail of decidedly cold water and stepped onto the smoothed floor to wrap herself in her dressing gown in lieu of a towel. Her supper, she'd been told through the locked panels of the door, would be awaiting her convenience on the stoop.

If some wild animal hasn't gotten to it.

She opened the door to find a wooden

bucket covered with a length of cheesecloth waiting for her.

It was a cold meal of ham and corn bread. Esther devoured it as though she hadn't eaten in a month. It filled up the empty places inside her for the moment. And the easing of the emptiness made her sleepy enough to want to sleep.

Perhaps she did sleep. The bed proved comfortable, the crickets in the grass and the distant hooting of an owl a lullaby.

The crack of a rifle shot was not.

She bolted upright, heart racing. The sharp report echoed off the hills and cliffs like more gunfire, growing distant. Then the night fell silent. Not even the crickets and owl had ceased their activities.

A scream pierced the stillness like a dagger through the heart. Gasping, Esther flew to the door. She stood with her hand on the handle before she realized how stupid it was to go into the darkness after a gunshot and then a scream.

And no one in the house had come to investigate. Through the dim glass, she saw no light, no movement by the moon's glow. She heard not so much as door hinges creaking.

"Didn't you all hear that?" she whispered. "Shouldn't someone go see what's happened?"

The scream had followed the gunshot rather a long time later. Surely the person shot wasn't the one who had screamed.

Shivering, she wrapped her dressing gown around her shoulders and retreated to her bed. Even beneath the quilts, she shivered, her ears straining for another crack of a rifle, dreading the shrieking scream again.

Instead, the wind kicked up, hissing through the trees like the soft hiss of the sea against the sand. The quiet soughing lulled her back to sleep.

Another scream yanked her awake moments before dawn edged its way over the treetops and a rooster crowed its greeting.

She gave up trying to rest. How everyone else could sleep through the shrieking that crawled across her skin like a colony of spiders, she couldn't comprehend. They should all be awake, running out to find whoever was being . . . well, surely ripped to shreds.

Or perhaps they were all cowards like her.

With her face washed, her hair neatly coiled at the back of her head, and her person tucked into a gown and petticoat for the first time in weeks, the horror of the screams faded and she was ready to face the day. The tiny mirror above the washstand showed her eyes with dark circles beneath and red-rimmed lids above. She hadn't meant to weep the night before. Fatigue and hunger had been her excuse then. In the light of day, she admitted to homesickness. She missed her parents. She missed her brothers and nieces and nephews.

She did not miss Seabourne — the looks, the whispers behind hands, the occasional spit as though the sight of her left a bad taste in the person's mouth.

"Lying harpy," they'd said.

"I didn't lie." Esther closed her eyes. Her stomach cramped.

Not to the people of Seabourne, she hadn't. But she had a bit to Griff Tolliver. She did want to go back to Seabourne, but only if she could go back in time too, back before January. Other than aching for a family of her own, to find a man who loved her as much as Papa loved Momma, she had been happy, contented with her life, loved.

But she couldn't go back in time; therefore, she must go forward. Breakfast with the Tollivers, a look around the area in the daylight, a close inspection of her school.

A door slammed in the direction of the house. Childish voices rose in the misty morning light, then footfalls raced across the hard-packed earth. They ran toward Esther's room and schoolhouse, the giggling and squeals announcing the children intended to awaken her or fetch her to breakfast. She decided to let them knock first and waited for them in the doorway to her chamber.

Nothing happened. The voices stuttered to a halt. Feet scraped against the stone stoop, but no one spoke. No one knocked.

Stomach convinced she hadn't eaten a mouthful of food since the day before yesterday, Esther grew weary of the apparent game and yanked open the door. The two boys stood there on the threshold with scrubbed faces and water-slicked hair, clean shirts and trousers in a homespun fabric, and identical expressions of bewilderment.

"May I help you?" Esther asked in imitation of a lady of the manor.

They shook their heads, dark curls bouncing out of their momentary control from a ruthless comb, and pointed behind her.

"Look," the older one said. "I don't read good, but I think that ain't nice."

"What . . . isn't nice?" Slowly Esther turned and followed the youth's pointing finger.

Someone had tacked a scrap of dirty paper to the door of the school. In a scrawling but surprisingly fine hand, the person had written, *Keep running.*

9

Griff noticed his brothers Ned and Jack standing more still than he ever saw them, even when they slept, and staring at the teacher. She too stood motionless, poised on the balls of her feet as though she were about to gather up her wide skirt and run.

"What — ?" He saw the note pinned to the door and stopped.

Run indeed. She was running away and someone knew it. He had guessed it. Females who looked like Esther Cherrett didn't take positions in the mountains unless they thought they were doing some kind of missionary work as if none of the people in the Appalachian Mountains knew about God's grace. They were poor and uneducated, but they knew the Lord.

Whoever had written that note wasn't uneducated. The handwriting was clear, even if the paper looked torn from another sheet of something and the pen needed trimming to get rid of the blotches of ink.

"Did you just find that?" Griff asked.

Esther jumped as though he'd pulled her hair down. She turned on him. "You shouldn't creep up on people."

"I'm right sorry, Miss Esther, but I never creep anywhere."

"He just walks quiet," Ned said. "I wanta walk quiet too. Better hunting that way."

"Do you know where this came from?" Griff kept his gaze fixed on Esther's face, her eyes with their gold lights in the morning sunlight, her skin flawless and glowing as though some of that sunlight shone from within, her hair shimmering with hints of copper and bronze amidst the glossy deep brown like polished wood. It all made his mouth go dry. And if he dared look at her mouth or her form, he would want to take the advice of the note writer and keep running.

She clasped her arms across her middle, held on to her upper arms, and gazed past his shoulder. "I don't know. I found it when the boys came to fetch me." Her vibrant voice had taken on a bit of a tremor. "I don't know who wrote it or where it came from or when it got here or — or anything but what you see."

"It don't — doesn't look like the writing

of anybody around here." He narrowed his eyes. "Do you — Ned, Jack, go back to the house and get your breakfast."

"We have to gather the eggs," Jack said.

"Then gather them and go back to the house."

The boys, raised more by Griff than their father, obeyed.

Griff turned back to Esther, who hadn't moved. Even the light tendrils of hair framing her face seemed to hang motionless in the breeze off the ridge.

"Do you have enemies, Esther Cherrett?" he demanded. "Did you bring trouble to my family?"

"No." She didn't meet his eyes at first, then shifted her gaze to hold his with an intensity that turned his insides to pine sap. "I can't say I have friends either, Mr. Tolliver, but I couldn't bring more trouble to your family than you already have."

"You'd best be right."

"A warning of some kind, Mr. Tolliver? Or else what?"

He shrugged. "You can find your own way back east, and fast."

"You're telling me —" Her voice rose in pitch, and she paused to take a deep breath. "You have someone stab you. You tell me there's a feud. Your older sister isn't mar-

133

ried and is likely . . . in trouble she shouldn't be in, and you're concerned about me bringing you trouble? I have never in my life known anything like this, and gunshots in the middle of the night and women screaming in the woods without anyone caring to find out — you're laughing at me."

He was. He couldn't help himself. "Women screaming in the woods?" He held his side, which suddenly didn't feel as healed as he thought it was. "Oh my, that's a good one."

"What is so amusing?" She took on that high and mighty city lady voice, and surely her nose went a bit elevated. "I did not imagine it."

"No, I'm sure you didn't." Griff made himself stop grinning. "I expect the gunshot was someone keeping a fox away from their chickens, and the screaming was a mountain lion."

"A mountain lion?" Her cheeks took on the same rosy hue as the sunrise. "Only a mountain lion?"

"You wouldn't say *only* if you came face-to-face with one when it's hungry and you're hunting."

"But they don't hurt people, do they?"

"Not usually. They just kind of make the skin crawl when you hear them."

"Yes, that's just it. Like spiders all over."

Griff grimaced. "I don't much care for that. Don't much like spiders."

"Me either." She smiled, and tension seemed to drain from her. "Did you say something about breakfast?"

"Yes, ma'am. Momma said to bring you to the house so it'll be hot. And you can meet Pa." Griff hesitated. "I should warn you that if Pa's in pain, he can be kind of ornery."

"People in pain usually are." She spoke with the authority of someone who held experience in that area.

Griff opened his mouth to ask, then thought better of it. He was leaving her to Zach. The more Griff talked to her about herself, the more difficult that could be.

Except he needed to know a bit more to understand why someone would pin that note to the schoolroom door. No, he'd tell Zach and leave that to him. The less Griff had to do with her, the better, which meant he should be taking his meals somewhere else. Seeing her over the dinner table three times a day might be a bit too much time looking at her face, listening to her voice.

Could she sing? With a voice that rich, she should be able to sing. If he pulled out the dulcimer one evening —

He drew himself up short and turned his back on her. "Come on. The day is wasting." He didn't wait to see if she followed him but strode across the hard-packed earth of the ground between the old cabin and the new house, scattering half a dozen cats feeding on something feathered. He wished he had one of those fine gardens like some of the houses close to town had, not herbs and vegetables like Momma and the girls kept, but flowers and bushes and useless things. Everything here was for use, not beauty.

And he'd never cared until the woman behind him had stepped from the cloud of fire smoke and leaf shadow and into the sunlight before him.

Esther's cheeks felt too warm for the temperate morning air. Likely she would blush forever over being so panicked about a mountain lion's cry. Not that she wanted to encounter one. The idea sent a shiver up her spine. They might not have much to do with people, but they were still potentially dangerous wild animals. The most she'd had to worry about before was the occasional poisonous snake — easy to spot, easier to avoid, and not terribly difficult to kill. One couldn't outrun, outclimb, or outkill a mountain lion.

Tangling her feet in her petticoats to keep up with Griff's long stride, Esther rubbed her arms inside their narrow sleeves. Woman in peril or not, those screams were going to give her nightmares.

If the note didn't.

Another missive. Cryptic. Mean. Too similar to the ones she had brought with her to keep her parents from finding them. She didn't recognize the handwriting, but then, she hadn't recognized the handwriting of the letters she had secretly received back in Seabourne. Yet surely no one could have located her. Not so soon.

She slipped her hand into her pocket and touched the scrap of paper she had tucked into it. Regardless of who had sent it, she would add it to the others tucked away beneath her mattress. She would say nothing about it, pretend she hadn't received it, as she had pretended she hadn't seen the others. Griff wouldn't say anything either if she asked him not to — perhaps.

She'd forgotten about the younger boys having seen the note. They said they couldn't read much, but they could read enough, and they brought it up the instant they slid onto the bench at the far end of the breakfast table.

"Miss Cherrett got herself a note this morning," the younger one, Ned, said.

"It weren't nice," Jack added. "Said she was to keep running."

"I'm sorry." Griff met her gaze from across the long table, which was polished and embellished with carving enough to belong in a mansion dining room but hand-made by Mr. Tolliver. "I should have warned them not to speak up."

"I'm glad you didn't." Mrs. Tolliver glanced around the table. "What is this about?"

"Nothing important," Esther said at the same time Griff said, "Likely a prank."

"But why would someone want her to keep running?" Ned asked. "I ain't seen her run nowhere."

"I haven't seen her," Liza corrected him. "You gotta speak good in front of the teacher."

Esther would have to tell Liza that one spoke well, not good. At that moment, though, she appreciated the distraction and offered the middle Tolliver daughter a bright smile. "That's what I'm here to teach, I think."

"Only if we want to go to school in a city," Jack, somewhere around twelve years old, pointed out. "I don't wanta go to the city.

They smell bad and got too many people."

"But the ladies wear such pretty clothes." Liza sighed. "Like your dress, Miss Cherrett. What do you call this stuff?" She touched one finger to Esther's sleeve.

"Muslin." Esther shifted on her chair.

One didn't talk about clothes and the like with men seated at the table. At the same time, it stopped them from talking about that note burning a hole through her pocket.

"Can we have some, Momma?" Liza asked.

Mrs. Tolliver glanced toward her husband.

He sat silently in his chair, his shoulders hunched like someone trying to hide. Pain lines etched a face that bore the same spectacular bone structure that had produced his beautiful children — all beautiful except for Bethann. His hair was red like hers, his eyes green. The children's eyes too. Like Bethann's, his mouth was thin and pursed.

He pursed it further. "We didn't bring her here to give our girls notions about wearing fancy clothes. They can wear those if they get themselves husbands who can afford it."

"But Pa," Brenna whined, "those kind of men don't go for girls in homespun."

"You're too young anyway." He pushed back his chair. "I'm going to the workshop."

He stalked from the room, every footfall sending a twitch through his shoulders as though he flinched from the pressure of putting each foot down.

Perhaps she could persuade him to drink an infusion of white willow bark. Or get him to go to the mineral baths in Bath County or Berkeley Springs. Many people with painful backs enjoyed relief —

But she was no longer a healer.

Esther stared down at her half-empty porridge bowl. It was corn porridge, something she wasn't fond of, but she'd eaten as much as she could to be polite. Sweetened with molasses, it wasn't too bad, though now that she couldn't swim, as she'd loved to do in the ocean, she would have to walk a great deal so she didn't get too plump for her gowns, or she'd be wearing homespun too.

"Maybe for Christmas," Mrs. Tolliver was saying.

"But the Independence Day celebration is coming," Liza protested. "I'd like something nice for that."

"You have something nice for that." Mrs. Tolliver stood and began to gather up dishes. "Brenna, it's your turn to wash, then get out there and weed —"

Griff slammed his coffee mug onto the table hard enough to rattle the flatware on the plates. "We were discussing someone sending Miss Cherrett a note. Since the boys mentioned it, we need to talk about it."

"We don't know nothing about it," the children chorused in a way that sounded rather too practiced and coordinated not to have been performed before.

Mrs. Tolliver scowled at them. "I've heard that once too often to believe it. If I find out any of you know —"

"We don't this time," Liza said. "We never left the house until the boys went to fetch her, except for Griff last night."

"Bethann wasn't even gone," Brenna added.

"Where is Bethann now?" Griff asked.

Liza curled her upper lip. "In bed. She says she has a headache."

Esther started to rise, certain she knew what ailed Bethann. Perhaps if the sickness was bad enough, she would accept help, a cup of ginger tea, or some mint —

She gripped the edge of the table as though a riptide would suck her up the stairs to Bethann's bedside. "May I help with something?"

"No, ma'am." Mrs. Tolliver smiled at her. "You go on and tell us what you need for the schoolroom. We got our four youngsters here, and my sister is sending her two boys. If you need supplies, Griff can go up to Christiansburg to get them."

"Christiansburg?" Esther's head shot up. "Aren't there any other towns closer?"

"Not that'll have schoolbooks and things," Griff said, watching her from beneath half-lowered lids. "Is something wrong with that?"

Only the doctor and midwife, who had literally known Esther since her birth. One of them, Phoebe Lee Docherty, had delivered Esther into the world.

"No, I just thought it rather far away." Which was partly the truth.

"It is. Seventy-five miles will take me more time than I should be away after being gone these past six weeks." Griff rose. "I'm off to the fields and may look in on the mine. Don't expect me for dinner." Without a word or a glance at Esther, he strode from the house, his curls lifting from his head in the breeze from the opening door.

He needed a brush and a pair of shears. Esther could neaten up those curls. She'd done so for her brothers often enough.

But Griffin Tolliver wasn't her brother. She had no business touching his hair, let alone running her fingers through it. But it looked soft and springy. Pulling out one of those curls and watching it rewind itself —

She jerked her shoulders straight and clasped her hands behind her back as though they had actually reached for a curl. "If you have some black paint and a smooth board, I can make do without books and even paper for a while. I have chalk."

"We got slates," Jack said. "The chalk's kinda broke into small pieces, but we got it."

"Then we'll manage fine." Esther smiled at him.

A flush ran up his neck.

With a silent sigh, she turned away. "I'll go inspect the school and see what supplies are there."

"We'll come with you," Ned offered.

"You have chores," Mrs. Tolliver reminded them. "Get to 'em." She flashed a sympathetic glance at Esther. "Just tell them to get out of your hair if you need to. And make 'em work hard at their schooling. The younger ones need to get off this mountain if they can. There ain't room for everyone now, and if the fighting continues . . ." She raised the corner of her apron to her eyes. "God surely sent you to us."

Esther murmured something she hoped appropriate or incomprehensible. She didn't think God had anything to do with her being there. He wouldn't approve of her leaving home as she had, disobeying her parents. Even if she was twenty-four, she had lived under their roof.

She beat a hasty retreat first to her room to stash the note under her mattress with the others, then to wander through the ten-by-fifteen-foot space set aside for a classroom, a space the size of her bedroom at home and far more sparsely furnished. Nothing covered the floor except dust. Hard benches were all the students would have to sit upon, unlike the comfortable chair in her father's study she had enjoyed for her schooling, as he taught her arithmetic and philosophy, literature and history, the Bible and French. As if a village midwife would need to know a foreign language.

Momma had taught her chemistry as they worked in the stillroom making medicines and preserving food. Momma taught her the workings of the human body and, of course, the art of birthing children, as her mother had taught her, and her mother before her, and back for as long as any of them remembered. Back when physicians scarcely ever delivered babies and midwives ruled the birthing chamber.

Not so much now. Now women preferred doctors with their forceps that could ease a difficult birth — but could destroy the woman if the doctor were not properly educated, which far too few were.

"Women should be doctors too," Esther had once told her mother. "I know more than any physician I've met."

Momma had laughed at the notion. "Females don't go to college like doctors do."

But Esther had heard tell of a college in Ohio that let women in to study right alongside men. A fascinating prospect.

But what would be the use? She wouldn't be allowed to get medical training and be called a physician. She would only be able to teach, and she didn't need to waste money on schooling to do that.

And here lay her school — barren and stuffy, lacking in proper books and writing materials. But she would have six students and perhaps an entire mountainside to use as a classroom when the weather permitted.

She stroked one of the benches. Perhaps she could find some of that homespun cloth everyone wore and make cushions for these benches. Discomfort did not promote better attention. After all, she didn't know how else she would spend her wage of five dollars a month, which was paid, Zach had informed her, from the mine profits. She supposed she should save some for the day she needed to leave. Until then, she would enjoy making her classroom more appealing.

Planning when and how she would conduct her first day of class, she wandered outside. Perhaps the children would have time to take her for a walk up one of the trails. Surely they didn't have chores all day. Otherwise how could they attend classes?

The chatter of young voices drew her back to the schoolhouse. Across the yard, Zach stood at the gate, his hands at his sides but not relaxed. Three of the younger Tollivers surrounded him, and the voices weren't welcoming. Even as Esther gathered up her skirts to run, Brenna picked up a stone the size of her fist and aimed it at Zach's face.

10

Esther grabbed Brenna's wrist and spun her around. "What do you think you're doing, young lady?" Her voice rasped. Her heart raced. She glared into the girl's set face. "You never, never, never throw anything at a person's face."

"Or anywhere else," Zach added in his quiet drawl.

"Um, no, nowhere else either." Esther's face heated, perhaps from the rush across the yard, perhaps from the embarrassment of implying that throwing rocks at other body parts was all right.

Brenna tugged against the restraint on her arm. "Let me go. He's a Brooks. We hate Brookses."

"We don't hate anyone." The words popped out reflexively. Esther expected the retort before Brenna jerked herself free and faced her with hands on her hips, one hand still clutching the stone.

"You aren't we. You don't know nothing about this, how a Brooks shot my daddy and probably stabbed my brother and killed my other brother and Bethann's baby and —" Tears starred in the girl's eyes, and she loosed the rock then. It thudded to the ground. She covered her face with her hands.

Esther jerked a half step backward. "Bethann's —" She closed her mouth. This wasn't an appropriate discussion to have with a female not yet a woman, with a man listening nearby. She was, after all, supposed to teach the girls deportment.

"Jesus taught us to turn the other cheek," she said instead. "No matter what someone does to us, we are not, as Christians, supposed to fight back."

Hypocrite that she was. Trying to fight back had gotten her nowhere but publicly shamed.

"And," she added for good measure, "I don't think Mr. Zach has done anything."

"Remember," he interjected, "I stabbed Griff, or so Bethann claims."

Esther looked at Zach's face — just rugged enough to not be pretty, his striking blue eyes, his gentle smile — and shook her head. "Griff doesn't believe it, and neither do I."

"You don't know him," Brenna wailed. "They're all slippery as eels."

"Brenna —" Esther swallowed down the tightness of anger in her throat to gentle her voice. "You need proof to accuse a body of trying to kill someone."

"Bethann has proof."

"Your brother doesn't accept it." Esther stepped forward and laid a hand on Brenna's shoulder. "Now then, go into the house and wash your face." She turned to the silently gaping boys. "Jack and Ned, if you've finished your chores, will you take me for a walk around the area?"

"I'll take you." Zach's eyes glowed. "I came over to see if you wanted a look around. The walk down to the ferry is right pretty."

"You shouldn't go anywhere with a Brooks." Brenna dashed her sleeve across her eyes. "They like to hurt us Tollivers."

"Ah, but I'm a Cherrett, not a Tolliver. Your feud has nothing to do with me."

"You might find wild berries on the walk," Ned added. "I'll bring a pail."

"You boys are as bad as Griff and her." Her wide skirt flaring out like a sail bellying in the wind, Brenna spun on her bare heel and dashed for the house.

Zach frowned, then his shoulders slumped

in an expression of resignation. "I've never hurt a Tolliver in my life."

"Momma and Pa say that," Jack said. "And Griff. The ones who caused the trouble are all gone."

"Not quite," Zach answered. "But if the rest of us can be an example, there won't be more fighting."

"I'd rather shoot bears than people." Ned lifted his hands as though aiming an imaginary rifle.

Esther smiled to cover up a quaking in her middle. "Run along, boys, and ask your mother if you may come along. And say, 'May we go?' "

"Sounds funny to me," Jack muttered, but he sprang into a hop, then a jump that ended in a cartwheel, then another, all the way to a perfect landing at the door of the house.

Esther watched him, her smile genuine. "I always wanted to learn to do that, but my mother wouldn't let me. Too unladylike, and I could hurt my hands."

"Do you play an instrument?" Zach asked.

"A little pianoforte. Not very well, though I can sing some. Why do you ask? Are you a musician?"

"No. I can't sing or play anything, but you mentioned your hands."

"Oh, that." Esther stared down at her long, slim fingers and narrow palms traditionally required of a midwife. In defiance of that tradition, she had grown her nails out past the ends of her fingers. "A lady needs nice hands."

The truth, as far as that went.

"You are a lady." Zach stared into her eyes. "I saw that straightaway. I mean, we figured you were, and, well, you're right fine, Miss Esther."

"Thank you. But I'm nothing special. My father is a preacher and my mother comes from simple folk. Her father was a schoolmaster. Quite ordinary."

As if anyone would consider her parents ordinary. Despite living in a small seaside village as its pastor for more than half his life, Papa was still very much Lord Dominick Cherrett. And Momma! Momma was kind and gentle and strong — independent, yet a true helpmeet to her husband. They were smart and loving and —

Esther's throat closed. Her heart ripped open a little more.

"Is something wrong?" Zach asked.

Esther thought of the note — the new one — tucked beneath her mattress, and the pain eased. She was here to make her family's lives easier. She must not mourn.

They would understand the wisdom of her decision to leave quietly now that she had gone.

She shook her head. "I'm all right. I simply miss my family a bit."

"I expect they miss you too." Zach's gaze held hers with brilliant blue intensity like the hottest of flames.

Esther shivered despite the growing warmth of the day. So he liked her — too much. She should tell him now that he possessed no hope of anything more than superficial friendship with her. If she didn't, she just might have to keep running, as that note had said.

Could Hannah have sneaked over and nailed it to the door, not wanting Esther to attract her brother?

The idea was ludicrous. She shook it off like the chill of a cold wave washing over her and turned toward the house. "I'll see what's keeping the boys."

"I'd rather they didn't come along." Zach fell into step beside her. "They'll scare off any hope of us seeing some of the birds or maybe even other wildlife along the way."

"That's quite all right with me. Well, the birds might be nice, but not wildlife. I'm, um, not used to animals that aren't domesticated except for fish and the occasional snake."

"We got plenty here. Mountain lions, bears —"

Esther skittered to a halt. "Bears? I thought Ned was joking."

"Naw, he's shot at least one, maybe two. The skins'll be put away for the summer, but come winter, they come in right nice on a cold night."

Running sounded like a grand idea at that moment.

Esther glanced toward the line of trees beyond the stockade. Mrs. Tolliver mentioned how it was to keep wild animals away from her chickens, but she thought the older woman meant foxes and badgers — unpleasant enough, but not large enough to harm a person. But a ten-year-old boy shooting something the size of a bear?

Zach squeezed her hand. "They're just little black bears."

"Just." Esther emitted a nervous laugh.

"They won't hurt you if you don't get between a momma and her cubs."

"Right. I think we'll collect the boys."

They came flying out of the house then, Ned banging a leather bucket against his leg. "Momma says we can go."

"Grand." Esther glanced down, decided

her ankle-high boots were sturdy enough, and took the arm Zach offered.

They departed from the compound, the boys racing ahead, then circling back to join them, energetic despite the steadily uphill climb. Zach pointed out the variety of trees, all of which he knew the names of, too many for Esther to remember.

"I'll have to come with you again and make notations with some drawings." She paused in the shade of an oak at least a hundred feet tall arching overhead to entwine its branches with another ancient deciduous tree. Together they formed a canopy like a cathedral roof with sunlight peeking through the leaves in a green glow. "One could hold a church service here."

And in that moment, the boys too far ahead for their voices to carry back, Zach calm and still beside her, the presence of God touched Esther's heart for the first time in months. It was a mere breath of awareness like the brush of a fingertip across the cheek, the tender hand of a parent against the face of a sleeping child, or a voice just soft enough for the ear not to catch.

" 'And he said, Go forth, and stand upon the mount before the LORD. And, behold, the LORD passed by, and a great and strong wind rent the mountains, and brake in pieces the rocks before the LORD; but the LORD was not in the wind: and after the wind an earthquake; but the LORD was not in the earthquake: and after the earthquake a fire; but the LORD was not in the fire: and after the fire a still small voice.' "

She recalled that that voice had gone on to ask Elijah what he was doing there on the mountain.

She crossed her arms over her middle and grasped her elbows. She knew what she was doing there — being selfless for the first time in her life. The Tollivers and Brookses needed her. Well, they needed someone to teach their children.

"Is that from the Bible?" Zach asked in his own still, quiet voice.

"The first book of Kings, yes. I had to learn a great deal of Scripture."

"I never did. We don't always have a preacher here." Zach slipped one hand beneath her elbow and started walking again.

Esther's arm tensed, and she pretended to wrap her shawl more tightly around her shoulders, though the day was warm. "But you have Bibles, don't you?"

"Yea, Momma has one, but I don't — she reads to us sometimes."

"You could —" Esther puckered her lips as realization dawned.

He couldn't read, at least not well enough for something as difficult to manage as the Bible. "No teacher. No preacher," she said instead. "That must make learning things like Scripture difficult."

And here she had chafed at the hours she'd been forced to spend reading and memorizing verses. Too often she hadn't — and paid the consequences for neglecting her lessons.

"I wanted to be running around on the beach instead of studying," she confessed. "But I couldn't escape when my parents were my teachers and everyone in town knew me."

"Nice thing about growing up on a mountain. Lots of places to escape to."

Like places to hide.

Pine needles and last year's leaves, damp in the shade of the trees, cushioned each step, making them mostly silent.

The cool shade beneath the trees suddenly stifled her, hemming her in like the walls of Papa's study when she wanted to be diving into the Atlantic. She needed to run, swim, climb a tree.

The boys broke through the underbrush, Jack carrying something cupped in his hands. "It fell out of its nest, but it ain't hurt or nothing."

He held a baby sparrow, gray and insignificant but with its head held high and its mouth opening and closing as though it shouted in protest at its captivity.

"Can I keep it?" Jack asked.

"May I," Ned corrected him.

"Yea, may I?" Jack persisted, gazing up at Esther as though she were truly in charge of him.

"I, um, don't know." She lifted her hand palm up. "My only experience with birds is listening to them or watching them catch fish. I've never tried to keep one."

"You shouldn't." Zach stepped forward and slid the creature from Jack's hands to his. It disappeared into his broad palm. "He needs to be fed, and he's meant for the trees, not a cage."

"I could keep him in my room." Jack's eyes shone. "It has a tree outside the window he could fly to."

"He isn't old enough to fly or take care of himself." Zach raised a finger to touch the bird's head. "He's still young. Where did you find him? We should put him back before he smells too much like human for his momma to want him."

"It was down this way by the waterfall."

157

Ned plunged into the underbrush.

Jack and Zach followed, leaving Esther standing alone on the path, the woods quiet save for birdsong high above and the soughing of the wind through the branches. No, not the wind. The leaves didn't so much as tremble, so the breeze must lay still across the forest. Yet that rushing-water sigh poured over her ears with familiar sweetness.

Rushing water. The waterfall, of course. Ned had said they found the sparrow by the waterfall. But she couldn't follow them through the shrubbery growing along the ground and over fallen logs. She would ruin her dress.

She glanced up and down the trail in search of a path leading deeper into the trees and on to that glorious, sighing tumble of water.

She stumbled upon the graveyard first.

11

Griff found her kneeling beside one of the plain wooden crosses marking the graves of previous Tollivers. Carved upon them with varying degrees of skill were the names and dates of those whose remains lay beneath the soil, from Griff's great-grandparents twenty years earlier to a few cousins, some dead from sickness, others from outbursts of fighting.

She paused beside the grave of Griff's nephew. "He was so young," she said. "Was it a fever?"

"No, it was a fall." Griff's voice emerged far more harshly than he intended.

She jumped and twisted around, her face pale beneath the overarching canopy of branches and leaves. "I thought you were Zach."

"I thought you were with Zach. Not kind of him to leave you alone." The roughness wouldn't leave his voice.

"He went to restore a sparrow to its nest for the boys." She rocked back on her heels, her gown billowing around her in soft blue folds like a wind-ruffled pool. "I heard the waterfall and tried to find it."

"You will if you keep going."

"I thought so. But I saw these, and Brenna mentioned something about a baby dying?" One curved brow rose.

Griff stared at a lightning-struck tree he should cut down before it fell in a wind-storm and crushed the crosses. "Bethann's. She was twenty-five and too ornery for anyone to marry, but it happened, and the fighting started."

Esther gasped. "And they killed an infant? You must have a wonderfully forgiving spirit to make peace after that."

"Not anything special. I just know an accident when I see it."

Father falling. The baby falling. Bethann screaming. Griff holding her back from leaping off the cliff.

"Whatever you say of Bethann, she loved her baby," he added. "And she was always good when the others were babies. She just scares off the men."

Esther muttered something that sounded suspiciously like, "I understand." But he must be mistaken. Esther Cherrett couldn't

160

scare off men. Her beauty alone must draw them in like bees to a hyacinth.

"And Bethann wasn't pretty," he added. "Even up here, looks matter."

"She's scarcely ugly." Esther placed one foot flat on the ground as though she intended to rise. "She'd be prettier if she gained some weight and smiled a bit."

"And didn't look like she was chewing an unripe persimmon." Griff smiled.

Esther smiled and started to rise. The toe of her foot pressed down on a fold of her gown, throwing her off balance.

Griff caught her hand to steady her. A jolt, like he was standing next to that tree when the lightning struck it, raced through him. A flare of light in her eyes and a hint of pink in her cheeks suggested she felt it too. She tried to snatch her hand free of his grasp.

"Don't be a fool." He held fast. "You'll fall over if you do that."

Her complexion grew darker. She ran her tongue over her lower lip, then bent her head. "Please let go. I don't like to be touched."

"I noticed that."

He'd also noticed her trotting off into the forest with Zach like they were a courting couple. But she hadn't looked anything more than interested in what he said to her.

No flush. No blaze in her eyes, no tongue peeping out to moisten dry lips.

"But you're going to have trouble getting up on your own," he pointed out.

"Not at all."

And she didn't. She tugged her gown free, then rose in one graceful motion, her gaze averted from him the entire time.

"I think I'll continue to the waterfall," she said.

"I'll go with you." He offered her his arm as he'd glimpsed Zach do earlier. He hadn't been spying; he'd been coming out of the barn and caught a glimpse of them through the gateway. "You shouldn't go walking through here on your own."

"The wild animals?" She walked beside him but didn't tuck her hand into the crook of his elbow.

He glanced at her, hesitated, then gave her the truth. "No, they won't bother you, especially not in the daylight. I'm talking about the kind of animal with two legs. We have a lot of pretty girls on the mountain, but none who —"

She held up a staying hand, probably the first female he'd met who didn't want a compliment.

"Some men haven't any manners," he finished instead.

"What men? I haven't seen a soul."

"You will. They're around. Tollivers. Gosnolls. Brookses. Neffs. We're scattered through these hollers like dandelion seeds on a breeze."

"Cousins?"

"Cousins, aunts, uncles. Momma had eleven brothers and sisters, and most of 'em lived."

The path narrowed, and he moved ahead of her to hold branches out of her way and clear out spiderwebs strung across the trail, foul and sticky, some bristling with unfortunate flies. Neither of them spoke. Only an occasional trill of birdsong broke the stillness beneath the trees.

Then the trees ended in a cascade of irregular steps created from the natural rock sprouting out of the mountainside like gray-brown flowers. Saplings and scrubby bushes sprang from the rocks, clinging to life in meager soil. But those bushes, for all their spindly size, shone green in the early summer sunshine, and at the foot of the hillside a pool sparkled and shimmered, foaming white at the base of the waterfall and smoothing out to a clear blue reflection of the sky farther out.

Griff turned back to catch the wide-eyed expression of wonder on Esther's face, and something twisted in his middle. He couldn't breathe. His offer for help caught in his throat. He held out his hand, and she took it. Wordlessly they descended the rocks. He clung to her hand. If she spoke, the burbling splash of the cascade drowned out her voice.

Then they reached the bottom, the jumble of rocks that surrounded the edge of the pool, and she snatched her hand free. She tucked her fingers beneath her own upper arms as though hugging herself, and studied the scenery, her head moving slowly from side to side, scanning the vista as though it were a book she intended to put to memory.

Griff stood beside her and watched and waited. This was his retreat, his escape from the chaos often reigning in the house, the cares of being in charge of his family instead of seeking a wife to build his own. This was where he talked to God about his fears and frustrations with Bethann's behavior, Brenna's growing sullenness, futures for the boys and the girls, and his pain-racked father. The only one he didn't worry about was Momma. Momma was strong in body, mind, and faith in God's promise to take care of a body.

Griff wished he were that strong. Everything from whether or not Henry Gosnoll would cheat them over the lead to whether or not they would grow enough corn to last the winter, even though they could now afford to buy it, concerned him. Now he had one more person to worry over — Esther Cherrett. She lived on his land. She was his responsibility. She too seemed strong, capable of taking care of herself. She captivated him like those flies caught in the spiderweb — an unpleasant image.

Attraction to her was unpleasant. It was the uneasy tenseness of knowing something was amiss and not being able to put his finger on exactly the cause of the discomfort in his middle.

The water gleamed before him, and he longed to dive into its icy depths, swim off the tension plaguing him, lie in the sun to warm, and talk to God about what ailed him.

Talk to God about the woman beside him.

He turned to her beside him instead. "There's no bottom to the pool that anyone's found. The stream must go underground here and end up in the river. It's not far off."

"It's lovely. I want to come back with my drawing things." She laughed. "Not that chalks could do justice to this."

"Paints? Painters come through here

sometimes. They want us to show them places like this."

"Do you bring them?"

"Not here. This is . . . private."

"Is it your land?"

"Probably. Hard to say where the Brookses' land ends and ours starts. We never much cared about boundaries before . . ." He fixed his gaze on the narrow but deep cataract of water foaming down the sheer cliff of rock, then below to the pond that the force of the water had carved over hundreds, maybe thousands, of years or more — a force far stronger than he. "Miss Esther, we were wrong to bring you here. We never should have done something so unfair without telling you the whole truth about the fighting."

"But it's quiet now." She tucked her hands beneath her arms again. "Isn't it? Nothing's happened — oh." Her gaze dropped to his side.

He pressed his hand to the healed wound. "That could have been someone intent on robbing me who got scared off."

"Are robberies on the trail common?"

"Common enough. Hannah came back to see where I'd gone and found me. Her coming might have scared the ambusher off."

Or she knew her brother had done something wrong and wanted to save him.

But no, he mustn't let Bethann's suspicions taint his thinking. Zach wouldn't hurt him. The fighting had never stopped him and Zach from being friends, as they had been friends since they were infants only hours apart in age. Zach would never assault him like that.

"Yea, robbers, most like. That's why you shouldn't go about on your own. This may be Tolliver and Brooks land, but all sorts of folk hide out here in the woods, bad men running from the law sometimes. There's a hundred caves they can camp in." A shudder ran through her, and he touched her shoulder. "I don't mean to scare you. Nothing happens much. Just warning you to be cautious and at least come here with the boys. They'll protect you."

"Two children will protect me?" He couldn't hear for sure but thought she snorted. "I'll manage."

"Those boys never go anywhere unarmed. They both carry knives."

"And you?" She scanned him from head to toe as though searching for a bristle of blades or the protruding butt of a gun.

The perusal warmed him, and he fixed his attention on the icy water. "Yea, but I never tell anyone where I keep my blades. Easy to disarm me if a body knows where to look."

A half smile curved her lips, then she stepped closer to the pool, her skirt swaying. He expected her to bow her head. Instead, she raised her face to the sky, a golden disk of sunlight blazing from the pale blue. She held out her arms as though embracing the pool, the waterfall, the surrounding rocky cliffs.

And Griff feared he could too easily be attracted to a girl like her.

But then a shout followed by another broke their wordless camaraderie beneath the gushing water, and his brothers and Zach burst onto the ledge atop the waterfall. Esther glanced up. Griff noted the stillness of her body, a tight pose, not relaxed. He could not see her face. But he could see Zach's.

Zach's expression lit as though he faced the sun and wasn't looking down. He called something inaudible over the water, then ran back to the tree line. A few moments later, he appeared, the boys following, on another shelving path descending to the pool. He scrambled too quickly, sending pebbles and dirt cascading ahead of him. His boot heels slid the last dozen feet, and he sprinted forward to clasp Esther's hands.

"We went back to the path and you

weren't there. You should have stayed put."

"You shouldn't have left her." The roughness had returned to Griff's voice. A band had tightened around his chest. "You know it's not safe."

Zach laughed and shrugged that off. "She was right safe in broad daylight, Griff. Weren't you, Miss Esther?"

"I thought I was, but Mr. Tolliver tells me I wasn't."

Zach shot Griff a cold glare. "You shouldn't go around scaring her. She'll leave when she's barely arrived."

"Someone wants her to." Griff set his hands on his hips and glowered at his cousin. "Didn't she tell you about the note?"

"Note, what note?" Zach switched his attention back to Esther. "You didn't say anything."

"It was nothing. A prank. I'm certain me finding this place was worth any small bit of danger anyway." She tilted her head toward the waterfall and smiled — because of the waterfall or Zach standing so close to her?

For the first time in the past ten years, Griff understood Bethann's hostility toward the Brookses and Gosnolls. They had taken all that was precious to her. Though saying Esther Cherrett was precious to him was a bit premature, Griff suspected she could be,

169

and a Brooks had taken away his chance to even attempt to find out, because Griff Tolliver had principles.

He was supposed to trust in God for this. God would provide a wife, Momma always told him from the time he started thinking of such things — later than most men on the mountain because he was too busy helping out his family. He believed her. He believed in God's promise to supply all a man's needs.

Maybe God thought he didn't need a wife.

Feeling as though someone had filled his boots with lead soles, he motioned to his brothers to come with him and headed up the mountain without a word of farewell to Zach or Esther.

12

Too late, Esther realized Griff and the boys were leaving. She pulled her hands free from Zach's, marveling how she'd forgotten he still curled his fingers around hers, and turned.

The others were already too high up to hear her call to them, even if she would raise her voice in a shout. And she wouldn't do that. She'd been too well-trained to raise her voice for any reason. The one time she had since she was a child had brought down wrath and a disaster, but not her parents' wrath. They said she had done the right thing.

It wasn't enough to counteract the wrong she had committed.

So she remained silent and still until the Tolliver males vanished into the trees at the top of the cliff, then she turned back to Zach. "I should go back too. Surely it's getting on to dinnertime. I should help."

"No one hired you to be a servant, Miss Esther."

"Helping is not servitude, Mr. Brooks." She sounded priggish and stiff.

"And sending you unkind messages is not a welcome. Why didn't you tell me about it?" He took her arm.

She experienced nothing above the now-familiar distaste for the pressure and warmth of human closeness, not the lightning jolt and residual tingle that raced from Griff's hand.

She shuddered at the memory, the flash of thought that something was wrong with her for feeling thus, for not exactly disliking Griff's touch despite what she claimed. Surely something was wrong with her.

She stepped away from Zach, far enough he couldn't take her arm again.

"I'd like to know who sent you an unkind message," Zach continued.

"It wasn't sent. Someone nailed it to the door of the schoolroom." Esther ground the toe of her boot into the gravelly earth beside the pool. "All it said was that I should keep running."

"Keep running?" Zach sounded bewildered or perhaps disbelieving. Difficult to tell with the rainfall gurgle of the waterfall. "What does that mean?"

Esther shrugged. "Someone thinks I'm running from something."

Someone knew she was running from something.

"Are you?" Of course he had to ask.

Esther started walking, watching where she placed her feet on the uneven ground with its rocks strewn about like the stones from an ancient and tumbling cathedral. "I needed to leave Seabourne." She chose her words with care, telling enough of the truth. "No one asked me to. That is, my family didn't want me to leave, as I told you. But I didn't feel I was doing any good there."

Zach kept pace beside her, his long, strong legs making the rough track seem as smooth as a city pavement. "Surely you had a dozen men courting you?" His smile teased her.

She couldn't help but smile back, even as she shook her head. "Not one."

"What's wrong with the men out there?"

"Not easy to court the pastor's daughter, you know, and my mother is the local midwife. She . . . well, she knows more about everyone in town than makes them comfortable."

And so did Esther.

"So," she continued, "I was running away a bit. But there's no need for me to keep running." She paused atop a boulder step.

"I'd like to stay."

She stood above him, their faces level. He locked his gaze with hers, and the blue that could be so icy in his cousin's gaze looked like a warm pool in Zach's.

"I know we all think you'll do right well here," he said. "You proved yourself on the journey here, you know."

"Was that a test?" She laughed and resumed climbing, still feeling nothing other than a comfortable warmth from being in Zach's company. "Was it the fire building, the coffee, or burning the pan bread?"

Zach laughed and strode ahead of her to give her a hand over the last terrace of rocks to the relatively level ground and trees. "Burning the bread for sure. Showed us all you're human and not an angel."

Esther made a face. "I'm no angel, Mr. Brooks. Never think it."

"I can't help it. You're —"

"You don't know me yet. Not like you think. I — I'm —"

She wanted to say bad-tempered, possessed of a vicious tongue, unfriendly. None of it was true. Yet she couldn't explain why she was no female to court, that she feared everything marriage entailed, for she was beginning to think that with him, she needn't fear. He was such a gentle soul, kind of innocent of the world despite his age.

"You're pretty and kind and not like any girl I've met," Zach said.

"I don't have the relationship with the Lord I know I should."

That might do it, stop these compliments.

"None of us has the relationship with the Lord we should. I . . . well, I —" He looked away, and the tips of his ears reddened. "I don't read well enough to study my Bible. I'd like to, but Momma doesn't have the time, and I . . . You're going to be busy enough with the children, so never you mind what I said."

"No, Zach, don't say that." Her heart melting over his simple confession, a confession that must have cost him a year's worth of pride to admit, Esther reached out to him. "I can't imagine not being able to read well and not having anyone to teach me. I can't remember when I didn't have a book in my hands. I'd love to teach you to read well."

"You would? You could?" Joy lit his face even beneath the dark green canopy of tree leaves.

Esther wanted to hug him, odd for her when she hadn't reached out to anyone for months. Zach's pleasure in her promise gave her a jolt of joy, something she hadn't experienced for too long to count.

No, not quite true. The sight of the water-fall had filled her with warmth. No, heat of a burning excitement to see such beauty. An unexpected gift.

God, are You looking out for me after all? Will my spirit heal?

She made herself tuck her hand into Zach's arm as they retraced their steps down the mountainside. Though their gait was steady, her heart skipped ahead. A beacon of light seemed to shine for her, guiding her forward and out of the slough of despond that had gripped her since January.

If he could have carried a tune, Zach would have sung or whistled all the way from the schoolroom door, where he left Esther, to the barn, where he came across Griff muck-ing out a stall. Without a word, he picked up another pitchfork and joined in the messy, smelly business. They didn't speak. Often since the time they were big enough to wield the heavy clods of manure and straw, they had worked side by side, enjoy-ing the companionship.

Today, for the first time, Zach grew con-scious of his sweat, the reek of the muck, the way his hair plastered to his head and the back of his neck. If Esther saw him now, she would find him revolting. All along the road to Brooks Ridge, she always looked as neat and clean as the local women did when a preacher came through and held Sunday services. He had washed up more than ever before on the trail. Now he hoped he could get to a stream before seeing her again. If he encountered her looking like he did, with straw and worse sticking to his arms and trousers, he would never help Griff again.

"You should hire someone to do this," he told his cousin as they hung up their forks and leaned against the shady side of the barn with cold cups of water. "You got the money to do it now."

"Why pay someone to do a job I can do myself? I like the work." Griff swiped his sleeve across his forehead. "It reminds me that I have mules and horses needing cleaned up after."

Zach inclined his head in acknowledgment of the rightness of Griff's words.

Silence fell between them again. In the distance, a hen let out a loud cluck signaling she had laid an egg, and the boys' shrill voices pierced through the heated air. Short silences between the men were common. This one stretched beyond the usual.

Zach straightened and hooked his cup

beside the bucket of fresh-drawn water. "Guess I oughta be on my way. Momma'll expect me for dinner."

He waited for Griff to extend an invitation for him to stay. He could clean up enough to be fit for the table, borrow something from his cousin. But the invitation didn't come.

"Expect I should get cleaned up" was all Griff said.

Neither of them moved.

Zach fisted his hands on his hips and demanded, "Why didn't you tell me someone sent her that note?"

"Didn't have a chance. Why didn't she tell you?"

"I don't know. She don't trust me yet, I expect."

"She doesn't trust anybody, and maybe with good reason."

"What do you mean?"

Griff straightened. "Why would someone tell her to keep running if they didn't think she had cause to run in the first place?"

"Oh, right." Zach felt like a fool for not thinking of that. "I can't believe she's done anything wrong."

"Because she looks like no other female you ever saw? Handsome is as handsome does, Momma would say." Griff's mouth set in a grim line.

Zach stiffened. "Are you saying you think she is running away from something?"

"She wanted to leave in the middle of the night, didn't she? No one to know and all that? She didn't scare off when you told her I'd been stabbed. What's that about? Most females would have gone screaming back to their mommas."

"She keeps her word?" Zach didn't say it with the confidence he wanted to.

Griff snorted. "She owes us nothing. She didn't need to come out here, but she wanted to. Since when do girls who look like her come to these mountains?"

Zach wanted to say since God prompted them to do so, but Esther Cherrett hadn't talked about God leading her anywhere. Still, sometimes God led one unexpectedly, took one's misdeeds and turned them into good.

"You don't trust her?" Zach asked.

"Depends on what you mean by trust. Do I think she'll murder us in our beds or steal from us? No. I think she'll make a right fine teacher. She's smart. She's kind. She knows a lot about a lot of things. But she has something behind her that ain't right."

"I don't believe it." Zach's fists tightened.

Griff flexed his shoulders. "Then you

explain that note."

"It don't matter. She —"

He started to admit she had offered to teach him to read his Bible, but not to Griff. Griff knew how to read good. He could talk and charm and get every girl at a celebration to dance or sing with him, especially when he pulled out his dulcimer and sang. They flocked around him like hens after grain.

But Esther had remained with Zach at the waterfall pool.

Taking comfort in that, he demanded, "So what do you think's wrong with her?"

"You don't want to hear me thinking bad things about her, and I gotta get cleaned up." Griff started toward the house, apparently not minding if Esther saw him all mucked up.

"Wait." Zach fell into step beside him, caring who saw him but needing to follow. "Tell me what you're thinking."

"It's not kind." Griff paused, half turned back.

Behind him and across the compound, Aunt Lizbeth called from the kitchen doorway, and the younger boys began to race toward the house.

Griff glanced over his shoulder, then looked at Zach. "I think the word is *indiscre-*

tion. It's why unmarried girls go away from here, ain't — isn't it? They commit an indiscretion."

"But that's when" — Zach's ears warmed — "they're in a certain kind of trouble. You don't think —" The notion made him feel sick.

"No, not that, but I think maybe she's running away from an indiscretion."

Zach gave his head a violent shake. "Not her. She's too good, too kind. Besides, that don't explain the note. How would anybody know?"

"I don't know." Griff sighed. "I wish I did. But however or whyever news got here, there's something wrong with our new schoolma'am, and I'm going to find out."

"Don't." Zach's hand lashed out and gripped Griff's shoulder. "Don't do it."

Griff glowered, and Zach braced himself for a justifiable blow. It never came. Of course it didn't. Griff would never strike out at him any more than he would strike out at Griff.

He released his hold. "Don't," he said more gently. "I don't care, and if she's done something wrong, God can forgive her. And I intend to make an honest woman of her."

13

Esther woke sweating and shivering from a dream. From *the* dream. She swallowed hard to keep the bile down. Her eyes burned, but no tears came. They lay stopped up in her chest as though she had tried to swallow a rock or, more likely, a chunk of broken glass.

"God, I thought You cared about me, that You'd make this go away." She cried out the words to the empty room, the silent cabin.

Beyond her window, open for a breath of wind in the warm night, leaves on the trees rustled, yet no air reached the chamber.

Gasping, afraid she was about to be sick, Esther stumbled to the window and leaned out over the frame. A shadow darted through the moonlight, too small to be a person, too small for anything truly dangerous, but too large to be a rodent. Probably a cat. Every farm owned a cat. They slept in the cool shade of a barn by day and hunted in the darkness of the night. No wonder some people thought them evil.

The people of Seabourne had come to think ill of Esther for going out at night too. No matter that her mother had done so for forty years, had apprenticed at sixteen — two years before she began Esther's training — and then gone out on nighttime calls alone from the time she was eighteen. For no logical reason, Esther was supposed to go only to those women who entered their confinement during the day. But Momma was still at a confinement and had been there for the better part of a day, and Mrs. Oglevie, whose husband owned half the fishing boats and three-quarters of the businesses on the eastern shore — or seemed to — claimed she was having her pains a month early.

Esther didn't want to go. Mr. Oglevie had tried to court her once. She had believed she wanted him to, as he was good-looking and educated, but once he did begin to court her, she discovered he was no gentleman despite his money.

He married another young woman, but as soon as her condition became known and he called in the midwives to assist her, he began to flirt with Esther. More than flirt. When she had occasion to talk with him, he touched her hair, her face, her hand, despite her efforts to deter him. He offered her carte blanche.

"I can't go there again," she told Papa. "He looks at me like I'm not wearing anything. Like I'm his mistress."

Papa's face had whitened, and his eyes blazed. She feared he would do something foolish like assault the man. He didn't. He simply spoke with him. Oglevie accused Esther of leading him into temptation beyond endurance. Momma and Papa didn't believe him.

People in Seabourne did. They had seen her casting a few glances his way from beneath her eyelashes, once or twice peeking at him from over the edge of her fan, or completely ignoring him at village fetes before he married. Harmless flirtations — or so she thought, until she got his attention and realized he was not the sort of man whose attentions she wanted.

But he owned the livelihoods of many in Seabourne. He employed more men than anyone else in the county, and several women too. No one would believe anything against Alfred Oglevie.

But they believed ill of the female whose looks were too fine, who sang too well, who could draw and recite poetry and Scripture, and who had learned the art of midwifery in her own right. Too many females had lost beaux to Esther Cherrett's looks, charm, and endless hunt for someone good enough to suit her.

So she'd stayed away. That night, however, someone had to go to Mrs. Oglevie. Against Papa's wishes, Esther went.

And learned that Mrs. Oglevie slept peacefully upstairs, while her husband —

Esther lost the fight with the bile. She doubled over the sill, coughing and gasping and thanking God this house faced the rear of the compound, away from the main house. She wouldn't wake anyone up.

She wouldn't sleep again. Sleep, as it had for the past four and a half months, brought dreams — bright canvas images of the Oglevie house, the kitchen, reflections in the night-dark windows. Always a face glowed in that window on the other side of the glass, watching, witnessing, waiting to spread lies calculated to ruin Esther Cherrett's life.

She ran from it, and someone knew. Someone told her to keep running.

"What comes in my next week here?" she asked the moving shadows, whether living creatures or shifting branches she couldn't quite tell now. "A note that says my sins will find me out?"

But they had. Someone on the mountain knew more than they should and wanted her to know it. Only Zach and Hannah had been in Seabourne. Hannah might have gleaned some gossip and be willing to spread it abroad. Zach wouldn't. Zach believed her pure and innocent, an idyllic female.

"I wish I were."

She wanted to be the female Zach saw. She felt like the female he saw when she was with him. Earlier she'd believed if that continued, she might be in a good place. Now, in the dead of night, with the dream reverberating through her mind and images flashing past like a magic lantern show against a wall, she knew she was wrong. Zach was fooled by her looks, attracted to them more than her character.

If she made herself unattractive . . .

She'd been trying for months, wanting to slip into the background in the hopes people of Seabourne would forget her and the great scandal she had caused, the least of the disasters that cold winter night. In Seabourne, though, she had parents and brothers to stop her. If she didn't brush her hair until it shone, Momma or Papa would tell her to make repairs. They expected her to

186

dress neatly, and the only soaps in the house smelled sweet or fresh, pleasant and apparently alluring to some people's senses. Her clothes must always be neat, washed, pressed, free of obvious repairs. In the habit of a midwife, she kept her nails short and her hands scrubbed clean at all times.

She couldn't compromise on her hands. But as for the rest . . .

As the night slipped into dawn, she began to ready herself for the day. She washed with the lye soap the Tollivers had given her for her bath the first night at their house. It irritated her skin, stung her nostrils, and made her feel nauseated to smell it. A good first step.

She bundled her hair into a knot and skewered it with hairpins without the benefit of a mirror or brush. To the touch, the texture felt rough. Her cheeks burned from using the caustic soap on her face.

She could do nothing about her dress. She had only brought a few of her plainest dresses. She chose the plainest, a gray one she had worn to more than one lying-in. Near the bottom, if anyone looked, a bloodstain that had resisted her efforts with warm salt water made a minutely darker splotch on the slate-colored fabric.

Still without looking at a mirror, she

declared herself ready for the day. Everyone else seemed to be ready, awake and going about their morning chores. Brenna and Liza milked the cows. The boys fed the chickens and gathered eggs. Griff passed the school cabin with a bucket in either hand, empty from the way he swung them. He returned moments later with them weighed down. Water, perhaps. Once he departed again, empty-handed this time, his stride long and purposeful, Esther crossed the yard and arrived in the kitchen in time to assist Mrs. Tolliver in preparing breakfast.

The older woman glanced at Esther. Her eyes widened, but she said nothing other than, "If you insist on helping, you can stir that porridge."

Esther stirred. Steam rose from the pot of corn mush. Her face grew damp and hopefully red.

"What gets you up so early?" Mrs. Tolliver asked. "The children are barely up doing their chores."

"I think it was a cat chasing some poor creature that woke me early."

Bless the creature for dragging her out of the dream before the end, the pain of her head hitting the floor, the screaming wife that had too often been Esther crying out in her sleep.

"I didn't mind it, though," she added.

"You look a fright." Mrs. Tolliver took the spoon from Esther. "Go scrape those potatoes for frying. It's cooler at the table."

"Yes, ma'am." Esther crossed the room in two strides. "Should I slice them too?"

"Yep, knife's in that jar and pan's hanging overhead."

Esther scraped, carried the peels to a bucket on the back stoop presumably full of slops for pigs, and set to slicing the potatoes paper-thin like Papa preferred them. She caught a glimpse of herself in the gleaming blade of the knife, a tiny image of a female with a ruddy face and wildly frizzing hair. Distorted by the beveled edge of the knife, or did she truly look that bad? She wanted a mirror.

The kitchen didn't possess one, but the pots had been scrubbed to a coppery sheen. Not as good as a silvered bit of glass, but close enough.

Esther took one down suitable for the potatoes. Before she filled it, she gazed into the bottom.

"That, my dear," Mrs. Tolliver said from across the room, apparently without turning around and looking, "is pure vanity to gaze upon your reflection in a mirror. Not the kind of example we want for our young'uns."

"You misunderstand, ma'am." Cheeks hotter than they were when she stirred the porridge, Esther dropped the pot onto the table with a clang. "I'm ensuring that I don't look like anything vain."

Mrs. Tolliver dropped her spoon and spun, her full skirt coming dangerously close to the hot stove in the breeze of her motion. "What are you talking about, gal? You don't look as neat as you did yesterday, but you couldn't be unattractive if you wore a flour sack and tied your hair up in twine."

"Don't say that." Esther pressed her potato starch-covered hands against her cheeks and added a belated, "Please."

"Odd. Never met a body who didn't like to be told she's pretty. You don't want to be pretty?" Mrs. Tolliver's eyes seemed to grow even wider. "Never heard the like."

"I don't want the young men to be attracted to me. That is . . ." Esther concentrated on laying the potatoes in the pan just right. "I know you and Mrs. Brooks had thoughts about your sons finding a finer female now — now that you have the lead mine, but I don't think I'm ready to be a wife."

She didn't know how she could ever be

ready, despite dreaming to the contrary at times.

Mrs. Tolliver's face softened. "My dear child, even if you don't want to take one of our sons as a husband, you can't go around looking frumpy. You need to be an example of neatness and cleanliness to our boys and girls."

"Oh no, I didn't think." Esther's hands flew to her hair this time, feeling a knot she hadn't brushed out, a straggling strand creeping down her neck. "But I have to hide it."

"No you don't. Beauty is a gift."

"It's a curse if it leads men astray."

Mrs. Tolliver snorted. "Men lead themselves astray. If they're wanting to stray, they don't need no pretty female to make them do it. Now go back to your room and fix —"

An unpleasant noise from upstairs brought her up short. She tilted her head back, and her face twisted as though she tried not to weep. "Speaking of not needing beauty to have a man stray — that's my Bethann. We raised her on the gospel, but she went her way anyhow, and now . . ." She shook her head, and a tear slid down her surprisingly smooth cheek. "She won't tell me and she won't let me help her. But I shouldn't even hint at this to an unmarried girl."

"My mother —" Esther stopped. "Mrs. Tolliver, I'm a fully qualified midwife. I learned it from my mother."

"And you never mentioned a word of it when you wrote?" Mrs. Tolliver's pale blue eyes narrowed, grew a bit cold as her eldest son's could. "Why didn't you tell us?"

"I — I've left that behind. A few months ago —" Esther's stomach cramped. "We don't talk about patients to others unless the court demands it, but I decided I shouldn't practice anymore."

"Did you have someone die on you?"

Esther started at the bluntness, but nodded. "One mother. Babies, yes, a few . . . Sometimes they are just too small. Sometimes they are born too early and never breathe. That's happened to me a few times."

"Once too often?" The blue eyes warmed a fraction.

Esther hesitated over the absolute truth. "I decided I'd rather teach those children who survive than risk working with those who don't."

"I lost a few early on." Mrs. Tolliver returned to stirring the porridge. "Makes me love those who live all the more."

She'd lost a few infants. The poor woman.

A groan and a thud sounded from above. Mrs. Tolliver jumped and headed for the door. "Not that she'll let me do anything for her."

"May I?" Esther whipped off her apron and strode toward the back door. "I have some ginger. If you can get her to drink tea, it should help."

She wasn't still practicing midwifery if she gave the other woman a ginger tea to settle her stomach. If Bethann lost more weight, she would die. It happened.

"I'll get her to drink it and tell me who the father is too." Lips pressed together so hard they all but disappeared, Mrs. Tolliver stalked from the room.

Esther raced for her cabin and her precious store of ginger. She didn't know how she would replenish her supplies. But the mountains surely yielded many herbs she could use. And she had brought her copy of *Gerard's Herbal.* It might help, even if it was written by a British man who didn't know about many plants growing in North America. Surely some were the same, or local women would know what worked on what.

But what was she thinking? Those were a healer's thoughts. She. Was. Not. A. Healer. God had taken that from her as certainly as

Alfred Oglevie had taken her innocence from her because no one said no to him and got away with it.

Feeling as sick as Bethann seemed to be, Esther collected the ginger and carried it back to the house. She shaved a minute amount off the root and set it in a cup of boiling water to steep. The sweet, pungent aroma filled the kitchen, clean and refreshing compared to the greasiness of lard and the blandness of corn mush and potatoes. Corn mush that needed to be stirred and removed from the heat. Potatoes that needed to be set on the stove and fried along with slices of ham.

First she carried the ginger tea upstairs. She could guess where Bethann's room lay — along the back wall and in the corner — to be above the kitchen. The chamber formed the bottom edge of an L-shaped hallway with rooms opening on both sides — not an imaginative design, but large and growing more comfortable as work progressed. The doors stood open along with the windows, so a pleasant breeze swept along the corridor. No curtains hung at the windows, and the walls shone a uniform white. But every bed bore a neatly spread quilt in bright colors and intricate designs.

Esther reached Bethann's room, the only

one with a closed door, and knocked. Mrs. Tolliver opened it.

"Tell her to go away," Bethann called from inside. "I don't need no witch doctoring."

"She'll drink it." Mrs. Tolliver took the pewter mug. "You fetch Liza to help with the breakfast as soon as she's done scrubbing out the milk pails."

"Whatever it is I can do." Esther nodded and turned away.

Again she caught the neatness of each room — plain and swept floorboards with handmade rugs pounded free of dust.

Her hands flew to her hair. She explored the tangles, the frizz, more slipping pins. She would get Liza, all right — get her to take over for ten minutes while Esther returned to her mirror and brush.

When she returned to the kitchen, the potatoes and ham sizzled in their pans, and Brenna stomped around the table setting out plates and flatware.

"There's a stain on your dress," Brenna announced.

Esther scowled at the blotch as though its presence were its own fault. "Blood is difficult to get out of cotton."

"Blood?" Liza squealed.

Brenna's eyebrows rose. "How'd you get blood on your dress?"

She shouldn't have said that.

"I got too close to someone who was bleeding." Esther hedged the response only a little.

"I can fix it," Liza said. "We can cover it up with some ruffles down the front. Wouldn't that be pretty?"

"Fit for a party."

Why hadn't she thought of that? Ruffles, some braiding, any number of decorations would have covered up the blood. Surely she didn't need that kind of reminder keeping her from making better use of her gown. And wearing the dress with its stain wasn't right in this neat-as-a-pin house and equally well-groomed inhabitants.

Female inhabitants anyway. The four Tolliver males came in, all grimy, uncombed, glowing from their morning's exertions, even Mr. Tolliver.

"Wash before you come to the table," she commanded, without thinking that she spoke to her employers and students.

She looked at her own hands. Clean. Good. She must be an example. They had hired her to be a good example of civilization so their children could go out and find their place in the world and not be shunned for their rough talk or appearance.

"Where's Momma?" Jack asked.

"Busy," Esther said. "She left me in charge of breakfast and everyone."

"Including me?" Griff flashed her his heart-stuttering grin.

"If you want to eat, yes." She frowned back at him.

He smiled wider. "What if I just —" He reached for a slice of ham Liza was lifting from the pan.

She smacked his wrist with her heavy, two-tined fork. "You leave that 'lone, Griffin Tolliver. I ain't gonna throw no food away because your filthy hands touched it."

"Yes, ma'am." He snatched his hand back and glowered at Esther. "You teaching back-talk to my sisters?"

"I didn't need to teach them. I'm going to try to unteach them."

"You're gonna need my prayers with this lot." Chuckling, Griff departed from the kitchen.

"I'm a good student," Liza said, "when I can get schooling."

"I don't want no schooling." Brenna slammed forks onto the table. "I wanta get married and have a house bigger than this and real silverware."

"You need to be older," Esther said.

"And find someone who'd want to marry you," Liza added.

"I don't think she will," Ned piped up from the doorway.

"Are your hands clean, Mr. Ned?" Esther reached out to take the child's hands in hers. She pronounced them fine, and he charged to the table.

Mrs. Tolliver descended carrying an empty tankard. She nodded at Esther and took her place at the table along with everyone else gathering. Mr. Tolliver asked the blessing in his quiet, deep voice, and bowls and platters began to fly about so quickly Esther hoped no one noticed she didn't take a serving of porridge.

When everyone was eating, she asked, "When would you like me to start teaching?"

"Soon as you can." Mrs. Tolliver wiped her mouth on her sleeve, and Esther cringed. "Can't do it all day like some places, which is why we're wanting you here now."

"I thought as much." Esther toyed with a bit of ham. "I'll need some time to work out my lessons. Today is Friday. Would a week from Monday be soon enough?"

Mrs. Tolliver nodded. Mr. Tolliver's face twisted as though a spasm of pain had coursed through him.

"Are four hours a day good enough?" Esther continued.

"Four hours!" the youngest three children cried.

"That'll do." Mrs. Tolliver nodded. "And maybe a bit extra to my girls for — what's it called? Portment?"

"Deportment." Esther glanced at the girls. Liza leaned forward. "What's that?"

"Teaching you how to walk and talk and carry on conversation."

"I know how to carry on conversation." Brenna screwed up her face and started talking with an affected accent. "I seen a lady in town who was oh-so-fine she stuck her nose in the air and tripped because she couldn't see where she was going."

Everyone laughed except for Griff. He leaned forward and tapped his sister's arm. "The word is *saw,* brat. You *saw* a lady in town. That's what you need to learn how to talk like."

Brenna flushed. "I forgot, you beast. I hate you." She slammed her chair back hard enough to send it toppling, then ran from the room.

"Griff, you shouldn't have embarrassed your sister like that," Mr. Tolliver said. "She hasn't had much schooling."

"She can read, but she doesn't try." Griff sighed and rose. "If you excuse me, I'll go apologize."

He left the room and a silent table. No one looked at Esther. Blaming her for the conflict? They probably hadn't cared about grammar before she arrived.

"So, Miss Cherrett," Liza said too brightly, "do you have a pretty dress for the Independence Day celebration? If you don't, I can help fix one up for you. We got time."

"Perhaps —" Esther swallowed a sudden lump in her throat at the unexpected offer of feminine kindness. "I'd like that. You can look and see if I have anything appropriate."

She had celebrated the last Fourth of July with her family and a young seminary student helping Papa for the summer. The family threw them together so much that Esther suspected their intentions. But the shy young man never looked her in the eye without blushing. Annoyed, she'd stopped speaking to him.

Her conscience pricked her. If she treated all males that way, no wonder she was twenty-four and never so much as engaged.

Heavy-hearted, she stood and began to gather up the dishes. Mrs. Tolliver offered a protest, but with Brenna still gone, Liza had no help.

"I'll go see to Brenna and Griff." Mr. Tol-

200

liver rose and exited from the house with his stiff-legged gait.

With Liza chattering about her Fourth of July dress and how she could put her hair up this year, the cleanup flew by. Brenna never reappeared, but Bethann slipped into the kitchen and served herself a tiny amount of food. It was food nonetheless, and an equally tiny thrill of pleasure at the sight ran through Esther.

Finished with the cleaning up, Esther returned to her cabin with Liza, where they sorted through her few gowns until Liza declared that a white one with tiny blue flowers patterned across it was perfect.

"Now then," Liza announced with a sideways glance, "we need to get you an escort. Should I ask my brother to invite you?"

The clenching thrill that usually only accompanied his smile, his touch, the sound of his sonorous voice, leaped through Esther at Liza's suggestion, and a "No!" burst from her.

"You don't like my brother?" Liza asked slowly. "Or do you like Zach more?"

Esther didn't answer such a direct and potentially dangerous question. She began to return her dresses to their hooks behind a curtain along one wall of her room and talked to Liza about her hair for the celebration. "Do you have ribbons?"

The question distracted the young woman from talk of an escort for Esther. The celebration was more than a month away, after all. Much could change between now and then.

Talk of hair ribbons and her own mention of the day at breakfast reminded Esther of home, of the family readying itself for Sunday. Papa would be practicing his sermon in his study. Esther should be with the choir working on Sunday's music, though she hadn't sung before the congregation since January. She'd been gone for a month now. They would be looking for her. Perhaps Zach and Hannah had left some clues behind. They couldn't arrive in a town as small as Seabourne without a few people noticing them. Yet some people — too many of them — in the village wouldn't help the Cherretts find their prodigal daughter. They would consider her absence welcome.

"Do you have services here?" Esther abruptly asked Liza.

Liza ceased smoothing the ribbons laid across Esther's table and shook her head. "Not tomorrow. The preacher comes by when he can. He promised to be here for the Independence Day service this summer, but we aren't usually sure when there'll be services until the day before or so."

Esther schooled her features so her relief didn't show. "What do you do then?"

"If Pa is feeling all right, we have prayers and singing in the parlor. If he's in too much pain to get up, we just stay quiet all day after tending to the animals and the like. I don't know about tomorrow . . ." Liza's pretty mouth turned down at the corners. "He didn't look well this morning."

He hadn't.

"It's going to rain," Liza continued. "Rain always makes him feel worse."

Esther looked at the cloudless sky. "How do you know it's going to rain?"

"It smells like it." Liza's nostrils flared. "Outside, that is. In here it smells like your perfume. What is it?"

"Violets. Those little purple flowers in the woods? My cousins sent it to me from England."

Liza's eyes widened. "Truly? From England? Is that where your clothes come from? I ain't never seen such fine lace before."

"The lace is, yes." Esther ducked her head. "I'm the youngest girl in the family, so they spoil me."

Her uncles, her cousins, her brothers, and

her father all treated her like a princess. Even when she brought shame on them, they didn't blame her. "It's not your fault" had been their refrain in Papa's study, on long walks on the beach, in letters from abroad.

She thought they should be right. Except to treat his wife, she'd avoided Mr. Oglevie after he married. But she must have done something wrong. A great deal wrong. Why else would the rest of the town blame her?

The only reasons she could come up with in all these months of pondering and anguishing warned her yet again to stay away from Zach and Griff alike. Devote herself to her students, to Bethann if she could befriend the unhappy woman, perhaps even to Hannah.

"Miss Esther, are you all right?" Liza touched Esther's arm.

She jumped, blinked. "Yes, I'm sorry. Woolgathering. Did you pick a ribbon?"

"I like the pink one."

"Good. It'll match the color in your cheeks." Esther smiled, presented the younger girl with the length of satin, then shooed her out the door to go about her chores.

Esther worked on lessons and helped with supper, avoiding even accidental eye contact with Griff, then retreated to her room as soon as she could politely do so. She read *Emma* to the accompaniment of the rain Liza predicted, a watery veil between her and the rest of the world.

You wanted isolation, she reminded herself. *Don't go all weepy over getting it.*

She walked to the door to inhale the sweetness of the rain-washed earth and heard the distant strains of music, liquid sweetness conjured from a stringed instrument. Not isolated at all. Not with those notes reaching out to her. She could close the door and return to the aloneness she thought she wanted, or she could remain in the doorway and feel the embrace of the music. Her head said close the door for her own safety. Her heart said stay where she was.

She stayed.

14

"Don't you like her?" Momma asked Griff after supper Wednesday night.

He leaned against the back wall of the house, where he hoped to have a porch soon — a porch surrounded by a real garden with flowers and bushes and soft, green grass rather than trampled earth and pebbles. Then, and only then, would he feel he could bring a bride home. At least the kind of bride he wanted.

The kind he wasn't going to get anytime soon.

He shoved his hands through his hair. "I like her right well. She's about the prettiest thing I've ever seen. But I promised Zach he could court her."

"What are you talking about, Son?" Momma rubbed her right eye with a knuckle.

"He took a fancy to her, so I said he could have his chance to court her without me interfering." Griff hesitated. "For the sake of peace."

"Peace." Momma rolled her eyes. "You'll get peace — a piece of my mind. Zach has some fine qualities, but they ain't anywhere near yours."

Griff smiled. "You're my momma, of course you say that."

"No." She gave her head a hard shake. "I say it because it's true. Tamar says it, and she's his momma. You work twice as hard as he does. You are smarter, better-looking, sing like one of the angels must have sung to the shep—"

"Stop." Griff doubled over laughing to disguise his blush.

"Not a bit of that isn't true."

"I can't argue with my momma, but I'd like to, even if it mattered. Which it don't." He heard Esther's melodious voice and corrected himself. "Doesn't."

Momma slid a sidelong glance toward him. "What if I order you to ask her to the Independence Day celebration?"

He stopped laughing and straightened. "I can't risk trouble between Zach and me. We're the hope of the future of our families."

"That ain't saying much about hope, Son."

"Momma, you shouldn't talk so about Zach."

"He's lazy and spends more time hunting and fishing with Henry Gosnoll than he does working that ferry for his pa."

"Gosnoll works hard at the mine now," Griff pointed out.

"And I reckon Zach suggested you hire him despite what he's done to us."

Griff sighed. "That was a long time ago, and no one else on the mountain knows anything about mining."

"But hiring Henry Gosnell encourages the hard feelings with your kin."

"Don't they understand?" Griff slammed his fist into the palm of his other hand. "I'm working hard for all of them so they can have work and not starve or drink themselves to death."

But he'd heard about Brenna attempting to throw a stone at Zach's face. Brenna understood the tension between the families and took it out on any Brooks she encountered, even though it wasn't her fight.

"It's none of our fight," Griff said. "Not anymore. Yet there's Pa preaching revenge still."

"He don't when his back don't hurt so bad."

"These last two days, the weather's been

dry and not too hot. What about when that changes? Is he going to take shots at the next Gosnoll or Brooks he sees just for sport? Especially if Bethann's trouble is caused by one of them . . ."

Every muscle tensed at the memory of a decade earlier — Pa heading out with his shotgun with the intention of killing the man who had ruined his daughter. He hadn't succeeded. Henry Gosnoll had married Hannah Brooks, and they'd left the mountain for a time. So Pa took his rage out on Uncle Tom Brooks — or tried to. He failed. But Uncle Tom and his brother retaliated by shooting Griff's older brother. Then Pa retaliated further, and so it went. Ambushes, killings, woundings, and not a soul talking when someone called in the government men to put an end to it. No one knew for sure who shot whom, so not a body laid claim to any knowledge of shootings. Accidents happened.

But not with knives.

Griff put his hand to his side. A knife attack was new. So was attacking someone off the ridge. A true intention to rob, or someone trying to make the assault look like a random crime?

"We don't know who caused Bethann's trouble this time," Momma said quietly.

"She goes when and where she wills and won't talk."

"Will he wed her?" Griff was forever hopeful someone would make an honest woman of his sister, making her less a shame to the family for her immoral ways and, worse, for starting the feud.

Momma shrugged. "She says he'll go away with her, but she thought that last time."

"He was promised to be married to somebody else the last time."

"And you think that was the last time she went astray?"

"Ooph." The words struck Griff like a hammer blow to the middle. "I didn't think about it. She's my sister. The very notion . . . I thought she'd changed her ways."

"I wanted to think it. I've prayed for her every day and night, but her heart is like a stone against the Lord."

"There's something in the Bible about that. God said he'd break the hearts of stone."

"Ezekiel. He needs a mighty big hammer for her. But not you. You, Son, have a kind heart, a pure heart."

Not pure enough when he looked at Esther Cherrett. Not when he touched her. Not when he heard the musical tones of her voice and wondered if she could sing.

Not when he thought about Zach courting her.

"Ask her to the Independence Day celebration, Griffin."

"Oh no, you're using my whole name."
He tried to laugh it off, throwing up his
hands as though to ward off a blow. "I gotta
obey or suffer the consequences."

"No consequences except you're a man
grown and too much alone. Your pa and I
had three children by the time we were your
age. You need a wife. And not one of these
mountain girls. You got money now. You'll
want to go into town and not have your wife
shame you. You need a pretty and truly good
girl."

"More like I'd shame her."

"Not as much as Zach would."

Griff gripped his wrist behind his back.
"Momma, don't you understand? I like
working in the fields. I like mucking out the
stalls. We could get as rich from that mine
as — as Governor Gregory, and I would still
like to do these things. Do you think a prim
and proper female like Esther Cherrett
wouldn't find that shameful? Can you think
of her taking me back to her father? She
talks like she's some kind of princess."

"Like I said, don't you like her much?"

Griff took a few paces away from the

house, then swiveled on his heel and stalked back. "I like her too much. I'm half tempted — no, more than half — to take my dulcimer and play it under her window to convince her I'm the better catch. But she runs away from me like I'm a bucket of turpentine next to a fire, and then clings to Zach like he's keeping her afloat. There. That convince you I'm right to leave her to Zach to take his chances with her?"

Momma smiled. "Not at all. Now go ask her. She's out feeding the cats."

"She's feeding the cats? Doesn't she know we'll get overrun with 'em if she does that?"

"Maybe she's lonely and doesn't care." Momma patted his shoulder and turned toward the back door. "Be a good son and do what I say."

He figured he could find a way not to obey Momma, such as wait for Zach to invite Esther so him doing so too would be nonsensical. But then, he did want to find out what she was running from and why someone would find it bad enough to pursue her to the ridge.

So he waited for three days. After two, he wondered how they had managed mealtimes without her. She cooked, she served, she ensured the young'uns came to the table neat and clean. Sometimes he caught glimpses of her seated in the classroom going through her books and writing things on sheets of paper. Another time he encountered her seated on the porch with Liza, their needles flying in and out of bits of material, making fancy stitchery work. Was there nothing she could not do well? She seemed so perfect.

Too perfect. Instinct warned him to keep his distance until he knew her better. The Independence Day celebration was a month off. He had plenty of time to get to know her before attending an activity that proclaimed a couple was courting if they arrived together.

Zach, on the other hand, had those three weeks' head start on Griff. He knew her better. She seemed comfortable with Zach and kept her distance from Griff as much as the proximity of their living conditions allowed.

Which was part of the difficulty with Momma. She cornered him one night when he was coming in from a swim in the waterfall pool after a particularly hot day of work. "Did you ask her yet?"

"No, Momma, it's weeks off yet and I don't even know her that well."

"And you won't if you don't stick around of an evening and get to know her." She narrowed her eyes. "You mooning over someone else?"

Griff laughed. "No, ma'am, even though you've been after me to do so for two years now." He narrowed his eyes back at her. "What's the rush?"

"You wanta find a girl before that mine makes us rich."

"If it makes us rich."

"I reckon every female from Roanoke to Bristol thinks it will. And thinks she'll catch herself a rich husband who looks like you."

Griff squirmed like a schoolboy with frogs in his pockets at church. "So do you want me to ask Miss Esther to the celebration 'cause you want me to court her, or do you want me to ask her to keep the other girls away?"

Momma just smiled in response.

At the sound of footfalls crunching toward her, Esther rose so quickly blood rushed to her head and light danced before her eyes in the darkness. The two cats she'd been feeding scraps of her fish from supper wound themselves around her legs, butting her with their heads, and purring loudly enough to be mistaken for distant thunder.

"You'll bring on every cat on the mountain if you feed them fish," Griff said.

214

"Then someone will have to catch more fish." She scooped the smaller of the two felines, an orange tabby, into her arms. "They're precious."

"They probably have fleas."

"Not likely. I rubbed them with some cedar."

Griff propped one shoulder against the side of the cabin. "You know a lot about that sort of thing."

"It's part of being a good housewife. That is —" She buried her hot face in the cat's soft fur, inhaling the tang of the cedar. "A female trained to be a good housewife."

"Or a midwife."

She jumped, and the cat leaped from her arms and streaked into the night. "Your mother told you."

"You should have told us."

"Why? It has nothing to do with my ability to teach."

"It does if you lied about having teaching experience."

"I didn't. I helped teach the other midwife apprentices."

"Why did you keep it a secret from us?" He leaned toward her, all powerful male and smooth voice. "I'd think you'd be right proud of it."

Without a touch, he drew her to him. She

leaned his way, smelled lye soap and sun-
dried fabric, fresh and clean and compel-
ling.

She crossed her arms. "You didn't need to
know."

"Why? Aren't you proud of it?" He faced
her, one hand braced on the cabin wall,
scant inches from her head.

She swallowed. "I was."

"And now?"

She couldn't forget the sounds. Screams.
Sobs. The crack of a hand across the woman's face. Nor could she block out the
smells. Blood. Fear. Death.

She summoned up her strength, the core
of icy steel inside her for the past four and a
half months. "No one needs a midwife
anymore. Doctors do most of the work.
Some females are even talking of going to
medical school if they can get in. Midwifery
is no longer an honorable calling for a female."

"Hmm."

That he didn't believe her was obvious in
that single sound.

"Not that it's any of your concern, Mr.
Tolliver. I am perfectly capable of carrying
out my duties and more."

"Not if you've brought us trouble."

"I . . . haven't." His hand was suddenly

too close, the fingertips touching her hair. Breath snagged in her throat. The rough wall of the cabin loomed behind her, preventing her from backing away.

"May I help you with something, Mr. Tolliver?" she demanded in the coldest of voices.

He chuckled rather like one of the cat's purrs. "My mother told me to ask you to the Independence Day celebration."

"So are you asking me?"

And she had prayed he wouldn't ask her. She didn't need more evidence that God was ignoring her pleas.

"I still obey my momma." His teeth flashed in the moonlight.

Esther's middle fluttered, reason enough to say no. She should not feel this way with him, the wanting to be close to someone again, cared for, cherished — all those things her foolish pride had denied her. Because she deserved better than what Seabourne had to offer?

So much better she'd gotten herself into deserving nothing now.

Not that she wanted Griff Tolliver. He was a fine man, hardworking, and even finer to look at. But he attracted her. Once before, disaster came when she thought she had met someone she wanted to be close to.

Until she knew more of him than his looks and superficial charm, and then her hopes failed. Worse than failed.

She licked her dry lips. "May I say no?"

"You may, but it'll be difficult to say yes to Zach when he asks you."

"Perhaps I can simply stay home."

"No one stays home. There'll be two hundred people there if there's half a dozen. They'll all want a look at you." He tilted her chin up with a forefinger.

She couldn't jerk away or she'd smash her head against the log behind her. Ah, but how that infinitesimal touch felt as though it would leave a mark behind. The flutter in her middle turned to jumping grasshoppers.

"I'll say no to both." Her voice emerged in a whisper. "I can watch out for the children."

"But you can't miss the dancing. We'll all want a turn on the floor with you."

"Of course."

Reels, quadrilles, any number of dances moved so quickly and changed partners often enough she could manage that without trouble.

"All right then. Something to look forward to." He ducked his head.

For a heart-stopping minute, she feared he would kiss her. Her heart began to race, and she flattened herself against the logs of the cabin, her lips pinched shut.

With another one of his purring chuckles, he touched his brow as though he were a city gentleman with a top hat and strode away.

Esther slid to the ground, heedless of getting dirt on her skirt. It was an ugly gown anyway, her oldest and ugliest. Liza was right. She should add some trimming to make it pretty, to cover up the bloodstain. She simply needed the reminder of her foolishness, her bad behavior, and the consequences.

"I never saw anything wrong with flirting," she had sobbed against Papa's shoulder. "I thought . . . I never guessed . . ."

"Neither did I. But I nearly cost your mother her work and her home. And the nature you have inherited from me has been a much dearer cost."

The sins of the father, one letter had reminded her, obviously someone who knew Papa when he was a bondservant in Seabourne. *The sins . . .*

And there she stood aquiver at Griffin Tolliver's proximity, his rich voice, his light touch, and she had come too close to flirting with him despite her promise to take more care with the hearts and desires of men. Her actions might be taken as playing hard to get. Considering that she liked his response to her, she surely trod too close to falling into her old habits.

She wrapped her arms around her legs and dropped her brow to her knees. "Lord, are all those people in Seabourne right? Am I wholly without moral fortitude? Was it all my fault?"

If so, she would have to take the advice of whoever had pinned the note onto her door and keep running.

15

On Saturday night, Zach came up with a good idea for getting to see Esther sooner than Monday morning, when he intended to deliver his younger brothers to the school. The following day was Sunday. It being a day of rest taken seriously, few people stirred on the mountain unless a preacher was around to give a service. For the following morning, however, no sermon would be forthcoming.

But what about a lesson on the Bible for the children? Esther was a pastor's daughter. She should know what sorts of things to tell the young'uns.

Pleased with himself, Zach set out across the ridge to the Tolliver compound. He was tired from a day of working the ferry back and forth across the New River, but the prospect of seeing Esther after more than a week filled him with renewed vigor.

He reached the Tollivers' a little before

the sun slipped behind the western mountains and discovered Esther cross-legged in the rocky soil outside her cabin door, two cats on her lap. Her dress and face glowed in the twilight, and a final beam of sunlight touched a copper highlight in her hair.

She was just too pretty for him. He really wanted a wife who was plainer, not likely to cause trouble. But he couldn't let Griff have her. She would bring more to the Tollivers, things they didn't deserve, like connections to fine folk in the East.

But she was kind too, with the way she stroked and murmured to the animals on her skirt.

"They probably have fleas," he greeted her.

She glanced up at him and laughed. "You sound like Griff."

"Then I take it back. If they had fleas, you wouldn't be petting them."

"A clever man." Her smile melted him, melted the moment of resentment toward his cousin for seeing her like this first.

He crouched down in front of her. "How did you get them to come to you?"

"I lured them with fish. The boys spent all afternoon catching it and cleaning it, and I fed it to these cats. But they appreciate the gift." She rubbed one cat's belly. It purred

excessively, and Esther drew her brows together.

"Is something wrong?" Zach asked.

"No, but I think she's —" She shifted her
shoulders as though casting off a burden.
"What brings you here so late in the day?"

"Tomorrow is Sunday and we don't have
a preacher this week."

"Yes?" Her hand stilled, but her fingers
must have tightened, for the cat meowed
and scrambled away.

"Is something wrong about that?" Zach
asked. "We're back here in the hills and not
too able of supporting a preacher. Uncle
John here takes a notion to say a word, but
mostly folk like to just rest."

"Only the menfolk preach?" She slumped
back against the cabin wall. "I was afraid
you might ask me to do it because of my
father, and . . . well, I'm not that much of a
hypocrite."

"How could you be a hypocrite?" Zach
reached out his hand, so wanting to touch
her fingers lightly curled on her lap where
the cat had lain, but he couldn't be that
bold and not risk offending her.

She snorted. "Easily. But how may I help
you?"

Ah, her lovely, precise speech.

Zach's insides surely held as much

strength as pine sap in the spring. "Will you teach the little ones about the —"

The atonal melody of a tuning instrument drifted from the far side of the big house. *Twang, twang, twang.*

Zach shot to his feet. Unfair of Griff to bring out his dulcimer on this warm, dark night. Surely it would lure her to him, away from Zach.

She didn't move. She made no indication that she so much as heard the first soft cord drawn across the strings.

Zach moved to lean against the wall beside her and gazed down upon the top of her head, the coiled hair still shining in the last glimmer of twilight. "I'm thinking you could tell stories from the Bible to the children tomorrow."

Slowly she shook her head. "I won't do it without asking a preacher first."

"Sure, I understand that." Zach suppressed a sigh of disappointment.

Griff began to strum and pluck the dulcimer, and Esther's head shot up. "What is that? It sounds a bit like a Spanish guitar, but maybe softer."

"It's a dulcimer." Zach couldn't suppress this sigh. "Griff plays. And he sings. I can't carry a tune in a bucket, but I'm a fair dancer if — if you'll consider going with me to the celebration, that is. Maybe the Independence Day service too, and I can introduce you to the preacher, though I suppose Mrs. Tolliver will . . . want . . ." He laid his head back against the logs and closed his eyes, wishing he knew when to shut his mouth.

With one graceful motion, she rose and glided to her door. "I already told Griff I wouldn't go with anyone. I'm here to teach, regardless of what your mommas want me here for. I'll take the children." She lifted the latch and flashed him a smile. "But I like a good reel as much as the next person." Then she slipped inside and closed the door behind her. A bolt shot home.

A reel was hardly compensation for her not arriving on his arm, yet better than nothing. But what stood out most in Zach's mind was that she had already turned down Griff — Griff, who promised he would let Zach court her and had gone ahead and asked her to the Independence Day celebration.

He followed the lure of the music around the house and up the front steps of the porch. Griff perched on a low stool, his dulcimer flat across his lap. None of the other Tollivers ranged about him, though Zach suspected Bethann wasn't far off. She loved music. She sang in a high, clear voice and often used to sing in church. Then Henry Gosnoll married Hannah, and Bethann sang no more in front of other folk, just her family.

Griff did sing, in smooth, resonant tones he kept to a low pitch in the settling quiet of the night. A ballad passed down from the Old Country: "Barbara Allen." Sweet and sad and with a warning embedded in the lyrics, a warning to maids not to be heartless. Or perhaps to young men not to be foolish over a maid.

And from his grave grew a red, red rose,
From her grave a green briar.

They grew and grew to the steeple top
Till they could grow no higher.
And there they twined in a true love's
     knot,
Red rose around green briar.

Zach stood with one foot propped on the top step and waited for the last note to die away before he spoke. "Why did you ask her?" he demanded in the ensuing stillness.

"Momma told me to." Griff strummed the narrow, flat instrument. "She doesn't abide me telling you you can court her. But she

226

said no, as I knew she would."

Zach's heart lightened. "She did? When I saw you two at the pool . . . well, I thought you looked pretty friendly."

"As when I left." Griff laughed and set the dulcimer aside. "I had to ask to keep Momma happy, but I ensured she wouldn't say yes."

"How?"

"I told you. She's running away, and I pushed to find out why. She's right secretive about it, so she doesn't want to be around me much. Happy now?"

Zach wanted to say yes. Instead, he felt like punching his cousin in anger for the first time in his life.

Esther leaned out her window, but only the faintest strains of the music drifted through the night. Each soft note plucked at a cord in her heart, drawing her as though she were attached by a rope and being pulled out of the door, across the yard, and around the house.

She didn't come from a musical family. Papa sang well enough, Momma and the boys not much at all. But Esther had learned to lift her voice in songs of praise from the time she was a small child and figured out she remembered Bible verses better if she sang them.

Now, gripping the sill to keep herself anchored in her safe little chamber, she made up her own melody to go with the arpeggiated chords crowding through the window and battering her ears.

Can anything be more lovely than music in the night . . .

She gritted her teeth to stop herself from singing aloud. She possessed such a loud voice that if she sang, someone in the house might hear her.

If only the musician were one of the girls or even Mrs. or Mr. Tolliver. She could slip out and listen closer. But Zach said it was Griff with complete certainty, as if he knew no one else would play the gentle stringed instrument. That Griff could draw such tender notes from strings with those broad, calloused fingers seemed impossible. She thought musicians had long, slender hands, white and smooth hands.

No one on the mountain possessed smooth hands except for her. She rubbed lotion into them every morning and night to keep them soft and smooth. Habit. Only habit. Never again would she need to worry about scratching a patient or marring a newborn's skin with a sharp nail or rough callous. She had ripped that part from her life, from her heart.

She would fill it with the mountain children. They needed a teacher, education, even the basics of reading. Enough reading so they could pick up their Bible and study what it said.

And now she had promised to ask about teaching a Sunday school.

"What was I thinking?" She pressed her hands to her temples. "Me teach Sunday school. Papa would laugh hard enough to fall off his chair."

And be pleased.

You'll do well, my dear. His voice came through so loud and clear her heart squeezed.

"Oh, Papa. Momma." She rested her head on her folded arms and shuddered with dry sobs. She should be home in her room readying herself for Sunday, a busy day in the Cherrett household. She shouldn't be standing at a window in a cabin all on her own, listening to soft strains of music and wanting to join the musician.

But she was there, and she would keep her word. She would fill up the emptiness inside her with work and the presence of children. She would go over her lessons for Monday on Sunday. Without church, the previous Sunday had been quiet at the Tolliver compound. She expected the same of the morrow.

She couldn't have been more wrong. After morning chores and breakfast the next day, Mr. Tolliver gathered the family in the parlor. For at least half an hour, they sang hymns — old ones Esther knew, ones that might have slipped up the mountains from the work Francis Asbury did in America the previous century. Even Bethann, still too thin and pale but up and about, sang in a surprisingly pretty soprano. The family broke into harmonies, even the children, and their faces glowed with the joy of the music.

Esther's heart glowed with the joy of listening to the music from Griff's and Mr. Tolliver's smooth baritone, to the piping notes of the boys, to Mrs. Tolliver's alto.

"If you know the words," Mrs. Tolliver said between songs, "join in."

"If you can carry a tune," Brenna muttered.

Griff smiled at Esther. "I'll be surprised if she can't."

Esther's mouth dried. She swallowed. She licked her lips. She shook her head. "I'd rather just listen this first time."

No one forced her to sing. They continued, and then from atop a chest Mr. Tolliver pulled down a Bible that looked old enough to have come from Europe a century earlier. It was the size of a gravestone — or not much smaller — and his hands shook as he set it on a table before opening the leather-covered boards. He flipped through the fragile pages and began to read. " 'Rejoice, O ye nations, with his people: for he will avenge the blood of his servants, and will render vengeance to his adversaries, and will be merciful unto his land, and to his people.' "

As Mr. Tolliver read the words in the halting manner of someone not used to reading aloud, Esther laced her fingers together and pressed them hard onto her lap to stop herself from jumping up in protest at the glee in his voice. She didn't recognize the passage. Early Old Testament, judging from the pages on either side of the spine. Yet she doubted it meant what she guessed he thought it meant — that the Lord stood on the side of the Tollivers.

Peace. Don't you want peace? she wanted to cry.

How could he — crippled up from his injuries, having lost a son and a grandchild and a handful of cousins — want the fighting to continue, to renew after a long hiatus?

Breakfast roiled in her middle. Scenes

flashed before her eyes. Oglevie's face. His reflection in the window. His hands reaching . . .

A hand landed on her shoulder, and she emitted a gasping squeak of surprise.

Mr. Tolliver stopped reading and stared at her. Everyone stared at her.

Griff, close at hand, stared the hardest. "You've gone pale, Miss Esther. Do you need some air?"

"It is hot in here," Mrs. Tolliver said. "The reading's about done. Take her outside and get her some cool water."

"No, truly, I'm all right."

Esther's protest fell on deaf ears. Griff's hand beneath her elbow practically lifted her from her chair. At least it placed enough pressure on her to rise that not doing so would have created a scene. So she rose, murmured an apology to Mr. Tolliver, who nodded a response, and stumbled from the room on the heels of shoes wholly inappropriate for the mountains. They exited the front door, descended the porch steps, and rounded the house to where a pump had been installed close to the back door.

Griff drew a cupful of water. He handed it to her without letting their fingers touch, but his gaze caught and held hers, ice-blue enough to cool the May day.

"So," he said, "tell me what upset you about my father's reading from Deuteronomy."

16

Esther's eyes shifted to the right, then dropped. "I'm not comfortable with vengeance," she murmured. "It's wrong. It hurts no one but the person getting the revenge. It's up to God —" She broke off from a speech that sounded much like someone assigned to recite — no emotions, no conviction in her words, more like a child repeating something her parents told her to know.

Griff gazed down at her, the smooth coil of her hair and a bit of her brow being all he could view from his height and with her head bowed. Not enough to show him any truth in her words, any conviction.

So whatever she was running from stemmed from a situation bad enough for her to want revenge, and she'd been lectured against it. A reasonable conclusion. Instead of acting something out, had she run away instead?

His tongue burned to ask. Instead, he slipped his fingers beneath her chin and coaxed her head up so he could look into her face, try at least to get her to meet his eyes. "Miss Esther, I don't hold with this revenge. What happened to Bethann happened a long time ago. It was wrong. The man responsible shouldn't have been permitted to go about his business while Bethann is shunned here, but much about how men and women are treated ain't — isn't fair and right."

She held his gaze for a moment, then closed her eyes.

Who has hurt you, you beautiful lady?

An ache for her started in Griff's heart. He had wanted to find out why she was running to the mountains so he could protect his family. Now he also longed to find out because —

He thought he could fix it for her? Of course he couldn't. Girls like her hired men like him; they didn't marry them.

He shook his head and stepped away from her, half turning from her. "I gotta get back to the family. We sing all sorts of songs now, and I'm teaching Jack and Ned how to play the dulcimer. You're welcome to join us. We can use a voice like yours."

"Thank you." She rubbed her upper arms

as though she were cold. "Why aren't you teaching your sisters to play?"

"They never asked."

"And if I asked?" She tilted her head, her half smile teasing.

Flirtatious?

He started from the impact. "Um, I — I . . . think I could." Stammering like Ned being caught not having memorized his music. "Do you have any . . . can you play any instrument?"

"The pianoforte."

"I heard one of those once. I liked it right much, but there's no way to get one up these tracks without pounding it to pieces. So we make do with the instruments we can build ourselves."

"You built your — dulcimer, did you call it?"

"Yea." He shrugged. "Pa had one made by a German fellow, but it got smashed, so I made another one."

"How? I mean —" Her gaze dropped to his hands.

"How can I do such delicate work with these hands?" He laughed and held them up. "God has blessed me, I suppose. It's like the voice to sing He gave you." He reached his hand out to her. "Will you join us and use that gift for His glory?"

She hesitated, glanced past him toward her cabin, toward the woods beyond the fence. For a moment, he expected her to simply walk around him and into her room, out of his reach. Her small teeth clamped down on her lower lip a moment, then she nodded and turned toward the house without taking his hand.

He followed her, collected his instrument from the cupboard in the parlor, and carried it onto the porch, where a fresh breeze cooled the afternoon. The rest of them joined him, arranging themselves on stools and steps or standing, Pa in the only chair, his face losing its pinched look as the music rose and swelled and echoed off the hills.

In times like this, with the music swelling to the heavens, family discord didn't matter, didn't exist. God's presence and love poured down. Even the trees seemed to lift their heads and listen, and the hens ceased their cackling.

Sneaking glances Esther's way, Griff caught how her head lifted, her shoulders straightened, tension ran away from her as though cleansed by a torrent as powerful as the waterfall. It sucked the breath from his lungs. He was a man drowning in the beauty of her face and form, the sound of her voice, the depth of her singing.

His fingers faltered on the strings, and he handed the dulcimer to Ned. "You take a turn. My hands are tired."

"I can't play in front of — of her," Ned whispered, shooting a look toward Esther.

"You can too." Jack poked Ned in the arm. "She's your teacher."

"I'll leave." Esther rose. "Shall I fetch everyone some water?"

"We should be getting dinner going anyway. You menfolk take to your lessons." Momma led a procession of females into the house.

"Whew." Ned heaved a sigh, then began to strum and sing in his high, sweet voice.

Jack followed, Pa listening intently, nodding his approval, even smiling once or twice. Yes, for peaceful afternoons like this with his family gathered, Griff would sacrifice a great deal.

Then everyone scattered after dinner, the women to clean up, the men to their evening chores that even Sunday couldn't stop on a farm. Cows needed milking, eggs needed gathering, all the animals needed feeding. By the time everyone finished, Momma had put the children to bed — Brenna insisting she wasn't a child, Liza wanting to finish a bit of needlework on her dress for the Independence Day celebration. Bethann had disappeared, a cup of something sweet and pungent in her hand.

Irresolute, Griff stood on the back stoop, gazing across the kitchen garden to the cabin where he had been born and lived until the past two years, when his family got the foundation and walls of the house up. Esther crouched on the side not quite out of sight, no doubt feeding those useless cats. He could approach her, ask her if she truly wanted to learn to play the dulcimer, offer to teach her. His feet refused to move. His heart raced forward like Ned after a bird, but his feet had grown roots to his doorstep.

Momma's hand, almost as big and calloused as his own, landed on his shoulder. She smelled of yeast dough and whey, sun-bleached homespun and lye soap — scents as familiar as the pine trees around him. "Why are you hesitating, Son?"

"I promised her to Zach. And I —" He shrugged. "Momma, she's scared of something."

"This place is new to her."

"No, I don't mean the mountain lions and bears, or even the chance of real fighting between our families. I'm talking about something she's running from."

"You mean that note?"

He nodded.

"Well, she won't be the first person who's come to these mountains to escape their past, and she won't be the last. It ain't none of our business if she don't want to tell us."

"It is if it puts us in harm's way."

Momma stepped outside beside him. "You think so little of her you think she'd risk us thatta way?"

"Well, no." He bowed his head. "I don't think little of her at all."

"I'm thinking you don't." Momma laughed. "Maybe you're thinking too much of her. And that's all right. Likely all she's running from is a broken heart. Some reason why a pretty girl like her ain't married yet."

"Yes, but why the note here?"

"Dunno. But she'll tell us when she's ready and not before." Momma pointed up to the ridge, where the Brooks land began. "And if your cousin Zach can't win her and you can, it's no reason for feuding."

"As if these families need reasons much." Griff's mouth tightened. "The mine just might make it worse, you know. Kill off all the Tollivers and you got yourself a lot of money."

"Griffin Tolliver, that ain't charitable thinking."

"Naw. It's just honest. Goes t'other way

too. It's not just our money; we got all those cousins who want their share."

"We can only do our part, Griff, and leave the rest to God."

"Who Pa thinks is on our side." He realized his hands had curled into fists at his sides and relaxed them. "Sorry, Momma. I'm being disrespectful."

"Did you ask Miss Esther to the celebration?"

Despite the abrupt shift in subject, Griff understood why — not asking Esther would have shown Momma disrespect.

"I asked. She turned me down. She turned Zach down too. She says she'll go with the children."

"And they'll leave early." Momma grinned and gave him a little push. "Go talk to her. She's gotta be lonely."

And for the first time since he could remember, so was he.

As he tramped across the yard, his footfalls sounding like rock slides compared to the stillness of the evening, the lack of trustworthy companionship weighed on his shoulders like a cliff side's worth of boulders. Zach was his friend, but their work kept them apart more days than not, and always the barrier of their families' hostility toward one another rose as immovable as the rocky ridge between their lands. When any other two men wanted to court the same girl, they took their chances with pleasing her more than the other. With Zach and him, one had to sacrifice for the sake of peace. He wouldn't court her, and keeping away from her . . .

That would be her decision.

She must have noticed him coming, as though she couldn't help but hear his footfalls. Two cats wound around her legs, their purrs like distant thunder, their glances upward adoring.

She looked down and laughed. "I like animals."

"I never think much about them. Horses are to ride. Cows to milk and eat. Same with pigs and chickens — they're for eating. Cats keep the varmints away and dogs can protect."

"But you don't have any dogs."

"We used to." A sharp pang hit him. "They got dead."

"They got dead?" She stared at him. "Old age? Disease? Bearing puppies?"

"One shot, one poisoned. By Brookses or Gosnolls." He tried not to show any emotion, as he tried not to feel emotion.

She pressed one hand to her lips. "And did you all . . . retaliate?"

"I didn't. Pa didn't. I don't know if anyone else did."

"Why? How?" The words shot from her in explosive bursts. "What can be so awful that it is worth killing a human or an innocent animal?"

"Family honor. At least that's what I'm told. My sister was dishonored by one of their family. Forever we must seek revenge until they confess and repent."

"Because you're God?" Her spine bowed as she drew away from him without moving her feet.

He shoved his thumbs into his waistband to stop himself from reaching out to her. "It's not my fight. I've never harmed a soul or even an animal except to put food on my table, and sometimes a body feels bad about that. But I can't stop my father. It just gets worse, Esther. One man is killed, and that means another one must pay. One man's injured, and so it goes. Endless. It's gone on amongst the clans in Scotland and Ireland and probably other places for centuries. Just continues here, I s'pose. All I can do is pray and do my best to make peace."

Like not try to win her to him for Zach's sake. Zach, so shy and awkward with females despite the fact they looked at him and threatened to swoon, judging by their behavior.

"And in the name of peace, I wanted to know if you want a lesson," he finished with less passion.

"I'd like that."

Not speaking, dusk settling around them with a tang of rain in the soft air, they strolled around the house and onto the porch. Griff retrieved his dulcimer once again and motioned for Esther to sit.

"You hold this across your lap flat like this." He demonstrated, setting the slant-sided instrument onto the skirt of her dress, then crouched before her. "You make the notes by holding your fingers over different frets — these things." He indicated the raised bars that ran all the way down the neck and across the body. "To make chords, you hold several fingers down. We'll start with this one."

He took her left hand in his. She felt as stiff as a statue.

"You need to be able to move quickly, not stiff," he admonished her. "Flexible?"

"Yes." Her fingers trembled in his hold, trembled like they had been exposed to cold weather. And they were cold.

He chafed them between his. She resisted for a moment, then began to relax. Her fingers warmed, grew pliant. His heart raced. Instead of crouching before her, holding her hand, he needed to be running, pounding up the mountainside until he couldn't breathe, until this wonderful, terrible, exciting warmth and racing heart calmed.

He stayed where he was before her, close enough to smell the sweetness of her skin and hair, catch the way she swept her lashes down a beat before their eyes would have met. Provocative. Coy. Distracting.

Yet she was an apt pupil. She grasped the idea of how to press on the frets with more than one finger at a time with one hand, while strumming with the other.

"You have a good ear for the music," he told her.

This time she met his gaze. Her eyes shone. "I like this. It's more personal than a pianoforte. Gentler."

"It's what we got here. And we like it right well."

He liked her right well. Too well.

17

Six children perched on the benches before Esther — Ned and Jack in the front, Sam and Mattie Brooks on the second one, and Brenna and Liza on the third. The Tolliver boys gazed at her with wide-eyed anticipation. The Brooks boys kicked their feet and fidgeted with their hands, never meeting her gaze or returning her smile. In the back, Liza sat prim and proper, her back straight, her hands folded in the lap of her best dress except for the one she was saving for the celebration next month. Brenna had brought in a stick and was doing her best to gouge holes in the hard-packed dirt floor.

After she announced the day had begun, Esther spent the first thirty seconds trying to stare Brenna into submission. All it did was make the Tolliver boys kick their feet and fidget and Liza begin an elbow-shoving match with her younger sister.

"Begin as you intend to go on," Momma

had advised Esther to behave with expectant mothers. "You tell them, not the other way around."

Esther marched around the first two benches and snatched the stick from Brenna's hand. "You bring nothing into my classroom I don't invite you to bring, or you will leave my classroom with whatever you bring." She then raised one foot to the bench beside Brenna and broke the stick across her thigh.

From the corner of her eye, she noted the two youngest boys jump at the crack of splintering wood. Good. They wouldn't be inclined to attempt any distracting actions — she hoped.

She tossed the broken pieces of the branch into the yard, closed the door despite the warmth of the day, and returned to the front of the room. "Has anyone else brought something he would like to give me now or let me give his mother and father later?" She fixed her gaze on Sam, a golden-haired imp of nine.

"Don't do no lookin' at me, ma'am." Sam fidgeted some more, rubbing his pocket.

That pocket moved.

"Are you certain of that?" Esther pressed.

"She talks right funny," Mattie whispered. He had stopped fidgeting and tucked his hands under his legs.

Esther laid her hand on Sam's shoulder, thin but sturdy inside his blue-dyed shirt. "Do I need to turn you upside down to get at your pockets?"

"I don't got nothing." Sam stuck out his lower lip.

The others sat perfectly still, watching, lips sealed as though someone had glued them closed. They wouldn't tattle on their cousin. They wanted to see what the new schoolma'am would do.

"Then here is your first grammar lesson, Samuel Brooks and the rest of you. When you say, 'I don't got nothing,' that is a double negative, and in English and arithmetic, two negatives create a positive." Esther hauled the boy to his feet. "That means you have something. So what is it?"

His pocket quivered.

"I don't understand what you just said." Sam's lower lip protruded further and quivered. "That's a lot of fancy words."

She was tempted to give in to the plea for mercy in those pale blue eyes. He was angelic-looking, which probably meant he was a bit worse than an imp.

"What's in your pocket, Sam?" she asked more gently. "Shall I have your brother pull it out?"

"Uh-huh." He blushed.

"Mattie?"

Fourteen-year-old Mattie, homely face split into a grin, dove his hand into his brother's pocket and emerged with a tiny green frog. It hopped feebly in Mattie's hand, its eyes bulging.

"I believe," Esther said, "this fellow needs some water. Liza, will you please fetch a bowl?"

"Yes, ma'am." Liza scrambled over Brenna and raced out the door.

Esther frowned down at Sam. "You nearly killed one of God's creatures for what reason? Trying to scare me sometime in the day?"

"It's just a frog." Sam could give Brenna pouting lessons.

"Frogs have a purpose on this earth, as does each of us." Esther began to turn the moment into a lesson. "Frogs eat things like flies and mosquitoes."

"And then they get et by bigger things," Jack pointed out.

Esther nodded. "That's right. Fish and snakes and other creatures that we might use for their skins, or animals we catch and eat."

"We don't eat no mountain lions," Ned said.

"No." Esther worked to suppress a shudder.

That humanlike scream had disturbed her sleep again the previous night.

"But they have a different purpose," she continued.

Such as?

She didn't know.

"They keep the varmints like rats away," Mattie supplied.

Esther favored him with a brilliant smile of relief. Before she needed to continue, Liza returned with a bowl of water, and Mattie deposited the suffering amphibian into it, then carried it outside. Once he returned, Esther swept back to the front of the room and fixed each child with a stare until he or she met her gaze.

"Next time I will take the object home with you while you explain to your parents why you needed to bring it to class. Understand?"

"You ain't gonna tell my momma?" Sam asked.

Brenna curled her upper lip. "She'll tell mine. And I was just trying to draw."

"We have time for drawing later, Brenna — with the appropriate implements."

The children gave her blank looks.

"We'll use chalk and slates for drawing,"

she clarified. "Right now we are going to see what you can read."

She had created sheets of paper with various paragraphs from the simple to the more complex. Copying each by hand had been painstaking but necessary for efficiency. She passed them out and the testing began. Liza, as expected, read the best, then Jack. Ned and Mattie read poorly, and Brenna somewhere in between. Sam couldn't sound out a single word, which reminded Esther that Zach wanted her to teach him to read. She hoped he knew more than his youngest brother. Sam would be a challenge to teach from the beginning.

But not in arithmetic. He worked out the answers to her sums faster than anyone else and was accurate every time. By the time she declared the day over, he was grinning with triumph at his ability with numbers, and so was Esther.

She was also worn to a thread and wanted nothing more than to take her own drawing materials into a quiet place and be left alone, no one talking to her, no one asking her questions, no one demanding her time. But Mrs. Tolliver wanted to know how the day had progressed, if any of the children gave her trouble, if she thought her young'uns could learn.

"Of course they can. All of them are intelligent."

The truth. Whether or not they wanted to learn remained to be seen after only one day.

It remained to be seen after two, four, five days. With a sigh of relief, Esther closed the door behind the last Tolliver on Friday afternoon. Whether it was risky or not, she intended to go for a long walk. The path up the mountain and then down again to the river was clear and well-traveled enough that she should be safe. She just must not stray off to the waterfall or any other alluring cathedral of nature. That much she had gleaned from the children and Mrs. Tolliver during the weeks she had been on Brooks Ridge. Two hours of solitude was all she asked.

She donned her half boots, hooked the buttons up the insides of her ankles, tied a poke bonnet over her hair, and exited her cabin with her sketching materials tucked under her arm. Two of the now four cats she fed scraps to each night wound themselves around her ankles. She bent and patted them, checking for flea bites and sores. One might be expecting kittens. In a few weeks, her sides would bulge indelicately.

"You should keep to your den soon, Momma," she murmured to the gray-striped tabby.

"Meow?"

"Yes, I've seen that handsome tom. He'd better do right by you." With a scratch behind the pointed ears, one a bit ragged from an old fight, Esther straightened and slipped behind her cabin and out the small back gate of the stockade fence, which was built to keep out marauding Indians that had bothered settlers to the mountains not that many decades earlier.

Cool, sweet air met her beneath the trees. Weaving around rocks and in and out of the rocky ground, a stream babbled along beside her path. Few birds summoned the energy to sing in the afternoon heat, so her footfalls crunched loudly on dead leaves and loose stones. No one could truly walk silently on this ground, but Griff came rather close. She rarely heard him approach no matter the terrain. Zach, on the other hand, whistled and tramped along as though announcing his presence. He didn't surprise a body. She appreciated that about him. She didn't appreciate Griff's stealth.

And she didn't appreciate the way her mind turned to comparisons between the two men. She would choose Zach if she were to choose either of them, which she would not. She held no more feelings for Zach so far except mild liking. He'd come by twice that week for her to give him a reading lesson. He knew his letters and could read simple words, but not much more. He was intelligent, though, and learned quickly. Teaching him was no effort, yet when he read his first verses from the Bible, he gazed up at her with an expression of such admiration and longing she had cut the lesson short and made excuses for him to stay away.

As for Griff . . . She warmed at the memory of sitting close as he positioned her fingers on the dulcimer strings. She tensed at the memory of how he pretended she didn't exist half the time during meals.

Shoving the two men out of her head, Esther chose a fallen log beside the stream at which to stop and perch her sketchpad upon her knees. Sunlight shafted through a break in the canopy overhead. Dense underbrush shielded her from view from the path, and peace settled around her. She concentrated on capturing the scene around her. If — when? — she told her parents where she was, she wanted pictures to send them. *I am well, Papa and Momma. Well.*

And right then, she was happy, more

peaceful than she had been in months. Warm and drowsy and lulled by the gently chuckling water beside her.

Too warm and lulled by the gently chuckling water. Her charcoal dropped from her fingers. The pad fell from her knees. She leaned back against an oak and let the serenity of the mountains wash over her until she experienced a hint of God's presence with her. A hint . . . A hint . . .

The voices jerked her from her doze. She started upright, then ducked her head so her pale face didn't shine beyond the bushes.

She recognized one voice — Bethann Tolliver's, but not sounding like anything she had demonstrated around Esther before. No anger. No bitterness. Not even the grudging and rough kindness she showed her younger siblings and parents.

She was crying and speaking in staccato bursts between sobs. "You promised . . . me. You — you . . . p-promised." Her voice swelled then faded as she passed Esther's hiding place, then moved on with two sets of footfalls accompanying the accusation.

Promised. Promised. Promised. The word seemed to echo off the hills. *Promised. Promised. Promised.*

Slowly Esther rose to her knees and

peered through some branches, trying to glimpse Bethann's companion, but they were already too far down the hill, all that was visible being a shock of red hair.

Esther didn't know anyone on the mountain with red hair other than Mr. Tolliver and Bethann. Bethann was not likely to be talking to her father out on the mountainside in the middle of the afternoon. And what had her companion promised? To marry her? And now he had changed his mind?

Not my concern, Esther told herself and began to rummage in the old leaves and fallen pine needles for her charcoal pencil. *Not my concern.*

Yet if she saw Griff and he chose not to ignore her, she would probably tell him. And at the upcoming celebration, she would look for a tall man with red hair the color of a sunset.

Before Esther could mention to Griff what she'd seen, Saturday night arrived and he came to her door smelling of spring water and the woods, his hair still wet from his swim. He held his dulcimer under his arm. "Ready for a lesson?"

"Won't we wake up the children?"

And didn't he awaken something she

thought dead inside her?

"I mean, it's late. You must be tired." She offered him a smile.

"Never too tired to play on a Saturday night, with the work done and a day of rest ahead." He ran his fingers down a string, making the instrument sigh. "If you get good enough, you can teach the children."

"Perhaps you should."

That single note reverberated through her ears, her head, her soul — a soft cry for someone to release . . . something.

"All right." She couldn't say anything else. "We can drag one of the benches outside."

Griff handed her the dulcimer while he brought out one of the school benches. He set it beside the door and waited for her to seat herself. Not until he joined her did she realize her error — the benches were large enough for two females or two half-grown boys to share, but not a full-grown man and woman. They were too close to both fit. Shoulders, hips, thighs touched. Their arms entwined as he laid the instrument across her knees.

"Show me what you remember from last week." He curled her fingers around the neck.

She gave him good G and D chords, then her fingers slipped on the C. They were sweating in the sultry June heat that was waiting for a storm to strike.

"Like this." He turned to face her more. His knee pressed harder against hers.

She tried to edge away. Her skirt caught under his leg, and she slipped to the edge of the bench.

"Careful." His arm shot out and encircled her waist, drawing her back onto the seat, pulling her close to his side.

Just as Zach sauntered across the yard.

"I think," he said coldly, "that she wants you to let her go."

"I think," Griff responded with the flash of a smile, "if I do she'll tumble onto the ground." He rose with languid grace, drawing Esther up with him. "But you're right. This bench is too small for decency."

Esther gripped the dulcimer hard enough to untune the strings and stared from one male to the other. If they were stags, they'd have locked horns by now. Moonlight behind them obscured their expressions, but they carried themselves with the identical stance of men on the edge of combat.

I'm not worth it, she wanted to cry. *Don't be fooled by this face and form. I hurt those who care for me.*

"You two are absurd." She made herself laugh. "Griff was giving me a dulcimer lesson, and the bench was a bit too small for comfort. Did you come to listen, Zach?"

"I can't tell one tune from another, just the rhythm for dancing," Zach admitted. "I just came to talk."

"Then we can all have a nice talk." Esther smiled. "My father calls it a *cose*. He's English, you know."

She no longer added that he was born the son of a marquess, and now his eldest brother bore the title. He and the next brother in line all had girls — grown women now — so they faced the danger of Papa inheriting the title, and some people found the connection impressive.

Griff and Zach wouldn't. In the few weeks she'd been in their company, she'd learned that how a man conducted himself brought far more honor to his name than any form of inherited title.

How a man or woman conducted himself or herself. If they truly knew her, they wouldn't be fighting over her attention with glass-edged voices and belligerent stances. And they wouldn't know, if she could help it. This was a good place to hide from the past.

She offered them both a conciliatory smile. "Being English makes my papa talk funny."

259

"Is that why you talk funny too?" Griff's tone suggested he was laughing at her.

"She doesn't talk funny," Zach protested. "It's charming."

"It's funny," Esther admitted. "He gave me most of my education."

"My pa can't read," Zach admitted. "Momma tried, but we was too busy working."

Griff took the dulcimer from Esther, his head bent. "I wish mine couldn't. I'm right tired of his vengeance readings from Scripture."

His light touch on the strings, setting them back in tune, may as well have been his fingers plucking at her heart. What pain he must suffer in wanting peace, wanting to spare his family further grief, and having a father who regretted his injury, not because it made his oldest living son have to work harder, but because it stopped him from destroying his enemies — enemies who were his family by marriage, if not blood.

"He should've just sent Bethann away," Zach said, "like Pa did Hannah and Henry."

"Or your pa should have made Gosnoll marry my sister and make things right instead of letting Hannah wed him." Griff sat on the bench and began to play as softly as the breeze through the trees — like a

260

distant moaning of branches bending to a greater power. "But the past can't be undone. No sense in trying to by hurting others."

"Except Henry still swears he's innocent." Zach took a step closer to Esther. "Will you go walking with me tomorrow, Miss Esther? That's what I come to ask."

"I . . ." A walk was always lovely, but she'd so enjoyed singing with the Tollivers last Sunday, she didn't want to miss it again.

"Go ahead." Griff tossed a smile her way. "We can play together anytime."

Esther caught her breath at the implication of his words.

"That," Zach ground out, "was uncalled-for."

"It was. I'm sorry." He sounded genuinely contrite with his head bent over the dulcimer. "I was just teasing a wee bit too far."

Esther stepped over the threshold of her cabin. "I am turning in for the night, gentlemen. I'll see you both tomorrow then." She closed the door in their faces but lingered shamelessly to listen.

"I thought you weren't going to court her," Zach said.

"I'm not." Griff strummed the dulcimer with the strings open. "She likes music and so do I, is all."

"You were mauling her."

Griff laughed. "I was keeping her from falling off the bench."

"But you like her, don't you?"

"Like her?" The music stopped.

Esther held her breath.

"Zach, if I thought she'd take either of us, I'd say forget anything I claimed and court her myself. There, that satisfy you?"

"Yea, I reckon it does."

"Good. Now go away. I'm for my bed."

But he didn't go after Zach departed. He remained on the bench, playing softly, so softly the music likely didn't carry to the house. But it carried to Esther's chamber behind the schoolroom like a fragrance soft and sweet, lilacs or roses drifting through the window, elusive like violets.

She'd never been wooed with music. Its power made her glad she needed to keep her distance from the musician. Too easily that music could lure her as nothing ever had, and that wasn't just out of the question, it was dangerous. She would get her heart broken when the truth inevitably came out.

For now, however, she would enjoy the fact that neither man repulsed her. Griff's nearness intimidated her because she liked it, but it didn't make her stomach curdle.

Momma had said it would happen — the healing — but she hadn't believed it was so. Yet it was happening there in the clear mountain air so far from the sand of Seabourne.

Tomorrow she had music to look forward to, and a walk in the forest. She was happier than she had been in nearly five months.

18

Nothing feels so much like a rabbit that two dogs claimed as their kill. Esther wrote an imaginary letter to her parents as she washed out her chemises and stockings and hung them to dry in her room to preserve her modesty. *They circle around me and snap and growl at one another, and I want nothing to do with either of them.*

It was too much like home, too much like the time before her final contretemps with Alfred Oglevie. Only it was worse. These were cousins from families barely managing to hold a peaceful coexistence on the same mountain, and she was supposed to help that peaceful process progress.

"If the boys will settle down and get themselves family," Mrs. Tolliver said one night over the washing up, "this feud talk'll end. Neither of them wants it. 'Course now . . ." She rolled her eyes toward Bethann's room above the kitchen and shrugged.

"Well, the boys will never carry things on no matter what."

Mrs. Tolliver hadn't seen the way Zach glared at Griff when he came across her taking another music lesson. Griff, fortunately, didn't interfere with Zach's reading lessons. In fact, he stayed away from the schoolhouse, preserving his cousin's pride. But he hadn't let her be in Zach's sole company at any time since that first Sunday walk.

"I'm responsible for you," he told her. "I have to make sure you're safe."

"Of course I'm safe. I'm with Zach. He's the most polite man I know."

"Uh-huh" was all Griff responded.

"We don't trust Brookses and Gosnolls," Brenna said later. "They're all liars and cheats."

"Then why does Henry Gosnoll run your mine?" Esther asked.

Brenna shrugged. "He knows more about mining than anybody around, and Griff didn't want some outsider cheating us."

"He'd rather a Gosnoll cheated you?" Esther responded before thinking perhaps she shouldn't say something like that to a child.

But Griff overheard and responded for himself. "I'd know where and how to find Henry if he does. It keeps him honest knowing that I know. And speaking of the mine, do you want to ride up there with me tomorrow?"

"As long as I can stay above ground. I don't want to go down any shafts."

Griff laughed. "It's not that deep yet, but no, you don't have to go down anywhere. It's just a ride."

They left after breakfast, passing through a part of the forest Esther hadn't yet seen. Much of the path led along the edge of a ravine that dropped off to more forest and a few plumes of smoke that suggested habitation.

"How do they get down there?" Esther asked.

"Walking, mules. Those are mostly Gosnolls and make their living cooking whiskey."

"Isn't that against the law?"

"It is, but nobody ever finds a thing if they come looking. You can't approach a holler like that without giving yourself away."

"No, I suppose you can't." Esther shivered.

Men died trying to clear out illegal distilleries.

But the scenery was stunning, so lush and green and majestic. Trees opened out into meadows full of wildflowers, and every tree seemed to hold a flock of some kind of bird.

Then they rode right up to a cliff overlooking the river clear and sparkling fifty feet below. "No wonder you love this place," she breathed in awe.

Griff turned in his saddle and smiled at her. "I thought you'd understand. It's a pity to spoil it with the mine, but times was so hard, we couldn't say no. What's a few trees gone if my family can eat?"

His eyes held such a bleakness, Esther reached out and touched his hand on the reins. He released them and curled his fingers into hers. For several minutes, they sat there in silence, then his roan gelding began to shift. Griff released Esther's fingers and headed along the cliff path. "We'll only be a short time," Griff tossed over his shoulder. "I know you have school in a bit. But I wanted to show you this and had to come pick up some ledgers."

And she had come because she was curious to meet the infamous Henry Gosnoll, who had gotten himself mining experience in Georgia. That and spend some time riding — with Griff.

She had yet to meet any of the Brookses or Gosnolls other than the boys, Zach, and Hannah. Tamar Brooks suffered from rheumatism, though she was younger than Mrs. Tolliver, and rarely left their house, and Esther hadn't seen Hannah since her arrival.

Henry wasn't in the mining office, a log shack perched atop a shaft gouging an ugly hole into the forest. But Hannah was, writing something in the ledgers she handed to Griff without looking directly at him. She didn't speak to Esther.

Hannah did speak to Esther the Sunday before the Independence Day celebration. She strode through the Tollivers' gate as though she called daily, then leaned against the post a hundred feet from the front porch, where the family had gathered for their afternoon singing. She lifted a hand, and Esther excused herself, figuring Hannah wanted to ask about the boys' progress with their lessons — fair at best — or perhaps was having trouble with her hand.

"How are you?" Esther asked by way of greeting.

"All right." She looked a little pale but otherwise healthy. "My hand's healed up right well." She held it out. A few marks showed where she had burned herself.

"It's the elder leaves. They do wonders." Esther smiled. "Do you want to come up to the porch?"

"No, I want to talk to you. Can we walk?"

"All right." Esther waved to the family

ranged before the house — with the exception of Bethann, who had vanished from sight — then turned back to Hannah.

"That female better disappear from my sight," Hannah muttered.

"I beg your pardon?" A stupid response if ever Esther had given one.

Hannah didn't respond. She didn't need to. Bethann disappeared from the sight of anyone who came to the Tolliver house. Her family let her stay with them because they were kind and loving toward one another, but she shamed them with others. The outspoken mountain folk weren't afraid to say what they thought of such a wayward female who had started a small war.

"So how may I help you today?" Esther broke the silence between them.

Hannah picked up a stick from the ground and began to whack it against the underbrush as they entered the woods. "I want to tell you to stay away from my brother."

"I . . . beg your pardon?" This time the response was not stupid. Esther stopped on the path and stared. "But I thought —"

"You thought our mothers said you'd make a good wife for one of them. Well, you won't."

"Of course not. I said weeks ago I wasn't

interested in anything but what I'm hired for."

Hannah's pale blue eyes flared. "But you lead him on like you do, giving him ideas."

"I make it clear there's nothing —"

Esther closed her eyes. What she said and what she did didn't always match up. She only took Zach's arm as they walked, but he'd seen her sitting side by side with Griff during lessons and once just talking without the dulcimer between them, and perhaps Zach thought —

"I didn't think." She rubbed her eyes. "Is he angry with his cousin or me?"

"Zach is always angry with somebody."

"What?" Esther's hands dropped. Her jaw dropped. "He never says an unkind word about anyone. When he's with me, he's the most cheerful person I know."

"He pretends good." Hannah jabbed the stick into the ground. "If a girl who looks like you ain't the marrying kind, there's something wrong with you, and maybe we made a mistake bringing you, 'specially if you make Zach and Griff stop being friends."

"I see." Esther leaned toward Hannah, trying to see more. "Hannah, did you leave that note on my door my first day here?"

"Note? Me?" Hannah opened her eyes too

wide. "No, ma'am, I can't write."

But when Esther had gone to the mine with Griff, she had seen Hannah making notes in a ledger.

"Why do you want me to go?" Esther asked.

"Strangers always cause trouble here," Hannah said, then snapped her stick in two and walked away.

Esther gazed after her, certain Hannah had left the note because she had heard something in Seabourne. Worse, Hannah seemed to know something she wouldn't say.

Like perhaps she knew Bethann was right and Zach had been the one to throw the knife at Griff.

When Esther said she would go to the Independence Day celebration with the children, she never considered that Griff would come along. The entire family came to the worship service at noon. Along with perhaps two hundred other people, they squeezed onto backless benches set up on the hillside sloping down to the river at Brooks Ferry.

"What do you do in the winter?" Esther asked as she attempted to maneuver herself into the center of the children.

"We don't usually have any preaching in the winter," Jack explained. "Too hard for folk to get here."

Esther raised her brows. "Too difficult? Why?"

"Ice mostly," Jack said.

"And snow." Ned bounced on his bench. "Snow, snow, snow. And we go sliding down the hills and Momma gives us hot cider. Do you like to sled, Miss Esther?"

"I don't know. I've never gone. I've never seen more than a few flakes of snow."

The whole Tolliver clan and a number of others stared at her. Never having seen snow appeared to be some kind of peculiarity no one comprehended.

"Easterners," a bearded old man muttered. "Who needs 'em 'cept my uppity nieces."

"That's Great-Uncle Neff," Liza whispered. "He doesn't like nobody who ain't — isn't from here." She gave Esther an anxious glance. "Did I say that right?"

"Almost." Esther smiled at the girl who was trying so hard and doing well at speaking proper English. "He doesn't like anybody."

"Oh. I'll never get this right."

"Of course you will. You —" Esther realized a hush had fallen over the congregation and everyone was staring at her. Her cheeks heated, and she wanted to crawl under her bench.

Griff rose. "The new schoolma'am," he announced, standing at the end of the bench. "Miss Esther Cherrett. Esther, stand yourself up."

"I, um, would rather not." Esther kept her head down.

"They want a look at you," Brenna said too loudly. "You're like some new kind of bird to them."

A bright child.

"Come." Griff edged his way to stand before her and took her hand to draw her to her feet.

She tried to keep her head down so as not to meet the hundreds of eyes she felt boring their way into her back, her head, her soul, trying to learn what they could from simply looking. But not to raise her head was rude, and she didn't want to shame the Tollivers.

She lifted her chin and smiled at the gathering. A murmur rippled through the crowd, rising like the wind before a storm.

"That's right," Griff murmured. "Stun 'em."

Esther bowed her head again. "I don't want to stun anyone."

She wanted to run down the aisle between

the benches and hop onto the ferry and escape across the river. But the preacher had emerged onto the ferry's deck and raised his arms for silence.

Esther sat — hard, her ruffled skirt billowing around her like frothy ocean waves of blue sprig muslin edged with the white foam of lace. It was her favorite dress, and she couldn't resist bringing it with her. It was far too fancy for the people. She never should have allowed Liza to talk her into wearing it. Or she should have modified it, removed the lace or a few ruffles and embroidered over the stitch marks — anything to make it less rustley, less fluffy, less ostentatious.

"Is she a princess, Momma?" a child asked from the back of the makeshift sanctuary.

"I'll bet she thinks she is," someone old enough to know better said across the benches.

"Welcome to Brooks Ridge, Miss Cherrett," the preacher shouted from the ferry deck. "I know Tamar and Lizbeth prayed a long time for you to come." His voice echoed off the hills and tree-clad ridges, amplifying it. "Now let us lift our voices in worship through song."

The singing began, raucous and rhythmic, heartfelt and joyous. After a moment when she realized seating herself in the middle of the children made her stand out for being taller than they, Esther settled into the pleasure of the singing. An hour passed. Then the preaching began and another hour passed. The afternoon grew warm despite a pleasant breeze blowing down the river. Surely the children would begin to fidget. They certainly did in her classroom. But they remained motionless, engrossed by the rise and fall of the pastor's piercing voice, his words of sin and redemption.

They were words Esther tried not to hear. Papa said she hadn't sinned. Momma and her brothers supported the same. No one else did. Others believed she had tried to destroy the reputation of a good man, a fair and generous man, simply because he married someone else. But she hadn't. She needn't repent of lying.

But what of not telling all of the truth? Surely her earlier games, the coquetry she'd practiced before he met and married his wife, had caused the rest to happen, and she reminded no one of that — of how she'd once pursued out of pride, out of arrogance, out of confusion over looks rather than character.

Pain drew her attention to the nails digging into her palms. Never before had her

275

nails been long enough to do that. She turned her palms up on her lap and stared at the crescents of red. Her stomach roiled. In another minute, she would have to run from the service and find a quiet thicket in which to be sick.

Heat, nothing more. She was simply hot and thirsty and missing home.

"Now let us pray for this nation to repent, that we may keep it free for all men, as Jesus keeps us free." The preacher's voice rose in a prayer filled with such devotion and passion he surely talked directly to God, believed God stood right beside him on the boat deck.

The congregation called out amens and other agreements as though they too experienced God's nearness.

A chill wrapped around Esther despite the July heat. She glanced up to see if clouds suddenly obscured the sky. No, the sun still shone as yellow as Zach's hair, the sky as blue as Griff's and Zach's eyes, as warm as the looks the men gave her.

She forgot to suppress her sigh of relief when the congregation rose to sing a closing hymn.

"Didn't you like it, Miss Esther?" Ned asked.

"I liked it fine." Esther ruffled the boy's

curly, dark hair. "I am simply a bit sleepy."

"We'll see that changes." Griff held out his arm. "Let me escort you out. You might be stopped too much or surrounded by children if you don't go with me."

She hesitated. His arm, muscular and as solid as a tree trunk, appeared capable of sweeping any obstacle from her path. The children couldn't hold back a tide of hens, let alone men, women, and children.

She touched his forearm as lightly as possible with her fingertips. Griff grasped her hand and drew her closer to his side, close enough for her skirt to brush against him with each step. Too close. Too intimate. They looked like a pair, a couple.

They came face to face with Zach, whose tight expression pronounced how he felt about her clinging to Griff's arm. "Right kind of you to help her, Cousin." Sarcasm dripped from his tone.

Esther started to snatch her hand free.

Griff caught her fingers in his and held them. "Did you think she could get through this crowd without it?"

"You don't need to be holding her hand." Zach spoke in a low voice so it didn't carry to others swirling around them, but they knew something wasn't right. Many stopped to stare, leaned forward to listen.

Griff thrust Esther's hand toward Zach as though it weren't attached to her arm. "Don't make a scene and embarrass her."

Zach clasped Esther's fingers, and Griff stalked away.

Esther would have yanked herself free, voicing the words burning on the tip of her tongue — *I don't belong to either of you like a dog bone* — but she didn't want to make a scene.

"Would you like something to drink?" Zach asked as though nothing discomfiting had occurred. "We special-ordered lemons just for today. Once a year we get 'em up here."

Lemons once a year when they weren't much of a treat to her.

"Thank you. I am thirsty." Head high, Esther followed Zach from between the benches and into a clearing laid out with tables groaning under the weight of the food upon them. Simple fare but lots of it. The pastor asked a blessing, and lines formed around the tables.

"Go sit with Mrs. Tolliver," Zach said. "I'll bring you food."

"But you don't know what I like," Esther began.

"I'll guess." And Zach was gone.

Gritting her teeth, Esther located Mrs.

Tolliver — easy to do with her height — and helped her spread out quilts for sitting upon. She rounded up the boys from the game of tag they played with several other boys who looked like them. Cousins, most likely. Neffs, judging from the sky-blue eyes and dark hair. Tall, agile, energetic, they made her smile. Her annoyance with Griff and Zach manhandling her vanished. If she remained with the children, she would enjoy herself.

And she did. After she consumed as much of the meal as she could manage, she joined the throng of young people swarming over one end of the clearing. For the sake of her dress, she didn't participate in any games, but she directed and supervised several, organizing teams for races, helping judge athletic feats.

"How d'you know so much 'bout them things?" one pretty young lady with honey-blonde hair asked Esther.

"I have four brothers. I learned or got bored." She held out her hand. "Esther Cherrett."

"Maimy Tolliver." The young woman shook Esther's hand with vigor. "I'm kin to your Tollivers. D'you wanta sit a spell? I'm fair worn out myself, and we've still got the dancing."

They found a bench someone had dragged up from the ferry landing and settled on it.

"I've been wantin' to come pay a call," Maimy said. "But we don't have no momma, and I've got six young'uns to see to."

Since she looked about eighteen, Esther asked, "Siblings?"

"Huh?"

"Brothers and sisters?"

"Not my own young'uns." Maimy laughed from her belly, then sobered. "Can't marry 'til someone else gets old enough to see to things. Pa needs me at home." She sighed. "Two years or more, and I'll be too old by then." She gazed across the clearing, her face a picture of longing.

She was gazing at Zach engaged in conversation with a handful of men who looked a great deal like him.

Esther's stomach knotted. Her dinner landed in the pit of it like lead from a mining tower. "Were you two courting?" she dared ask.

Maimy snorted. "With our families at one another's throats half the time? No, ma'am. But he's been right nice to me, and if this feudin' ever stops . . ." She sighed, shrugged, and laughed. "But listen to me mournin' on. Tell me why you came up here."

"To teach."

Maimy gave Esther a sidelong glance.

"I wanted to see someplace besides Sea-bourne."

"You're getting old. Lookin' for a hus-band?" Maimy's glance went to Zach again.

"Not looking," Esther assured her. "I'll teach here as long as I'm needed or wanted, then move along."

"Then I guess we can be friends if you don't want to take the man I want."

Blunt. Honest. Open. Enough to take aback a body used to subterfuge of most people, but Esther's heart warmed toward the younger woman.

"Yes, I'd like a friend here closer to my age. Do you want to send your brothers and sisters to my school? I'll ask Mrs. Tolliver if it's all right."

"I'd like that, but it's a long walk and we need them to work."

"How long?"

"An hour, maybe more. Maybe when the harvest and butchering are in." Maimy looked wistful. "Someone in our family should read."

No one in their family read?

Esther knew that some of the fishermen and their families on the coast had little education, but usually at least one person had made a way to get some knowledge of letters.

More and more, as the afternoon drifted into evening and people overcame their shyness enough to talk to Esther, she learned that in Maimy's family, the fact that no one recognized the letters for anything more than what they were — the alphabet — was more common than not. Only the Neffs seemed to have some book learning because of a relation who had gone away to work and then had come back knowing all about letters making up words. Maybe if a few people asked, she could teach a little reading and writing to the adults too.

Even without reading, though, they knew about song and poetry, storytelling and music. Right at sunset, someone brought out a fiddle, others produced more fiddles, and the true festivities began. From children to grandmothers many times over, people got up and danced. Liza, Brenna, and even Jack and Ned joined in for a while, then the younger ones went home with Mrs. Tolliver, and only Liza and Esther remained with the dancers. Griff was nowhere to be seen, but Liza looked so pretty and happy in a white dress she had stitched with pink flowers, she seemed to float on a glowing cloud.

Zach presented himself to Esther and

asked for a dance. "You promised me," he reminded her.

So she had — before her conversation with Hannah. Before she began to wonder if Zach were as gentle and kind as he seemed. Before she was certain Hannah wanted to be rid of her but didn't know why.

Zach proved an excellent dancer, guiding her through the steps that differed from the ones she knew already, but her old ease with him had gone. His touch made her uncomfortable, especially with the way he kept looking at her — too boldly, his gaze not on her face as though she wore some décolleté gown instead of one with a modestly rounded neckline and a ruffle adding to its modesty.

"I want to sit down," she said when the movement of the dance brought their hands together again.

"You can't. It's the middle of the set. You'll ruin it for everyone."

And so she would, so she continued, avoiding his gaze, looking for Liza or Griff and a way to leave.

But no one was leaving. In between dances, to give everyone a rest, the assembly paused to sing ballads, some old, some Esther knew, some local. One young man with sunset-red hair that made Esther's eyes narrow stood up and began to recite a poem about two families in strife. The rhyme and meter were imperfect, but Esther's fingers itched for a pencil to write down the words, preserve them in the event the strife of the families exploded into full violence once again. Without writing implements at hand, she leaned forward to ensure she caught every word in an attempt to commit them to memory.

When the dancing recommenced, Zach appeared before her again and held out his hands. "You promised me another dance."

"I did?" She didn't recall doing so. On the contrary, she was quite certain she had said no such thing.

So why would he lie?

She couldn't get out of going onto the dancing area with him. It would have made a scene, which she didn't want.

He behaved himself this time, though, introducing her to several of his cousins. She danced with a few of them too. The night grew dark. More mothers took the younger children home. Old people either departed or nodded on benches and quilts. And the music continued to play. Esther continued to accept invitations, more and more of them from Zach, as many of the men went home, no doubt, as work recommenced the next day. Some returned, their faces flushed. She suspected why. When one approached her in the movement of a dance, she caught a hint of spirits and understood — someone was serving liquor in the woods. She braced herself for trouble.

None came. The music slowed. The dances grew more focused on couples staying together throughout the piece, and Esther found herself with Zach for the fifth, perhaps sixth, time.

"I'd rather not," she began.

But he gripped her hands and drew her onto the trampled flat grass and slipped his arm around her waist. It was a waltz, but he held her closer than the dance required, closer than she liked.

"Let me go, Zach," she said in a quiet voice.

She tried to pull free but couldn't draw too much attention to herself. She'd done enough of that already tonight. All the couples seemed to be dancing that close, including Liza with a young man who bore the golden hair of the Brookses. And there was Griff at last, his arm around Maimy's waist. She laughed up at him, and his smile for her held pure affection.

Esther's middle twisted. He hadn't come near her, hadn't once offered to dance with her, but appeared to waltz with his cousin several times removed.

Not that Esther cared with whom he danced. If he didn't want to dance with her, he was free not to. But her teeth hurt from clenching them, so she tried to turn her attention back to Zach.

The figure of the dance brought her line of sight to Griff. Across the clearing, their gazes met, held, until they had to turn away, and Esther missed a step, treading on Zach's toes.

"So sorry," she murmured.

She wasn't. She didn't care at that moment. She needed to sit down, get away, do something to clear her head of the notion that she was jealous of Griff choosing to dance with pretty Maimy Tolliver over Esther Cherrett, who had always had more dance partners than any girl needed.

"I need to stop," she said aloud.

"When this dance is over." Zach drew her closer.

She stiffened her spine, grateful for her corset for once in her life.

"Did I tell you how beautiful you are today?" he murmured too close to her ear.

His breath fanned tendrils of hair away from her cheek, and she jerked her head back. "No, and I'd rather you didn't."

"But it's the truth." They turned and spun through the other dancers, along the edge of the clearing.

"Zach," Esther said through her teeth, "take me to one of the benches. I'm weary of dancing."

"We can't stop in the middle." One more turn, and he had them beneath the spreading branches of a sycamore tree. "We can stop here."

They ceased dancing, but Zach kept his arm around her. Once again, Esther's gaze tracked Griff around the clearing until the figure of the dance turned him to face her. She caught his eye, then glanced up at Zach and smiled. "Thank you. I'm growing weary."

"I can walk you home."

"I must wait for Liza."

"Griff's here." Zach raised his hand from her corset-protected waist to her unprotected shoulder. His thumb caressed her ear.

She slapped it away. "Stop that."

He did and turned to face her. "I'd like to court you, Esther. You are just the sort of girl —"

"I'm twenty-four, not a girl, quite too old for marriage around here." She tried to sound like she did in the schoolroom.

He simply smiled and brushed a stray curl

off of her cheek. "That's not too old for me. There's no one better here."

"There's Maimy Tolliver. She's young and very pretty."

And looking up at Griff as though he were Prince Charming from a fairy tale. He bent toward her to catch something she said, then straightened and looked directly at Esther.

Her heart skipped a beat, and she crossed her arms. "Please, Zach, enough of this talk. I'm your friend, nothing more."

"I'd like it to be more." He cupped his hand beneath her chin.

"If you try to kiss me," she said through stiff lips, "I — I'll —"

She remembered Griff tilting her chin up that way, how she thought he might kiss her, how she feared it and then was disappointed when he simply walked away.

Oh no, no, no, she couldn't want Griff Tolliver to kiss her. That was wrong. So terribly wrong. So terribly —

"I've never met such a perfect, lovely . . ." Zach leaned forward. He was going to kiss her.

"Stop." Esther stumbled backward.

"Esther, don't run off." Zach reached for her again.

She took another step back. "I'm not

anything like perfect. I — I'm . . . just not. And if you persist, I — I won't be able to see you at all."

"But you spend more time with me than anyone. Your eyes. Your smiles." He curled his hand around her arm.

Another hand grasped his wrist. "The lady said no," Griff said. "Now let her go."

Zach glared at his cousin. "Don't interfere."

"She's under the protection of my family. Of course I'm going to interfere if she looks upset. Now let go." Griff must have squeezed Zach's wrist, for his face pinched with pain and he released Esther.

She flashed Griff a grateful smile. "I shouldn't have danced with him so many times."

Though the fiddling continued, the dancing had ceased. The crowd circled around, gaping, listening.

Griff gave her an indulgent smile in return. "Playing the flirt can get a girl into trouble."

"I wasn't . . . I don't . . ." She gave Griff a wide-eyed stare. "Or perhaps I was a little. It happens in the dancing, you know."

"Yea, I know. It's why I didn't ask you."

The music ground to a halt, and in the eerie stillness Zach spat out, "Him? You

289

prefer him?" He turned on his cousin. "You promised. You said you wouldn't court her."

"I haven't," Griff said at the same time Esther exclaimed, "He hasn't."

Except perhaps in those dulcimer lessons, with him right beside her, his hands curled around hers, the air crackling between them.

"It's nothing," she insisted to herself as much as to Zach. "Truly, Zach."

He didn't seem to hear as he glared at his cousin. "So maybe Pa is right and Tollivers can't be trusted to keep their word."

"No, don't say things like this because of me!" Esther cried.

She clutched at the folds of her skirt. She glanced right and left, taking in the faces — curious, accusing, angry, everything but sympathetic. She was a stranger, a female who had come into this isolated community and apparently had taken the most eligible bachelor on the ridge. No one would listen to her explanation. No one would accept her protest as the truth. One choice faced her, the choice that had brought her there.

She spun on the low heel of her dancing slipper and ran.

19

Esther plunged into the trees, into the darkness, away from the crowd, all staring eyes and moving lips. All the angry notes she'd received in Seabourne raced before her mind's eye even as her real eyes probed the blackness for a path, a clearing, a place to hide. The notes turned to faces, the words rang in her ears.

Bad woman. Scarlet woman. Go away.

She paused in a thicket and clamped her hands over her ears. "I'm . . . none of those . . . things. I'm . . . not." Her protest emerged in panting gasps.

Yet perhaps she protested too much. Always in her heart ran the relentless fear that she was all of those things. She had been too friendly with Zach, teaching him to read, sitting beside him on the bench instead of across from him. Just because his nearness made her feel nothing didn't mean hers didn't affect him.

And at the same time, she flinched from Griff's touch because she liked it too much, met his gaze with hers and thought about meeting his lips with hers. Wanton, sinful thoughts, unacceptable behavior to have danced with Zach once, let alone half a dozen times, when she had Hannah's warning. He would make assumptions about her intentions, and rightly so. She had made the same mistake again, not considered the other person in her own pursuit of pleasure.

"I didn't know how to say no politely," she protested to the night.

But he and Griff looked to come to blows over Zach's unwanted advances and Griff's interference. Blows, a flaring up of the feud because of her.

She folded her arms across her middle and bent over, sick. As her breathing slowed, the night sounds of crickets, a distant owl, and the faint rustle of leaves brushed against her ears, calming and soothing.

Not knowing where the clearing lay was not calming and soothing. She had run. She presumed others had pursued. Yet the woods lent one a hundred directions, and she had taken one the others hadn't, if they had left and not decided to let the scarlet woman lose herself in the woods, come face-to-face with one of those screaming mountain lions and —

She must go back. She must find her own way back. Downhill would surely lead to the river. The river would lead her back to the celebrants.

She started walking slowly, carefully, her hands out to protect her face from swinging branches. Thorns and twigs ripped at the lace on her gown. A ruffle caught on the limb of a fallen tree. She yanked the fabric and herself free. Her gown was hopelessly ruined. No matter. She would never want to wear it again. She had ruined Zach's enjoyment. Perhaps Hannah was right and she had ruined Griff and Zach's friendship.

If she did, then she would keep running. She would not be responsible for the feud starting up again, or live with the guilt and let it turn her ugly and bitter as it had Bethann.

Despite her efforts, she sounded like one of those black bears crashing through the underbrush. Twigs snapped beneath her feet. Branches cracked like rifle shots. Rustling, snuffling, gasping, she pressed on, down the hill she had fled up, pausing to listen for the rush of water.

Voices drifted to her during one of those pauses.

"Whatzat?" A man's slurred speech rang

loud and clear through a fence of trees.

Esther blinked and caught the flicker of light now, a fire in a clearing. Fires meant people. People meant someone to help her find her way back.

She lifted her foot to take a step forward.

"Probably one of those spyin', lyin' Brookses," another man said. "Whatcha wanta bet?"

"Come out of the bushes," yet one more man called. "Come into t'light where we can see ya."

Esther didn't move. She dared not breathe.

"We won't hurt you iffin you didn't hear us plotting to rid this mountain of more Brookses and Gosnolls." The man laughed.

His companions joined him.

"Nothing important," one of them shouted.

More laughter followed.

Esther spun on her heel and tried to creep away. Lace caught on a thorny shrub and held her fast. She grasped it with both hands and tugged in an attempt to free it and herself. The ripping of fabric. Stitching screeched like a saw on metal.

And someone grabbed her from behind.

She kicked at him. She swung her fists back to strike his arms, break his hold. She screamed and screamed as she should have screamed in January. "Let go of me! Let go of me! Let me go!"

He eluded her attempts at blows with the grace of a fencer and carried her kicking and still screaming into the clearing. "Lookee what I got here. Prettiest rabbit I ever snared."

"And the loudest." One of the men rose and clamped his hand across her mouth.

She tried to bite him. Her teeth wouldn't sink far enough into his calloused palm to hurt him. He simply chuckled and stayed where he was, too close, close enough for her to smell his sweat and whiskey breath.

"Which one of us gets to skin the rabbit?" he asked.

"I catched her," her captor said.

"Yea, but iffin you let go, she'll run. I think I should." The man with his hand across her mouth raised his other hand and hooked his fingers into the modest neckline of her dress.

Esther's stomach rebelled. She swallowed, tensed, made her whole body go still. She couldn't stop them at that moment. If she seemed to comply, perhaps they would lower their guard.

"I like to skin them right down the middle." The man gave her gown a tug.

"Yessir, right down the front to get to —"

The click sounded like a slamming door in the night. The three men froze except for their heads snapping around to the other side of the clearing.

"Let her go, Jake and Jeb Tolliver," Griff said, stepping into the clearing. "I've got two barrels with this scattergun and won't hesitate to use both of them."

No one ever looked as good as did Griff Tolliver at that moment. Her knees weakened. If Jake and Jeb let her go, she would fall flat on her face and probably hug Griff's calves, or feet, or whatever she could reach.

Neither of them released her. "You wouldn't shoot kin," Jake or Jeb said. "Not over a stranger."

"She's not a stranger to me — to my family." Griff shifted the bell-shaped barrel of the gun. "I'm taking responsibility for her. Now let her go."

"We was just havin' some fun," the third man objected. "We wouldn't have harmed her."

Perhaps he wouldn't, but Esther was too close to Jake and Jeb not to know otherwise.

She twisted her shoulders, then her hips, trying to loosen their combined hands on her waist and neckline. Both tightened their grip. Fabric tore.

And Griff fired.

Leaves and twigs showered down on them.

"Are you crazy?" the man behind Esther bellowed. "That nearly got me."

"The next one will." Griff shifted the gun. "If you remember how to count, you have until three. One. Two. Th—"

Cursing, the men released her and scooped up a jug from the ground, and all three hightailed into the trees.

Esther dropped to her knees, gagging, fighting the urge to retch to clear her mouth from the taste of the man's hand — salt and spirits and grime. Her hair tumbled around her face, her pins gone. It seemed to reek of smoke and sweat and whiskey. And her fear. The ripping, tearing terror of knowing exactly what would have happened if Griff hadn't come across her.

"It's all right now, Esther." He stooped before her, and with the same kind of gentleness that plucked music from the dulcimer, he brushed the hair away from her face. "They're gone."

She grasped his hand like a line for a drowning man. She should shove it from her, tell him she'd had enough of men taking liberties with her person. Except they weren't liberties if she allowed it, if she wanted it.

She clung to his fingers, pressed them against her cheek, and began to tremble as though the temperature had dropped to freezing.

"Shh. Hush now." He knelt and gathered her against him, holding her close, stroking her hair down her back, murmuring, murmuring over her keening wails. "Hush now. Hush."

"I" — she gasped — "can't."

"Yea, you can. You don't want nobody else finding us like this. They'd have us before the preacher by morning." His tone was light, teasing.

It worked. Her shuddering diminished. She managed to swallow the wailing sobs. If he released her, she wouldn't tumble over or be sick. She would get to her feet and start walking.

He didn't release her. He slid his hand beneath the fall of her hair and cupped the back of her head, tilting her face up toward his. Too close to his. His breath brushed her lips. His eyes gazed into hers. He was going to kiss her. She must stop him. It was wrong. They weren't even courting. If the mere touch of his hand made her insides quake, how much more would his kiss do to her body, her heart, her soul?

His lips covered hers before she worked

that out, and then she couldn't think. She could only feel — warmth and excitement. She could only taste — lemons sweet and tart on his lips. Despite her head saying, *No, no, no,* she wound her fingers through his ragged curls and held him near for the first closeness she'd allowed herself in nearly six months, a closeness she thought she feared, believed she didn't want.

Knew she shouldn't have.

She tensed and dropped her hands to his shoulders.

He raised his head only enough to break the contact. "I expect that was a right foolish thing to do."

She nodded.

"Should I apologize?"

She shook her head. "I didn't stop you."

"I'm right glad about that." He brushed his lips across hers. "I've been wanting to kiss you practically since I met you. But you've been running from me since you got here." He cupped her face in his hands. "Why?"

"I . . . I'm . . ." She jerked away and grabbed for her torn neckline. "Please. Please forget this happened."

"Forget?" He smiled. "If you think I can forget that, you don't know noth— anything about men."

"I know too much about men, like the intentions of your cousins. They thought they could — they thought I was the kind of female they could —"

It came to her then, the full impact, the irrepressible nausea. She scrambled to her feet, tripping over and tearing her gown further, and darted into the bushes.

She might have crawled beneath a convenient rock and stayed there until Griff gave up on her and went away. She couldn't face him again. She'd let him kiss her. Aching for arms around her, she accepted his touch and too much more. And she didn't want to pull away this time. She wanted to stay, kissing him again and again.

Oh, the people of Seabourne were right. She was a conscienceless woman leading men astray. Oglevie and Zach, the Tolliver cousins and Griff. Griff, who drew her to him like a full moon drew the tide up the sand. She couldn't run fast enough or far enough to get away from him, the first man who made her feel as others had said she made them feel. And if she gave in again, if they gave in to temptation again, if someone like Zach caught Griff touching her, a lifelong friendship — the slender stem of hope for peace on the mountain — might shatter.

She must get back to the Tollivers', gather what of her things she could carry, and leave.

She started to push her way through the trees.

"Esther." Griff reached her before she had gone two yards. "You can't get back by yourself. You'll be lost in half a minute."

"Downhill to the river?"

"Downhill into a holler full of Gosnolls."

"Oh." She scrubbed at her lips, wishing she still tasted lemon. "They wouldn't harm me, would they?"

"Like those Tolliver cousins wouldn't."

"Oh." She hung her head. Her loose hair seemed to weigh down her scalp. "You wouldn't have truly shot them, would you?"

"Nowhere it would have done any harm. Well, not much anyway. They're a lot of lazy varmints hoping to get their hands on the lead mine, or some of the profits."

"By killing off Brookses."

Griff's hand closed over her shoulder, and he turned her toward him. "What did you say?"

"I heard them making some jokes about doing away with Brookses and Gosnolls."

"Well, that's right troublesome." He released his grip and slipped his arm around her shoulders.

301

Make him stop.

She rested her head on his shoulder, too weak and weary in body and spirit to remain upright, forthright, create distance between them.

"Come along." He urged her forward. "We need to get you home."

He led her back into the clearing, where he paused to scoop up his shotgun.

She shuddered at the stench of spent powder. "How did you get that so fast?"

"I had it with me in the things we brought down for the picnic. Wasn't about to go through the woods at night without it."

"But I was."

"Not too wise of you." He wrapped his arm around her shoulders again. "C'mon. Those rascals might take a notion to come back."

That was enough of a threat to get her going. They entered the blackness of the woods and started uphill on a path too narrow for them to walk abreast. Griff took up a position behind her, his hand on her shoulder, guiding her as though he were a cat and could see in the dark. Up, up, up they climbed. Perspiration ran down her spine and beneath her hair. Breath rasped in her throat, and the sole of one shoe flapped loose. Just when she thought she couldn't go on, they crested the ridge, and the bubbling splash of tumbling water greeted her like a blessing.

He had brought her to the waterfall.

20

Hands clasping the gun barrel, Griff stood with his back to the waterfall pool. The rush of water drowned out any sounds Esther made. She could be simply splashing water on her face, or she might have gone for a swim. He'd asked her if she could swim.

"Like a dolphin," she replied.

He understood that to mean yes, but he had no idea what a dolphin was. Not that he could admit that to her. It only emphasized the gulf between them — her education and his only passable ability to read; her respectable family background and his disreputable family, fallen sister, vengeance-seeking father, and his own bleak future regardless of how much money the mine might bring the Tollivers.

He had taken too much of a liking for a woman he had declared he wouldn't pursue. He had gone further, too far. He had held her close and kissed her. What might be worse, she had kissed him in return. Weeks of her darting away from him like a minnow in a pond racing from larger fish, then welcoming his nearness with glances from beneath those ridiculous eyelashes, followed by abrupt evasions from catching his eye, had ended like a thunderstorm concluding with a cliff tumbling into the river — disaster and repercussions yet to be known.

"I only meant to give her comfort, Lord." Griff spoke to the night, knowing only God could hear him above the plunging cliff of water. "I lost control."

And then some. Her scent like those tiny purple flowers that grew in dim places in the spring, her softness save for where she wore one of those corset contraptions, her willingness to let him hold her — all served to break down the will he'd worked to strengthen when around her. And once his lips touched hers and she didn't resist, he was lost to reason that tried to tell him she had just had two men assault her and didn't need a third manhandling her.

She didn't consider his touch manhandling this time.

"Why this time, Esther Cherrett? Why did you let me kiss you?"

"I've been asking myself the same thing." She appeared beside him.

He started. "I didn't hear you over the water. Some watchman I am."

"You were being a gentleman." She smiled at him, automatic brilliance like something she practiced on all men and not just him. That her hair hung in sodden hunks around her face and over her shoulders, and she stood in a tattered cotton gown, did not detract from her beauty. It was a face and form a man could happily wake up to every morning and see passed along to his children.

The skin-deep beauty was there and then some, but what of the spirit of the woman inside?

Uncertainty about that was all that kept him from drawing her to him and kissing her again. If he kept telling himself that she flirted with all men, or most of them, and that she had led Zach to believe he could pay her compliments and then had run from him as though he'd insulted her — a coy act if ever there was one — he could talk himself out of caring for her. He was nothing to her. She had probably returned the embraces of many men.

"It wasn't the first time for you, was it?" He sounded accusatory but didn't care.

She shook her head. "I've been kissed before. I'm . . . I've been . . ." She took several quick steps forward, then caught the toe of her slipper in a crevice between two rocks and stumbled to a halt, her back to him, her hands gripping her upper arms. "I shouldn't have done it. But those men were so rough, and you were so gentle. And they smelled so bad, and you — you tasted — that is . . ." Her voice dropped so low he couldn't hear the rest of her words over the waterfall behind them.

He should move closer to her, yet with her talk of how he tasted to her, he dared not close the distance. He ached for no distance between them. But being there on their own in his favorite place, being near her, might prove more disastrous to them both at that moment.

"We should go," he snapped out. "We'll be missed if we're gone much longer, and the others will want to know I found you."

"I disrupted the party," she exclaimed. "I am so sorry."

"Zach disrupted the party. He shouldn't have been making advances to you when you said no." Griff had to close the distance between them now. He strode past her, then held out a hand to help her over the rocky climb to the top of the gorge.

She laid her fingers in his, hers ice-cold on that warm night, and a jolt came, an impact to his belly, his heart. At that moment, nothing would please him more than to warm her hands between his. She should never be cold when he was near.

He gazed down at her. "I think I'd have kissed you sooner if not for Zach. I thought you wanted him to court you with all that book learning you're giving him."

"I think everyone should learn who wants to. If I can help, I will."

"And the dancing?"

Even in the minimal light, he saw her glare at him. "You never asked."

"I didn't dare. I think you know why now."

"You don't want to upset your cousin or fight with him."

"Especially not over a female who is likely to run off without saying a word about it."

Her silence was enough of an affirmative response for Griff.

He released her hand as soon as they reached the path down the mountain. Over the ridge, the gurgle of the waterfall diminished and the intermittent night sounds of the forest took over.

"I'll tell you when I go. I'll leave in the morning," she said into the stillness. "If you all will lend me a horse, I'll hire someone to bring it back once I reach a town."

If she felt the same pull toward him as he

did toward her — and her kiss suggested she did — then her decision was best. Yet the hoofbeats of her riding away already seemed to pound into his chest, crushing it, interfering with his breathing.

"You can't ride off alone," he said. "And the children need you here."

He needed her there. But so did Zach.

"I'll stay away from you if you stay," he added. "I promise not to touch you."

She walked beside him for a hundred yards or more, the crunch of their footfalls doubly loud, her gown swishing, brushing against his legs, before she asked, "Can you?"

His lips formed the word *yes* — silently. It was a stupid vow he couldn't keep.

"I'm not certain I want you to, and that's the trouble," she answered for him. "Zach thinks he has some kind of claim on me, and if I stay, I'll make trouble between you." She stumbled again and caught her breath. "I'm afraid I gave him too much reason to."

Oh yes, she had, with her smiles and her hands in his, her warmth in greeting his arrivals, the time she had taken to help him with his reading, their heads bent close over a slate and chalk, the way she held his arm when they went for walks. No wonder Zach thought he could pay her compliments and have her accept the way he wished to hold her in the dance, perhaps even steal a kiss in the shadow of a tree.

She had flirted with him. She had flirted with Griff until he kissed her. And she had kissed him back out of gratitude, out of curiosity to know if it would scare her off, because she wanted it right down to her toes.

No wonder God had deserted her. She was everything the people of Seabourne claimed, leading two men in a merry dance, then deciding to run away from the trouble she caused. Surely it was nothing more. She couldn't love Griff Tolliver. She no longer had a heart to give to anyone. And yet she wanted nothing more than to have him hold her, kiss her again, beg her to stay.

"Esther?"

"Ye-es?" She tripped on her broken shoe, and the word emerged more a gasp than a word.

He faced her on the path. "Why did you leave Seabourne?"

"Not because I had to." She looked straight at him. "My parents didn't want me to go away."

"Then why did you?"

"It doesn't concern my ability to carry out

my duties here." She delivered the pronouncement in icy tones, then brushed past him and continued down the path.

For half a dozen yards of uneven footfalls. Then she brought down one foot and gasped loudly enough to be a soft cry, and dropped to her knees.

"Esther." In an instant, Griff was beside her, on his knees, reaching for her hands. "What is it? Did something bite you? It would be unlikely to have a snake here in the dark, but a body never knows how wild creatures behave."

She shook her head. "No bite. A sharp rock. My shoe." She took a long, shuddering breath. "I broke my shoe. The sole's come clean off, and I stepped on something sharp."

"Why didn't you tell me you broke your shoe?" Frustration infused his tone.

"What could you have done about it?"

"Likely more than you're doing. Are you bleeding?"

"Yes, I think I am." Her voice was tight, strained.

"You're in pain," Griff said.

"I'll be all right. I can tear off a strip of my petticoat and bind it."

And grit her teeth hard enough to not express the pain that would cause.

"And walk another mile to the house?" Griff stood.

Esther tore off a ruffle of her petticoat. "I will walk, thank you very much."

"Ah, her royal highness is back." He laughed and reached out as though he had a right to embrace her for the pure pleasure of her taking on her uppity way of speaking in the middle of the forest, in the middle of the night, while wearing a torn-up dress.

"You won't get a dozen feet, Esther."

She stood with less than her usual grace, took one step, and stopped. "Or a dozen inches."

He handed her the scattergun. "Hold this."

"You're going to leave me here?" Her voice rose in pitch. Panic. Fear. Weakness.

"No, sweetheart, not that." He laid his hand against her cheek. "What? Is this a tear?" He smoothed it away with his thumb. "I'm going to carry you," he told her softly.

Her heart began to race. "You can't. I'm too —"

He pressed his thumb to her lips. "Don't tell me I can't. I got to or leave you here 'til I get help." And with that, he scooped her into his arms.

She squeaked a protest. His arms tightened around her, strong, warm, protective.

She dropped her head onto his shoulder. Her wet hair soaked through his shirt.

"It smells fresh like the water of the pool." He pressed his cheek against the top of her head for a moment.

"I couldn't resist the chance to swim. I miss the sea."

"Enough to go back?"

"Not to Seabourne. Somewhere else, perhaps."

Though having him hold her felt too good to make that a desirable action right then.

"You can't go anywhere," he whispered.

"You won't be able to go anywhere if you hold me much longer," she returned.

"True, true." He laughed and started walking. "Good thing it's downhill all the way."

She pressed the stock of the gun into his chest a little harder than necessary. "I said you couldn't carry me. I'm not a little thing like your sisters."

"You're just right." He stumbled over a rock. He caught his balance and Esther before he dropped her, and he let out a grunt of pain.

She shifted and wrapped an arm around his neck. "What's wrong?"

Besides his face being too close to her right then, too tempting.

"Nothing much unless you count me thinking of kissing you again."

"You shouldn't."

"No, ma'am, I reckon that's a bad idea." He kept walking, but his breathing gathered a hitch in it.

"It sounds like you're in pain. Did you hurt — oh no." She struggled to free herself. "You had that stab wound. It's likely not healed properly. You can't carry me with that wound. It could open up again. You could start bleeding and not be able to walk anywhere. I'll have to go for help, and I'm useless in these woods. I'm scared to pieces I'll come face to face with a mountain lion."

"You can always talk him out of attacking you," Griff said drily.

"Not if I can't talk you out of carrying me." And she should. Having him holding her so close to his heart gave her odd notions of wanting it longer, perhaps forever — notions of things a nice girl didn't think about.

"Truly, Griff," she pleaded, "I can walk the rest of the way."

"Not with a cut foot." If anything, he held her closer. His lips brushed her hair.

No, this couldn't continue. "Please?" She dropped her voice to a murmur like a purr, then she smoothed the hair on the back of his neck, marveling at its softness, its springy thickness, and the power of the flesh beneath. "I really need to walk."

A shudder ran through him, and he began to walk faster. Firs replaced the birches and walnut trees, pungent in their scent. The ground leveled in the holler. He paused. He was sweating from the effort of carrying her or from the warm night.

Gooseflesh raced up her arms and down her spine. Fear. Anticipation.

"I can walk now," she exclaimed in desperation.

"No you can't." He started up again. Muscles rippled across his shoulders.

She squeezed her eyes shut. She would not, not, not get interested in another man, not like this. She must use some of her arsenal, whatever the consequences. If she was lucky, they would disgust him as she should.

"Griff, you must be in pain." She touched his cheek with her fingertips, trailed them across the strong bone of his jaw to his ear and behind.

"Stop it," he ground out between his teeth. "Esther Cherrett, you stop it right now."

"Stop what?" She twined her fingers in his hair again. "Trying to persuade you to let me down?"

"What do you think?" He clenched his teeth together and fairly sprinted across the field to the compound and the house.

He kicked open the kitchen door and deposited her on the bench beside the stove. His hands on her shoulders, he leaned toward her, his face close enough for her to feel his breath on her lips but too far away to kiss. "Don't you never — ever play those tricks with me again to get me to do what you want."

She widened her eyes. "Do what again?"

"Don't you go teasing and tormenting me into a state where I can't think right so I'll jump when you say jump."

It had worked. She'd made him angry enough to turn him from her. And it hurt. Knowing her wiles had lost her the only man she knew she could love sliced her open inside.

Tears she didn't have to manufacture sprang into her eyes.

And Mrs. Tolliver, Zach, and half a dozen Tollivers burst into the kitchen.

21

Esther stared into Griff's sky-blue eyes, only vaguely aware of others crowding into the room, only dimly hearing their voices. The end of the world would have suited her just fine at that moment. Her world had ended with the slamming realization that she had crossed the line again in her attempt to cajole him into letting her down.

She could protest that he should have listened to her. In the end, the result was the same — she had let down her barriers with him. In her distress over the drunken men's assault, she had clung to the only familiar and kind person near, as she had clung to her parents and brothers back in January.

Only Griff wasn't her brother, and her response to him bore nothing close to feelings of kinship. Clinging to him stirred the attraction she'd been fighting since she met him. She should have stayed away from him.

But she hadn't.

"I meant nothing by it." Her voice emerged in a rasp. "Believe me, I —"

Even if what seemed like a score of people weren't firing questions at them like shotgun shells, she couldn't have gone on, for she *had* meant it — the kiss, the affection in stroking his surprisingly soft hair, wanting to be out of his arms before she begged him to kiss her again, despite her throbbing and bleeding foot.

"I'm sorry," she croaked out.

"What are you doing to her?" Zach's voice rumbled through the fray of voices.

"What's happened to her?" Mrs. Tolliver demanded.

"Your pretty dress!" Liza cried.

They all came closer, the oldest ones anyway, Zach first, grabbing Griff's shoulder and yanking him back. "Get your hands off of her, you —" He raised his fist.

Esther grabbed his wrist with both hands. "No, don't. It's not as bad as it looks. He wasn't hurting me."

Her foot was, but she couldn't bring herself to mention it at that moment.

The adults stopped talking at once and stared at her. The children hushed except for giggles from Brenna and Jack.

Griff's lips curved into a half smile. "I

don't think they thought I was hurting you, Miss Esther."

"He was going to kiss you," Brenna said in a singsong chant.

"Ewww," the younger boys chorused.

Esther pressed her palms to her flaming cheeks. "He wasn't."

Mrs. Tolliver turned toward the children. "You all go to your rooms. And no sneaking down the steps. That includes you, Brenna."

"But M—"

"Do as I say," Mrs. Tolliver snapped out.

Face mutinous, Brenna followed her younger brothers and cousins out of the room.

"Liza." Mrs. Tolliver turned to her middle daughter. "Go see that they get into bed and settled down for the night."

"Yes'm." With a last glance at Esther, Liza trudged from the room.

Mrs. Tolliver set her hands on her broad, bony hips. "So were you about to kiss her, Griffin Tolliver?" his mother demanded.

"No, ma'am." He crossed his arms over his chest. "I was . . . uh . . ." His glance collided with Esther's, must have read her plea, for he relaxed his stance enough to touch her lightly on the shoulder. "Miss Esther has had a right bad time of it tonight, no thanks to you, Zach."

Zach's face turned red. "I didn't mean to offend her. Guess I lost my head a bit."

Because she'd been flirting with him, dancing with him more than anyone else, giving him reason to believe she'd accept his compliments and kiss. After all, she'd been letting him pay court to her for weeks.

Griff refused to pay court to her and didn't give her pretty speeches. He was more rude to her than not. He just took a kiss, and she freely responded.

Oh, she was shameless.

"I'm so mortified." Tears proved too easy to produce. "I shouldn't have run off. I was so afraid they were going to fight because of me, and — and — I want to go home."

It was true. Every word of it. By morning, things would be just as bad on Brooks Ridge as they had been in Seabourne, and she wouldn't have her family to protect her.

"There, there, gal." Mrs. Tolliver sat on the bench beside Esther and wrapped a ropy arm around her shoulders. "I'm sure you're missin' your kinfolk, but there's no call for you running off just 'cause some flirting at a celebration got a tad out of hand."

"Just a tad," Griff muttered.

His mother glared at him. "You mind your manners, Son. What were you doing when we walked in? And don't tell me comforting

320

her. She looked like you were about to pick her up and drop her out the door."

"Tempting," Griff drawled. "But those cats she loves so much might drag her in."

"Griffin Tolliver, I never raised you to talk about a female thatta way." His mother sounded horrified. "You apologize right now."

Griff said nothing.

Zach's face twisted, and his hands balled into fists. "Apologize."

"Griffin," Mrs. Tolliver barked.

"I'm sorry, Momma, but I'm going to disobey you," Griff said and walked out of the house, letting the back door slam behind him.

Zach charged after him.

Esther's tears weren't manufactured. She buried her face in her hands and sobbed. "Go after them. They'll fight."

"No, they won't. Griff won't touch Zach."

"But he nearly struck him for — for trying to kiss me at the celebration."

"So maybe you'd better tell me what happened, Esther." Mrs. Tolliver kept her arm around Esther, but her voice held the note of a woman who would take no nonsense protests.

Esther took a deep breath. "I'm a terrible flirt. Momma says I get it from Papa. I don't even know I'm doing it. I think I'm just being friendly, and . . ."

"Because you look like you do, men take it the wrong way."

Esther nodded. Oh, how so very wrong some took it. "I should have been more careful with Zach. I knew he had a bit of a *tendre* for me, but —"

"A what?"

"A fancy for me. I told him I don't want to be courted, but I've been teaching him to read, and we were together all that time on the road here, and . . . I should have said no when he kept asking me to dance."

"But you're young and miss your kin, and he's a handsome young man."

Esther nodded.

"So you ran off into the woods so the boys wouldn't fight over you," Mrs. Tolliver concluded.

Esther nodded again.

"And Griff found you."

"Yes, but not before I'd stumbled into some of your relations. Some Tolliver cousins." She pressed her fingers to her lips. "They were inebriated," she whispered. "They . . . tried to take liberties."

"They never! Who was it? I'll skin 'em alive." Mrs. Tolliver leaped to her feet as though intending to do so right then and

322

there. "Griff stopped 'em quick enough, I hope? Your dress?" Her gaze dropped to the tear in the neckline that ended just short of making it indecent.

"Yes, he had a shotgun."

"Which one did he shoot?"

"No — none." Esther stared at the older woman, who looked pleased at the prospect that her son had perhaps shot one of his own cousins.

"Well, that's probably a good thing," she said. "We got troubles enough with other families. We don't need 'em amongst our kin."

"But I've made trouble between Zach and Griff." Esther pressed her cold hands to her hot cheeks and dropped her gaze to the stone floor of the kitchen. "I need to leave."

The sound of voices rumbled from outside — harsh, but not angry, not fighting. Childish laughter and a few thumps sounded from overhead.

Mrs. Tolliver cleared her throat. "You and Griff were alone an awful long time. Did my son dishonor you in any way?"

Esther shook her head.

"Hmm. I wonder why I'm not believing you. You two looked right close when we walked in here."

Esther ducked her head further.

"Look at me, Esther." Though gently spoken, the command suggested Mrs. Tolliver would take no disobedience from the schoolma'am either.

Esther raised her head and crossed her arms. "Yes, ma'am?"

"Did Griff kiss you?" Mrs. Tolliver asked.

Esther ran her tongue along her lower lip, recalled the taste of lemon, the tang of the flavor, the sweet pressure upon her mouth, and she grew warm all over — longing, shame, humiliation.

"I'm gonna tan his hide." Mrs. Tolliver strode to the back door.

"Ma'am," Esther called after her, "I'm afraid my foot is still bleeding and I've gotten some on your floor."

Zach encountered Griff at the well, pumping water into a pair of buckets as though trying to win a contest.

"Why?" Zach asked.

Griff exchanged a filled pail for an empty one and resumed pumping without saying a word.

Zach tried another tack. "You took my girl from me."

Griff paused with the pump handle raised and his gaze fixed on the distance. "I didn't take her from you, Zach."

"You were holding her."

Sickness ran through Zach's guts at the memory of walking into the kitchen and seeing Griff with his hands on Esther's shoulders, his face so close to hers, her eyes wide, her lips parted as though anticipating a kiss. She certainly wasn't trying to escape, as she had from him.

"You were practically nose to nose," Zach pointed out.

"We were." Griff dropped the pump handle into place and set his hands on his hips. "She broke her shoe and cut her foot when she ran away from you pressing your advances on her after she said no. I was setting her down after carrying her for near a mile. Does that satisfy you? 'Bout broke open my wound doing it too. She's heavy."

"She's perfect."

"Yea, I think you were saying something 'bout that before you tried to kiss her." Griff took a pace forward. "I should have knocked you down for that. She's under a Tolliver roof. She's under my protection, and you drove her right into danger."

"Is she all right? Her foot? The rest? Her dress looked torn to bits." Zach half turned toward the house. "I should go —"

Griff grabbed his shoulder and spun him back. "Leave her alone. You've done enough damage for one night."

"I'd like to apologize."

"You can wait until she's not hurting and isn't wearing a tore-up dress and —" He started to move away. "I got work to do."

"At midnight?"

"I'd rather be mucking stalls than talking about that female with you."

Zach fell into step beside him. "Why've you taken to not liking her?"

"You don't want me to tell you." Griff walked faster. "Just go home, Zach, and come back tomorrow to say you're sorry for being a fool around a female tonight."

"Not 'til you explain yourself." Zach reached the barn door first and stood in front of it, his arms crossed over his chest. "You were as mean as I've ever seen you be with a female in there tonight. I oughta knock you down for talking about the cats dragging her in."

"Go ahead if it'll make you feel better. I probably deserve it, and I won't hit you back."

Zach's innards twisted up like a scrap of rope. "What d'you mean you probably deserve it?"

Griff remained before him, tall, sturdy, silent, his hands at his sides but not relaxed. Every muscle in his body, etched against the starlit sky and distant light from the house, spoke of coiled muscles ready to snap.

Zach dropped his own arms, fists clenched. "You did kiss her, didn't you?"

"That female in there you think is so perfect ain't anywhere near." Griff moved in closer and lowered his voice. "If you insist on knowing, then I'll tell you. I did kiss her, and I wasn't the first man she kissed back. She's more'n happy to use her pretty face and her soft little hands to get a man to —"

Zach lashed out. Griff swayed to the side, and the blow landed on his cheekbone rather than his nose. But the skin split and blood flowed.

"Don't you ever talk about her that way again." Zach braced himself, waiting for a retaliatory strike.

Griff simply yanked off his shirt and pressed the cloth to his face. "Don't believe me. Court her and find out for yourself. Now get out of my way." He shoved Zach aside and stalked into the barn.

The door closed and the bar dropped into place behind him.

Zach stared at his knuckles. One was swelling. Swelling because he had hit his cousin, his lifelong friend, had broken his vow before the preacher and God to keep peace between the families.

"You don't speak against any female like that," he said aloud.

But he had done all he could for the moment to raise tension between the families, to start the feuding again — short of acting like his brother-in-law and dishonoring a female, which he just couldn't bring himself to do.

Apparently unlike his cousin.

"I'm glad I struck you, Griff Tolliver." He spat in the direction of the barn.

His anger, his apprehension that he might indeed have started up the feuding again, however much he wished not to, sent him striding up and over the ridge like it was flat ground. He didn't care how long they'd been friends. Griff was still a Tolliver, and the rest of his family didn't like Zach's kin, so Griff might have joined them in taking what he wanted without caring for vows or friendship.

Lost in a whirlpool of anger, envy, and speculation, Zach didn't hear the crunch of rock beneath someone's foot, the snap of a branch, and the rustle of leaves until a moment before a knife slammed into his hip.

22

Griff slammed the pitchfork so hard against the barn's stone floor, the ash handle broke with a splintering rend of wood that sent the horses and mules whinnying and kicking their stalls. Griff tossed the shattered pieces into a corner and contemplated kicking or striking something himself.

But he didn't need a busted-up foot or hand. He already sported a busted-up face with blood flowing down his cheek in a slow but steady trickle. He was going to have a black eye too, thanks to that lovesick fool of a cousin.

And his own stupidity.

He dropped to his knees in the center of the barn with the warm hay and manure and horse smell around him, and pressed both hands to his face. "Oh, Lord, why did I do it? If I'd kept my hands off of her, if I didn't give in to temptation, I wouldn't be thinking now maybe I love her."

And he wouldn't be so hurt by the way she had given him her attention, stroking his hair, touching his cheek — the affections of a beloved — just because she wanted something he refused to give her: setting her down to . . . what? Satisfy her pride, avoid the embarrassment of being carried like a child?

His face throbbed. His heart ached. His conscience stung.

Zach wasn't the only one who needed to be asking the girl for forgiveness.

At that moment, with the bleeding refusing to stop, he needed to ask her for purely practical help.

Light-headed, he staggered to his feet and made his way back to the house. He didn't know how he'd be greeted. Momma probably wanted to get out the stick she used for tanning the deer hides and use it on him. And Esther was likely to slap his face as soon as doctor it, as she should have done in that clearing.

He opened the door with caution and peered around the edge. "Momma? Can I come in?"

"Maybe on your knees."

"Yes, ma'am." He opened the door wider.

Momma crouched on the floor, finishing wrapping a strip of clean rag around Esther's foot. A smell like something they'd feed the pigs reeked in the kitchen.

He grimaced. "What's that awful smell?"

"Comfrey. Heals like nothing —" Momma glanced up, and her jaw fell open. "Did Zach hit you?"

"Yes'm."

"What's he look like? Does he need doctoring or burying?"

Esther gasped.

Griff half smiled. "Neither. I didn't touch him." He met Esther's gaze across the room, tumbled into the pull of her beauty like a body caught in a spring river current. "I deserved it."

"Humph." Momma snorted. "Not sure turning t'other cheek's so good when you get yours busted open."

"You need stitches." Esther reached for that black satchel of hers. "And cold water. I guess there won't be ice. Come sit down. I'll —"

"Not without a shirt he won't." Momma stood between him and Esther. "You should know better'n to come into a room with a lady without being all dressed."

"I forgot." Griff looked down at his blood-streaked chest.

"It's all right." Esther stood, favoring one foot. "I have brothers and I — I took a bullet out of a man's shoulder once when he shot himself cleaning his gun and Momma was out of town. Come sit down, Griff."

"I'll fetch you a shirt." Momma headed for the steps, tossing over her shoulder, "You be respectful, Son."

Griff sank onto the bench Esther had vacated and gazed at her busying herself with things in her bag until she noticed him. When she glanced up, he gave her a lopsided smile. "If you want to leave the ridge, I don't blame you a bit. We haven't been too kind to you."

"You all have been very kind to me." Esther began filling a needle with a thread as fine as a spiderweb strand.

"I'm right sorry about tonight. Will you forgive me?"

She kept her head bent low over her task. "Depends on what you're sorry for."

"Everything, maybe."

"I see." Without looking at him, she set the threaded needle on a cloth, where it caught the light from the candle lantern and shone like a miniature spear she intended to stab him with. She pulled a square of cloth from her bag and poured something from a flat bottle that smelled almost like spirits.

"What's that?" he asked with some trepidation.

"Witch hazel. It'll sting." She laid it against his cheek.

Breath hissed through his teeth, clamped shut against an exclamation he'd regret later.

"I warned you." She sounded too cheerful.

"Is that revenge for what I said about the cats, or for kissing you, or both?"

"Neither. It's to clean away any dirt and stop the bleeding so I can see what I'm doing."

"Do you know what you're doing? I mean, this is going to hurt, ain't it?"

"A great deal." She sponged gently around the bruised and split skin. "And I expect you'll have a scar. But it won't take away from your handsome face. In fact, I think it'll make you quite dashing."

Even if she was flirting with him again, his heart stopped aching. He barely felt the first bite of the needle, but she paused and rested one hand on his shoulder. "Are you all right? You're not going to faint on me or anything?"

"No, ma'am. I've known worse."

"Like what?" She took another stitch.

He closed his eyes. "The time the ax slipped when I was chopping wood and cut a gash in my leg. Momma don't have such a light touch with the needle as you."

"You're lucky you didn't lose your leg." She again drew the thread through his skin. "You still all right?"

"Yes'm." If he held on to the edge of the bench with both hands.

"Two more. Let me know if you feel weak."

Of course he was weak. Not two minutes had gone by in her company, and he was like a rotten log she could crumble between her fingers. Soft in the heart. Soft in the head. He needed to say more to her.

"Esther, I —"

The fourth stitch might as well have been a butcher knife to his entire skull, and he couldn't think for a moment. Then Momma returned, a clean shirt over her arm.

"You're gonna need to be buying ready-made shirts in town if you keep ruining them with blood." She draped the shirt over his right shoulder since blood smeared the other side. "At least you're halfway decent."

He was going to be halfway unconscious if the fifth stitch hurt as much as the last one.

"Thanks, Momma," he murmured, bracing for the stab, the bite, the drawn-out agony of the thread pulling through. "I hate spiders," he muttered.

Esther started. "What? Are you going out of your head? I forgot to ask if you're hurt elsewhere." She placed one hand on the back of his head. "Did you hit your head when you fell?"

"I didn't fall and I'm not injured anywhere. I was thinking of that thread. It's like having a spider spinning a web through my face."

"Ah." She smiled. "It's silk. You need something fine for stitches on the face or head. Ready for the last one?"

"Ready as I'll ever be."

"Mrs. Tolliver, perhaps you'd better put your arm around him. He's looking a bit green. If he faints, I'll never catch him."

"If I faint," Griff said, "I'll die of shame before I hit the floor."

"You kind of look like a body does before he keels right over. Those pretty eyes of yours are going to just roll up in your head and you'll slide right down —" She stuck the needle in.

He clenched his teeth hard enough he should be cracking his molars. His eyes watered, but he remained upright.

She said he had pretty eyes.

"You are all right." She smiled at him. Though Momma's arm encircled his shoulders, Esther laid her hand on his upper arm and looked straight into his eyes. "I'm going to clean that up a little more and put a sticking plaster on it. We'll keep it clean for a week or two, and it should be all right. But it's going to hurt. The swelling's just setting in."

"It'll learn him to mind his tongue," Momma said, rising. "I'll fetch some water so you can clean yourself up."

"There's two full buckets by the well." Griff spoke to Momma but kept watching Esther as she cleaned her needle and wrapped it in a square of soft cloth, then took a packet of papery stuff from her bag and moistened one side with some water.

"Did you tell Zach you kissed me?" she asked as she stuck the paper on his face.

"I'm afraid I did."

"Is that why he hit you?"

"He didn't like it. But he hit me because I told him you're a shameless flirt."

"I'm not shameless."

"You weren't shameless when you were petting me like one of those cats when you want it to sit on your lap, just to get me to set you down?" The surge of disappointment and anger roiled inside him again. "What do you call it then? Taming me like some kind of beast?"

She bent low over her satchel, peering

inside as though searching for a lost coin the size of a pea. "I'm not making myself understood."

Momma was coming back, bucket bales rattling.

"I can't say now." She spoke quickly. "My foot hurts. I'm worn to a thread, and your mother is about to walk in. So answer me this before she does: will this start the feuding again? Because if it does, you know I have to leave."

"Zach will see good sense by morning. It'll take more'n a little spat over a female, even you, to start up the fighting again."

" 'Course it will." Momma swung through the doorway, carrying two buckets and a stout stick from the woodpile. "My nephew's not a fool. Now, see here, I've brought you a stick to help you hobble around. Can you get back to your cabin on your own, or do you need Griff to carry you?"

"I can manage," Esther said. "He shouldn't strain himself."

Or be that close to her again.

Except that didn't matter. The grace of her movements, the sweetness of her voice, the way she had been so kind to him after what he'd said about her, lured him like a trout to a fly. More like to a butterfly. Despite being convinced she wasn't as good a girl as the preacher's daughter should be, nothing stopped his heart from wanting her.

"Good night," he said. "And thank you."

"You're welcome." She limped across the room, leaning on the stick and clutching that satchel she had so clung to on the journey to the ridge, according to Zach. "I suppose I'll see you all in the morning."

Griff relaxed. She wasn't going to run away, not yet anyway. "In the morning."

"We'll bring you your vittles," Momma said, "so's you don't have to walk too much. And there won't be no school. The young'uns are worn out anyhow."

"I can teach," Esther protested. "Perhaps if I have a chair."

"You just rest a day or two and see how that foot does. Now git yourself to bed before you fall down yourself."

"I'll bring you the dulcimer so you don't get tired of doing nothing," Griff offered.

"I'd like that." Her smile was warm, reaching all the way to her eyes.

Their gazes held for only a heartbeat, but she might as well have stitched herself right to him, so powerfully did he feel her nearness.

Griff rose and opened the door for her. From ten inches away, he didn't look at her. "You don't need me to walk with you?"

"You'd better not."

She was right in that.

"Then I'll stand here until you're there and have a lantern lit."

She nodded and started across the yard, past the garden and the well and over the patch of barren ground he wanted lush with grass one day. A cat meowed in greeting. Her voice murmured through the night. Then the cabin door latch clicked. A few minutes later, light flared through the window. Still Griff remained in the doorway with his back to Momma and his face to the night.

"Are you going to do right by her?" Momma asked.

"How can you ask? I scarce know her."

"You seem to think you know her well enough to take liberties with her."

"Yes, ma'am, I thought she might be willing. And that's what's wrong. She ran away from Zach. She still might run away from me." He took a deep breath to ease the constriction around his heart. "Until I know why she ran here, there can't be anything else but what we got now, maybe less. 'Cause I'm afraid it's something bad."

23

Pounding on her cabin door dragged Esther from sleep at dawn, only an hour after she'd managed to fall asleep. Eyes still half closed, she swung her legs over the side of the bed and cried out as her injured foot hit the floor.

"Miss Cherrett? Miss Cherrett, come quick." The voice belonged to a boy, and not one of the Tollivers. Neither Jack nor Ned called her Miss Cherrett. "Please." The latch rattled.

Lips compressed to stop another cry of pain, Esther snatched up her dressing gown and wrapped it around her as she limped to the door, calling, "I'm coming. I'm —" She raised the bar.

The door flew open, and Mattie Brooks tumbled over the threshold. "Praise Jesus." He grasped her hand with both of his. "You've got to come now."

"Come where?" Esther rubbed sleep from

her eyes. "Mattie, what are you doing out this time of night?"

Not even the roosters had crowed their greeting to the day.

"Zach. It's Zach. He's been stabbed."

"Not another one." Esther's hand flew to her side as though a knife might be sticking out of it. "When? Where? No, never you mind all that now. Let me get dressed."

She returned to her room. Once there, she stared down at her bandaged foot. She could never walk across the mountain to the Brookses' home.

"Mattie," she called through the door, "go to the barn and saddle a horse. I can't walk."

"I don't want to get shot by no Tolliver for stealing."

"You won't. I promise. But I can't walk that far right now. Hurry."

"Yes'm." The outer door banged. Most likely, his racket had already awakened someone in the house who would be down any moment to learn what was afoot. But they wouldn't shoot a boy even if it looked like he was stealing. Of course, at fourteen, Mattie wasn't considered much of a boy any longer, certainly not a child. And shooting him would start up the feuding.

But if Zach had been stabbed, someone had already recommenced the feuding.

No need to ask whom. Those Tollivers the night before talked about getting rid of more Brookses. Drunk enough, angry with Griff for shaming them by making them run away from him, they might have retaliated on a Brooks caught out alone in the night. Or another Tolliver might have retaliated for a blow to his face. And a stab wound from over two months ago?

Esther's fingers fumbled on the buttons of her dress. Not Griff. Surely Griff would never do anything so violent. If he were inclined that way, he would have struck back in the yard, not ambushed his cousin in the night.

Or perhaps he had struck out — with a blade — and left Zach bleeding in the yard. None of them would know. No one had gone outside except to the well and Esther's cabin.

"No, I won't believe it." She tossed a shawl over her shoulders, bundled her hair into a knot on the back of her head, and snatched up her satchel. By the time she hobbled to the front door, Mattie was waiting with a horse bridled. It was the dark gray one Griff had been riding on the journey from the east, black in the dawn light. Mattie's face was ghostly pale in comparison.

"C-can we both ride?" His stammer said as much as his pallor — he was scared to death.

Esther was going to a patient, nothing more — not a young man she had hurt the night before, not a young man whose spurt of violence caused an injury she had repaired. He was a patient in need of help — if the distance didn't mean she was too late to provide it.

"Yes, we can both ride," she said. "We'll have to. But let's walk outside the compound first."

They exited through the rear gate so as not to pass the house. A tree stump offered Esther a mounting block, and she swung up behind the saddle with only a little clumsiness and a small flash of ankle. Her soft slippers, all she could wear over her bandage, were not suitable for riding, so Mattie used the saddle and stirrups, and they headed along the well-trodden track that served as a road — up, up, up the mountainside, past cleared fields with their ripening corn, through high pastures with a few sheep, goats, and cows, then into the forest where night still reigned.

"What happened?" Esther asked under cover of the trees.

"We dunno." Mattie's tall, gangly frame

trembled as though he were cold in the misty morning. "Pa found him when he come home this morning."

Whatever Mr. Brooks had been doing out all night, his coming home in the wee hours of the morning proved fortuitous for Zach.

"Zach was lying on the path bleeding like a stuck pig," Mattie continued. "He was outta his head, but he kept asking for you, so Momma told me to come fetch you."

"Where was the wound?" Esther asked. "Chest, belly, a limb?"

"Kinda to the side of his belly, I think. Couldn't tell for all the blood. Momma's doctored him some, but she's not so good at it."

"He was conscious?"

"Ma'am?"

"Awake?"

"If you count talking nonsense awake, then sure."

"What sort of nonsense?"

Ask questions, gather facts. It kept her from thinking of the worst cases.

Mattie bent his head to avoid a low-hanging branch. "Just asking for you mostly, and how you was really an angel. And something about Griff —" He shut up as though someone had laid a hand over his mouth.

Esther tensed. "What about Griff?"

Mattie shrugged.

"Mattison Brooks, what did Zach say about Griff?"

"Momma said not to say. She don't think he did it."

"But someone else in your family does?" Now Esther shivered too, though heat from the day before seemed trapped beneath the tight canopy of leaves without a breeze stirring.

"Pa and Henry," Mattie whispered.

"Oh no." Esther closed her eyes and didn't duck in time to avoid low-hanging leaves from catching in her hair and tugging it loose from its pins. It tumbled down her back in abandoned waves, messy, inappropriate for a sickroom.

If not worse.

No, she would not consider that for a moment. Zach. Must. Not. Die. The consequences of that, the repercussions, would prove disastrous for everyone.

"Mattie, believe me, no one at the Tolliver house left last night. I was awake until a little over an hour ago and heard nothing."

"They ain't the only Tollivers."

Too true, and some had been planning to be rid of more Brookses.

"Can we go any faster?" Suddenly she

needed the horse to gallop, take flight, and leap over the mountain to the next hollow.

"No, ma'am. It ain't safe."

"Then let's hope I'm a better healer than teacher."

"Ma'am?"

"Your grammar, Mattie," Esther tried to say with some cheerfulness. "It's appalling."

"It's what?"

"Bad. But at least you learned what grammar is."

"Yes'm. I'm doing my lessons, but if Zach's laid up, I can't come to school. Gotta work the ferry."

"Aren't you too young?" She couldn't imagine a lad of his age in charge of safely carrying wagons and horses and people across the swift waters of the New River.

Mattie stiffened. "Zach's been doing it since he was younger than me. I wanta be there now, but Momma and Pa said I should be getting book learning first."

Even with a lead mine starting to produce money for them, they insisted their children work. Good in many ways, yet it denied them the gift of reading and writing and learning about the world around them. The latter would intrude on them soon enough. The mountains couldn't remain isolated forever. The more people moved west, the more traffic the river would get. Towns grew. New ones sprang up. The Tollivers, Gosnells, and Brookses would want to spend their lead mine income and needed to learn not to be taken advantage of.

She should be in her classroom in another five hours helping with this, but Mrs. Tolliver had canceled classes because Esther's foolishness had injured her. She was supposed to be resting, and yet she was riding across the mountain on Griff's horse to practice a skill she had sworn she would leave behind. Next thing she knew, she would be delivering babies.

"A sad joke, God?" she murmured.

Mattie made no indication that he heard.

Surely God had taken her profession from her, rejected the skill she had worked to gain for years to make her mother happy and both parents proud. They had loved her and given her so much, it was the least she could do in return, but she had failed them. God had rejected the gift she'd dedicated to Him when she took the midwife's vow practiced by women in her family for centuries.

And yet there she was close enough to one more patient to see smoke from the Brooks house curling into the pale blue sky and rising to mingle with the mist still lying along the ridges. Cows lowed, begging to be milked, and the rising cackle of chickens suggested their eggs were being gathered and grain spread for their breakfast. Mattie guided the gelding around a curve in the path, and the Brooks compound opened up below with a pale finger of sunlight centering on a small pond of water surrounded by green grass and other vegetation.

It wasn't the only place green grass grew like the most luxurious of eastern lawns. All the way around the house, it grew still green from spring rains. Closer in, a kitchen garden promised an abundance of fresh produce ripening, and fanning from that shone the bright colors of flowering plants.

Mrs. Brooks enjoyed a true garden meant for nothing greater than beauty.

"So pretty," Esther said.

"It's all right." Mattie reined in. "Can we dismount here? They'll recognize the horse, and I don't want to get shot for a Tolliver."

"They wouldn't."

They just might.

Esther dismounted, wincing as her right foot reached the ground. She should have brought her stout walking stick. She had to settle for taking Mattie's wiry arm and gritting her teeth. It couldn't be half the pain Zach must be feeling, if he were still in a place to feel pain. That would be a blessing, odd as it seemed. It meant he still lived.

She clutched at her satchel and began running through the remedies she might have on hand. She had no laudanum and only a minute amount of opium powder. White willow bark tea wasn't strong enough to ease Zach's kind of pain. Surely something else could serve. She and Momma had rarely dealt in matters requiring the reduction of pain. Opiates risked the stopping of labor, which could kill both mother and child. Whiskey? The mountain seemed to contain enough of that. It dulled the senses but was surely not good for an injured man. She needed a stronger thread for stitching up a knife wound than she had used on Griff's face, but if the knife had struck an organ, all she could do was try to keep Zach comfortable to the end.

If she had any say in the matter, the end would not come.

As they approached the house and Hannah flung open the door and started toward them, Esther remembered that once she would have prayed before seeing a gravely ill or injured person. She didn't know when she'd last prayed. She had given up on good things from God.

"We were praying you'd get here." Hannah's greeting seemed to be a taunt. "Didn't know if they would let you."

"I'm not a Tolliver prisoner," Esther responded a bit too sharply.

"We didn't wake anyone, as you told me not to," Mattie added. "But we had to bring one of their horses. Miss Cherrett's hurt her foot."

"Then I'm twice as glad you've come." Hannah grasped Esther's arm and urged her forward. "We got him in the parlor. Didn't think it'd be good to carry him up the steps."

"Have you sent for a doctor?" Esther posed the question she always did when called to an injured person's bedside. It was the one way she and Momma had kept the physicians on the eastern shore from saying the women overstepped the bounds of their training.

"Ain't no doctor to call." A tall, thin woman with the kind of bones that suggested she had once been beautiful emerged from a door to the side of the front entrance. Her hair, more silver now than gilt, was thinning and drawn tightly back from a deeply lined face, the grooved lines around her mouth signifying pain. Dark circles like bruises emphasized the sky-blue of her eyes.

"Mrs. Brooks?" Esther ventured.

"I'm Tamar." She shook Esther's hand.

"Should have come introduce myself, but my sister and I don't visit much no more. Mostly communicate through our boys." Her voice cracked. "While we got 'em."

"He won't die, Momma," Hannah said. "Esther has a healing gift. You saw my hand."

Esther ground her toe into the floorboard. "A burn is far different from a stabbing, but I'll do my best."

"And the Lord will use you according to His will," Mrs. Brooks said. "Come in."

A number of lanterns added to the natural heat and stuffiness of a closed room in the summer. No curtains hung over the windows, but the shadow of the mountain and trees kept the room dark. In an hour or two, the light would be good. She didn't have an hour or two, more than likely.

"Please open the windows," Esther said. "Fresh air is more healthful."

The two women stared at her.

"No, ma'am," Mrs. Brooks said. "The night ain't healthy."

"It isn't unhealthy. I've been out in it many times and am always well." Esther marched over to the closest window and threw up the sash.

Cooler, sweeter air streamed in, and she marched to the second and third until sweet, fragrant air from the garden swirled around them, dispelling the greasy odor of the tallow dips.

Once she could breathe, she braced herself, schooled her expression to blandness no matter what she discovered on the mattress someone had carried into the room, and dropped to her knees beside Zach.

His face was as white as the homespun pillowslip beneath his head. Once shining golden hair lay limp and dull around his head, and his eyes were nearly colorless.

But those eyes were open and gazing right into hers. "You . . . came."

"As soon as I could. Where does it hurt?"

"Right side. Above . . . bone." His voice was breathy. His pulse was thready and too fast, his skin clammy and colorless.

She glanced up at his mother and sister standing across from her, their hands clasped at their waists, the mother's tiny, the daughter's far more sturdy.

Esther narrowed her eyes for a moment, but she shoved the thought aside and asked, "What have you done for him? Is he still bleeding?"

"I stitched the skin together," Mrs. Brooks said. "It ain't bleeding much now, but it don't look right. But I told him it ain't right for an unmarried girl to look at him there."

"She's . . . healer," Zach whispered. His hand reached out, fingers groping.

Esther covered them with hers, wishing they weren't so cold, so clammy. He'd lost too much blood. He needed restorative broths, but she couldn't recommend that until she saw where the knife had gone in. If the stomach had been compromised, food would only kill him faster.

Which meant she didn't dare administer a pain reliever yet.

"I can't help him if I can't look, Mrs. Brooks." She made her voice as authoritative as she could. "It won't be the first time I've seen a male torso. I have four brothers and I extracted a bullet once."

Their eyes widened. Their jaws dropped.

"My mother and her mother and her mother were all healers as well as midwives, and I have learned." As she explained, Esther pulled back the quilt that covered Zach.

She glanced over his bare chest, smooth and muscular, only long enough to note if any other injuries had occurred. All seemed well other than how he seemed oddly vulnerable without his shirt.

Unlike his cousin —

She clamped down a lid on that memory and focused on Zach's belly. The bandage was dark with old blood. She touched it with her fingertips. Nothing fresh. Nothing else oozing. A good sign.

"Hot water," she directed. "Fresh bandages. Zach, I'm going to hurt you as little as possible, but this has to come off."

"It'll start the bleeding again," Mrs. Brooks protested.

"It may. We have to take that risk." Esther began to search through her bag for a heavier needle and stronger thread than she'd used on Griff.

She located a tiny vile of clove oil and closed her fingers around it as though she had found a diamond the size of her palm. Clove oil would numb the wound area if she did need to rework the stitches. She should have remembered it and used it on Griff. That she hadn't pricked her conscience. Yet surely she wasn't so lost to propriety that part of her had enjoyed the stitch that made him flinch. If so, she needed to beg his pardon.

And repent of such a wicked thought.

Hannah brought in a kettle of hot water and set it beside Esther. She shook her head, sending her hair tossing back behind her shoulders, and set to work.

Although Mrs. Brooks's stitching had stopped most of the bleeding, she had only sewn the skin together, and blood had pooled beneath the surface. This might mean something vital had been struck and his bleeding would never stop until he slipped away. She must find out.

She snipped away the stitches. Fresh blood poured out onto the quilt beneath him and like as not through to the mattress.

And behind her, Hannah fainted.

"Get her out of here," Esther said without looking around. "I don't have time for someone who faints at the sight of blood."

Zach had fainted too. Good. Easier to work on him.

With smooth efficiency, Esther mopped up what she could and pulled the wound apart. She smelled nothing bad. Perhaps a good sign. She didn't have enough experience with knife wounds to know for sure, but logic and her knowledge of anatomy said she might smell foulness if the knife had glanced off the hip bone and cut into the belly cavity. And blood didn't continue to flow. Indeed, the knife hadn't gone all the way through. The wound was serious but, if no infection set in, wouldn't be fatal.

Thrown from a long distance? Deflected off his hip bone? She couldn't ask Zach until he woke, but the latter seemed likely. He was still alive, weak, too weak, but had been alive for hours after the wound.

"God, I need direction . . ." The prayer slipped out unbidden.

"Amen," Mrs. Brooks said. She knelt beside Esther. "Tell me what you need, and I'll give it to you."

"Shouldn't you see to Hannah?"

"She'll come around soon enough."

Most likely. Few people stayed in a faint for long.

Esther sprinkled a few drops of the clove oil on a clean cloth and dabbed it onto the wound. The pungent aroma of the spice filled the room, blotting out other less pleasant smells. Her nostrils flared, stung. But her eyes focused on the task, and her hands were steady.

"Hold him in the event he wakes," she directed Mrs. Brooks.

Momma, you'd be proud of me.

"You have such a healing touch, Esther," Momma had said often. "I wish you could be a physician."

But she hadn't been good enough to save Mrs. Oglevie, only the baby, that dear, sweet baby boy so alive, as his mother was not.

If I can save Zach, I'll have paid for some of my wrongs, my failures.

She stitched. She mopped. She murmured soothing nonsense to him when he woke and groaned with pain. She drew the last stitch tight and wound a bandage around his body with Mrs. Brooks's help.

"Now it's up to the Lord," she pronounced, smoothing damp hair from Zach's face.

He caught hold of her hand. "You won't run away?" he pleaded in a murmur.

"No, I'll stay," she promised.

And as she spoke the words of reassurance, she accepted that she didn't want to run for the first time in months.

24

Griff found the empty stall first. His favorite horse had disappeared in the night. His heart a lead weight in his belly, he sprinted from the barn and across the yard to the cabin.

The empty cabin.

The door stood ajar, her night things strewn across the unmade bed. Clothes still hung on their pegs, books laid on the table, one open with a sketchpad beneath. All that was missing was her precious satchel.

"Oh, Esther, you didn't need to run." He raised his hands to shove his fingers through his hair, wincing as he brushed the cut and bruise on his face. His left eye was swollen shut and suddenly began to burn along with the right. "I'd've gone away from you if you'd only stayed."

"Griff," Liza called from the schoolroom, "you shouldn't be in here with —" She stopped in the bedroom doorway. "Where is she?"

"I don't know, and Sunset's gone too."

Liza gasped. "Did someone steal her along with your horse?"

"I don't think so. She took her doctoring bag."

"Then maybe someone was sick and fetched her." Liza tiptoed to the desk table as though Esther were sleeping across the room. "She draws pretty pictures." She drew the sketchpad from beneath the book. "Look, it's the waterfall."

"Liza, put that down." Griff snatched the pad from his sister.

The pages fanned open, and he caught a glimpse of himself on the page beneath the waterfall. He was wielding an ax to chop wood, and he looked like a wild man or some warrior going into battle, before guns were used for fighting.

Was that how she saw him, all wild hair and fierce expression, not a bit of softness in him? No wonder she ran, after the night before. He'd kissed her, then accused her of being a wanton because she kissed him back and used her female wiles on him.

His ribs squeezed around his heart, and he set the drawings on the table. "I gotta go find her. She can't go out on the mountain alone. Even on a horse, it ain't safe."

"Isn't," Liza said.

He stared at her. "What?"

"Isn't." She set her hands on her non-existent hips. "Miss Esther always says *isn't,* not *ain't.* If you don't want to sound like an ignorant mountain man to her, you gotta — have to say *isn't.*"

"Yes, ma'am." He tugged the single braid she wore down her back.

She touched his face. "What happened?"

"Zach didn't like something I said."

"Did you hit him back?"

"No."

"Why not?"

"Because I deserved it."

"Huh." She glanced around the room, then back at him. "Did you kiss her? Is that why she ran away? She's in love with you and don't — doesn't want to be?"

"I think part of that's the truth. Now run back to the house and tell Momma I gotta go looking for Miss Esther. If she's alone, she'll never find her way into anything but trouble."

"And if she's not?" Liza tossed over her shoulder.

"He'd better start running before I catch him."

Griff glanced around the room. Odd she

360

would leave it in such a mess. Every time he saw her, she was as neat as the kitchen after being washed up, except the night before. Her ruined dress lay in a crumpled heap, half kicked under the bed. He bent to look at it. Maybe Momma or the girls could use some of the fabric for quilting. It sure was pretty with all those blue flowers on it, and in it Esther had looked like some princess from another land, so graceful in her dancing she seemed to float over the ground. He'd watched from afar and hadn't dared ask her to dance. She seemed quite content with Zach as her partner most of the time. Too content and happy for Griff's liking.

But she had kissed him, and his heart had been so full he wanted her to be as perfect as Zach thought she was.

He retrieved the dress, caught a whiff of her sweet flower scent, and started to shove the gown back under the bed.

That was when he caught sight of the slip of paper.

Maybe she hadn't simply run off with his horse and no other word. Maybe she had written a note, and his racing into the cabin had sent it sailing beneath the bed.

He reached to retrieve it and felt a stack of papers there. Wrong to look, of course. But she had gone without taking these, which seemed strange if she were running off. Leaving clothes behind was one thing. A body could get new clothes. But these looked like letters, and folk liked keeping letters from family, from sweethearts. Momma had one from her great-grandpa to her great-grandmomma when he was off fighting the English. Nobody could hardly read it now, but Momma kept it anyway.

Griff drew the bundle toward him. He would put these where he could send them to her family if, God forbid, he didn't find her.

A word on the top sheet of paper leaped out and struck him as though Zach's fist had landed squarely on his nose. *Jezebel.* That was all. The single word scrawled with thick, black lines.

He couldn't stop himself from glancing through the other letters after that. Some said more. They couldn't say less. The meanings were the same, the message clear.

Esther had run from Seabourne for a reason.

Something bad, he'd told Momma. The letters before him were proof. They just didn't say why.

And now she'd run again.

He shoved the letters between the mattress and bed frame, feeling more paper already there, and charged to the barn. He would take the other horse they'd bought for riding. Bethann used it often, though not so much lately. Of late, she'd been walking out alone, though Griff suspected she was meeting someone. He supposed he should have been following her to find out who was responsible for her trouble this time, but he knew what was expected of him if he learned the truth — a forced marriage at the end of a shotgun if necessary. Unless the man wasn't free.

Griff didn't want to know the truth if it was that last possibility.

He tossed a saddle on the mare. She was a bit small for him, and he couldn't ride her far. He hoped he didn't have to ride her far. He headed for the gate.

"Griff," Momma called from the house, waving a bundle.

He rode up and took it from her. "I'll find her, Momma, never you fear."

"You'd better." Momma scowled up at him. "And you'll do right by her when you do."

"I can't do that. She's made it more than clear she don't want me."

"Doesn't," Liza called from inside the kitchen.

■ ■ ■ ■

Zach's fever started in the middle of the afternoon. Dozing on a sofa, Esther started up at the sound of his restless thrashing and mumbling about heartless wenches.

"I'm not heartless, Zach." She dropped to her knees beside his makeshift bed and touched his brow.

It burned like a sunbaked stone.

"Water," she called to whoever might overhear her. "As cold as you can get it."

Ice would be better, but they got precious little of it there in the winter months, certainly not enough to save for the summer.

"And lots of cloths," she added.

Footfalls pounded down the hall, those of a child from the sound of it. Someone had been assigned to sit outside the sickroom parlor and wait for her instructions. Esther had gone out only once to freshen up with some cold water on her face, a trip outside, and a bowl of stew. The rest of the time, she remained with her patient, watching, waiting, knowing the fever would come. He was young and strong and he might overcome it, but fevers took a body without warning. They sapped the greatest of strengths, and

Zach had lost a great deal of blood, weakening him already. Beef or other red meat broth would help eventually. For now, however, he seemed able to stomach only sips of water.

Hannah entered with a pitcher of water and a stack of cloths. "Is this enough?"

"If you keep replenishing it every few minutes." Esther took the pitcher and dipped a cloth into it. "He's burning up."

"That's bad, ain't it?"

"I won't lie to you. It isn't good. But you don't look well yourself."

Hannah shrugged. "I'll do." She sank onto the sofa with a yawn. "Tired, is all. We didn't none of us get much sleep last night."

"Did any of you get anything out of him about what happened?" Esther began to bathe Zach's face and chest with the cold water.

"You mean like who did it?" Hannah returned. "No doubt about it. It was a Tolliver."

"Did he say so?"

"It weren't no Gosnoll or Brooks. Might have been a Neff since they've sided with the Tollivers, for all they're my mother's people too."

"Why are there sides, Hannah? You're all family. This isn't medieval Scotland."

"What?"

"Scotland a few hundred years ago when the clans feuded with one another for territory. There's lots of land here."

"Not good land. Can't hardly grow a thing here, and the ferry don't bring passengers all the time." Hannah curled her legs beneath her on the hard cushion of the sofa. "The trees might be valuable. Walnut makes for fine furniture. But they're too hard to get out to folk."

"So there's the mine." Esther continued to sponge cold water over Zach.

He continued to mutter and try to thrash.

"He's gonna break open that wound," Hannah said, her voice tight.

Esther nodded. "I'm concerned about that too. It's like he's trying to get away from something."

"He was trying to get home," Hannah said. "He kept saying he had to get home for his lesson. Don't know what he was talking about."

"His reading lesson." Esther's eyes swam just a little. "Didn't he tell you I've been giving him reading lessons?"

"No." Hannah shook her head, grimaced, and pressed her hand to her brow.

"Headache?" Esther asked.

"Like a horse galloping through my skull."

"I have some willow — horse!" The cloth dropped onto Zach's chest with a splat. "What's happened to Griff's horse?"

"Griff." Zach spoke loud and clear. "May that horse break his neck."

"Zachary Brooks!" Hannah exclaimed. "I don't care if he is a Tolliver, you don't talk thatta way if you're a-dying."

"He's not dying," Esther said to convince herself as much as Hannah.

The fever had come on too fast, too strong for her comfort and skill.

"But you still shouldn't talk that way." She recommenced bathing him in cold water. "He's your cousin."

Clarity shone in Zach's eyes at that moment, a good sign. "He stole you."

"I'm not yours, Zach. I'm not Griff's either."

"He kissed you."

Hannah caught her breath.

"He was distracting me from the behavior of his drunken cousins, is all. And I'm a passably pretty girl he was alone with in the woods at night. It meant nothing to him."

There, she'd said it aloud, put voice to her fears about Griff's intentions.

But Zach wasn't listening. His eyes clouded. His lids drooped.

"About Griff's horse?" Esther asked.

"Mattie took care of it," Hannah said. "He walked it back over the ridge and let it go."

"He just let it go? That's a valuable animal."

"It'll go home."

"I'd have sent a message if I realized. Since I left without a word, they'll be wondering where I am."

Or would they? She had told Griff she would leave. No doubt he thought her capable of wanting away from him so badly that she would abandon her possessions save for her medical bag, that she would ride off the mountain on his horse, then send the beast back. He would no doubt be relieved to have her gone, especially if someone unearthed those letters beneath her mattress. They would confirm his belief that she was everything he thought of her and worse.

All the preaching about how a body could make a clean start in life was false. She had traveled about four hundred miles from home, gone to a place remote from anywhere else in the country, and yet her past had followed her.

She picked up the pitcher of water and a packet from her satchel. "I'll get some fresh water and make you some white willow bark tea."

"Can't you use it on Zach if it helps the pain?" Hannah asked.

"I've given him an opiate. I don't have much or I'd give him more."

It wasn't enough, with the way he kept mumbling and moving as though trying to escape the ache in his side.

"And I'm not certain if I should mix the two."

Perhaps a little wouldn't hurt. For the life of her, she couldn't remember what Momma had said about that. They only used the tea for headaches and when a woman's cycles pained her too much. Surely a little would be all right.

The Brooks kitchen lay quiet in the mid-afternoon, too early for supper preparations. Finding the water in a bucket by the door too warm, she set a kettle to boiling for the tea and went outside to pump fresh water.

Mattie appeared and took the handle from her. "You shouldn't be doing that, Miss Cherrett. You'll blister your hands."

"Thank you." She returned to the house and made the white willow bark tea for Hannah, stirring in some honey to counter the bitterness. She added honey to another cupful and carried both cups back to the parlor, Mattie following with the water.

"Drink this." She gave Hannah a cup of

the tea. "It tastes rather awful, but it works better than anything except for maybe feverfew, which isn't as easy to get."

"You're talking a funny language to me." Hannah smiled. "So tired of these headaches. Do you know what makes them happen?"

"Perhaps." She glanced at Mattie in the doorway, gazing at his brother. "We can talk about it later."

Hannah nodded, sipped the tea, and grimaced. "You sure this ain't poison?"

"I'm sure." Esther returned to Zach's side. She spent another half hour bathing him with cold water, then inspected the bandage and the wound beneath. It was puffy and red but showed no sign of a serious infection. Along with the fact that the wound wasn't deep, her hope of his survival grew.

But he woke later and complained of the pain. He clutched at Esther's hand hard enough to hurt. "Like I keep getting stabbed," he whispered.

"I'm afraid to give you more opium. A man can become dependent on it too easily, I know, but I don't know how much that takes."

She didn't remember that part of Momma's lessons either. She was forgetting too much.

No, it didn't matter. She wasn't supposed to be doing this anymore. She was a teacher now, not a healer, not a midwife.

"Give him the willow stuff." Hannah spoke up from the sofa, where she half reclined. "It's made my headache go away. Sure enough it'll help him some."

"Well, perhaps it won't hurt." Esther leaned down to tuck her arm beneath Zach's shoulders and lift him, as she'd been doing all day to give him sips of water. "It tastes awful, but it helps other kinds of pains, so it might work."

"Anything." He sipped at the cooled tea and coughed. "Bitter."

"Very."

He sipped some more. "But I can think it's sweet because you gave it to me."

"You're feverish to say such nonsense." Esther tipped the cup to his lips again so he ceased speaking of her. "But if you're awake enough to give me compliments, you are awake enough to tell us what you know of who did this to you."

"Didn't see nothing." He slumped against her. "Nobody around, then — whack. Gotta be . . . someone . . . quiet."

"Like Griff," Hannah said.

Esther eased Zach onto the pillow but remained with her face close to his, staring, watching for signs of him hiding something. "Like Griff?" she repeated as a query.

A caterwauling was set up in the yard, a dog barking, someone yelling.

Zach's eyes drifted shut. "Griff."

The parlor door banged open, and there he stood in the opening. "I didn't stab him," Griff said. "Which of us are you going to believe?"

25

Griff clasped his hands behind his back to stop himself from striding forward and yanking Esther from Zach's side. The man was clearly ill, and she was tending him. Yet the sight of her face so close to Zach's on a pillow sent Griff's innards churning like the water of the pool beneath the waterfall. Waiting for her response turned that water to acid burning through him.

She took too long to extricate herself from Zach, set a cup of something on the floor, and rise with only slightly less grace due to her bandaged foot. She faced him, though, her hands before her, palms up. "I think Zach is out of his head with fever and doesn't know what he's saying. And no one left your house last night. So no, I don't believe you did the stabbing."

Hannah emitted a snort of derision.

Smiling, Griff took a step toward Esther. "Thank you."

She raised her hands to ward him off. "But I do think it was one of your kin. I heard those men talking —" She glanced at Hannah and shut her mouth.

"You know something?" Hannah demanded.

"A group of drunken fools is all I know of." Esther waved one hand as though erasing a slate. "Nothing important."

"Except it might lead to knowing what varmint stabbed my brother," Hannah protested. "A left-handed thrower, seeing as how it's his right side that's been hit."

"As with me," Griff said.

"They were too inebriated to have come this far." Esther turned her back on them and knelt again to fuss over Zach, drawing up the quilt and tucking it around his shoulders.

His bare shoulders. Whether or not Zach was injured, Esther should show more decency than being there with a half-naked man, tending him, touching him, her soft hands caring for Zach as they had cared for Griff's face.

He raised his hand to the sticking plaster on his cheek, the blackened eye above it. "I can't hardly see where I'm going. Took me nearly all day to find you."

"I'm sorry." Esther stilled with the back of

her wrist to Zach's brow, the sort of gesture a mother would perform on a sick child, or maybe a wife for her ailing husband. "I should have left a message."

"You did," Griff snapped. "Several of them."

"What?" Esther surged to her feet, came down hard on her injured foot, and gasped.

"What did you do to her, you beast?" Hannah cried.

"Nothing," Griff and Esther answered together.

"I stepped on a sharp stone last night, is all." Esther gave Hannah a tight smile and hobbled forward. "Will you tend to Zach? He needs more cold water on his brow. He's still burning up. But the willow bark tea seems to be helping with the pain. Will you give him some more in a few minutes?"

"You're leaving?" Hannah's eyes widened. "Esther, you can't go now."

"No, no, but Griff must. He's not welcome here."

Esther wouldn't be either if Griff spoke one word about those notes beneath her bed. The temptation to ask her about them in front of Hannah ran hot through his veins. Aunt Tamar suffered from rheumatism and rarely left her house, but she was one of the most God-fearing woman Griff knew and wouldn't tolerate a fallen woman in her house, teaching her children, or courting with her son.

He gazed at Esther — her gown specked with blood, her face drawn with fatigue, and her hair spilling over her shoulders in tangled waves — and the notion of her being a fallen woman uprooted itself from his brain. She must be innocent, or so good her past didn't matter. She had spent all day tending an injured man after patching Griff up until late the previous night. She wasn't complaining. She was thinking of him, of getting him away from his hostile kin.

He wanted to get her away from his hostile kin even if they weren't hostile to her. He closed the distance between them and took her hands in his. "Do you need me to carry you?"

"That doesn't sound like a good idea. But I'll accept your arm."

He offered her his arm. She leaned upon it heavily and half walked, half hopped out of the sparsely furnished parlor and onto the front porch. Coolness met them there from a breeze blowing down the mountain. It carried the scents of sun-warmed pines and roses from Aunt Tamar's garden, the sort of place he wanted on his side of the ridge, the sort of place for a man to ask a girl for courting rights.

He couldn't ask anything courting-like of Esther now, with the words of those messages burning his eyes.

Heart heavy, he released his arm from her hold, crossed both arms over his chest, and leaned against the side of the house. "I thought you ran away with one of my horses."

"I couldn't walk here." She rested her hip against the porch railing and gripped the bar, her knuckles white. "I didn't take the time to write anything, so what do you mean by me leaving you a message?"

"I went looking for you. They was spilling out from under your bed."

"They were?"

"Yea, right, *were* spilling out."

"I wasn't correcting your grammar, Griff, I was expressing surprise. They were tucked up too tightly to fall out by accident."

"They weren't tight when I went hunting you. They wa— were spilling all over the place bright as pennies."

"And you read them, as someone hoped you would." Her face was so pale, her eyes and hair appeared black in contrast. "That person must know — you know —"

"That you weren't welcome in Seabourne, yes, ma'am, that was clear from the start.

What I don't know is why." He leaned forward, though a yard and a half still separated them. "Why do they hate you so much?"

"I told them a truth they didn't want to hear. They wanted to believe anything but that the man with the goose that laid the golden eggs was guilty —" She pressed a hand to her lips. "I can't talk about it. It hurts." She pressed her other hand to her middle. "Because you won't believe me either."

"I need to know. I have brothers and sisters to protect."

"From what? A female with loose morals, when your own sister has had one child without benefit of a husband and appears to be —" She shut her mouth.

Griff sighed and rested his head back against the log wall of the house. "I shouldn't have read your letters. I thought you'd run off. I wanted to know why."

"You know why, Griff." She dropped her voice to a murmur so low he had to move closer to hear. "If I had run away, you would have known why."

"Because I kissed you?"

"Because I kissed you back. Because I used your attraction to me to persuade you to do what I wanted. Because you thought me a wanton for it."

"I didn't."

"Your anger said as much."

"That's because I —"

He gazed down at her, so pretty and so tired, her shoulders slumped as though carrying the Tolliver clan on her shoulders, and knew he had compounded her burden with his accusation. He also knew he didn't care about whatever had driven people to write the vicious words in those letters and sent her running to the mountains. He loved her. He had known he loved her since he'd thought she was gone.

He opened his mouth to tell her so, but then he recalled how she had touched Zach's brow, had smoothed the quilt over his bare shoulders with loving tenderness, and he couldn't humiliate himself that way. She had run to Zach's side without so much as thinking he, Griff, might worry about her.

She had kissed him, but maybe that was just the moment, gratitude for his rescuing her, the night woods. She'd wanted away from his hold soon enough after that.

"You lowered yourself to teasing me to get away from me," he said at last. "That made me angry with you."

"Why? Because I used my wiles on you or because I wanted away from you?"

He smiled and stroked his thumb down her cheek. "Because you didn't want me holding you."

"You read the notes. Maybe now you know why." She turned her face, and he held his breath, thinking she might kiss his palm. Then she tilted her head away from him. "I wish they were wholly untrue." She slid sideways along the rail and placed distance between them. "There now, you may not want me to come back, but for now I'm the best chance Zach has of surviving this attack, and I'm staying until he's well."

"Then you'll return to us?" he asked.

She gazed at him from beneath her lashes for a long moment, then inclined her head. "If you still want me . . . to teach your siblings, that is."

Oh, he wanted her to teach his siblings, to grace his table, to sit beside him and sing in the evenings. He simply wanted her.

"Come back to us," he said. "And don't let Zach win your heart while you're here."

"My heart isn't a prize to be won. It's a cold, unfeeling lump of beating muscle inside my rib cage, and I intend to keep it that way." She said it so seriously Griff laughed.

"Ah, Miss Esther Cherrett, you don't lay out a challenge like that to a man from these mountains and not expect him to rise to the occasion."

For Griff Tolliver, winning her heart was no challenge. If she dared, she would give it to him in a moment. But he knew about the letters. Added to her behavior the night before, he would believe them the more he thought about them.

Esther expected a message to arrive at the Brookses' at any time telling her not to return to the Tollivers', that despite Bethann's behavior, they wouldn't tolerate a schoolma'am with a questionable past. But the message never came, and the days turned into weeks.

Zach did so well the first two days, Esther thought he would heal quickly. But when she changed the bandage on the third day, her heart dropped to her middle, feeling like the cold lump she had told Griff it was.

"I need to make a poultice for this." She spoke calmly, not wanting to distress Mrs. Brooks. "It's not healing as I'd like."

It wasn't healing at all. It bore all the signs of sepsis.

"What do you need?" Mrs. Brooks asked. "Onions? I got lots of onions from last year still."

"Let's try something gentler first. Milk

and stale bread. Maybe a bit of cinnamon."

She applied the bread and cinnamon poultice, and his fever climbed. She used an onion poultice, and he thrashed about in pain so much he broke open his stitches. The ensuing gush of fluid made even Esther's gorge rise, and she had experienced all sorts of human frailties. Hannah had been helping her but fled from the room, her hand to her mouth, tears flowing down her face.

Esther didn't know what else to use. She was a midwife, not a physician, but her pleas for them to send for a doctor met with resistance. Doctors didn't come to the mountains. Not worth their time and trouble. Doctors took too long to get there. Doctors cost too much money.

Esther knew of a doctor who would come and not cost them a penny. But by the time anyone sent for Rafe Docherty, Zach would likely be dead. Still, she must try somehow to get a message to him.

The consequences to herself didn't matter. Dr. Docherty would, of course, tell her parents where to find her. She wouldn't then be surprised to find them on the Brookses' doorstep telling her to come home. It didn't matter. Saving Zach did.

"Can you get a letter up to Christiansburg?" she asked Mrs. Brooks.

It was at least seventy-five miles away through rough mountain terrain. That could take as long as three or four days to get there. More than a week there and back. Zach didn't have a week. He grew thinner and weaker every day. She would have given her hiding place away for nothing.

But she would have tried.

"There's a physician there, a kind and godly man," she explained.

At the least, Dr. Docherty and his wife Phoebe could pray. No doubt they were already praying for her.

"How do you know a doctor in Christiansburg?" Mrs. Brooks asked.

Esther smiled. "His wife is a midwife and brought me into the world. She and my mother have been friends for over thirty years."

"Ah, then they are trustworthy people." Mrs. Brooks retrieved pen, ink, and paper from somewhere and brought them to Esther. "I'll send Mattie."

Esther stared at her. "He's only fourteen. He can't travel all that way on his own."

"He's a man grown. He'll do right well. His pa went clear to Roanoke on his own when he was younger than that."

"I think," Esther said, "I have been too

protected."

"Of course you have. You're a female."

Esther wrote the letter with a hand that shook from fatigue and anxiety over the consequences. She kept it brief.

I am living on Brooks Ridge along the New River and have a patient with a septic stab wound. What do I do? I'm afraid he'll be dead by the time you get this, but I have to try. Although you will ignore this request, I ask that you please not tell Momma and Papa where I am. I can't go home.

Esther Cherrett

If Zach died, she couldn't stay. The Brookses wouldn't keep her to teach one child, as only Sam would need schooling since Mattie would be needed on the ferry. And Griff wouldn't want her back, whatever he claimed. She would have to move on, maybe southeast to Charleston, lose herself in a city, with one more death on her conscience.

She walked outside for a breath of fresh air. In mid-July, it was warm and sticky, emphasizing the onion stench of her hair and clothes. The Brookses had provided her with a bath whenever she liked, but a swim in the waterfall pool lured her. A good thing she didn't know how to find it from the Brooks compound. Otherwise, the temptation to go might prove too great to resist. She couldn't leave Zach for that long.

With a sigh that didn't even lift her shoulders, she returned to his sickroom to find him barely breathing.

If something didn't change by morning, Mattie wouldn't need to fetch Dr. Docherty.

26

Griff finally tracked his cousins down at the abandoned one-room house of a Neff uncle who had died years before at the hand of a Gosnoll. They appeared to have been doing nothing but drinking for the past week. The house stank of liquor and unwashed bodies.

And worse. They didn't even rouse themselves when he knocked and walked in, but started up cursing when he flung the door open wide to the sunshine.

"Why aren't you all working?" he demanded.

They groaned and covered their heads. He hoped they hurt.

"You aren't getting a thing from the mine if you don't give a thing to the mine." He scanned the room, picked up three empty jugs before he found a fourth still mostly full. "If you aren't at the mine tomorrow morning, don't any of you go back, and don't expect a penny."

They stared at him through red-rimmed eyes. All three were younger than he was by half a decade. All three had lost someone important in the worst years of the fighting — a father, a brother, a sweetheart by accident — to a Brooks. Momma had done her best to help them, but she had her own hands full, and the three had ended up wastrels. Griff got them work in the mine. They were gone more than they were there.

"We won't work for no Gosnoll," Jake grumbled. "He gives us the worst of it."

"Ya shouldn't trust our fortunes to a Gosnoll," Jeb added.

"He's the only one who knows anything about digging up the lead," Griff said. "You know that. And if we don't have workers, it doesn't get dug up, and if it doesn't get dug up, we don't get any money."

"You hear that?" The cousins exchanged glances. "He's talkin' like he's some city feller, all fancy-like."

"Must be that pretty girl of his." Jake leered. "Never seen anything so pretty here on the mountain. Wish you hadn't come along quite so fast. We was fixin' to —"

"Don't. Say. It." Griff ground out each word.

His shoulder muscles twitched with the effort of not lashing out and knocking Jake's teeth down his throat. Griff would not be violent. Nothing was served by striking another man. Except if he had struck Zach, his cousin wouldn't have been stabbed and wouldn't now be dying with Esther at his side.

"If any of you ever touches her," Griff said, "you will be looking for another place to live."

"You don't own this mountain. We does," said the youngest of the three, Seth. He was quiet and shy and did whatever his elder brother Jake told him to.

"Not enough of it." Griff took a further step into the room and looked each man in the eye. "So which one of you stabbed my cousin Zach Brooks?"

Blank stares were the only response he got.

"Don't play the fool with me." He stepped a bit closer, though their stench made him think of taking a swim in the waterfall pool. "Miss Esther heard you all talking about doing in more Brookses, and then Zach was stabbed."

"We just want rid of Henry Gosnoll," Jake said.

"He works us too hard," Jeb added.

"Which. One. Of. You?" Griff repeated.

More silence. More blank stares.

Then Seth shook his head, wincing. "We

388

didn't know he were stabbed."

Griff glanced from face to face and knew they spoke the truth. They'd been holed up drinking for a week. They hadn't been prowling around the mountain throwing knives at opposing family members.

"All right then." He headed for the door. "If any of you hear who did, I'll pay a reward for the information."

"Snitch on our kin?" Jeb sounded shocked.

Griff didn't look back. "Snitch on our kin to prevent a feud from starting up again. We've had peace for two years. I want to keep it. And you can come work the farm instead of the mine if you come tomorrow."

It was the least he could do for the Lord, who had given him so much.

He left, taking the fourth jug of corn whiskey with him. He poured it out along the trail. Like as not, the cousins didn't have money for more. That should drag them to the farm or back to the mine.

Griff dragged himself to the waterfall pool, where he indulged in a swim in the icy water. If Esther were his wife, they could swim there together, sun themselves on the rocks like lizards, or warm themselves —

He dressed and returned home to more news that Zach was worse than ever.

"Esther sent us a nice letter," Momma

said. "She said she's watching over him day and night with Tamar and Hannah's help. But he's not doing too good."

"It isn't right." Griff perched on the bench where Esther had stitched up his face. The sticking plaster had come off and the stitches itched, but the swelling had gone down and was turning all shades of green. "She shouldn't be doing this."

"She wants to." Momma busied herself at the stove, stirring salt and precious pepper into a pot of something smelling of onions and chicken.

"She thinks we won't want her back," Griff finally admitted.

Momma stirred the stew. "Why not? She's doing a fine job with the children, and your pa especially likes her singing."

"I especially like her singing."

And the smoothness of her hands beneath his as he positioned them on the dulcimer strings.

"But she thinks she's shamed herself," he confessed.

"Ha." Momma slammed the lid onto the kettle. "She ain't the one who's done the shaming, what with you taking advantage of her like I didn't teach you to treat a female better."

"I forgot myself." Griff shoved his fingers

through his hair, touched the back of his neck where Esther had stroked his hair like one of her cats.

Cats he continued to feed as though she were there.

She had forgotten herself too, teased him, excited him, angered him because — God forgive him — he felt guilty for taking advantage of her. He'd been shamed when he found the letters and wondered if she had taken advantage of him, of the attraction to her that he didn't try to hide.

"She should have slapped me," he said.

If she had, he wouldn't believe for a minute that anything in those letters was true. But she had returned his embrace as though she liked it, sought it, hungered for it as much as he had.

"She shouldn't have needed to," Momma said.

Griff rose. "No, ma'am. I know that. And you shouldn't need to be telling me to get to work, so I'll be about it."

He departed for the barn and the hard, physical labor that eased the gnawing ache inside him crying out for a mate, for someone at his side in work and play, raising children and worshiping the Lord. He'd never met a girl he could put in that place until he came face-to-face with Esther

Cherrett. Now the thoughts roamed at will through his head, waking him at night, distracting him during the day.

Distracted now, he was halfway across the barn before he noticed Bethann in one of the empty stalls. She stood with her back to the door, making no noise, though her shoulders heaved and shook in silent weeping.

Instinct told him to run from a crying female, especially his elder sister. She wouldn't thank him for catching her showing such weakness. Yet he couldn't walk away from such misery.

He laid a hand on her shoulder. "You all right, girl?"

"Right stupid question," she muttered.

"Yea, that it is. But what else does a body say when he finds a crying female? Why are you crying?"

Bethann's hand dropped to her belly. "I think you know."

"Yes'm, I guessed." His ears went hot. "He, um, won't marry you?"

Bethann shook her head. "I made a fool o' myself begging him to go off with me. But he thinks he'll get rich staying here, with the mine producing and all."

"You don't have to run off to get married, Bethann. I can . . . well, I can persuade him it's the best choice if you tell me who it is."

She shook her head. "I won't start no feuding again 'cause I'm an ugly spinster nobody wants. 'Cept him when he's lonely."

"That's no excuse." Griff's body tensed. "I get lonely too, and I don't go around ruining decent women. Or any women at all."

"Decent?" Bethann emitted a high, piercing laugh that bore no resemblance to amusement. "I ain't been decent for ten years, Griff. You know that."

"That wasn't your fault."

How he'd wanted to take up arms against the man who'd ruined her and started the feuding, but he'd left the mountain with his new bride, and when he returned a year later, he seemed invincible. One or two Tollivers had tried to gun him down. Both times he had evaded the shots, and then no one seemed to recall who was to blame for starting the fighting, as grudges formed and got settled with fists and knives and the lead they dug out of the mountain.

"I want to go away, Griff," Bethann announced. "I ain't no good to Momma or the young'uns or you. Can you spare me some money so I can go away?"

"I . . . can. But where would you go?"

"Don't matter. Away." She pulled away

from him and exited the stall. "I don't need much. Fifty dollars? Twenty-five?"

"I can't get it straight off. It's in a bank in Christiansburg, you know. And I can't leave right now. Maybe you should wait until . . . um . . . after . . ."

"And see another one die? I'll go without your money." She stalked from the barn on silent feet like a cat, far too thin.

When had he last seen her eat more than a few mouthfuls?

She might be better off going away, finding a fresh start where no one knew her, where no one knew how she had started a family war. Somehow he would find a way to make a trip to the city and get out some of the money the mine was bringing in. What good, after all, was having the extra if he didn't use it for the good of the family?

He should leave now, maybe put his cousins to work in the fields and with the animals instead of the mine, to keep them away from Henry Gosnoll. The different sights and sounds and smells of the journey might clear his head of the image of Esther smoothing the quilt across Zach's bare shoulders as though she possessed more than the right of a healer to do so. Or, worse, was used to performing such actions.

He trekked back up the mountain to bring

his cousins back to the farm, then packed his saddlebags and rode out the next morning.

27

Esther met Henry Gosnoll and Mr. Brooks around Zach's bedside. They had been gone on mine business for a few days and hadn't darkened the doorway of the sickroom until she admitted that the rest of Zach's recovery was in God's hands.

"Unless Mattie gets back in time with the doctor."

And Rafe Docherty knew what to do.

"Or the Lord gives us a miracle," Mrs. Brooks amended.

"Of course."

A good thing Esther had stopped practicing her profession. She had stopped praying for her patients when God failed her the last time. At least if Zach died, she couldn't blame God, for she hadn't asked Him for a thing.

She knelt at Zach's side, remembering the few words he had spoken to her over the days of his illness. "Beautiful. Perfect.

Angel." Nonsense he wouldn't have to learn was untrue. She could go through life knowing one person thought those things of her.

"What's wrong with him?" Gosnoll asked. "Other than being ambushed and stabbed."

He was a strapping man of around thirty-five, with hair that glowed like a sunset even in the flickering lantern light, and a bony, handsome face. An intelligent man if he was running the mine, but an inattentive husband. He wasn't even standing beside his wife, who wept silently into her apron.

"His wound has taken an infection," Esther explained. "The fever has burned away all his strength."

"You can't bring it down?" His tone held an accusatory note.

Esther stiffened. "I am a midwife, Mr. Gosnoll, not a physician. I know a few things about healing, but not enough for this kind of illness."

"Seems to me, missy," Gosnoll returned, "that if he's hot, he needs to be cooled down."

"Yes, you're right, sir." Esther spoke in her most imperious tones. "But you all have no ice, and the bath is too small and the pond too warm."

"What about the waterfall pool?" Gosnoll asked.

Esther arched her brows. "You expected us womenfolk to carry your brother-in-law up there?"

"We're sorry we weren't here." Mr. Brooks cleared his throat. "Didn't know he was bad off."

"Or who done it to him. But we'll find out, won't we, Pa?" Sam piped up. "And we'll kill 'im."

Mr. Brooks cleared his throat again but said nothing.

"I'll carry him up," Gosnoll said. "He can't weigh more'n a girl now. Less than my wife." He snorted as though he'd made a joke.

Esther's mouth opened. Hannah was nicely muscled and rounded, but far from heavy for a female of her height. She was as beautiful as her siblings, with blonde hair and blue eyes and flawless skin save for a few natural lines.

"Well?" Gosnoll snapped. "Do I do it?"

"It's on Tolliver land," Mr. Brooks pointed out.

"Griff's gone," Sam said. "Ain't none of the rest of 'em go up there save maybe Bethann."

Griff was gone?

Esther's heart leaped and twisted with a struggle between relief and fear. Now she knew why she had heard nothing from the Tollivers, but the idea that he would leave in the middle of the summer wasn't right.

"Saw Ned fishin'," Sam explained. "He says how his brother's gone up to the city for something he won't say."

Definitely more on the fear side than the relief.

"Hope he don't hurt Mattie on the way," Sam plodded on.

" 'Specially if he thinks one of us stabbed him back in April," Gosnoll said.

"What does it matter?" Esther cried. "Zach is dying while you worry yourselves over a ten-year-old fight. We've got to get him to the pool." She lowered her voice. "It may kill him, but staying here isn't going to save him."

Gosnoll wrapped Zach in the quilt as though he were no larger than a child and carried him from the house. The rest of them followed, silent save for Mrs. Brooks praying and the occasional groan from Zach. Yawning, Hannah leaned on Esther's arm, though Esther still limped a bit on her injured foot.

They reached the waterfall pool after dark. Moonlight bathed the rocky hollow and turned the waterfall into a cascade of silver, the spray to sparks. Kneeling beside the water at the still end of the pond, Esther held Zach's head while Gosnoll eased the rest of his brother-in-law's body into the frigid water. Through his hair, Zach's head burned from the fever. Surely water this cold would help, if bathing in cold cloths did with lesser fevers.

Something has to work, Lord, she prayed at last. *Please.*

Sam had voiced what no one else would say — if Zach died, the Brookses would want revenge. They wouldn't rest until they discovered who had given the killing blow. More men would die, perhaps even Griff.

Griff, who only wanted peace, who had refused to blame anyone for his own stabbing, who had refused to strike back at Zach. Griff, who sincerely believed God would work things out if he only kept the peace and believed.

When had Zach stopped believing that too?

The answer doubled Esther over as though she too had received a knife thrust in the middle, right through her vital organs — Zach had stopped believing in peace between the families when she came along and he fancied himself in love with her.

400

Keep running.

The one who had penned that note was right. She should go, and keep going. Change her name so as not to accidentally shame her parents. Let them believe she died. It would hurt them for a time, but they would recover. The townspeople would be sympathetic to parents who had lost their daughter to a tragic accident or illness, unlike losing her to sin.

"How long do we leave him in?" Gosnoll asked.

Esther started upright. She touched Zach's brow. It felt cooler. So did his shoulder. Suddenly his teeth began to chatter as they often had during the fever. So strange, the body, with teeth chattering from too much cold and too much heat.

"Not any longer," she said, "or we risk a lung fever."

They wrapped him up again and carried him back. Once he lay on the mattress, Esther asked for another quilt, then another. Still he shivered.

"Let's get some hot tea in him." She kept her tone neutral so as not to show her fear that she had gone too far in her treatment in taking him to the pool. "Any kind of tea."

"I'll fetch it." Hannah scurried away.

"We don't have any real tea," Mrs. Brooks

said. "There's some of your herbs and the like."

"It doesn't matter. Plain hot water will do." Esther chafed Zach's hands. They were beautiful, long-fingered hands like Griff's, like their mothers'. Holding them triggered a warm glow of affection like she held for her four brothers. Only touching Griff's hands made her feel like she was a Lucifer match and he the rough surface needed to strike a flame. "Stay with us, my dear friend."

His eyes fluttered open and looked straight into hers for a moment, then drifted shut.

"He knows you, girl," Mrs. Brooks said. "He told me how he feels about you. You save his life and he'll be wanting you around forever."

"If he gets well," Esther said with care, "he'll owe it to the Lord, not any skill of mine."

"True, true." Mrs. Brooks nodded. "But he won't see it all thatta way."

Hannah entered the room carrying a pewter mug from which steam rose. "This was all I could find to use. There weren't no broth left over."

Esther's nostrils flared. Poor Zach. It was willow bark tea and without any honey. It hadn't seemed to help him much before, not being strong enough to ease his pain for long, but it was hot and wouldn't hurt him.

She took the cup and, with Gosnoll holding Zach upright, guided the rim to his lips. "Just a few sips to warm you. It's that awful bitter stuff, but it's warm." She talked and cajoled in her sweetest fashion, and the contents vanished down Zach's throat a few drops at a time.

Gosnoll lay Zach down and stared at Esther with a bemused expression. "You're good at this."

"I've had a great deal of practice." She fussed with Zach's covers and with his hair. Still Gosnoll gazed at her. The more he gazed, the more she took up little things to occupy her.

And the further across the room Hannah retreated until she perched on the edge of the sofa beside her dozing father and brother.

They all looked exhausted. None of them had known much sleep over the past two weeks. The floor, even without rug or blanket, looked appealing. Esther sat crosslegged and made notations in her midwife's notebook.

Soaked in cold natural pool for thirty minutes. Removed when shivering grew intense. Wrapped in blankets and gave one cup of white willow bark tea.

And right before dawn, Zach's fever broke.

Griff reached Christiansburg in two days. He and his horse both dropping from fatigue, he spent money on a room and slept until hours past daybreak. From the one other time when he'd gone to the bank — that time with Zach and Henry Gosnoll — to open accounts for themselves and the mine, he knew to dress in a linen shirt and a coat and trousers made from wool despite the heat of the day. The other men wore neck cloths. Griff didn't own one. Perhaps he should purchase one. And since he was there, he would buy ribbons for the girls, one for Esther too, some of that fancy thread Momma and Liza liked, and new slates and chalk for the schoolroom.

If they still had a teacher when he returned.

He certainly wanted her back. So did the children. Even Brenna admitted she missed the stories Miss Esther read to them, and Ned liked the way she let him bring bugs and things into the classroom if he could tell her something about them. Griff missed her voice when they sang. It was so rich and pure and smooth like fresh cream. He missed her woodland flower scent, her light step, the way she spoiled the stray cats like they were beloved relatives. He missed all the kindness she was lavishing on Zach.

If only the ridge had a doctor.

As though he conjured it from his imagination, he saw the shingle announcing that a doctor's place of practice lay within. A rather good doctor, judging from the size of the house beyond the surgery — two stories and painted white with green shutters, two chimneys, and a profusion of roses in the front garden. A man like that would never come to the ridge to see the victim of a family feud. But Griff could ask him questions, perhaps buy some fancy medicine, anything to free Esther from her sense of obligation to remain at Zach's bedside.

If she wanted to be free.

If she did, then he would find the opportunity for her. If she did not, he wouldn't have wasted his time and would have aided his cousin.

He knocked on the door to the office.

A young woman perhaps three or four years older than Liza opened the door. She had eyes the color of moss and hair like the red stones they sometimes dug from the rocks, a startling and pretty combination.

"I'm so sorry. I was expecting someone else." Her voice was pretty too, lighter than Esther's but just as smooth. "If you want to see the doctor, he's still up at the house. Momma just got home from a lying-in and they're having breakfast." She looked him up and down. When her gaze reached his face again, it held interest. "You don't look injured or ill. Can you wait a wee bit?"

Ears hot from her perusal, Griff shifted from one foot to the other and shoved his hands into his pockets. "I can come back later. I have some business that I can do first." He started to turn away.

"Whom should I tell him to expect?" she called after him. "I'm forever forgetting to ask people their names."

"Tolliver. Griff Tolliver."

"Oh?" The little word held a page of curiosity.

Griff nodded and went about his business at the bank. They remembered him and ushered him in with the same respect they showed other customers, but he noted the differences in his appearance and theirs. Besides no neck cloth, he wore boots, not shoes, beneath his trousers, and he'd forgotten to cut his hair again.

On his way back down the street, he saw a barbershop and considered going in for a haircut, but the memory of Esther's fingers twining through the hair on the back of his neck, then smoothing it down again, stopped him. If she liked it, he would leave it. If she liked it and it wasn't just a distracting ploy on her part.

He continued to the doctor's office.

This time a different woman answered the door. She was in early middle age, also strikingly pretty with dark red hair and brighter green eyes than the younger female. "Are you the Mr. Tolliver here to see my da?" she asked in a Scots burr.

Griff blinked. "Yes'm. Um, yes, ma'am. Doctor —" He hesitated, not sure he knew how to say the name on the door.

"Docherty. He's waiting for you. I'm his eldest daughter, Melvina Docherty Mc-Wythie." She led him along a narrow corridor with doors closed on either side until it reached an open room at the end. She dragged one foot a bit but otherwise moved with grace. "Da, this is Mr. Tolliver come back to see you."

A big man rose from behind a desk. Light from the windows shone on gray hair still bearing enough red to show where the daughters had gotten theirs, but the eyes were pure, winter-day gray. He held out a broad hand. "I'm Rafe Docherty. How may

I assist you?" He too spoke in that broad Scots burr so common in the mountains. "As my daughter said, you look hale and hardy to me."

"I saw your sign and thought to ask for my cousin's sake." Griff glanced at the woman.

"I'm going back to my ledgers so you two can talk." She smiled at Griff. "Do not let my da frighten you. He has not been a pirate for nearly thirty years." With that odd remark, she swept from the room.

Griff arched one brow at the older man.

Docherty laughed. "I was ne'er a pirate, only a privateer. Now sit you down and tell me what you are asking for your cousin."

"He's got an infection from a stab wound," Griff began.

"That sounds bad. Where is it?"

"Right above the hip." Griff touched his own side. "Got a wound there myself but didn't suffer from the infection."

"Odd, that, the two of you getting stabbed in the same place, no?" The gray eyes fixed on Griff, piercing as arrowheads, as Docherty picked up a quill pen and uncapped an inkwell.

Griff met the gaze and ignored the implied question. He wasn't about to tell an outsider about the feuding. "The best thing to a doctor we have is a midwife with some healing skills."

Docherty's hand stilled in the act of dipping the quill. "A midwife, you say? An older lady then?"

"No, she's right young. A bit younger than me."

"So nae so much experience." Docherty wrote something on a clean sheet of paper before him, his head bowed. "And you're asking advice on how to treat a wound sepsis?"

"He has a fever eating away at him."

"Ah, then 'tis throughout the body. Ver' bad. We have not the medicines to treat such systemic fevers. We can only treat the symptoms and trust in God and the strength of the patient." Docherty dipped his pen, wrote another word, then looked up. "What has this midwife healer young lady done for treating the fever?"

"I . . . don't know." Griff shifted on his chair, suddenly uncomfortable in his middle as though his breakfast weren't settling well. "Wiping down with cold water. Some hot drinks."

"Some willow bark tea, some cinnamon perhaps." Docherty rose and crossed the room to a cabinet with dozens of tiny drawers. He began drawing them out and scooping fragrant powders into paper pokes. "I doubt she has much of the willow or cinnamon with her. What else? Feverfew? Aye, for certain." He continued in this manner for several minutes, rattling off names of powders and liquids, until he had filled a basket with paper packets and tiny vials. Griff watched, his gut and mouth growing tighter by the moment.

Finally, Docherty carried the basket back to the desk and set it before Griff. "There now. That'll suit her fine."

"Will she know what these are all for?"

A stupid question. Of course she would.

"Aye, I am thinking she will. Now then, do you leave for home straightaway?"

"Yes."

"Then come up to the house for some coffee and food before you go. My wife and other daughter would like to be meeting you, I am thinking."

Him? A common man from the mountains, who didn't know the right way to talk or dress? Griff eyed the basket, his hand twitching with the urge to grab it and bolt for the door before he learned what was wrong here.

But hot coffee and food sounded good before he made the long journey back into the mountains.

He followed Docherty to the house, where a pretty woman whose hair still showed flashes of its former gold greeted them with a warm smile and curious sidelong glance at Griff. The flirtatious younger daughter kept her gaze demurely downcast in front of her parents.

"Sit down, Mr. Tolliver," Mrs. Docherty told him in a honey-and-cream voice like Esther's. "Do you like anything in your coffee?"

He said he didn't. He sat at a fine walnut table before a deep window overlooking the red and pink roses and other flowers he couldn't name. Mrs. Docherty served him coffee. Miss Docherty served him warm rolls with butter and strawberry jam, slices of ham, and fresh raspberries. They gathered at the table, Dr. Docherty asked a blessing upon the meal, and four pairs of eyes fixed themselves upon him.

"Tell us about your mountains."

"Tell us about this young midwife."

The two eldest women spoke at the same time.

Griff looked to the doctor for help.

He smiled. "I'd like to know where you're from first, Mr. Tolliver. Where is it?"

"Southwest of here," Griff answered with care. "Along the New River. Some surveyor told us once it was seventy-five miles from here."

"And no roads?" Miss Docherty exclaimed.

"Just a track," Griff admitted.

"Do you have wild animals there?" Miss Docherty persisted.

"Sounds to me," Mrs. McWythie murmured, "like they have some wild people."

Griff's fingers tightened on his knife. Fixing the elder daughter with a fierce glare, he said in his best mountain drawl, "We're gettin' civilized, ma'am. My family owns half a mountain and half a lead mine."

"And you hired a teacher."

Griff's head snapped around to face Docherty. "You've . . . heard?"

"News travels." Docherty's smile was warm, encouraging. "But my wife would like to know about your midwife healer. She's one herself."

The gut tightness returned. "I don't know what to tell you," Griff hedged.

"Let's make this easy," Mrs. Docherty suggested. "Start with her name. I may know her."

"She's not from around here." Griff set his knife down and curled his hands around the edge of the table. The gazes upon him were too intense, the faces too set for something not to be wrong. "Her name is Cherrett. Esther Cherrett."

The younger daughter gasped. The other three exchanged glances.

Griff gave up thinking he could eat. "You know her." It was a statement stemming from a suspicion he'd carried from the doctor's office.

"Aye," Dr. Docherty affirmed, "we ken who she is. She's the missing daughter of our dear friends."

28

Esther turned the page and began to read yet one more of Shakespeare's sonnets. These and several of the playwright's dramas, all appearing old enough to have belonged to the bard himself, were the only reading materials in the Brooks household other than the Bible. She'd been reading that to Zach. It kept him awake. Shakespeare sent him to sleep. And he needed his sleep, as much of it as he could get. He needed broth and milk and eggs, and she, his mother, or his sister spooned those down him in small portions several times a day. He was far too thin and weak to do much for himself, but his recovery seemed more likely each day.

"I said you're an angel," he had told her when he woke after his fever broke.

"You can thank your brother-in-law for carrying you up to the pool, not me. I'd run out of ideas on what to do."

And sent Mattie to Rafe Docherty for no reason. By now Rafe and Phoebe and at least their daughters and son-in-law, if not their sons too, would know where to find her. No doubt a message was on its way to her parents even as she read one more sonnet in the heat of the summer afternoon. No doubt they would arrive in as little as four and no more than six weeks. She had that long before she had to make up her mind whether to stay or keep running.

"Esther?" Zach's voice was as weak as he.

She raised her gaze from the book. "Yes?"

"You stopped reading."

"I thought you were asleep."

"Thirsty. Please." He reached toward the cup of water beside his bed, his hand trembling.

"I'll get it." She set the book aside and crossed the room to kneel beside him.

He'd lost so much muscle she could lift him. She held him with one arm beneath his shoulders and her other hand holding the cup.

He smiled at her from half a foot away. "I feel like a child."

"You won't for long."

"I hope not." He curled his fingers around her wrist holding the cup to his lips. "I love you now more than ever."

"No, Zach, you do not." She tried to ease herself away from him, but he held on. Her heart began to pound, her stomach clench. "You're confusing love with gratitude. Now let me go."

"I don't want to."

"Zach —" She couldn't breathe.

A commotion sounded in the yard, horses' hooves, men shouting.

"Let me go, Zach." Esther's voice rose on a note of panic. "You have callers."

"Not for me." He leaned closer to her. His breath brushed her cheek, stirring the hair she no longer owned pins enough to keep bundled into its knot, and bile burned in her throat. "Just kiss me so I can truly feel alive."

"I c-can't kiss —"

The parlor door burst open and Griff Tolliver strode in — tall, broad, vigorously strong and healthy with his wind-tossed hair and sun-bronzed skin. The very air in the room seemed to crackle and swirl.

Then it settled to unnatural stillness. "I beg your pardon for interrupting." Griff closed the door behind him. "I crossed paths with your brother on the trail and brought him home, Zach."

"You didn't need to come in and tell me that." Zach's voice, though weak, held

416

enough ice to fill a barn.

Esther's face and neck burned as though she had caught Zach's fever, but the panic slipped away. She tried to pull away from him again. He held her with more strength than he should possess. If she struggled, she would likely spill the water all over him. If she didn't get away, Griff would think the worst of her.

She sent him a pleading glance. "Welcome back, Griff. I trust you had a safe journey?"

"Safe enough." He plucked the cup from her hand. "I think she wants to get up, Zach."

"Only because you walked in." Zach sank back against his pillows, and Esther scrambled to her feet, smoothing back her hair.

"I think," she said with her own hint of frost, "you can get your own water now, Zachary Brooks."

"Aw, Esther, you can't blame a man who's been a-dyin' for trying."

"You . . . can if she's not wi-willing."

"But was she unwilling?" Griff murmured.

A tremor raced through Esther, and she backed to the door. "Excuse me. I need some air." She jerked up the latch.

Zach grinned at Griff. "She saved my life, now I'm going to marry her."

"I didn't . . . I'm not going to . . ." She ran out of the house and into the yard.

No one was there now, and she dropped onto the lowest porch step, her face buried in her hands. She was shaking for no good reason. That was Zach, weak-as-a-new-calf Zach, not some healthy male. She could have gotten away even if it had made a bit of a scene. He wouldn't have hurt her. He wanted nothing more than what Griff had taken.

No, what Griff had given and she'd taken before giving back.

A low moan escaped her.

"What's amiss?" Griff was there beside her, silent as ever in his approach, his hand light on her hair. "Are you ill? Mattie said you've been at Zach's side constantly."

"I'm not ill. Worn to a thread, is all, and not much liking the way Zach thinks he has a claim on me."

"Miss Esther Cherrett . . ." Griff crouched before her, coaxed her chin up, and met her gaze. "I'm only an ignorant mountain boy compared to the fancy, educated friends you have, but I know fear when I see it, and you was — were scared in there." He tapped her chin. "Since when have you been afraid of Zach?"

Esther sank her teeth into her lower lip.

Griff rubbed it with his thumb. "Your eyes are about twice their usual size, and that's right big. Now tell me what's happened this week."

"Nothing. That is — since his fever broke, he's gotten too insistent."

"Then slap his face."

"I can't slap a patient."

"You sure can if he's bothering you."

"If it's my fault, though . . ."

Griff's face tightened. "You been petting him like you did me?"

"No, I never — I wouldn't. But I'm certain it must be something."

"You should have your hair pinned up." He lifted a handful of the loose strands and allowed them to flow through his fingers. "It gives a man notions about seeing it spread out on his pillow."

She swung her palm toward his cheek.

He caught her wrist, laughed, and kissed her palm. "That's right. I shouldn'ta said it. Even if it's true, it's the sorta thing a man keeps to himself until he's married to a girl. Just like his hands if she says no."

She didn't say no to him, not before, not then. He pressed her palm against his cheek, and she remained still, a two-day growth of his beard prickling her palm, his skin warm and smooth beneath. If they'd been anywhere but on the Brookses' front steps, she would have brought her other hand to his face and kissed him. For being understanding, for being kind, for being there.

She'd missed him. Now that he was there, she felt where he'd been lacking, the empty place in her heart now filled.

Oh no. No, no, no, no, no. She. Did. Not. Love. Him.

But of course she did. Why else had she let him kiss her? Why else had she so desperately needed him to let her down when she knew she couldn't walk on her injured foot, needed to get away from her own wish to have him hold her closer?

She couldn't love anyone. He was a good man who deserved a respectable wife. He was a Christian man who deserved a wife who still believed God cared.

Yet had God not shown He cared with Zach?

Zach was good and kind and hardworking. He too deserved a wife who wasn't sullied by scandal.

Scandal. Her parents. The Dochertys.

She jumped back from Griff. "Did you meet Dr. Docherty?"

"I sure did." He smiled. "And his wife and daughters."

Esther narrowed her eyes. "Both of them?"

"Both of them." Griff winked. "Miss Janet is a right pretty girl."

"She's a minx." Esther tossed her hair back over her shoulders and rose. "Let me guess. She looked you up and down like you were her luncheon, and all the while her fiancé is off seeking his fortune at sea."

"Not anymore. She was right happy to tell me that he's on his way home." He took her elbow and started her toward his tethered horse by the gate. "After she finished looking me up and down like I was her luncheon."

Esther kept her gaze on the roan gelding and its bulging saddlebags. "And her parents? What did they tell you?"

"That you're their dearest friends' runaway daughter."

"Like I'm a child."

"You shouldn't have come without telling them where you are, you know. Mommas worry about their young'uns."

"And so do fathers, but mine are better off —" She drew her lip between her teeth to keep it from trembling. She couldn't stop the tears from springing to her lashes. "Are they coming here to drag me away?"

"Naw, they don't want to drag you away."

"What?" She flashed a glance up at him. The unshed tears scattered.

He caught one on the pad of his thumb. "They said it ain't —" He let out a sigh of exasperation. "It isn't their place to do anything of the kind to a woman grown. And it sounds like we need you here."

Esther's knees wobbled with her relief. She didn't need to run after all. Not yet. Not unless she couldn't manage her feelings for Griff.

"But they will write to your parents and send it by special courier," Griff concluded.

"Of course they will." Esther rubbed her eyes.

"And they'll come to get you?"

Esther nodded. "Not that they can make me do anything, but my father can be . . . persuasive."

"Esther." Griff laid his hand on the small of her back.

She wasn't wearing her corset and jumped at the heat through only her gown and petticoat.

"Dr. Docherty said you didn't need to run off," Griff continued softly.

"Did you tell him about the letters?"

"No, of course I didn't. What kind of man do you think I am?"

Honorable, kind, generous, loyal, and far, far too good to look at.

They reached the gelding, and she stroked

his neck as though he were her long-lost pet. "He must be weary. Will you take him home now?"

"I want to take you home now. After what I saw in the sickroom there, I think it's time."

"I think it's time too. He won't believe me. Perhaps if I go."

"Then go fetch your things, and we'll be gone."

Esther hesitated, not wanting to enter the house, hear Mrs. Brooks or Hannah pleading with her about how much Zach needed her still. He didn't. They were fine nurses. All he needed now was nourishment and strength. If she wasn't around, perhaps he would come to his senses.

She laid her hand on Griff's arm and gazed up at him from beneath her lashes. "Will you go fetch them for me? There isn't much, and —"

Griff snatched her hand from his arm and stalked toward the house, his long legs eating up the ground, his back stiff.

Esther stared at her hand, still curved as though gripping Griff's muscled forearm, and a verse from the fifth chapter of Matthew's Gospel kept running through her head. *And if thy right hand offend thee, cut it off, and cast it from thee: for it is profitable for thee that one of thy members should perish, and not that thy whole body should be cast into hell.*

Why did she think she needed to cajole and flirt and tease to get someone to do something for her? She never used to be so bold. Before January, she simply smiled and asked, and half a dozen men appeared to do her bidding. Then Alfred Oglevie ruined her reputation, and if she needed help with a parcel, with finding something, with mounting a horse — anything — men expected a reward from the pastor's wanton daughter.

Like the kiss she had given Griff after he rescued her. Could it truly have been nothing more than her believing she needed to reward him for his aid? No, surely not, not when she felt about him the way she did.

And she knew how deeply those feelings ran for certain the instant he reappeared, her satchel in one hand, a small bundle of her things in the other. Unkempt and dusty from the journey, he was still a fine sight to her. Her ears ached to hear his gentle, deep voice. Her whole being yearned to be close to him, feeling his strength of mind, spirit, and body.

But she dared not. She was ruined, not good enough for him.

Choking down a sob, she turned on her heel and headed out of the compound.

29

Griff stowed Esther's gear onto the saddle and swung onto the back of the horse. He needn't hurry. She couldn't get far walking. She still limped. He noticed that as she turned and headed out the gate as though a mountain lion pursued her.

Aunt Tamar pursued him. "Griff, why are you leaving so quick? Where's Esther?"

"She left." He hesitated, then decided he may as well tell the truth. "Zach is making her uncomfortable with his courting talk."

"That boy." Aunt Tamar shook her head. "I told him not to, but can you blame him for falling in love with her?"

"No," Griff said. Raising his hand in farewell, he wheeled the gelding around and set out after Esther.

He reached her in less than a mile. She had slowed her pace and her limp was more pronounced, but her head was high, her long waves of hair lifting and drifting in the afternoon breeze.

He didn't give her a choice about riding with him. She'd say no, the stubborn woman. He simply rode up beside her, leaned down to grasp her around the waist, and swung her onto the saddle in front of him. She shrieked and managed to deal his knee a painful kick. Her skirt billowed, showing a bit of lace on the edge of a petticoat ruffle and trim ankles in white stockings, but she sank into place at once, shoving down petticoat and gown as far as she could manage. A bit more of her lower limbs showed than was decent. Griff tried not to look.

Her hair helped in that. It caught the wind and veiled his face, tangled in the buttons at the neck of his shirt, wrapped itself around his neck like a ribbon or a noose.

Laughing, he took the reins in one hand and gathered the shining mass of waves into a queue. "No wonder females scarce ever carry weapons. They can kill a man with this stuff."

"There's a Scandinavian legend about a king who killed his enemy with his hair. Strangled him."

"I believe it was the truth." He smoothed the tail of her hair over her shoulder. "Hold it. You think Hannah or Aunt Tamar could have given you some pins."

"They offered, but I hated taking from them. They have so little."

"They have so little?" Griff laughed. "They'd have twice as much as us even if they didn't have the mine too. That ferry brings in a tidy income."

"But their house. It hardly has any furniture."

"Aunt Tamar is frugal and keeps her hand firmly on the purse strings. But she'll give Zach whatever he wants."

"That won't be me." Her tone was cold, her spine stiff.

"Why not?" Griff drew her back against him with one arm around her waist, a more comfortable way for them both to ride, more secure for her precarious perch ahead of him.

She didn't relax into his chest as she should, and Sunset tossed his head, snorting, feeling the tension atop his back.

"Settle yourself," Griff murmured into her ear. "You're upsetting the horse."

"How can I when you get upset with me for — for touching you?"

"Miss Esther, I don't get upset with you touching me. I like that maybe more than I should. I get upset with you using your pretty eyes and soft hands to do what you

428

want. I think it right tawdry of you, like — like —"

"Like those letters are true?"

If she behaved like that with the men of Seabourne, they probably held some truth. But why would she? The Docherty family so obviously loved her. Her own parents must too. Yet she'd run from that love to the arms of strangers.

Only something awful would drive a body away from family who cared. Like Bethann waiting for him to return with money so she could flee the mountain and her disgrace, even though they all loved her and told her she could stay.

Bethann had strayed on her own this time, but before it hadn't been that way, and it had started a war between families.

"Esther?" No, he couldn't ask a female such a thing. He could only protect her. "I don't care about what those letters said."

She said nothing in response, but her back relaxed, her head nestled into his shoulder. He kept Sunset to an easy pace, not caring how long he took to get them home.

Esther fell asleep against him. She trusted him enough to sleep in his arms. He would settle for that.

They reached home at dusk. The air smelled

of frying pork and rang with the joyous shouts of the children swarming out to greet them.

"You brought her home." Ned hugged Esther the instant Griff set her on the ground, then backed off, blushing.

She smiled down at him. "That's the nicest present I think I've ever gotten."

Ned glowed, and Griff loved her all the more.

"Did you bring us presents?" Brenna asked Griff.

"Why'd you have to go anyway?" Jack asked.

Esther shot him a look with arched brows that asked the same question.

"I had business to see to. As for presents" — he tugged Brenna's pigtail — "maybe."

"But you promised," Brenna wailed. "You'd think we were as poor as the Neffs, my ribbons all look so shabby."

"Brenna, that ain't nice," Liza said, then clapped her hand to her mouth.

Esther smiled. "I see I've been gone too long."

"Why are you wearing your hair down?" Brenna turned her big eyes on Esther. "Did my brother do that? It's indecent that you —"

"Brenna, go inside," Griff said with quiet

firmness. "If you've done all your chores, I'll see what I brought you and if you can have it. But only if you apologize."

"But it's true. Momma says — ouch, Jack, why'd you kick me?"

"All of you, inside." Griff clamped a hand on Jack's shoulder and steered him toward the house. "I'll be inside as soon as I rub down this poor beast and give Miss Esther her things."

"And kiss her good night," Brenna shot back as she slipped in through the back door.

Griff glanced at Esther, couldn't stop himself from looking at her lips. A kiss would please him greatly. She might even kiss him back again. But decency said he shouldn't now any more than he should have on Independence Day.

He swallowed down disappointment. "I bought some new pins for Momma and Liza. She's getting old enough to start putting up her hair. I expect there's enough for you too."

"Thank you. I seem to have lost a number of them since getting here."

"I'll bring them by later." He glanced at the darkening sky now that the sun had dropped behind the western mountains. "Or maybe it should wait for tomorrow."

"Yes, it probably should."

"Will you come to the house for supper?"

"No, thank you. I'd like to go to my room and sleep."

"Then I'll see you in the morning." He satisfied himself with a brush of his fingertips across her cheek, as soft as the petal of a flower, then stood beside his horse while she crossed the yard to her house. Once she was inside and the bolt shot home, Griff took the gelding to the barn and unloaded it. He had plenty of excuses to go see her in the morning. He still carried her satchel, as she'd forgotten it for once. He also had the basket of herbs and oils from the doctor.

He stowed the things for Esther in an empty stall, then carried the other packages to the house. Momma and Pa greeted him with nods and questions about his journey. The children clamored for whatever he had brought them, and from the far doorway, Bethann scanned his face with anxious eyes.

He inclined his head and dropped one hand to his breeches pocket. Bethann half smiled before slipping away. She could be gone in a day or two, and maybe, with her presence away from the ridge, the families could forget about the cause of the feud. Griff could correspond with her — she wrote well enough to do that — and ensure she had enough to support her and the baby if the father wouldn't support her.

Conscious of the money burning in his pocket, he realized he shouldn't give it to Bethann without telling Momma and Pa. Yet if he told them, he would break Bethann's trust and she might disappear from them forever. For all the trouble she had caused, Bethann was kin. He couldn't lose Bethann as Esther's parents had come so close to losing her.

Esther crawled into the bed and slept until past dawn. She hadn't been able to sleep in a real bed for more than a few hours in over two weeks. She had enjoyed no privacy. This was coming home.

To cap off the impression, the cats greeted her outside her cabin door, twining themselves around her ankles, purring like steam engines interspersed with squeaky meows.

She stooped to pet them, the skirt of her pink muslin gown billowing around her. "You two need more cedar. I hope I can find some. And you're going to have those kittens any day now, aren't you, momma cat?"

"Meow. Meow."

She rubbed chins, promised them breakfast, and glanced up to see Griff smiling down at her, his hands laden with parcels.

"May I help you?" She intended to sound cool; she sounded breathless.

"I can help you." He held out the packages. "Let's take 'em inside. Some of this is for the schoolroom."

"Chalk?"

"And new slates."

"Bless you." She sprang to her feet and flung open the schoolroom door. "That was so kind of you. The children probably haven't missed their lessons. I know Sam and Mattie haven't. But I've missed teaching them."

"They have, though. Even Brenna." Griff set the chalks and slates on the table, then returned to stand directly in front of Esther. "This basket is from your doctor friend. I think he suspected it was you the minute I mentioned you, 'cause he started filling this basket with all sorts of stuff."

"Uncle Rafe did?" Esther fairly snatched the basket from him and began to plow through it, lifting up the packets and sniffing them, looking at the labels on the vials of oils. "Cloves, cinnamon, thyme. Lovely."

"You going to cook or heal people?" Griff's eyes glowed like the sun-washed sky outside.

Esther laughed. "I could do both. These

434

are sovereign remedies for many things. Oh, a whole gingerroot. I suppose I'll have to write to thank him. And you for carrying it back."

"I'd have carried more." Griff ducked his head, his curly hair sliding across his brow. He tossed a smaller parcel from hand to hand, then thrust it at her without looking. "This is from me."

"Griff, you shouldn't. That is . . . is it all right?" Her hand shook, making the wrapping crackle.

"Momma said it was."

"Your momma has ideas I — well, thank you." Esther kept her own head bowed as she set the package on the table and pulled the knotted string apart.

The paper fell away to reveal half a dozen ivory hairpins and a length of ivory satin ribbon embroidered with purple violets. Simple. Elegant. Probably the most precious gift she'd ever received. Her throat closed, and she couldn't speak.

"It's the flower you use for your scent," Griff said tentatively. "Violets, I think?"

She nodded, her heart thumping at the notion that he recognized her scent and remembered it.

"It ain't much. Just a bit of fancy ribbon, but the girls like 'em, so I thought . . .

maybe . . . you . . ." He trailed off.

The cabin fell silent save for a fly buzzing against the window. The intermittent hum as it beat itself against the glass emphasized the stillness.

Then someone called Griff's name from across the yard, and he shuffled his feet without moving. "I should be going."

"Not yet." She forced the words out. "Please, I —" She swallowed and raised her gaze to his face. "Thank you. It's beautiful. It's perfect. It's — It's —" She held out her hands to him.

He started to clasp them in his.

"There you are. I should have known." Brenna stomped into the schoolroom. "Bethann is in the barn, and I can't get her to wake up."

30

Esther gathered up her skirts and charged for the barn, the others racing behind her. "Keep Brenna and the other young ones out," she flung over her shoulder.

In Bethann's condition, anything might be possible. Blood. Too much blood for children to see.

But no blood pooled around Bethann. She lay curled up on a pile of straw in one of the stalls, only a thready pulse in her neck indicating she was still alive.

"What's wrong?" Griff crouched beside Esther.

"I don't know. I don't know." She caught the edge in her voice, desired to beat her fist against the wooden partition, and took two long, deep breaths before speaking again. "I'm not a doctor. I'm a midwife, and not a very good one at that. My last patient died."

"Zach didn't."

"He was young and healthy. Bethann is starving herself to death." Esther lifted one of the woman's hands. "Ned's wrist is thicker than — what's this?"

Bethann's hand gripped something even in her unconsciousness. Esther pried it out of the bony fingers and stared at the hand-written label on the bottle. *Laudanum.*

Her head spun. Stars danced before her eyes. She swayed, and Griff wrapped his arm around her shoulders. "What is it?"

"Laudanum. It's a mixture of spirits and opium for serious cases of pain." She held the bottle to the light from the door. More than half of the contents were missing. "It must have been in that basket of things from Uncle Rafe. This is his handwriting. And I doubt he sent me anything but a full bottle."

"You think she took all of this?" Griff removed the flask from Esther's hand.

"It's unlikely she spilled it, or we would smell it." She bent close to Bethann, sniffing.

She caught the hint of spirits on the woman's faint breaths, but nowhere else. She reached to examine her as she had done for so many women, remembered Griff beside her, and stopped. "We need to get her someplace better than this. My room will do."

"Shouldn't we wake her?"

"Yes, we'll try, but let me examine her first in the event she's, um, terminating."

"She's . . . oh, of course." Head ducked, Griff lifted Bethann in his arms and left the barn.

The children gathered around, and Mrs. Tolliver headed their way.

"What's wrong?" the latter asked.

Esther met her and took her arm. "He's taking her to my room. I want to examine her. I'm thinking she perhaps started to terminate, the pain grew intense, and she took too much laudanum." She kept her tone neutral, professional, despite her racing heart, the fear slamming through her middle. "I'm going to examine her if you'd like to join me."

Face pale, Mrs. Tolliver accompanied Esther to her room. Griff laid Bethann on the bed, then slipped into the schoolroom.

Esther closed the door, washed her hands as Momma had taught her according to a code good midwives had followed for hundreds of years, and set about examining Bethann, palpating her belly, looking for more intimate details. She diagnosed nothing wrong except an expectant mother who was far too thin for good health. Certainly not an expectant mother who should have been in pain enough to need something as strong as laudanum to ease it. At least not a physical pain.

Holding herself tense so she didn't show her anxiety, Esther washed her hands again and remained facing the tiny square of mirror above the washstand as she delivered her report. "The baby seems just fine. Perhaps six months along. So now we need to work on waking her up."

"How do we do that?" Mrs. Tolliver asked. "Brenna said she shook her and slapped her, and nothing happened."

"No, I don't suppose it would." Esther gripped the edge of the nightstand.

Calm. Always be calm, Momma had said again and again. *At least pretend that you are.*

"All I know to give her is strong coffee. Lots of it. And get her moving. Griff can help with that." Esther opened the door. "Griff, I have work for you."

"I'll make the coffee." Face working, Mrs. Tolliver sped from the schoolhouse like she was running away.

Perhaps she was. She was an intelligent woman. Like as not she was thinking what Esther considered far too likely.

"What's wrong?" Griff asked.

Esther made herself meet his gaze. "I

think — please understand that I'm only guessing here because of the circumstances, but I think Bethann may have tried to kill herself."

"Naw. Never. She — we —" Griff closed his eyes, and his face twisted. "Why?"

"I don't know if it's even true."

But Bethann wasn't stupid. She could read the label and know better than to drink down three times as much laudanum as the label instructed.

"I could be mistaken," Esther tried again.

The pain on Griff's face sliced through her heart. Her arms ached to reach out and hold him, stroke his hair to soothe him, reassure him everything would be all right. The truth was, however, she didn't think everything would be all right if she didn't do something.

"We need to get her up," Esther said briskly. "We need to get her walking."

"She's unconscious."

"We'll do it for her at first. The coffee may — will — help. Coffee and — and —"

Momma's medical books had mentioned something else to do. Blisters on the arms and legs. No, logic said that wouldn't work. Too slow and painful. Swallow something to make her bring up the poison. But if she wasn't moving at that time, she could choke to death, and the poison seemed too deeply engrained in her system. But something . . . something . . .

Esther grabbed for her satchel and began to plow through its contents, scattering packets of herbs, vials of oil, and a paper of needles until her fingers closed over a flat, green bottle. It was too little too late, but worth a try.

She sprinted for the bed and uncorked the bottle. The stench of ammonia flooded the small, hot room. Esther coughed as she held the vinaigrette under Bethann's nose. "Breathe. Breathe." She cupped the back of Bethann's head and lifted it from the pillow. "Breathe."

Bethann's eyelids twitched. Her head remained as heavy as a rock, the neck muscles not supporting it.

"Breathe, you ungrateful wretch. Your family loves you. You have no right to do this to them. Breathe." She practically stuck the neck of the bottle up Bethann's nostril.

Griff removed it from her hand and set it on the table. "I'll help her up. You go help Momma with the coffee."

"I won't let her die. I won't. I can't. I —" Esther pressed her shaking hands against her face and made herself breathe.

Calm. Calm. Calm.

She puffed out her breath. "I'll help you."

Together they dragged Bethann to her feet. She was as tall as Esther but weighed considerably less. With Griff taking most of her weight, she was no heavier than a child to hold upright and move. They walked her like she was a doll with sawdust filling her limbs instead of flesh and bone. Her legs buckled beneath her. Her head lolled.

Not wanting the children to see, they walked Bethann to the cabin door and back into the bedroom, back and forth, Griff holding her upright, Esther trying to get Bethann's legs to move. Spreading the poison more deeply into her body, or helping her system get rid of it? She didn't know. She had only heard tales of people taking too much of an opiate or hemlock. Most of them died, but not all. They didn't all die.

When they had finished a third circuit and set Bethann on one of the school benches so they could all rest, Mrs. Tolliver arrived with a pot of steaming coffee. "How do we get it down her?"

"We open her mouth and pour in a little at a time." Esther took the pot and cup and poured a bit from one to the other. "I've had a great deal of practice at this lately."

"I noticed." Griff's tone was dry.

Esther frowned at him. "An unconscious

patient will die without nourishment." She sounded prim.

He gave her a half smile and tightened his hold on his sister, alternately patting and shaking her shoulder.

Esther began to administer the coffee. One drop, two. A trickle of the heavy, dark liquid. Not enough to choke her. Esther rubbed Bethann's throat, murmuring for her to swallow.

Coffee ran out of the corner of her mouth.

Mrs. Tolliver wiped it away with the corner of her apron, then dabbed at her eyes. "Don't she know we love her no matter what? I never condemned her for it. Her pa will if he finds out, but I'll see to it he don't. Even last time, he loved that baby when it came. We'd have loved this one too."

Esther let Mrs. Tolliver go on and kept working at dribbling in coffee. "Swallow. Swallow." She rubbed the long, fragile throat. "Swall—"

Bethann swallowed.

Esther and Griff let out a shout of victory.

"Good girl. More. More," Esther urged and poured in more coffee.

Bethann swallowed, choked, and was sick.

"Very good." Esther hugged the older woman. "Get that poison out of you. Let's get her up and moving."

They got her up, stumbling and swaying, but not as much of a dead weight. They gave her more coffee. She swallowed without prompting.

In what must have been hours, Bethann opened her eyes, looked Esther in the face, and said something rather rude.

Mrs. Tolliver gasped. Griff compressed his lips and looked away.

Esther laughed. "I've been called worse when a woman's in the throes of travail. It doesn't kill me."

"I might," Bethann mumbled. "Want . . . to sleep . . . forever."

"That's not your decision to make," Griff said.

"Is that why you drank my laudanum?" Esther held up another cup of the now cold coffee. "Because you knew it could kill you?"

"It said —" Bethann swallowed. "Relief from pain."

"Oh, Bethann." Esther blinked several times, then held the coffee to Bethann's lips. "Drink."

When she refused, Esther poured it in until Bethann needed to swallow or choke. She swallowed, then fixed a blurry green gaze on her brother. "Why?"

"Why what?" Griff held her upright. "Or

more like why did you do it? I was going to let you go. I was going to help you."

"Couldn't waste your money." Bethann's head lolled against his shoulder, and her shoulders heaved with silent sobs.

Esther left Bethann to her brother and mother and went for a walk up the mountain. The boys joined her, and she welcomed their zest for life, their enthusiasm about everything they saw, from a fish visible in the clear waters of their favorite fishing stream to an ugly fungus growing on the side of a fallen log. She drank in their chatter about all they'd been doing while she was at the other side of the ridge, and breathed deeply of the sharp, sweet scents of the forest.

When they wandered off in search of something whose tracks they noticed on the path, she chose a sun-warmed rock beside a stream and stared into the sparkling spill of water, shallow now in the dryness of summer. A swim would refresh her. A swim would cool her. A swim would cleanse her. The waterfall pool called her.

She rose and returned to her patient.

Griff still held Bethann upright on one of the benches. A bowl of soup sat on another bench, half empty. Bethann's face held a hint of color. Griff's carried too many shadows beneath his eyes. Even the bruise and wound on his face, mostly healed now, paled next to the circles of fatigue emphasizing the blue of his eyes.

Esther touched his shoulder. "I'll sit with her for a while so you can rest."

"I have chores."

"Your cousins have done them." Esther settled on Bethann's other side and slipped her arm around the older woman. "Go ahead and get some rest and food and air. I can manage her."

"Like I'm a naughty child," Bethann grumbled.

"You acted like a naughty child." Esther's tone held no sympathy. "That was a stupid thing to do."

"Esther, do you think —" Griff began.

"I should talk to her that way? Someone needs to be honest with her." Esther turned and glared at her. "Your brother just rode a hundred and fifty miles to help you. And you throw that help in his face like it was worthless. Your mother has kept you close and loved you even though your behavior is appalling. And you thank them by shaming them, by interfering with God's plan for your life, by —"

"Esther." Griff rose and gently closed his

hands over her shoulders. "It's all right."

"No, it's not." Tremors ran through Esther, and tears burned her eyes. "It was a cowardly action that didn't take anyone else into consideration."

"Kinda like you coming out here," Griff said.

"I'm still alive."

"Your family doesn't know that."

Esther clenched her teeth against a bubble rising in her throat, which she feared might emerge as a howl or a shriek like a mountain lion.

And Bethann laughed — high-pitched and a little hysterical, but a laugh. "You think you're so smart coming here to teach us ignorant mountain folk how to talk and tossin' around your cures like you're some kind of saint. But you never had nobody hurt you so much that dying seemed better'n livin'."

Esther drew in her breath. She glanced at the orange and gold sunset visible through the open door. She glanced at the patch of gray-blue sky lighting the window. She stared at a stain of spilled coffee on the dirt floor. Then she finally managed to look Bethann in the eye. "You're right. I have never tried to end my life. But I have wondered if continuing to live was worth the effort when I woke up in the morning. I made a mistake that caused someone to die and ruined me so completely I tried hiding amongst you good people."

31

Esther's icy calm sent a chill racing through Griff. No female should be so steady, so unfeeling, after saying what she just had. But there she sat like a statue of a female, drawing him to her to offer comfort, yet repelling him with a chill that said no man could ever reach her heart, and if he stayed, she would wound him too.

He couldn't move, couldn't lift his hands from her shoulders. He tensed, expecting more from her, an explanation, a command to leave her alone.

"You ain't never had a man want someone else more than you," Bethann challenged, " 'cause you're not pretty enough or smart enough, nor got anything to offer."

"No, I haven't." Esther remained straight-backed, her head up, her eyes avoiding Griff's. "I was the one who found them wanting — too old, too fat, smelling too much like fish. Tabitha and Dominick Cherrett's daughter could afford to be choosy." She emitted a laugh a little too high-pitched, too sharp-edged. "Or so I thought until someone decided I needed a lesson in humility."

Griff saw himself on his horse and heading east to Seabourne to learn the identity of the man who had hurt her and teach him a lesson. And for the first time in ten years, he understood Pa's reaction to the man who had ruined Bethann. Love and loyalty could make a man fierce in his heart. He'd never felt this way for Bethann's sake — he'd been quick to find a way to have her gone in the hope of peace.

Guilt punched him in the gut. If he honestly cared about his sister, wouldn't he have wanted to keep her close, ensure she was safe and taking care of herself? No, for the sake of peace, he had been willing to buy her off. For the sake of peace, he'd been willing to simply let Zach court Esther without even considering he might care for her himself. He hadn't fought for her honor; he had robbed her of it, as if he or Zach had ever had a chance with her. Even without her wounded spirit, they weren't the sort of men a female like her chose.

He released Esther and stared at the scars and callouses on his palms and fingers that surely marred her flawless skin — too crude, too rough like other hands that might have, must have —

"Yes, you shouldn't touch me." Esther rose and placed the width of the room between them. "I am not the kind, selfless, and, above all, pure maiden you all thought you hired. I hid the truth for a new start in life, away from the scandal, so my parents could continue serving the Lord who abandoned their daughter."

"God doesn't abandon you, Esther," Griff began.

"It feels like it," Bethann said. "The preacher talks about Jesus loving us, but I never had anyone love me."

"We do," Griff said at the same time Esther exclaimed, "Your family does."

She glided toward Bethann, her hands outstretched, sympathy replacing the coldness her face had held moments earlier. "Bethann, your mother and brother just spent the day saving your life. How can you think they don't love you? They kept you here when they could have sent you away."

"But I was going to do just that." Griff folded his arms across his chest and leaned back against the wall. He understood Esther's expressed desire to run and keep running. The urge plucked at him now, prodding him to move, move, get away to the fields, the mountains, the purity of the waterfall pool, and maybe then find his soul clean.

"I asked you," Bethann admitted. "I wanted to go away."

"Of course you did." Esther brushed limp hair away from Bethann's brow. "A body always wants to run away from one's own guilt."

Bethann flinched but asked, "Were you guilty? I mean, did you deserve the lesson?"

Esther stared down at the floor, her still loose hair forming a veil to hide her face but not her hands, which twisted together at her waist. "I didn't think it was my fault at the time. Now, I don't know. You hear enough bad about yourself, you start to believe it."

"You sure do." Bethann's face softened.

"We never said —" Griff clamped down on the words. They just weren't true. They had all said things critical of Bethann. They had made her name a byword on the mountain with the continuation of the fighting. As apparently Esther's name had become a byword for an evil female in Seabourne, if those letters were only partly to be believed. He ached to help her. He needed to help his sister.

"I shouldn't have said anything against you, Bethann," he began, "even amongst kin. You belong here."

Esther belonged with her family — loved, cherished, guided to the kind of husband she deserved.

"You were happy enough to let me go away." She glared at him.

"I was." Griff cleared his throat. "I'm sorry. You don't need to leave us." He read her bleak expression and added, "I want you to stay where we can take care of you."

"Even now after I — after today?" Again the challenge with a hint of antagonism.

Griff closed the distance between them and took one of Bethann's hands in his. "Especially after today. If you'd like to go back to the house and your own room now . . ." He shot Esther a glance, but she didn't look up.

His heart skittered in his chest as though it were a caged bird. He longed to go to her, pick her up, and hold her until she was at home with him. She was too quiet. He didn't want to leave her. But he couldn't take care of his sister and stay beside Esther. If he left Esther alone, she might not be there when he returned.

And he would return if the Lord was willing. But right then, Bethann needed him, all of them — kin and evidence of God's love for them, for her especially.

"Will you stay, Esther?" he managed to ask.

She didn't answer but stopped twisting her fingers together.

"I don't want to leave you —" he began.

"Not the pretty girl," Bethann muttered with a sneer.

No, not the pretty girl, but the one who spoke her mind a bit and was often cool to cold yet warmed him with a glance. Of course he didn't want to leave her, after she had just admitted to something more awful than he'd imagined when he read the letters.

"Will you come to the house with us?" he asked Esther.

She shook her head, still not looking at him. "I need to be alone."

For a chance to run again?

"I'll be back," he said to Esther, then offered Bethann both his hands.

She took them, but her legs seemed too weak to hold her. She wouldn't let him carry her, so he lifted her to her feet and walked her to the door with his arm around her waist to support her.

"Feed her," Esther said at last. "Give her as much food as you can get her to eat. And don't let her sleep for at least another four hours."

"I'll stay up with her all night." Griff looked back at Esther.

She was pale but composed and looked as isolated and immovable as a rock in the center of the New River.

If he remained with Bethann to ensure she was all right, he would leave Esther in isolation, where she had placed herself. As she thought she deserved to be because . . . He could only guess from what little information she had given them, shared for Bethann's sake.

All the way across the yard, he kept glancing back at the schoolhouse in the hope of seeing her come to the door, raise a hand to him, ensure his patient was all right. He wasn't all right without her. He'd abandoned her. He'd abandoned Bethann. He'd abandoned Zach in his attempts to maintain peace, not trying to learn who had now stabbed them both, if the person were one and the same.

And how many left-handed throwers lived in the mountains?

Griff glanced back at the schoolhouse one more time. Esther had closed the door. It could have been a slap in the face. Yet he didn't blame her. She had shared something intensely private and painful for Bethann's sake, and they had walked away from her as though they believed the worst of her, like the people she must have considered friends had walked away from her. All those people, some of whom had gone to her church. No wonder she thought God didn't care.

No wonder Bethann thought no one cared. Her family defended her honor by killing one another off, and in the end, no one kept thinking it was for her honor; it was for personal revenge for previous injuries. The man who had seduced Bethann, the twenty-five-year-old spinster, was married — if not happily, as his wife had given him no children — and still walked free. Better than free. He was respected for his skills. Griff himself treated the man with respect and trusted him, gave him a position of authority, while being willing to send his sister away.

He held her close for a moment. "Bethann Tolliver, don't you ever do anything so stupid again. Promise."

"I might have killed the — the baby," she whispered in response. "Esther said it might not — I'm an evil woman, Griff. I should go away."

"Remember what the preacher says. God loves us. If you repent, it's all forgiven. And

457

He never stops loving us."

"Huh. Everyone always stops loving me."

"We haven't."

But they had, finding her an irritation, a burden they bore because she was kin.

They reached the back door, and Momma appeared, looking more rested than she had earlier. She drew Bethann to her for a long, silent embrace, then set her in Pa's chair with the arms. "I have rabbit stew for you."

"I'm not hungry." Bethann turned away from the table.

"Esther says we need to feed her," Griff pointed out. "As much as we can."

If Momma would stay with Bethann, he could return to Esther, assure himself she was all right. He kept seeing her standing alone in the schoolroom with the plain, hard benches and no adornment except herself, with her dark veil of hair hiding her face from him as though she were shamed by it.

And maybe she was. Maybe her beauty had led her astray.

He sank onto the bench beside the stove, though it was too hot there for the summer night. He watched Momma coax Bethann to take a few bites of the savory stew and wished for Esther to be beside him where he could protect her. If she could talk to him . . .

As though she would confide in a crude man like him. No wonder she had flinched away from him so much. The thought of a man touching her must have repulsed her. She hadn't said, and he was only guessing, but he figured his guess was right. Whereas Bethann had been willing, Esther had not. No wonder she ran off into the woods when Zach grew too friendly at the dance.

And yet she had let Griff hold her, kiss her. Before that, she claimed she didn't like to be touched, yet she sat close beside him and let him hold her hands when teaching her the dulcimer.

Because he was doing something for her. She was repaying him for his help, as she had repaid him for rescuing her on the mountain that night. And he thought she cared.

He scrubbed his hands over his face as though that could wipe away memory, thoughts, fears.

He surged to his feet and began to pace the kitchen. He needed a run up the mountain, a swim in the pool, anything but being caged there in the house while Esther was alone. Yet he must stay with his sister, help Momma watch Bethann to ensure she was all right and didn't do something crazy again.

He strode to the parlor and returned with his dulcimer tucked beneath his arm. "If you don't think it'll wake the young'uns," he said to Momma.

"Naw, go ahead. If it does, they'll like it."

So he played. He strummed and plucked and let the music flow from his fingers through the strings and then his voice and into the night.

I'm just a poor, wayfaring stranger.
I'm traveling through this world of woe.
Yet there's no sickness, toil nor danger
In that bright land to which I go.
I'm going there to see my father.
I'm going there no more to roam.
I'm only going over Jordan.
I'm only going over home.

I know dark clouds will gather 'round me.
I know my way is rough and steep.
Yet golden fields lie just before me
Where God's redeemed shall ever sleep.
I'm going there to see my father.
He said he'd meet me when I come.
I'm only going over Jordan.
I'm only going over home.

I want to wear a crown of glory
When I get home to that good land.

I want to shout salvation's story
In concert with the blood-washed band.
I'm going there to meet my Saviour
To sing his praise forever more.
I'm just a-going over Jordan.
I'm just a-going over home.

32

Esther stood in the doorway to the school-house and drank in the music like nourishment. The rich timbre of Griff's voice smoothed over her spirit like a healing balm, an ointment guaranteed to soften the tensest of muscles.

Or melt the hardest of hearts.

Run. Run. Run, her spirit cried. *Get away before you're lost.*

Her leg muscles tensed as though she would take flight that moment, race down the track leading back to civilization, back to a family who did love her, who always wanted the best for her. Yet she could not go. Could not. Could not. Could not. But how could she stay now that she had all but told them the truth about herself, told them how she had been broken beyond repair?

It revolted Griff. She felt his tension, knew the instant he released her he would never want to touch her again. He got himself and his sister away as fast as he could.

Yet he'd asked her to stay.

Of course he had. She was useful to them. Bethann still needed help. If the opium had destroyed the life inside her, she would find herself in serious trouble. Esther hadn't said so, but that could kill her where the laudanum had failed. Perhaps Esther's skills would be good enough to save Bethann in such a horrible event.

But she had helped to save Zach. Dear Zach, who thought her pure and innocent and next in line to the angels. She should have told him the truth straightaway, squelched any notions he possessed about making her his bride. But she feared being sent away. She wanted to stay. Knowing now that the Tollivers would likely ask her to leave, she wanted nothing more than to remain right where she was, teaching the children and learning the mountain by day, drinking the music by night.

I know dark clouds will gather 'round me. I know my way is rough and steep . . .

Not a cloud marred the sky, though the sultry stillness of the air and the rings around the three-quarter moon riding high above the treetops promised rain before dawn. It would keep them all inside, other than doing their chores. She would be shut out, away from the love and laughter, away from the music, away from Griff. All for the best. She knew better than to let herself care. He, like Zach, had been attracted to her outward beauty. When he learned what lay inside, the desire for her left.

She closed the door and slammed the bolt home, then retreated to her room. The hairpins and length of ribbon lay on the washstand. She snatched up the former and began to wind up her hair, draw it back, and skewer it into the most severe bun she could manage. If anything, that was worse. It emphasized the fine bones of her face rather than obscuring them. With her hair down, she looked like a wanton. What had Griff said? It gave a man notions about seeing it spread out on his pillow.

If the mirror had belonged to her, she would have smashed it against the wall.

She put out the light so she couldn't see herself and climbed into bed. Every bone and muscle in her body ached, her heart worst of all. She had known too little sleep over the past few weeks, and now sheer exhaustion overcame her will to keep listening to the music drifting through her window.

But sleep didn't conquer the rumble of thunder echoing off the mountains and the roar of rain pounding on her roof, blowing in through the open window, and pouring through a leak in the roof over the school-room.

"The new chalks!" She sprang from bed and ran barefoot into the other room. The storm had found a weak point in a corner, well away from anything important save the floor. Esther set the washbasin beneath the leak, then ran back to her room to light the lantern and dress. She needed a bucket. The basin wouldn't hold enough. The barn held buckets — maybe one rested outside the kitchen door too.

She tossed her cloak over her shoulders and drew up the hood. It didn't help much. Rain soaked through the wool in moments. Her boots dragged in a yard suddenly turned to a sea of churning mud, and the lantern became a useless metal burden with the candle unable to stay lit.

Esther could barely stay upright in the buffeting wind. She slipped and slid and used intermittent flashes of lightning to find her way to the barn, where relative dryness met her with the scents of horses and cows, hay, and the not altogether unpleasant odor of manure mixed with the straw on the floor. Horses stamped and snorted in their stalls at each roll of thunder. A hoof struck the wooden partition. She should get out. If the beast broke loose, he could run amok in a closed barn and trample her as she tried to escape.

She snatched up a bucket from beside the door and turned to go. A lull had come. She might reach her room without further soaking herself. And the horses had calmed for the moment.

She lifted the latch and then heard it, a low, groaning mew.

"Kitten?" She cocked her head, listening for the sound again.

"Ma-row." It sounded like it was in pain, injured. Perhaps by one of the horses? Cats were known to go into horse stalls in pursuit of mice trying to get at the grain. If so, she couldn't leave it.

She set down the bucket and moved forward, her hands held out before her to find her way between the boxes. "Kitten?" she called again.

"Ow-row." The sound dropped onto her ears.

It was in the hayloft.

Esther groped in the darkness until she located the ladder, then she climbed, her skirt tucked into her waist sash, her cloak neglected on the barn floor. "Where are you, little one?"

466

She heard a meow again, then a squeak. A mouse? Oh no, she wasn't moving toward a cat with a cornered mouse. The idea sent a shudder through her. She paused, heard the squeak again, and laughed. No, not a mouse, a kitten.

Outside, rain gushed and poured off the eaves of the barn. Lightning flashed, and the thunder rumbled and roared again and again and again as it bounced from mountain to mountain.

Inside the hayloft, Esther sat cross-legged beside one of the feral cats she had befriended and marveled at the ease and calm with which she delivered four damp, hairless balls. How she licked each one clean and guided it to nourishment.

" 'I will praise thee; for I am fearfully and wonderfully made: marvellous are thy works; and that my soul knoweth right well,' " she quoted from Psalm 139. "God's hand even in these tiny creatures."

If God cared about such tiny beings, how could He not care about the human beings He had created to have communion with Him?

Esther stroked the momma cat's head. She purred and snuggled more deeply into the nest of hay she had made for herself and her new family.

"If women gave birth so easily, little one, there'd be no need for midwives."

And the pain struck again, her lack of a place in the world. Midwives were growing out of fashion. In trying to help Bethann understand she wasn't alone in suffering pain deep to the heart at the hands of someone else, Esther had ruined herself there on the mountain, as she had in Seabourne. She had some healing skill, but she wasn't a doctor. As the mountain grew more civilized, one would come and resent her intrusion.

"So how can I believe You care, God?" Her cry rang from her heart, yet it was too quiet for anyone or anything other than the cat and her new offspring to hear. "You gave me so much — looks, intelligence, a loving and wonderful family. And now . . ."

A simultaneous thunder blast and lightning strike shook the barn. The horses' whinnies sounded like screams, and the cows mooed with as much emotion as placid beasts could produce. Silent now, the momma cat curled herself around the kittens.

Esther clambered to her feet. She had forgotten about the leak in the schoolroom roof. The place would be flooded.

She headed for the ladder but stopped,

nostrils flaring. Yes, she smelled smoke. Most definitely smelled smoke.

She tumbled down the ladder, snatched up her cloak, and charged from the barn, then ran back to grab up a bucket and departed again. The smoke burned stronger; the rain fell lighter.

Not now. Not now. If something was burning, they needed the rain, the wet.

She glanced around, seeking flames — the barn, the house, the chicken coop.

Her cabin. Against a patch of clear, starry sky, a plume of smoke bloomed as though someone had lit a fire on the hearth. Probably a lightning strike on the roof.

"Nooo!" She raced across the yard, slipping and sliding in the mud.

Everything she owned lay in that cabin — her pictures, her books, the curl of embroidered ribbon Griff had given her.

She flung open the door. No flames she could see, just heavy, oily smoke like burning pitch. Of course. Pine logs. A pine-shake roof saturated with the oil of the sap and smoky before bursting into flames. She might have minutes; she might have seconds.

She dropped to all fours and began to crawl. Her dress caught on the rough floor and ripped. Another gown ruined. They'd all be ruined if she didn't reach her room.

She pushed open that door. Less smoke. Cool, sweet air flowing through the window —

And a flash of heat behind her.

She whirled, caught the flame curling across the floor, and threw her cloak atop it. The wet wool smothered it, but another flame near the window burned more insistently, sparkling off broken glass.

A lightning strike that broke a window?

No time to think of that. She slammed the door and began snatching her things from tables and pegs. Books, clothes, and satchel ended up in a jumble atop the coverlet. She wrapped it together and tossed it out of the window.

A line of red-gold ran beneath the door. *No more time.*

She scrambled to her feet, coughing from the smoke, and stumbled to the window. Her skirt was still tucked inside her sash. She raised her leg to climb over the sill. A bit too high for that. And the opening was too small. Surely too small for her to go through. She beat on the frame with her fists. The nails groaned but held fast. She needed something stronger than she was. Someone stronger than she was. But the family slept, exhausted from the ordeal with

Bethann, the noise hidden by the storm.

She heard the flames now with only the door and fireplace between her and fire. In the darkness, she peered around for a ram, something with which to batter at the window frame.

She grabbed the washstand. The pitcher slid to the floor and shattered like the glass in the other room.

Don't think. Don't think. Don't think.

She hefted the stand and slammed it against the window frame. More glass broke. Arms aching, she slammed it again. Nails shrieked. Heart pounding out of her chest, she heaved the stand again.

The window frame and remaining shards of glass fell atop her bundle. She tumbled after them, catching her diaphragm against the edge of the opening. Winded, she hung there for a moment, arms, legs, body shaking, flames eating through the door behind her.

Somehow she must find the strength to crawl through the opening, get away, get her things away. Her breath whooped and wheezed through her lungs. She couldn't drag herself to safety. She was trapped with the building burning around her.

Then she heard it, the sound of Griff call-

471

ing her name, louder, louder, coming toward her.

She raised her head. "Here! I'm —" Her voice broke on a spasm of coughing.

But he was there, grasping her beneath her arms and hauling her through the open window. He held her tightly against him, murmuring something against her hair, then set her down. "Can you walk?"

"Yes. Yes, I'm all right." She sank to her knees. "My things. Must get my things."

"Here." Griff scooped up the bundle and strode away from the cabin.

Esther grabbed up a shoe, a mud-splattered book, and her satchel, which had fallen out of the bundle, then followed. Behind her, the fire burst through the door and into her room.

Griff deposited her things inside the kitchen, then snatched up the two buckets by the back door and left. The rest of the family save for Bethann streamed into the kitchen and fanned out the door, calling directions, asking questions, working as a team that had either practiced or had experience with fire. They pumped water. They filled pails and carried them to the fire. Even Mr. Tolliver participated.

After a moment's hesitation, Esther joined them. The building couldn't be saved. They could only ensure that between the soaking rain and the water they poured over the fire, they could keep it from spreading to the wooden stockade fence or one of the other buildings, now that the rising wind was blowing the storm across the ridge.

It took until dawn and then some to subdue the blaze down to nothing more than smoldering ruins, partial walls, and a collapsed stone chimney. Esther's hands and arms ached from the strain of carrying the heavy buckets by their wire bails. She plodded rather than walked. She couldn't run like Jack and Ned, tireless as always, shouting, exclaiming over every shower of sparks shooting into the sky like fireworks for a celebration. Liza and Brenna pumped, filled, and carried with the same energy as their younger brothers, at least twice as much as Esther managed. Slow. She was so slow. The mud splashed up to her knees, and she had to wade through it to move a step. Her head pounded and she kept coughing. Then she picked up a bucket and her hands gave way. Her fingers simply refused to curl around the twisted wire handle.

She dropped to her knees and held her hands to the crimson light fingering its way through the haze topping the mountains.

From the centers of her palms to the tips of her fingers, blisters covered her hands, blisters that had formed, broken, and re-formed. For the first time in her life, she didn't think about protecting her precious midwife's hands.

33

The schoolroom and Esther's chamber collapsed in on themselves with a final shower of sparks barely visible against the rising sun. The yard around it was a churned-up sea of mud. The air and everyone nearby reeked of smoke. And Esther discovered that besides her blistered hands, somewhere along the way her hair had gotten singed.

She sat on a chair outside the kitchen door while Mrs. Tolliver took a pair of shears to the frizzed and uneven ends. What felt like ten pounds fell from Esther's head and onto the ground. The waves turned to curling tendrils that bounced and coiled around her shoulders. She tried to pin it up, but it refused to stay in the pins as though it had a life of its own. After a lifetime of always being the neatest person in any room she graced, she looked like her brothers did when they returned from one of their merchant sailing excursions — unkempt and a bit wild.

"You need a ribbon," Liza said. "I have some."

"I have one." Esther retrieved the embroidered satin ribbon from her salvaged belongings. "It's so pretty."

"Too pretty to put on your hair until you can wash it. It's a bit sooty."

Brushing had helped some, but they all looked grimy without the time or energy to draw water for eight individual baths.

"Use this." Liza produced a faded bit of calico sewn into a long, thin strip.

Esther tied her hair back, her fingers stiff from the blisters. The lack of piles of hair atop her head gave her a sense of freedom. Dressed in one of Liza's gowns, a good enough fit except for being too short, she looked young, more Liza's age than her own, especially with a smudge of soot still running along her hairline.

"I look like a ragamuffin," she exclaimed.

Not the beauty of Seabourne, Virginia. Not a beauty at all. And not a midwife with her hands so sore and blistered. She should feel free.

She felt adrift, a part of nothing and very, very dirty. First she washed her clothes, a torture to her hands as she scrubbed her few remaining garments, then hung them

476

up to dry in the brilliant sunlight. Somehow she must obtain fabric and sew more. She couldn't possibly go about with only two dresses, and neither of them a good one. In the dark, she hadn't known what she snatched, and she hadn't taken her riding habit or her best dress. Her gray one with the faint bloodstain and a plain blue linen were all that had survived. Even her cloak was gone.

But she had her fine shoes. Silly creature that she was, she had managed to save all her shoes, from her riding boots to a pair of plain leather slippers to blue satin dancing slippers that had matched the one truly fine gown she'd brought along. And she had her books. Those were harder to replace than dresses.

"We'll manage more for you." Liza helped Esther hang up her petticoats. "Uncle Elias's wife makes the finest cloth on the ridge. And I sew a fine seam."

"You do. Your needlework is exquisite. How did you learn?"

Liza shrugged. "Momma taught me. I . . . well, I wasn't going to show you this yet . . ." Liza ran into the house and emerged a few minutes later to show Esther a length of fabric about six inches wide and covered with tiny blue flowers. "To sew on your gray dress to cover up that stain and make it pretty."

"Liza . . ." Esther's throat closed. She blinked hard to clear tears from her eyes.

She had received many fine gifts in her life. Her English relatives liked lavishing their wealth on their poor American relations, who weren't particularly poor at all, especially once her brothers started earning a living in trade. But they sent her patterns and the fabrics to make herself gowns too fine for Seabourne, fans from Paris, and hats from Italy. Her shoes were fashioned of the finest Moroccan leather, and she even owned a muff of Russian sable, which due to the mild climate of the coast never saw use. They were all the fripperies money could buy.

No money could buy the love and attention that went into this length of homespun linen stitched with cotton floss.

"You don't like it?" Liza's lower lip quivered.

"Liza." Esther cleared her throat. "I've never received a more precious gift." She hugged the younger woman. "Thank you."

"It's nothin', really." Liza kicked at the mud. "Bethann said as how you're not as good as we all thought you were and we should send you about your business, but I don't believe her?" Her declaration ended with a question.

"I suppose that's up to your mother to decide. You can ask her what Bethann told her." Esther busied herself hanging a chemise so gauzy and lacy, her face heated at the notion that everyone could see it. So far, she had hung her under things to dry inside her room to preserve her modesty. Now ruffles and beribboned trims fluttered in the breeze for all to see.

For Griff to see.

Except he hadn't been around all day. He'd inhaled a cup of steaming coffee in the kitchen, then vanished somewhere beyond the compound. If something went well for her, her clothes would dry before he returned.

She didn't have time to concern herself about that, for Mrs. Tolliver set them all to work cleaning debris from her kitchen garden and picking up fallen branches around the compound to use as kindling. Esther worked beside the others, but her hands hurt so badly, tears sprang unbidden to her eyes, and when she wiped them away, she saw blood on her fingers where more blisters had broken.

"I have to take care of my hands," she said to anyone within hearing distance and ran across the yard. Her satchel contained an ointment she thought might help — lavender and rose hips, fragrant and soothing. She stood at the kitchen table trying to apply it to herself.

"Let me help." Griff appeared in the kitchen doorway, filling it.

She glanced at him. "You've managed to miss out on the hard work."

"I've been inspecting storm damage at the mine and about, making sure we don't have flooding to worry us none."

"Oh." She regretted her acid tongue. "I should have thought of that."

"No reason why. You're a town girl." He touched her shoulder. "I need to talk to you."

"About . . . what?" She discovered she was trembling, certain he had drawn the worst conclusions from what she'd admitted to Bethann and was about to send her away.

He came to the table and took the salve from her hands. "About the fire. What do you need me to do?"

"Rub it in."

"My fingers are rough. I might hurt you."

"You won't."

She had hurt herself by letting herself fall in love with him.

"You have such pretty hands." He cradled

one in his palm and used the gentle touch he applied to the dulcimer strings to smooth salve over her blisters. "I hate to see them marred."

As calloused and scarred as his hands were, they were beautiful, so broad and strong, so tender and sensitive. He could wield an ax that split a log in two, or he could coax heart-stirring music from a set of thin strings. He didn't know Shakespeare or John Milton or Henry Fielding, but he knew a hundred hymns of praise and ballads. He didn't know much Scripture, but he knew the Lord loved him, the difference between the right way and the wrong way to treat people, and how to love. He worked hard without complaint and took the time to show someone else the grandeur of his mountains.

How could she have ever flirted with a soulless man like Alfred Oglevie — for however short a time she had considered him a potential suitor — when men like Griffin Tolliver existed?

She bent her head and kissed the back of his hand.

His fingers stilled. "Why? To thank me for helping you on Independence Day?"

"No." She looked him in the eye. "Because I have never met a finer man."

"A finer man would have protected you last night."

"You saved me. I was stuck in that window until you came along."

"You'd have gotten out, I reckon." He released her hand and lifted a strand of her hair to the light. "How did it happen, do you think?"

Esther shrugged. "I don't know. Lightning? I'm not sure where the fire was when I ran into the cabin."

"When you ran into —" Griff's hand dropped onto her shoulder. "Where were you?"

"I was in the barn. There was a leak in the roof, so I went for a bucket and then heard the cat in labor."

"So you went to help, of course?" His eyes were soft as they gazed down at her.

She licked suddenly dry lips. "She didn't need me, but I wanted to be there. New life —" She lowered her gaze to her blistered palms, considerably better for the salve. "It's beautiful to see happen. I mean, it's messy, but it's . . . special."

"I think you —" He touched her face. "Tell me exactly what happened after that." His voice was tight, his body tense.

Esther's brows arched. "I, um, smelled smoke and went hunting for the source."

482

His hand dropped to one of hers. "Did you know your room was burning before you went in?"

"Yes, but I had to save something of mine. It's all I have and —"

"You went into a burning building for things?" His eyes glittered, sparkled like moonlight — or was it firelight? — on broken glass. "That was right idiotic of you, wasn't it?"

"Yes, but I'm all right and have some things. But Griff —" She leaned away from a sudden intensity in his gaze. "I didn't tell you. With everything else, I forgot to tell you that something broke that window before the fire started."

"You mean someone." He spun away on his heel and began to pace the kitchen. "I knew it. I knew something was just wrong about that fire. And if you'd been there —" He swung toward her, wrapped his arms around her, and held her close. "That fire wasn't set by no lightning strike. Someone set it o'purpose."

"I know." She was shaking, and he held her more tightly. She could scarcely breathe and didn't care. "But they didn't want to kill me. Surely they didn't want to kill me. No one hates me that much. Please —"

"Shh." He tilted her head back and kissed

her, drawing away slowly at the sound of footfalls outside the kitchen door. He smiled. "One way to stop you from talking too much."

"I don't talk too much."

"No, ma'am, sometimes you don't talk enough, but talk now." He glanced past her. "Bethann, are you all right?"

"Right enough." She stepped into the kitchen. "I wanta hear about how that fire got started. It were a Brooks, weren't it?"

"We can't reach that conclusion." Griff caught Esther's gaze. "Your trouble back home didn't follow you here, did it?"

"No."

"There was that note," he pointed out.

"I think Hannah wrote it."

"Hannah!" the two Tollivers exclaimed.

"Why would Hannah want rid of you?" Griff asked.

Esther told them of her conversation with Hannah while she busied herself replacing the lid on the jar of ointment and stowing it in her bag. "She seemed distressed about something, but while I was there these past two weeks, she was . . . friendly. She's also —" She paused. That wasn't something she should share.

The Tollivers looked at her expectantly.

"Nothing important. The menfolk aren't

484

around much, is all."

And Henry Gosnoll barely spoke to his wife.

"I'm going over there." Griff strode to the door, his face a taut mask, expression inscrutable.

Esther gazed down at the dress whose skirt ended at the top of her boots. "I'd like to go too and ensure Zach is healing well."

And ensure Griff didn't do something stupid.

"If you'll wait long enough for me to change my dress," she concluded.

Bethann said nothing. She simply walked out of the house and across the yard, still appearing weak, but her head high.

"I'll wait." He followed his sister from the house, then crossed the yard to the burned-out schoolhouse.

Esther snatched her dress off the line and ran upstairs to change. How she would love a bath or a swim before donning the clean clothes. No time to concern herself about that. Griff might not wait for her. The day was wasting if they wanted to get over the ridge before sundown.

Perhaps she should stop him from going. He couldn't ride up and make accusations against Hannah without trouble.

Esther's fingers stilled on the hooks at her

neck. Making trouble. Someone had been trying to make trouble between the families since Griff had been ambushed on the road east. Everyone denied it. Yet someone was guilty. Bethann wanting revenge for being jilted again? Zach or Hannah? Griff? None should have any kind of reason for wanting trouble. They should want peace. Someone did not.

Heart heavy, Esther descended the steps to find Griff waiting for her with saddled horses. As though she weighed nothing, he lifted her onto the mare's back, then mounted and led the way up the track toward the Brookses' compound.

Riding single file on separate mounts, they couldn't talk quietly enough to keep their voices from ringing through the forest. Esther kept pondering how trouble could benefit anyone. Hannah had won over Bethann in getting the husband. Zach and Griff were friends. Or had been friends until she came along. Now they seemed at odds, trying to outdo one another in giving her attention. At least Zach had. Griff hadn't really pursued her. He had seen to her welfare. He had taught her the dulcimer because she wanted him to. But Zach had pursued her. Every time she and Griff seemed to be edging toward a line between friendship and courtship, Zach grew ardent in his attentions as though —

As though trying to make Griff jealous?

Esther edged her mare up beside Griff's gelding despite the narrowness of the track. "Why would the Brookses want to make trouble?"

"You mean start the fighting again?" Griff reined in and looked at her. "I've been pondering on that but don't know for certain. They'd have to get rid of all of us Tollivers to get ahold of the mine for themselves. And same with the land."

"What about why the feuding started?"

Griff bowed his head. "I'm ashamed to say my pa started it. He tried to shoot Henry Gosnoll at his wedding but got the bride's eldest brother instead. It was . . . bloody."

"I'm sorry." She rested her hand on his. "I can't even think how that must have been."

"I vowed that day to keep peace. Things'd be quiet for a while, then someone would get ahold of that Gosnoll whiskey and things'd start up again over nothing much. But the preacher tried to bring peace about, got Zach and me to make that vow." He flashed her a quick smile. "It's one I've managed to keep."

"But not Zach." She touched the healing mark on his face.

"Not Zach." He turned his head toward a stand of walnut trees, as solid as the mountain and a hundred feet high if they were twenty. "Zach has just never been as good at things as I am. Everything I've done, he's tried to do, and most of the time he don't do so well."

"Envy is a powerful emotion."

"I expect you'd know that, you being so pretty and smart and kind." The tenderness of his look melted her, scrambled her insides.

She worried her lower lip. "I'm not that kind, Griff. You're kind. Zach is kind. I'm probably thinking the wrong way."

"We can only know if we ask." He nudged his mount forward, and they began the downhill trek to the Brookses' holding.

They tethered their mounts outside the gate, where lush meadow grass gave them fodder. Then they approached the house side by side.

Hannah greeted them on the front steps. "What you doing here?"

"I came to see how Zach goes on." Esther offered a friendly smile and hefted her satchel.

"And we need to talk," Griff added. "To

488

all of you."

"Talk." Hannah curled her upper lip. "I thought Tollivers shot first and talked later."

"Maybe so, but I want to talk now."

"And I do need to look in on the patient." Esther's voice was too bright, too cheerful.

Wordlessly, Hannah twitched around and led the way into the house, into the parlor, where Zach half sat, half lay against the wall and a pile of pillows. He smiled at Esther but gave Griff a wary glance.

"How's the wound?" Esther asked. "Any more fever?"

He held out his hands to her. "I'll do better for you coming back to me."

"She didn't come back to you." Griff's tone was cold. "Twice you've foisted your attentions on her when she didn't want them. At least twice I've seen."

Twice he'd seen. Twice Zach had done so. The rest of the time, the times when Griff wasn't around, Zach was a perfect gentleman.

Esther sank to her knees on the floor beside Zach's bed. "Why, Zach? Why do you try to get me to kiss you or look like I will when Griff is around, but not otherwise?"

"I don't know what you're talking about." But his eyes shifted to the right, then down, avoiding her gaze. "Just a coincidence."

489

"I don't think so." She began to ache inside, struggling to set aside old images. "You think Griff likes me, and you want him to think I favor you. Why?"

Zach plucked at the quilt covering him and stared at his restless fingers as though sewing a fine seam. "I'm tired of pretending all's right between the families. It ain't and it ain't never going to be. I thought maybe for once I could get something he wanted."

"I didn't know I wanted her," Griff said. "Not at first."

"You thinking I'll believe that?" Zach glared at his cousin. "I saw the first day you met how it would be. You two flirting like we might as well have planned a wedding right then."

"I didn't — we didn't —" Esther shook her head and fixed her eyes on Hannah. "Is that why you wanted me to go away? So there wouldn't be trouble between them?"

"I heard things in Seabourne." Hannah met Esther's eyes, hers unnaturally bright. "Didn't think you was good enough for either of them if they was true."

"They are." Esther swallowed. "Mostly anyway. And I'm not."

Zach's head snapped up. The floorboards creaked beneath Griff's feet as he shifted. She didn't dare look at him.

490

"So you did write that first note?" he asked Hannah. "Did you start the fire?"

"We don't need strangers here stirring up trouble." Tears began to trickle down Hannah's lovely face. "Especially not her kind."

"Hannah, be quiet," Zach commanded.

"Did you want to start the fighting again?" Griff sounded accusatory, appalled. "Hannah Brooks Gosnoll, do you want more kin to die?"

"If it's the right ones." She twisted her hands together around her apron. Fabric tore, and she kept twisting. Her face twisted.

Esther stared at her. The woman was unwell in her mind. Too much pain from being married ten years to a man she probably was never sure cared for her, a man she knew had helped start a war. Perhaps the deaths themselves.

"Hannah." Griff took a step toward her, his body and voice controlled. "Did you stab me and your brother to make trouble?"

"I — I —" Hannah raised her apron to wipe her cheeks. "It's my husband I want dead, the cheating, lying —"

"Hannah!" Zach cried. "Stop it. You can't mean it."

"Then who stabbed them?" Esther asked.

Hannah's gaze slid past Griff. "Ask her."

They turned to see Bethann standing in

the doorway.

"I didn't do nothing but believe her cheating, lying husband," Bethann said. "He was going to go away with me, take the money from the mine ore sale this month and go off with me, but he decided to stay with his wife."

"He did?" Hannah's eyes widened. "You mean I . . ."

"You what, Hannah? Tried to start the feud again so one of us would kill him?" Griff speared his fingers through his hair. "Oh, Hannah."

"She didn't admit to nothing," Zach pointed out. "You need to ask your sister if she tried starting the feud again."

Everyone faced Bethann.

She looked paler than ever but held her hands on her hips in a belligerent stance. "Why would I start the feud again when I was thinking Henry was going off with me?"

"But I can't throw a knife any good," Hannah said.

"Nor," Esther murmured, "can you tell the truth. You told me you can't write, but that's a fine hand on that note I got. Why should we believe you over Bethann, who has always been truthful?"

"No she ain't!" Hannah cried, pointing her finger. "She lied about my husband ten

492

years ago, and she lied about him this time. He's done cheated on me, but not with her."

"He has!" Bethann cried. "He said he loves me."

"You're wrong," Hannah said. "You couldn't get into trouble with him 'cause he . . . can't."

"Then how is it you are preg— expecting, Hannah?" Esther asked.

"I — I'm not." Hannah whitened around her mouth.

Bethann made a strangled noise in her throat and stumbled out of the doorway, out of the house.

Zach stared at his sister. "You always said that's how you knew the Tollivers were lying, 'cause Bethann had a baby and Henry never fathered any young'uns on his women or you. But now, if you —"

"She's wrong. I'm not," Hannah protested.

Esther rose and crossed the room to stand over Hannah. "You've known since before you stabbed Griff, haven't you? You are far enough along that everyone would notice if you didn't wear that apron. But I know the signs. I've watched women for all my life. My mother taught me what to look for."

"I thought you were more interested in watching men," Hannah spat out. "Or is it having them watch you?"

"That's enough," Griff said. "This isn't Esther's fight."

"How could you want to see your baby's father killed?" Esther persisted. "Or his uncle or grandfather? Life is sacred, a gift from God. We can't waste it like that, toss it aside like it's rubbish."

"And what would you know, with your whoring ways that caused a baby's mother to die?" Hannah lashed out.

"I'm not . . . like that." Esther wrapped her arms across her middle as though Hannah's words were physical blows. "It's lies. What you heard, it's all lies. I never . . . I didn't . . ." She wanted to curl up on the floor and hide. She remained upright and facing the other woman straight on to watch her, to avoid seeing Griff's reaction to Hannah's words. "I made a mistake in going to the Oglevies' without my mother. I knew what he was like. I thought it was my duty, but I was wrong, and the consequences were tragic." She gasped for air, battered by the shock and horror on the others' faces. "Please, listen to me. What happened is how I know that this can't go on. Griff and Zach nearly died. I could have died in that fire. Many people could die in a feud, not just your husband. Maybe not him at all. He survived so far. How can you throw away the gift of life God has given us, given you now?" She dropped to her knees and laid her hand on Hannah's belly, firm and starting to round. "You can't carry this hate to another generation."

"Are you Saint Esther recommending forgiveness?" Hannah's lip curled in a sneer.

Esther's mouth twisted into a wry smile. "Yes'm, I guess I am."

Good advice she could never carry out, as she would never have another generation to bring up the right way — in love and forgiveness — now that Griff had heard too much about her and would want to know more. Regardless, she couldn't continue to hate Alfred Oglevie.

Some of her burden lifted.

"My own s-sister." Zach's voice shook. "Me trying to keep you from Griff is one thing. I did care for you, Esther, before Hannah told me what she'd learned, but this . . . my own sister . . . Griff, what do we do with her?"

"I think she and Henry need to go away from here." Griff's voice was too quiet, too calm. "We'll tell him the truth about what she's done and intended, and he can see to her."

Esther swung around and stared at him.

"But she's not right, Griff. There are places, special hospitals —"

His jaw hardened. "We take care of our own kin here."

"I'll give them my profits from the mine," Zach said.

"That's right generous of you, Zach." Griff bent down to shake Zach's hand, then crossed the room to take Hannah's arm. "Come along, Hannah." His demeanor, his voice, held that tenderness that would forever melt Esther's heart when she thought of it. "You need your momma right now." And he led Hannah, docile as a kitten, from the room.

Esther glanced at Zach. "What exactly did Hannah tell you?"

"She found your letters. She read them, even though she claims she can't read. They said enough to let me know you're not good enough for Griff."

She flinched and gave him a smile that quivered at the corners. "I knew that all along. I tried not to love him. But I failed."

34

Griff caught up with her before she reached the thickest part of the forest. The hooves of his horse beat against the hard ground like a drumbeat of warning, and Esther reined in to wait for him.

"When are you going to stop running away?" he asked.

"When my past stops catching up with me."

"Yes'm." He looked at her, his eyes luminous beneath the trees. "I can't believe you have a past worthy of such meanness."

"Believe it," Esther said. "It's what drove me here. It's what will drive me somewhere else."

"Nobody's driving you anywhere." Impatience edged his tone. "You're going on your own.

"In the end it's the same."

"Esther . . ." The path narrowed. He dropped back behind her and called out,

"You've got to tell me, you know."

"I know. I should have a long time ago."

But they went back to the house first to put up the horses and see if anyone had seen Bethann.

"She's in her room," Mrs. Tolliver said. "Came home looking like she was in one of them there trances and went right up. What happened?"

Griff told her.

"Is it over then?" Mrs. Tolliver asked, wiping tears from her eyes. "Will the fighting stop now?"

"I reckon it will without anyone fanning the flames." Griff kissed his mother's cheek. "I'm taking Esther up to the waterfall. She needs a swim to get all that soot off of her."

"It ain't right," Mrs. Tolliver said. "I should send Liza along."

"If you trust your son, Mrs. Tolliver, I'm safe with him." Esther retrieved the only bar of soap she had left, one salvaged from her satchel, and slipped it into her pocket.

The swim in the pool she would enjoy. Talking to Griff she would not. For the time being, she savored their closeness. Side by side they headed out of the compound. He tucked her hand into the crook of his arm, then covered it with his free one as they climbed the wide part of the track in silence.

Not until the path narrowed, and he indicated that Esther should follow so he could clear the way of branches fallen from the storm, did he speak.

"I've been a poor cousin to Hannah. I didn't realize how much she hated her husband for his wandering."

"Could you have stopped him?"

"I s'pose not. But maybe reined him in."

"He's a man grown, Griff, and not your responsibility."

Griff snorted. "Sometimes I think everyone on this mountain is my responsibility."

"And you take the burden upon yourself rather than letting the Lord do it for you?" Esther couldn't help but tweak him a bit.

"Miss Esther Cherrett preaching to me." He moved beside her and squeezed her hand. "I thought you believed the Lord doesn't care about us as individuals anymore."

"I think He must care about you, you're so good and kind."

"But not you?"

"I'm . . . lost somewhere."

The darkness beneath the trees surrounded them, a hush between birdsong and cicada chatter. Griff's muscled forearm rippled beneath her fingers, so sturdy, so dependable, carrying too much weight with even her hand.

"We are never lost to the Lord, only to other people and ourselves."

"I used to believe that." The constant ache of emptiness inside her tore a bit wider with the knowledge that she would lose this man too — all part of her folly that began two years earlier.

Griff stroked her hand. "Surely your parents have told you otherwise."

"My parents are the most loving people I know — next to you."

"That's kind of you to say so, but it ain't true, you know. If I'd been a better, more loving brother to Bethann, if I hadn't wanted rid of her, she wouldn't have drunk that laudanum."

"Perhaps not. Perhaps she would have. Most families would have gotten rid of her as soon as they knew she was, um, increasing."

"As I said, we take care of our own here." Griff lifted a limb as thick as his arm that hung precariously over the path. "Go ahead. I'll take this down before it falls on someone."

Esther took several steps beyond him, then turned back. He snapped off the limb as though it were a twig, then cleared it off the path, alongside a sapling half uprooted and leaning against its neighboring brother spruce. His powerful muscles moved as smooth as water beneath his simple clothes. He apparently had taken a swim earlier, for not a speck of soot marred his skin or dulled his hair. He was a strong man in body and spirit, intelligent and kind, sensitivity showing through his music and his love for his family. She would have thought him beneath her back home. Here he was a prince amongst other men. Back home he would still be a prince amongst other men, but she wouldn't have seen it there as the pastor's pampered daughter. Unlike all the others who had courted her, this one man had won her heart.

"I don't think you helping Bethann go away is why she took the laudanum," Esther said. "I think she wanted to avoid shaming all of you, but being alone was too bleak for her to face. You have such a loving family. When you all sing together —" She spun away from him as tears began to trickle down her cheeks.

With more haste than prudent in the fading light, she descended the slope until the trees gave way to the rocky hollow through which the stream gushed and then dropped into the foaming cataract of water and the deep, dark pool at its foot.

"No wonder you want peace so badly." Esther poised on the edge of the water, staring into the clear, fathomless depths. "How far down do you think it goes?"

"I reckon it's about a hundred feet or more." Griff remained on a rocky ledge above her. "If you want to swim, I won't look."

"Thank you."

He turned his back on her, and she removed her gown and petticoat, then plunged in with her chemise for a bathing dress. After the sultry heat of the day, the pool felt like diving into a vat of ice. It chilled her. It sent her blood racing through her veins. It cleansed her of grime and sweat and soot. She washed her hair with the cake of violet soap from her satchel. The grime and bubbles floated away on a current that drew them into an invisible channel to disappear and never be seen again.

Like Jesus's death on the cross washed away her sins. Yes, she knew it. She had accepted it. But she couldn't scrub the sins from her heart enough to believe God hadn't grown disgusted with her and left her to her own devices.

"It's not what the Bible tells us, Daughter," Papa had reminded her.

It didn't matter. She couldn't get clean in

her heart.

She glanced up at Griff. How could she think for a moment he would want her? Oh, he thought he did in part — wanted to touch and gaze at her. But for her to be his wife and raise his children? She was spoiled goods like a meat pie with a fine crust and rancid filling.

She dove again and again until her hands and feet numbed from the cold. Then she clambered onto the rocks, used her petticoat for a towel, and dressed.

"I'm decent," she said. "If you don't mind my hair." It hung in curling tangles around her face, surely nothing a man would want spread out on his pillow.

Griff leaped down to the rock she sat on and took her hands in his. "I reckon it's time for you to talk."

Her hands tensed in his, not trying to free herself, just not relaxing, as he wished she would. He could only hold her tightly and inhale that flowery fragrance of her hair in its tangled mess. He could only hold her to assure her that he would protect her from all the bad things going on around them.

She didn't let him hold her hands for long. After a few moments, she rose and walked to the cliff beside where the waterfall gushed from the rocks and tumbled twenty feet down to the pool. The dying sun created rainbows out of the spray, a fitting background for Esther's beauty. He fixed the image in his mind. If one of those limner fellas ever came through, he'd ask him to paint her like that.

If she was around. The way she poised with more weight on one foot, she looked about to run up the side of the ravine like a doe fleeing the hunter's shot.

But she spun on that foot and returned to his side. "I'm going to tell you something I've never told anybody. I think my parents know the truth, but I haven't given them all the sordid details of my shameful life. I didn't want to hurt them." She touched his hand. "I don't want to hurt you, and that's why I'm telling you, so you'll know for certain that I'm not good enough for you."

"If anyone's not good enough for a body, it's me for you."

"No." She pressed her fingers to his lips. "Listen to me, please." She started to stroke his jaw.

He caught her hand in his. "You don't need to entice me to listen. I will anyway." He smiled down at her, the shortened hair making her seem oddly vulnerable, more precious, her pale face warning him he

504

wasn't going to like what she said.

"I led you all to believe I fled Seabourne because a man broke my heart, and that the letters came from the family of a man whose heart I broke. It's actually true. I didn't lie to you as far as that goes." She moved a few inches away from him and folded her hands in her lap. "Papa talks about the lies of omission, and those I've committed aplenty."

Griff held his breath, waiting for her to speak. She didn't. She sat staring at the water, her hands still, her shoulders slumped. Cold where she had rested beside him for a moment, he reached out, wanting to take that invisible burden from her shoulders. He brushed back her hair, let his fingers twine a curl for a moment before allowing his hand to drop to his side.

"The sun's about to set." An obvious and stupid thing to say, but it filled the silence beneath the burble of tumbling water. "Momma will miss us."

"Don't worry yourself. Once she hears the truth about this fine schoolma'am she hired, she'll not expect you to marry me either, even if we stayed the night here."

"Esther, stop it. You're not like — well, you're not like Bethann."

"No, in many ways I'm worse. I learned

from a young age that I could get what I wanted with a smile, an embrace, a kiss on the cheek. My father was strict with the boys. Fair but strict, but he spoiled me because they so wanted a daughter and I took my time coming to them. And, well, I grew up." She sketched a female figure with her hands. "I got lots of attention from the male population. I was a shameless flirt. And I wanted to find a man who was good enough for me." She snorted. "I was the daughter of a man who came to this country as an indentured servant, little more than a slave, and a mother who is a midwife — and nobody in Seabourne was good enough for me. Too tall, too thin, too ugly . . . I let them take me on picnics and out sailing and to every fete the village had and some in Norfolk, but I never intended to marry anybody until — until —" A shudder ran through her. "Alfred Oglevie came along." She scrubbed at her lips as though she'd tasted something foul and were washing out her mouth. Then she fell silent.

The water continued to flow as it had for hundreds of years or more. The sun glazed the mountains in gold, then dropped out of sight behind towering trees and distant peaks. Still she sat in silence, her hand to her lips.

"Who was Alfred Oglevie, Esther?" Griff broke the stillness.

She jumped. "The man who owns half of Seabourne. Half of the eastern shore, I think. He was handsome and rich and, most importantly, not at all interested in me."

"You liked him because he wasn't interested in you?"

Would he ever understand females? Not if that was their logic.

She flashed him a quick smile that said she understood. "It makes sense when you remember that everything was too easy for me. I learned everything quickly. French. Mathematics. Anatomy."

He didn't even know what anatomy was.

"And beaux. They came easily. Papa was about to send me off to my relations in England, but I begged him to let me stay. I'd be some kind of provincial yokel in England. I was — well, I was a princess in Seabourne. And I wanted the prince." She laughed, high-pitched and not at all humor-filled.

The hysteria too obvious, Griff took her hand in his. She didn't resist. Nor did she curl her fingers in his. The poor, blistered fingers lay curled against his palm like a wounded creature.

Wounded, yes — his Esther was wounded

deep inside. He'd known it since they met, had seen a grief and pain inside her beautiful eyes and wanted to rescue her, spare her more grief. He never should have gotten even a little close to her, let himself care, fall in love with her. Zach was so much better at caring for wounded creatures. He let fallen birds learn to fly on their own. Griff tried to give them wings.

"Did you give up on him?" he prompted.

"I did." Her fingers suddenly tightened on his. "I all but threw myself at him at a party. No, I did throw myself at him. I asked him to dance. It was a leap year, after all, so it was all right for the lady to do the asking."

"I beg your pardon?"

This time her laugh held true amusement. "You don't know that tradition? Yes, every four years the female gets to do the asking."

"That sounds right silly."

She gave him a sidelong glance. "Humph."

"Though you could ask me even when it ain't a leap year."

"In Seabourne I wouldn't have, you know." She lowered her gaze. "Though you're so pretty I might have."

"Pretty? I think that's the meanest thing a female's ever said to me."

"It's not meant to be. You are. All those black curls and those eyes, and your manly form and —"

He touched his finger to her lips. "Stop. You're embarrassing me."

"You could have any female on this mountain in a minute."

"Except you?"

"Except me."

"Because I don't talk right and don't have book learning and money and —"

"I said I'm not the sweet female you thought I was. I'm a snob. I thought I should be the mayor's wife at the least."

"Did you ever ask God what He wanted you to be?"

"I did, and Alfred Oglevie decided to take up residence on the seaside." She flashed him a twisted grin. "I thought that was God's answer and Mr. Oglevie just wasn't listening. So I asked him to dance, and he did, and it was a waltz, and he held me too close. We went outside and —" She shrugged. "Who kissed whom doesn't matter, does it?"

That she'd kissed anyone else mattered a great deal. His gut twisted like rope.

"What matters," Esther pressed on, "is that I didn't like it. Suddenly there he was admitting he was playing hard to get because of my reputation for being a heartless flirt, and there I was finding out he tasted like tobacco and smelled like he didn't wash quite well enough. And kissing him felt like absolutely nothing to me. Worse, he was . . . crude. So when my father came out to take me home and probably lock me in my room, I said it was all a mistake. I made a fool of Alfred Oglevie, and he vowed he'd get even with me."

"He did."

She nodded.

"But that was two years ago."

She nodded again. She returned her hand to her lap and began to twist her fingers together, probably using some special skill to be performing the action on his innards at the same time.

"Esther, tell me."

"I will. I must." She breathed deeply. "Alfred Oglevie married someone else. A dear, sweet girl who was so very kind and pretty. She got . . . well, the natural outcome of most marriages occurred last year, and Momma and I attended to her. Mrs. Oglevie was a bit . . . nervous about the upcoming event and called us on the most ridiculous things. I shouldn't be telling you this much about a patient, but everyone in Seabourne knew anyway. And when I went over, her husband . . . was too friendly to me. He started out just touching my shoulder or my hand, and then he caught me in the kitchen making his wife some tea when he came home one night, and he cornered me and kissed me."

Griff's hands fisted on his thighs. "What kind of man does that when he's wed, let alone when she's bearing his child?"

"A despicable man. But Momma was with me that time and stopped him. She and Papa told me not to go over there again." She covered her face with her hands. "They told m-me." Her voice shook for the first time.

Griff speared his fingers through his hair, certain his head would explode if he didn't hold it together. He knew the rest. He knew with every bit of his being what she was about to tell him.

And she did. Sobbing, she told him the rest. "I went anyway. We got a message from them, and Papa said I should wait for Momma to come home, but it was near Mrs. Oglevie's time. Early, but close enough I thought I knew best and went. Except she was in bed sleeping, he told me when he let me into the kitchen. He had a plan for the two of us. We could have a little private supper together and discuss how I could repay him for humiliating him."

Griff couldn't breathe for wanting to ride

straight for Seabourne or simply to tell Esther to stop talking. He couldn't speak.

She kept talking in a voice that had turned to gravel. "I tried to leave. I screamed, and he kissed me to stop me. Then he knocked me down. My head hit the floor and — I don't remember much after that. I guess I can be grateful for that. But then Mrs. Oglevie walked in and saw — excuse me." She sprang to her feet and ran up the rocks like a mountain goat. She disappeared into the blackness of the trees at the top of the ravine.

Griff let her go for the moment. Sickness clawed at his own belly at the image she conjured — a gentle, pampered girl trained to heal, a strong man trained to have his own way.

His mouth tasted sour. He walked to the edge of the water and scooped up the cool, sweet liquid to drink, to wash his face.

He sensed her proximity before he heard her. She slipped up behind him, then around to splash water on her face and drink the cold, clear liquid as well.

"I'm sorry." She rocked back on her heels. "It happens sometimes."

"Like when my cousins got too friendly."

"Like then."

"Why not when I kissed you?"

She looked away. "Gratitude, I guess."

He wanted to call her a liar. He wanted to believe she was lying so he'd think she didn't care.

"Do you think this makes you not good enough for me?" he asked her instead.

"I'm ruined. I'm not pure and innocent as a proper wife should be. And there's more." She rose and turned her back to him so he couldn't hear her.

He moved up close behind and rested his hands on her shoulders. "I hear you, Esther, and thinking you're not good enough isn't so."

"If you think that, then no you don't hear me. But I'll tell you anyway." Her shoulders felt banded with steel rather than muscle. "Mrs. Oglevie started screaming — at me. She started calling me every horrible name I'd ever heard the fishermen use and then some. And then her water bro— oh, I'm sorry. I forget I shouldn't talk about these things to a man."

"I'm not going to faint." He smiled. "Blush maybe, but not faint on you."

"Oh, Griff, I —" She pressed one hand to his over her shoulder. "It was awful. She was early and the baby wasn't positioned right at first, and I was half dazed from my head hitting the floor and . . . everything.

513

And by the time Momma got there, Alfred was pacing the floor like any expectant father and Mrs. Oglevie was — was — gone."

"She died?"

Esther nodded too vigorously, her curls bobbing against his hands. "I saved the baby, but she . . . well, sometimes women bleed a great deal and it can't be stopped. Alfred Oglevie blamed me, of course, said I was incompetent. I told about the — the —" Her shoulders spasmed, and the next word was inaudible, though he knew it in all its ugliness.

He rubbed her shoulders with just his fingertips, more simple contact than in any hope of easing her tension. "From those letters, I guess nobody believed you."

"No, they said I made it up to put the blame on someone besides myself. And it's worse."

How could it be worse?

"Someone saw us through his kitchen window and said I was trying to seduce him."

"He lied."

"No, Griff, not really."

He jerked away. " 'Scuse me?"

She laughed and faced him. "I pretended to go along with him before I tried to get away. No, that's not quite right. I didn't fight him off at first, so it must have looked like I was compliant. I thought it would work, that he'd be softened up and let me go without anything for us to remember later. But it didn't work. It made things . . . worse."

"Then it wasn't your fault."

"Of course it was. I started it by my bits of flirting two years earlier. And everyone in Seabourne knows the truth they want to believe to save their livelihoods, and now Hannah and Zach know it and are likely to talk. Wherever I go, someone will know that I am little more than a — a —"

He pressed two fingers to her lips. "Don't say it, my dear. Don't call yourself that. You're not."

"Good wife material? No, I'm not."

"Esther."

"Griff." Her tone turned sharp. "Your mother wants her children to have a better life than they've had so far. She doesn't want Liza and Brenna to go the way Beth-ann did because she wasn't good enough for the man to marry her. She wants Jack and Ned to have more than the fighting and scraping a living out of these rocks. Do you think for you, her favorite and most reliable son, she will want a wife with my reputation?"

Gazing at her, loving her, he wanted to say that what Momma wanted didn't matter. With every fiber of his being, he ached to tell her that her past was in the past and they must leave it there, accept forgiveness for what she had done wrong, and forgive for what had been done wrong to her. But he'd known since he found the letters, as someone intended him to find them, that as much as he wanted to spend his life with her, he couldn't do it if his family disapproved.

35

She'd lost him. She knew she had. It was why she had insisted she protect her heart against caring for anyone. Except he'd won it with a few words, a few smiles, a lot of music and kindness. And the kiss that told her she wasn't afraid to be touched by him.

"I'll leave." It was all she could do — offer to go before he sent her away.

"Where?" He took her hand in his so gently she wanted to weep. "You can't go without somewhere in mind."

"I'll go to Phoebe and Rafe Docherty. They — they're as close as I have to relatives in this part of the state."

And Griff hadn't asked her to stay.

Run. Run. Run before you break down and throw yourself into his arms.

She didn't move. Her feet seemed rooted to the rock of the mountain, with the waterfall constantly refreshing the pool, keeping the water pure. To move meant ripping away a part of her soul and all of her heart.

"Griff, I can't go."

"Esther, I don't want you to go."

They spoke together. They stared at one another in the starlight, then Griff drew her against him with his arm around her waist and his other hand in her hair, tilting her head back so he could kiss her until she couldn't breathe. She cradled his face in her hands and continued to kiss him with a fervor she hadn't known lay within her. She let herself enjoy the moments, letting them last a bit longer than they should have, then she drew away.

"We can just say I left because of the fire," she said.

"You can't go. I can't wake up in the morning and know you won't be here. I want to wake up with you beside me. I want to marry you."

"You know you can't." She shook her head. "You have had trouble enough with Bethann, and I've caused trouble enough already. Having me in the family will hurt your sisters. It'll hurt the way other men respect you. And they need to for you to make the right decisions for the families and everyone who depends on you for work."

"Which makes me not much better than

that man who hurt you. Giving you up so others will respect my authority over them 'cause I have my own house in order ain't — isn't right. You should come first if I love you."

"I gave up being worthy of that kind of love, Griff." She turned her back on him and walked away, climbing the rocky slope with care so he wouldn't come help her, wouldn't have a reason to touch her.

He caught up with her in a few strides and didn't touch her. They descended the mountain in silence save for the crunch of their footfalls on the path. In silence they entered the house, where Mrs. Tolliver sat on the kitchen bench sewing and glancing toward the door.

"It's past time the two of you got back." She set her needlework aside and rose. "Are you hungry?"

"No, thank you." Esther kept walking through the kitchen without once looking back at Griff. If she caught a glimpse of his clear blue eyes gazing at her with even a hint of hope in them, she wouldn't leave.

As she had left her family for their sake, she would leave the Tollivers for theirs, especially for Griff's. He could marry one of those nice young women with whom he'd danced at the Independence Day celebration. Perhaps one was a Gosnoll and he could ensure peace on the mountain that way.

She climbed the steps and slipped into Liza's room. The girl slept on the very edge of her bed as though even in sleep she was polite enough to make room for Esther. She readied herself for bed and slipped beneath the quilt, though the night was too warm to need a covering. She wouldn't sleep. She mustn't sleep if she was going to leave before the family woke in the morning. But her body sank into the moss-filled mattress as though every fiber sighed in relief at lying down at last, and she drifted into slumber to the soothing murmur of Griff's and Mrs. Tolliver's voices below her.

Griff poured himself a cup of water, then leaned against the table, watching Momma slice bread and ham to feed him food he didn't want to eat. She would start lecturing him at any moment. Whether he was a man grown or not, Momma expected him to behave a certain way, and he had overstepped his bounds as far as she was concerned.

"You don't keep a nice girl out in the woods past dark," Momma began. "I done taught you better'n that."

"Yes'm."

Except Esther might not be considered a "nice girl" to Momma.

Of course she was. None of what had happened was her fault.

Except it was in a way.

"We brought her here to help teach the young'uns how to go up right like folk in the city," Momma continued. "The boys can't stay here. There ain't enough for them, and they need to know their letters and their manners and —" She turned around, plate of food in hand, and stopped. "What's wrong, Son?"

Even at age six, he hadn't laid his head on her shoulder and cried over a wound. He'd borne it like a man did — without a whimper, maybe even with a shrug and a grin. Now he wished he could forget about being strong, about carrying the weight of the family's fortunes and misfortunes on his shoulders.

"She won't marry me," he blurted out past a constricted throat. "I told her I wanted to, and she said no."

"She don't love you?" Momma's face showed surprise. "I was right certain she does."

"So am I. But she doesn't think she's good enough for me. She —" He couldn't talk.

521

He finished his cup of water, but his throat remained too closed for words.

Momma set the plate on the table, then wrapped her arms around him as she never had when he was a boy and suffered some bump or scrape or childish fever. She expected him to be strong over that.

Apparently a breaking heart demanded something different.

She held him while he told her Esther's story. She didn't say a word until he was done, then she moved away and pulled out a chair.

"Sit and eat."

"I'm not hungry."

"You need food. You haven't eaten all day."

Dutifully he took a few mouthfuls, then set down his knife and fork and rested his head in his hands. "How can she think she's not good enough for me when I have Bethann for a sister? We forgive Bethann for all she's done, and not once have I heard her say she's sorry. But I tell Esther I love her, and I hesitate before reassuring her that her past doesn't matter. It's no wonder she thinks the Lord has abandoned her. All those people she grew up with abandoned her."

"Her parents didn't, did they?"

"No, she left them because she felt she

was hurting their work. And that man goes free."

"You hired Henry Gosnoll to manage the mine," Momma pointed out.

"I needed someone I trusted to be honest."

"You trusted the man who ruined your sister to be honest?" Momma shoved back her chair. "It was a decision you and your pa made, so I didn't contradict, but I saw how it hurt Bethann every time you mentioned his name."

"And to this day he denies being responsible. His wife denies that he's responsible, as much as she knows he has a wandering heart and wants him dead."

And he had to tell Momma that story too. She wept through it for her poor sister's sake, for her niece's sake, for the waste of lives.

"If he weren't guilty," she asked at the end, "why did he leave the mountain?"

"To protect his hide. I'd have gone too if y'all hadn't needed me here."

Momma stared at him. "You would have? You'd have left us?"

"I've never wanted this fight. I want my family alive and well and prosperous. I want to be able to pay a preacher to be here all the time. I want a schoolma'am here all the time. I want Esther here all the time as my wife. But how can I convince her that her past don't — doesn't matter if she's determined to think different?"

"Let her go back to her kin."

"What?"

"You can't keep her here if she don't want to."

A simple and painful truth.

"She won't let you talk sense into her if she thinks she's leaving 'cause she loves you too much to stay," Momma continued. "Let them talk sense into her."

"Yea, like how it . . . isn't sensible to love a man from Brooks Ridge."

"If they can do that, then it's best she's gone, now ain't it?"

Another simple and undeniable truth.

The kitchen, the house, the entire compound of buildings and yard and kitchen garden shrank in on him. He needed air, clear, fresh mountain air, soothing to his soul like the balm he'd spread to soothe Esther's hands. If only he could find a balm to soothe her soul.

How could she believe she wasn't good enough to be loved? She was good enough for God to love her.

The answer came to him as he climbed the steepest path on the ridge, slowly enough not to stumble in the moonlight, fast enough to make his breath sear in his lungs and his legs burn with the effort.

She was all mixed up between people loving her no matter what she'd done and God loving her no matter what she'd done. People let a body down. Griff had thought Zach was his friend, and he'd been jealous enough to start a fight. When people abandoned Esther, she confused it with God abandoning her.

He reached the top of the ridge and stood, breathing hard, his hands on his knees. Sweat ran into his eyes, but his mind was clear.

If he let her go without trying to keep her with him, she would think he'd abandoned her too, and she might never get her heart right. One more time he had to convince her she should stay.

He straightened to run down the mountain again and heard a scream. His blood ran cold, and he knew it was a mountain lion a little closer at hand than he liked. Cautiously he started to walk, quieter than running, soft-footed on the carpet of pine needles and last year's leaves. He drew the knife from the back of his waistband, though a knife was a poor weapon against a big cat.

Another scream proclaimed the beast to

be on the hunt on the other side of the ridge, the opposite direction from him. He started to relax, to focus on getting back to Esther as fast as he could.

And then a gun exploded. Another scream followed. Not the eerily human cry of a mountain lion, but unmistakably that of a human female.

Esther woke to the chilling scream of the mountain lion. She lay beside the soundly sleeping Liza, her own body tense save for the occasional shudder running through her. It sounded too real, too much like a woman's cry of fear or anguish. Her own heart cried out.

The time had come to go. With the big cat in the distance, with the house silent from everyone sleeping, she could slip away. She would take one of the horses. The Tollivers — Griff — would understand. Once she reached Christiansburg, she would send the horse back.

As quietly as she could, she dressed, bundled her things together in her other dress, and caught up her satchel. One step creaked beneath her. She froze, waiting for someone to call out, challenge her. No one did. When she reached the barn without incident, a sense of peace washed over her, as though for once in her life she had made the right choice.

She wasn't really running away. She was going back. Rafe and Phoebe Docherty would give her shelter and help her find somewhere to go. Yes, they would tell her family, but it was past time they knew. She should never have rejected their love. It was the only anchor she possessed in the world.

You shouldn't be leaving Griff's love behind, a still, quiet voice said inside her head.

"But I don't have it," she said aloud. "He let me go without a fight."

Not that she wanted that fight. Not that he would fight for anything. He was a man of peace, a man who always took the peaceful road. The road with the least resistance.

Suddenly she was glad to be leaving. Outrage like she hadn't experienced since no one in Seabourne would believe her story against Oglevie ran through her veins. She could have run all the way to Christiansburg with the power of her anger.

But wasn't she a fool for wanting him to fight for her?

She saddled the mare, tied on her satchel and bundled clothes, and mounted. Riding astride was certainly easier than in a side-saddle. More secure, better for riding through woods lit only by moonlight.

She knew where to find the track. It led straight to the Tollivers' front gate, too narrow for a wagon, too rough for speed. Intermittent light broke through the branches like winking stars leading her way. The horse seemed to know it anyway. A docile, sweet creature, she picked her way down the hill — down, down, down until a sparkle of water in the distance proclaimed she had reached the path along the river.

Except it wasn't the sparkle of moonlight on water; it was the glow of banked coals and an occasional flame shooting from them.

She drew up. "Who's there?"

A rustle, a grumble, and the click of a gun being cocked answered her.

"I'm unarmed," she said.

"Then you're a fool for admitting it, lass."

"Uncle Rafe?" Esther flung herself from her horse and ran to greet her father's oldest friend and her honorary uncle. "What are you doing here?"

"Coming after you." He closed his arms around her.

And other arms joined his — Phoebe's, slim and strong — the two of them nearly smothering her.

At last Rafe let her go enough to rest his hands on her shoulders and give her a little shake. "What do ye think ye are doing out here at the back end of night?"

"I had to leave. I had to. They know everything. And I'm just not good enough for him." After her jumbled speech, she burst into tears.

Rafe led her over to a fallen log for a seat. Phoebe knelt to build up the fire and set a kettle on to boil.

"That wee explanation made nae sense, lass," Rafe told her, "so I am thinking you need to start from the beginning."

Esther looked at Phoebe across the rising flames. "I was standing by a fire in a place like this, and a man came walking through the trees."

Rafe groaned, and Phoebe hushed him with a glance.

"He looked like something out of a James Fenimore Cooper novel — a little wild. His accent was so thick I could hardly understand him, and his grammar would make Papa shudder. But he walks like he owns the mountain, which he rather does, and he has a smile . . ."

"Yes," Phoebe drawled in her genteel plantation accent, "Janet about swooned when she met him."

"Met —" Esther pressed her fingers to her lips. "Of course. How could I forget? Then you know why I — why I —"

If she said it, it would make the feeling too real and then it might not go away.

"Why you love him?" Phoebe supplied.

Esther bowed her head. "I didn't think I could. I knew I shouldn't. He deserves so much better than me."

"Oh, Esther." Phoebe had her arms around Esther again, holding her, cradling her while she wept, drank coffee as black and hot as lava, and told the rest of the story.

Dawn was breaking as she finished with, "And so I left."

"Then he will be coming soon, nae doot," Rafe said.

"No." Esther shook her head. "It's not Griff's way. He's spent the last ten years of his life seeking peace. He won't find it if he marries me."

"Aye, that is for certain." Rafe grinned at her.

"Ignore him," Phoebe said. "If Griff prefers peace to a little struggle for the lady he says he loves, then perhaps he just doesn't love you that much."

"From how I am seeing it," Rafe said, "Esther's trying to force his hand and make him come after her just like she is so fond of doing, you ken."

Esther's head shot up. "I didn't — I'm not —"

But perhaps she was.

Quivering inside, she asked, "What should I do?"

"Only you ken your heart, lass." Rafe rose and reached for the rifle. "Or perhaps you do not have the choice after all."

Esther heard it then, the hoofbeats pounding down the trail too fast for the lack of light, too fast for the rough terrain. A tendril of early sunlight flashed off a red hide, a roan coat.

"Griff." Esther clasped her upper arms with her hands.

But it wasn't Griff. Mattie Brooks slid from the horse's back and staggered into the camp. "Miss Esther, thank the Lord I catched you." He seized her hand.

"Griff?" Esther clung to the boy's fingers. "Is he all right?"

"Yes, it's Bethann. Her time has come, and she's . . . bad."

"Her time has come already?" Esther glanced at Phoebe and Rafe. "She can't be more than six months along."

Their faces reflected her concern. That far in advance rarely meant good for baby or mother.

"What happened?" Esther asked Mattie.

"Did she fall?"

Or was it a result of too much laudanum?

"Yes'm," Mattie said. "She shot Henry Gosnoll, and the recoil knocked her off a ledge."

36

Esther slid off the mare and started running before both feet hit the ground. Jack and Ned, Brenna and Liza tried to greet her as she raced through the gate and into the house. She didn't pause long enough to return a word, simply tossed out, "Where is she?"

"Her room," Liza called. "Griff carried her there."

Griff, who had sent a boy after Esther instead of coming himself. No time to think of that now. She must see to Bethann. Phoebe was coming too, a little slower. And Rafe, a doctor. He would have forceps if he'd brought his medical things.

Of course he had. She never traveled without her satchel. He wouldn't travel without his.

She gathered her skirt up to her knees and took the steps two at a time, the soles of her boots loud on the bare treads, announcing her presence. Mrs. Tolliver emerged from Bethann's room, her knuckles bulging as she twisted up her apron.

Esther made herself slow down and walk sedately into the patient's chamber, composed. Bethann lay on the bed, her body so thin she barely made a ripple in the quilt spread over her, and Griff sat beside her, holding her hand.

His gaze met Esther's, and he offered her a half smile. "I knew you'd come back for Bethann's sake."

"I was going to come back for yours, not that you asked me to." She approached the bed and brushed her fingertips over Bethann's brow. "Tell me what's happening, Bethann."

"My pains." Bethann's teeth sank into a lower lip that was already bruised. "I know it."

"Then you know you can have false pains." Esther smiled and made her voice sound a bit too cheerful. "I think it's a little soon for you to have that happening, but —"

"Her water's broke," Mrs. Tolliver interjected.

"Ah, I see. Well then." Esther grew brisk, though she watched Griff from the corner of her eye.

Not so much as the pink tip of his ear showing through a curl.

"It could be quick this time. I need to examine you." She glanced about for a washstand, clean towels, soap. They stood in one corner of the room. She headed for it, then glanced at her blistered palms.

She shouldn't be doing this with her hands such a mess. She never thought she'd need them pristine as usual again. She would have to let Phoebe do the examining.

But Phoebe wasn't there yet, and a woman's second child often came within an hour after the water broke.

"Griff, you should probably leave."

"She won't let me." He kept his gaze on his sister's face.

"All right." She could examine beneath the quilt. Doctors did it all the time to preserve the woman's modesty.

She washed her hands, then performed the examination. The baby was small. So was Bethann. The baby appeared to be further along than Esther guessed. But Bethann was weak, her contractions close together yet not as strong as they should be. Internal bleeding? Perhaps she had been injured in the fall that had commenced the travail.

Falling off a ledge after shooting Henry

Gosnoll.

He was dead. She'd used Griff's shotgun on him, Mattie had told Esther and the Dochertys before parting from them to head home. Gosnoll had been sneaking home after an assignation with one of his women. Bethann waited for him on the path and pulled the trigger.

"Were you injured in your fall?" Esther asked.

"No." Bethann's voice was as weak as a newborn's.

"Maybe," Griff said. "I heard her scream." A shudder ran through him. "Nothing's broken."

Not on the outside. Insides could break too — parts that caused a body to lose blood inside, where nobody could fix it.

If only Rafe would get there. Doctors knew so much more about the workings of a body's insides. Esther had some knowledge but mainly about the working of a woman's particular parts.

"Have you felt the baby move recently?" Esther asked.

"Yes'm," Bethann said. "Before the pains started."

That was good as far as it went, but the baby couldn't keep moving outside the uterus. Never had Esther seen a six-month, let alone younger, infant survive. She could only hope to save the mother.

Save her to hang for murder?

"There was a struggle," Griff said, still looking at his sister and not at Esther. "She said Gosnoll hit her belly."

Mrs. Tolliver started to cry.

Esther gasped. "Self-defense then?"

She and Griff exchanged a glance, swift, full of understanding.

He nodded. "If you find evidence she's been injured thatta way . . . I won't look."

She knew he wouldn't. He was a gentleman for all his homespun clothes and rough speech.

She drew up the quilt and Bethann's night dress. A purpling bruise marred her belly. It could have happened in the fall. But it was the size of a man's fist.

"Yes," Esther said. "There's a bruise I can testify to."

Griff's free hand curled into a fist on his thigh, and a muscle in his jaw bulged. "If Gosnoll weren't dead, I'd —"

"No, Griff." Bethann spoke more strongly. "It's done. Let it be done."

"And let's get this baby born." Esther brought back her smile. "It shouldn't take long now."

But it did. The morning wore into early

afternoon. Phoebe and Rafe arrived, and still Bethann's labor pains continued, but weaker. Bethann was weaker.

"Will you examine her?" Esther asked Phoebe. "Perhaps I'm missing something."

"I doubt you are." But Phoebe performed the same examination. When she straightened, she shook her head, then jutted her chin toward the door. "I'm going to get my husband."

"Why?" Griff asked the instant Phoebe departed. "Why's she going after Dr. Docherty?"

"Because this calls for a doctor, not a midwife." Esther dropped to her knees beside the bed and took Bethann's other hand in hers. "Your travail is going on too long, and your pains aren't strong enough to bring out the baby. So the doctor is going to use his forceps."

"Can't you?" Bethann asked.

"I'm not allowed to as a midwife. I'd have to be a doctor."

"She don't want no strange man touching her," Mrs. Tolliver said from the far corner of the room.

"He's a fine doctor, trained in Edinburgh, Scotland," Esther said. "He's helped many bairns, as he calls them, come into the world. He helped at the births of his own children —"

"Esther," Griff said quietly, "be quiet."

She was talking too much again, masking anxiety behind a spate of words.

She substituted actions for words — wetting a cloth and wiping Bethann's perspiring brow, laying her hand on the too-small mound of Bethann's belly and counting the minutes before the feeble contractions, washing her hands. She dropped the soap, picked it up, and started to apply it to her palms again.

Until it disappeared from her hand. "Sit down, Esther." Gently, his hand beneath her elbow, Griff led her to the chair he'd occupied.

"But where will you sit?" Esther protested.

"I can stand. She wants you."

"Me?" Esther dropped onto the chair and leaned toward Bethann. "What is it?"

"I'm a-dying," she whispered. "Must . . . tell . . ." A stronger contraction left her sweating and gasping.

Esther sponged her brow. "Good girl. Keep that up and we'll have that baby here in no time."

"Dead." Bethann's lips formed the word without sound. Then aloud she said, "I thought he killed it. So I . . . shot him."

Momma had never prepared Esther for

this situation. She'd had answers to everything imaginable in the birthing chamber. None of them had prepared her for this one.

Rafe and Phoebe entered at that moment, preventing further speech. For all his size and seafaring past, Rafe was the tenderest of physicians. He approached Bethann's side and took her hand in both of his, then spoke to her in an undertone. "So you are having a wee bit of trouble, are you? You have two ver' fine midwives here to attend you, but I have a trick or two us doctors wisely keep to ourselves. Otherwise they would be putting us out of business. May I try?" He glanced at Griff. "Mr. Tolliver, I am wondering if you would prefer to be elsewhere. This can be a wee bit unpleasant."

"No!" Bethann cried. "Stay."

Griff's face paled in the afternoon sunlight pouring through the window, but he crouched at Bethann's side and laid his hand on her head. Though he didn't so much as move his lips, Esther knew he prayed for his sister.

If ever a body needed prayer, it was Bethann Tolliver. Her baby was most certainly dead already. Her chances of survival weren't much higher. If this birth didn't kill her, the Gosnolls would see her hang. This time the mountain folk weren't likely to keep their information to themselves, or they just might hang her themselves.

"God, where is Your love right now?" Esther didn't realize she spoke aloud until Phoebe rested a hand on her shoulder.

"God is here right now with His love. It's we who don't ask for it."

"Don't . . . deserve . . ." Bethann cried out as Rafe took out the forceps.

"What's that?" Mrs. Tolliver exclaimed.

"They do look wicked, do they no?" He flashed Mrs. Tolliver his still charming smile. " 'Tis nae so bad and will help things along. Now just you lie there still, Miss Bethann, and let me do the work."

The forceps drew the too-small infant into a world it would never know. And with it came the blood. Too much blood. Blood that wouldn't stop as long as it had a supply to draw upon.

"I'm sorry," Rafe said, and his face and voice rang with sincerity. "There's damage inside from the look of it. A rupture."

Mrs. Tolliver began to sob. "My child. Not another one."

Phoebe went to her, not the first mother she had comforted.

"The last one," Bethann whispered. "It's over. I started it. It ends with me."

"You didn't start it." Griff spoke through clenched teeth. "Pa started it with his desire for revenge for ruining you. And the Brookses continued it, and —" He dropped his head onto the pillow beside Bethann's head. "Yes, it ends here, but you didn't start it."

"I did. God . . . not forgive me for this." Bethann's voice grew so weak Esther leaned toward her to hear.

The others stood in silence. The yard and forest beyond lay still as though holding their breath.

"God always forgives if we ask," Griff said. "There's a Scripture about no condemnation . . ." He gave Esther a helpless glance.

" 'There is therefore now no condemnation to them which are in Christ Jesus, who walk not after the flesh, but after the Spirit. For the law of the Spirit of life in Christ Jesus hath made me free from the law of sin and death.' " She and Phoebe quoted the words together from the eighth chapter of Romans.

A slight smile curled Bethann's thin and now bluish lips. "Then forgive me for this, Jesus." She turned her head toward Griff. "I lied. It was some artist man. It weren't never Henry's baby the first time." Her breath sighed out, and for the first time since she met her, Esther saw Bethann Tolliver look at peace.

Griff appeared as though she had ripped his heart from his chest with her bare hand. His face whitened, his eyes turned a colorless gray. Without a word, without a sound, he shot to his feet and strode from the room, allowing the door to slam behind him.

Mrs. Tolliver commenced to weep uncontrollably. Rafe led her from the chamber, murmuring something about a sedative draft. Esther and Phoebe remained to clean up the blood before flies swarmed through the open window.

"She found her peace," Esther said. "She died free of a huge burden."

"And what a burden." Phoebe removed the sheet and canvas from beneath the body with the ease of experience. "She lied to get revenge on a man who spurned her love and started a family war."

"Yet she never stopped loving him." Esther started for the door. "I'll fetch a pail of hot water."

"Don't." Phoebe glanced toward the window and the setting sun. "Go find that young man of yours before it gets too dark."

"I can't go after him. You said yourself —"

"I was wrong. Go." Phoebe made shooing

motions with her hands. "Rafe will come back and help me with the rest. If ever I saw a young man in need of being loved right now, it's him."

"But he rejected me the other night."

"Did he? Or did you run away?"

"I — he —"

The scene flashed through her mind, her leaving him. He hadn't spoken, but she had just burdened him with an unpleasant — to say the least — tale about herself. She hadn't given him time to think, just presumed and departed.

As she hadn't given God time to heal her wounded spirit, just presumed He wasn't with her and ran away from Him too.

The time for running away had ceased. The time for running toward was now.

Esther spun toward the door.

Griff wasn't in his room, the kitchen, or the parlor. He wasn't in the barn. The children swarmed around her, asking a dozen questions. She shooed them away as Phoebe had sent her packing, wanting the answer to only one question: "Have you seen Griff?"

"No, ma'am," Ned said, "we ain't."

"Haven't," Liza corrected him. "Is Bethann —"

"I need to find Griff." Esther started for

544

the forest. She knew where he'd be.

He sat cross-legged beside the waterfall pool with his elbows on his knees and his head in his hands. He didn't so much as lift a finger when Esther clambered down the ravine and slid down to the rock beside him.

Esther ventured an opening. "She died at peace with God at the end."

"Whereas I may never know peace in my heart again."

"Griff —"

"Esther, go away." He sounded weary. "Your fine friends are here. Go back with them. The scandal will go away in time. He'll hurt some other female and everyone will believe you. You can have your old way of life back."

"You mean the one where I thought nobody was good enough for me except the richest man on the eastern shore?" A surge of anger bubbled up in Esther's veins. "You mean the one where I flirted and teased and didn't care whom I hurt because I was amused? I don't think so."

"Well, you can't have a life with me." He turned to glare at her. "I don't want you."

Esther caught her breath. "B-because I was right? I'm not good enough for you?"

"No, because I'm not good enough for

545

you. I was a fool to think for a minute maybe it didn't matter. But now I know for certain."

"You don't know anything if you think that." The words burst from her loudly enough to echo off the rocks and be heard over the waterfall. *Think that. Think that. Think that.*

She liked the sound of it and stood to raise her voice a bit more. "My frivolous behavior led to a woman's early labor and death."

"And my sister is a murderer." Griff stood with his sleek grace and took a step toward Esther. "Did you get that? My sister lied, and four families have been finding reasons to kill one another off for years. Poor Hannah isn't right in her head. Lives are ruined."

"So what does that have to do with you?"

"I'm responsible for my family —"

She took a step toward him and poked a finger in his chest. "Did you make Bethann go astray? Did you make her love the wrong man? Did you make her lie and start a feud? Did you make your father go after Gosnoll with a gun? Did you —"

He caught hold of her pointing finger and pressed her own hand to her mouth. "Esther, be quiet. I can't think with you yammering on like that."

"Yes, you need peace." She didn't try to remove the sarcasm from her tone.

"If I truly wanted peace, I wouldn't have ever thought of marrying you."

The past tense of his words drained the fight out of Esther. She dropped her hand to her side and stared at the ground. "That's what Uncle Rafe said. If you're a man of peace, you won't want to marry me."

"A wise man." He shoved his hands into his pockets and turned away. "It's getting dark. You should leave."

"You mean run away?"

"Something like that."

If she looked up to find that the cliff side had crushed down upon her chest, she wouldn't have been surprised at that moment. She could scarcely breathe. She certainly couldn't move. She could barely keep standing.

"What if I want to stay?" she managed to ask.

"Then I'll go."

"Why? You love me. I love you."

"Esther." He faced her, his hands on his hips now. "You were right happy enough to leave me behind before. Why won't you go now when I want you to?"

"Because you don't want me to. You just think you shouldn't let me stay because of

Bethann."

"I let you go because I thought we couldn't bear up under another scandal here."

"Were you going to come after me?" She glided toward him a half step.

He braced his legs as though expecting her to throw herself at him. "I was going to come after you."

"And I was coming back."

Their eyes locked for a moment, then Griff looked away. "That was before we knew about Bethann. I reckon that changes everything."

"Not for me it doesn't." She slid another half step forward, tilted her head, started to caress his stubbled cheek, then stopped, tucked her hand behind her back, and gave him a direct look. "I'm here."

"You shouldn't be. You come from finer folk."

"Ha! I'll have to tell you about those finer folk, like my father fighting a duel and Uncle Rafe being a privateer — and Aunt Phoebe! No, Griff, those finer folk don't have spotless pasts either. And you know I don't. I'm ruined as far as most men are concerned."

"Not to me."

Ah, the rocky cliff finally rolled off of her chest.

She rested her other hand on his shoulder, sidled just a bit closer. "We didn't lie to Bethann at the end, Griff. The Bible doesn't lie. 'There is therefore now no condemnation.' That isn't a lie after all. We are not condemned because of what we've done or, worst of all, what others have done to us. Can you tell —"

He laid his fingers on her lips. "Miss Esther Cherrett preaching to me about God's redemption?"

"I am a preacher's daughter." She smiled at him.

His face remained grim. "But you thought God no longer loves you or cares about you."

"I did. I may have moments of doubt again. But when Phoebe asked me if you left me or I left you, I realized I'd gone away before you had a chance to think about all I'd told you and make up your mind for yourself. It made me realize how I thought God had abandoned me that night and I gave up on Him. He hadn't given up on me. Nothing can separate us from the love of God. Nothing. We can run as far and as fast as we can, and He still loves us. I don't have that same kind of all-forgiving love, Griff

Tolliver, but if you try to run away from me, I'll come after you, still loving you."

He grinned. "You'll chase me until I catch you?"

"Something like that." And she wrapped her arms around his neck and kissed him.

She kissed him until he kissed her breathless. Then they sat on the side of the pool with their feet in the water and watched the stars waltz across the sky and light the waterfall to liquid silver.

"We should go," Griff said. "Your reputation will be broke to bits."

"I guess you'll have to marry me then."

They laughed and stayed where they were, watching the sky, listening to the waterfall's continuous splashing and the sporadic noises of a forest at night.

"When will you marry me?" she asked.

"This ain't — isn't a leap year. You can't ask me to marry you."

"I didn't. I asked when you would marry me."

"Next time the preacher comes around?"

"Two weeks or so? I can manage that, except . . . I'd like my parents here."

"Then we'll go to them."

She stared at him. "You'll get off this mountain to do that for me?"

"I will. Gotta ask your pa for permission."

His hand closed over hers. "Will he give it?"

"Of course. I always get what I want."

He groaned. "Then I pray we don't have daughters to get spoiled like that."

"I want at least one. It's tradition to have a female healer in the family. Then lots and lots of sons to grow up just like you."

They talked about their future, what they'd build for a school, a place where Esther could do her doctoring, a new manager for the mine. They talked of how to heal the rift with Zach.

"Find him a fine wife," Esther said.

And when the sky began to pale and a few birds stirred in the trees, they gathered the strength and will to leave the waterfall to return to their families. Hand in hand, they strolled down the mountain and into the sunrise.

EPILOGUE

"I want . . . to see . . . my husband." Esther Cherrett Tolliver spoke through teeth gritted against the pain of another contraction. "Now."

"A birthing chamber is no place for a man," Momma declared. "He can see you afterward."

"*After* won't be for hours." Esther breathed more easily. "I don't have your ancient years of experience, Momma, but I know I want to see my husband."

"If he sees you in pain," Phoebe said, "he'll never come near you again."

"Ha." Esther started to laugh, but pain stopped her.

Momma leaned over her, gripping her hands, then smoothing a cool, damp cloth over her perspiring brow. "Hours, you said?"

"All right, perhaps sooner. But I still want . . . him."

"In a few minutes." With the brisk efficiency of experience, Phoebe examined Esther. "Sooner than you think. It's your first."

"And midwives make the worst patients." Momma brought Esther some water. "But you're doing well."

"Better than I did. I wasn't asking for Rafe. I wanted to kill him." Phoebe laughed.

"But you have six children." Esther managed a smile. "Now get my husband. Griff's hands are stronger than yours, Momma. I want to hold on to him."

The two older women exchanged glances.

"Esther," Momma began.

Esther glared at her. "Now you decide not to spoil me. After a . . . lifetime . . ."

"Never too old to learn." Momma smiled and caressed Esther's cheek. "And you didn't come up so bad in the end, did you?"

"No, but — please." Esther released Momma's hand for fear of crushing her delicate fingers and gripped the mattress. "Or perhaps I will kill him."

Except she couldn't imagine life without him, his love, his tenderness, the closeness that had produced this first baby. He honored her for her work on the mountain, which still didn't have a doctor. If the people couldn't cure something themselves, they came to her. She had saved Hannah's life after a difficult lying-in, and then the women asked for Esther to aid them in childbirth. She had accepted her calling as a wife and midwife, and now, Lord willing, as a mother.

"Please," she said again when she could speak. "Just for a minute."

"Men don't belong in the birthing chamber," Momma repeated.

"They tend to faint," Phoebe added.

"Then why do women call in male doctors?" Esther demanded. She raised herself on one elbow. "I'm going to get him myself if you don't —"

Momma pushed her down. "Do you want to drop this baby in the hall?"

"I wouldn't —" She gave in to the pain, then finished, "Or perhaps I would." She dropped back onto the pile of pillows behind her. "You'd think I'd know how bad this is." She blinked, and a tear slid down her face. "Just let me see him in case — in case I don't . . . survive."

Momma and Phoebe laughed.

"We know your tricks, child," Phoebe said. "Be a watering pot all you like. It won't change our minds."

"Besides," Momma added, examining Esther herself, "there isn't time."

"There must be. I've scarcely been in

554

labor —"

But of course Momma was right. For the next several minutes, Esther didn't have time to think about Griff or anything but pain, impossible discomfort, and her determination not to so much as whimper through it all. She failed at the latter. Somewhere in the haze of it all, the door banged open and hands stronger than Momma's gripped hers. That beautiful voice told her to hang on to him and she would be all right.

And she was all right because he was there beside her, holding on tightly, the two of them strong together. Momma was there too, scolding Griff for interfering, urging Esther to push just a bit more and more —

And there it was, her baby's first cry. Their baby's first cry. She gazed up at Griff's face, so beautiful to her, and managed a smile. "I love you."

"You must." He huffed out a breath. "To go through that."

"This once anyway." Esther closed her eyes, aching for rest.

"They always say that." Momma laid a bundle in Esther's arms. "This will change her mind. Your daughter."

"Daughter?" A surge of energy raced through her, and she accepted the bundle, surely too light to be made of flesh and blood, and drew down the folds of the linen wrappings. "She's quite hideous, isn't she?" she cried with delight.

"She's beautiful," Momma, Phoebe, and Griff exclaimed together.

"Because she's ours." Griff touched just his fingertip to the baby's cheek, then kissed Esther. "And you're even more beautiful than ever." He gazed down at them both, his eyes soft and shining with a suspicious brightness.

"She looks just like you did when you were born," Momma said.

"What are you going to name her?" Phoebe asked.

"Felicity," Griff said. "Esther tells me it means *happiness,* and that's right fine to me."

"Perfect." Momma took Griff's arm. "You can see her all you like later, but right now we've got to make her pretty."

Griff flashed her a smile. "She already is."

He left with a lingering look over his shoulder, one Esther returned with a weary but satisfied smile.

"I admit I wasn't sure about you marrying someone from the mountains," Momma said as she gave Phoebe the baby and began to help Esther clean up, "but he won us over."

Esther yawned. "I knew he would. He's as charming as Papa."

"Let's hope he doesn't spoil little Felicity." Momma began to brush Esther's hair. "But probably not since you didn't have to wait for her."

"Unlike your mother and I had to wait for our daughters." Phoebe sighed. "And now neither Melvina nor Janet wants anything to do with being a midwife. It's up to you to pass the tradition on to your daughter or daughters, Esther."

"Midwife?" Esther struggled to sit up straighter, though she ached in places she hadn't known could hurt before then. "My daughter's not going to be a midwife. She's going to be a doctor."

ACKNOWLEDGMENTS

The idea for this story goes back so far in my brain, I don't even know how many people helped me along the way. I think of Pat, who told me the fastest way to get a man from Appalachia to do something was to tell him he couldn't do it — and she should know, being married to one. Then I can thank Shelia, Pam, Kelly, Susie . . . The list goes on and on of all the wonderful women from the mountains who made me laugh until I cried with their commonsense wisdom and down-to-earth attitudes about life. Pam especially reminded me that God loves me, even in a spiritually dark time in my life. Rest in peace in Jesus's arms, my dear.

Closer to the present, I thank the Montgomery Museum and Lewis Miller Art Center for their valuable information, and the University of Kentucky Press for publishing *Days of Darkness: The Feuds of*

Eastern Kentucky by John Ed Pearce, which showed me that those feuds aren't just stuff of legends. They were violently, tragically real, and many of the perpetrators were educated and financially successful men.

To the usual suspects I owe a great deal, as always — Patty, Debbie Lynne, Louise, Marylu, and Ramona. Gina helped keep me so sane with her midnight emails and marathon phone calls that she gets her own line. As does my husband, who makes my writing possible by keeping my temperamental computer and DSL running, not complaining about my weird hours — much — and making me have fun along the way.

A huge thanks to my agent, Tamela Hancock Murray, for taking care of business so I can take care of being creative. Last but not least, I don't have enough space to express my gratitude to my editor Vicki Crumpton for being understanding about the insanity of this past year, with my two cross-country moves, family emergencies, writing in hotel rooms while seeking housing, and something new each month.

Above all, I thank the Lord for bringing all these people into my life.

ABOUT THE AUTHOR

Laurie Alice Eakes used to lie in bed as a child telling herself stories so she didn't wake anyone else up. Sometimes she shared her stories with others, so when she decided to be a writer, she surprised no one. *Family Guardian,* her first book, won the National Readers Choice Award for Best Regency in 2007.

In the past three years, she has sold six books to Revell, five of which are set during the Regency time period; five books to Barbour Publishing; and two novellas to Barbour Publishing and one to Revell. Seven of her books have been picked up by Thorndike Press for large-print publication, and *Lady in the Mist,* her first book with Revell, was chosen for hardcover publication by Crossings Book Club.

Laurie Alice teaches online writing courses and enjoys a speaking ministry that takes her from the Gulf Coast to the East Coast.

She lives in Texas with her husband, two
dogs, and two cats and is learning how to
make tamales.

The employees of Thorndike Press hope you have enjoyed this Large Print book. All our Thorndike, Wheeler, and Kennebec Large Print titles are designed for easy reading, and all our books are made to last. Other Thorndike Press Large Print books are available at your library, through selected bookstores, or directly from us.

For information about titles, please call:
(800) 223-1244

or visit our Web site at:
http://gale.cengage.com/thorndike

To share your comments, please write:
Publisher
Thorndike Press
10 Water St., Suite 310
Waterville, ME 04901